Praise for *Brown Sugar*

Brown Sugar 2

Great One Night Stands

A Collection of Erotic Black Fiction

Edited by Carol Taylor

WASHINGTON SQUARE PRESS

New York London Toronto Sydney Singapore

"Art, for Fuck's Sake," Copyright © 2002, by Leone Ross
"If He Only Knew," Copyright © 2001, by Preston L. Allen
"Transplanted," Copyright © 2002, by Tananarive Due
"Sit," Copyright © 2001, by Bernice L. McFadden
"The Most Beautiful Thing," Copyright © 2002, by Timmothy B. McCann
"Lula Mae," Copyright © 2001, by Shay Youngblood
"Mr. Good Lay," Copyright © 2001, by Zane
"Next Time Take Flesh," Copyright © August 2001, by Jenoyne Adams
"Letters & Remembrances," Copyright © 2001, by Kathleen E. Morris
"It's Never Too Late in New York," Copyright © 2001, by Nelson George
"Counting Days," Copyright © 2001, by Shawne Johnson
"Ella by Starlight," Copyright © 2001, by Willie Perdomo
"Passing Through," Copyright © 2001, by Sandra Kitt
"Simply Beautiful," Copyright © 2001, by Michael A. Gonzales
"Zoe," Copyright © 2001, by Nicole Bailey-Williams
"Prelude To . . . ," Copyright © 2001, by Reginald Harris
"Don't Stop 2 You Get Enuf," Copyright © 2001, by Yolanda Joe
"Mr. Man," Copyright © 2002, by Rebecca Carroll

A WASHINGTON SQUARE PRESS *Original* Publication

WSP

A Washington Square Press Publication
1230 Avenue of the Americas, New York, NY 10020

Compilation and introduction copyright © 2003 by Carol Taylor

ISBN: 0-7394-3327-X

Brown Sugar 2 is dedicated to those we've known and loved, and those we've loved, *then* known.

CONTENTS

ACKNOWLEDGMENTS

Many thanks to my agent, Tanya McKinnon, for her smarts, savvy and guidance, and to Rosemary Ahern for her continued editorial wisdom. Thank you, again, Tracy Sherrod, for being a good friend. Thanks to my family for making me who I am; without you I am nothing. Thanks Ellis, Monika, and Carla, for the great dinners, unwavering support, and inspiration. Much love to Peter for more than I can say here. My deepest thanks to all the writers who have so diligently and fearlessly created the original stories in *Brown Sugar 2;* you are on the cutting edge.

"Brown Skin, you know I love your Brown Skin,
I can't tell where yours begins. I can't tell where mine ends."
—India.Arie, "Brown Skin"

INTRODUCTION

It Feels Good to Be Bad

So, here we find ourselves again: The morning after the night before. Sprawled out, the sheets a mess. Your contacts in, your clothes half on, half gone. You've given up all preconceived notions of time and place. Your brain turned off as your senses turned on, a smile bright as the morning on your face. No longer worrying should or shouldn't, if he is or isn't. Living now only in the moment, your brain on stun as your body takes over.

To deny our impulses is to deny the very thing that makes us human. When we've acted first and thought later. When we went with the flow and lost ourselves in the moment. There are few things that unify us; one is the irrational, impractical, out-of-character impulses that we've given in to. One of those irrational impulses is a one-night stand. We've all had them. And if we're lucky, they've been great. I'm not gonna lie, I've had one or two or twelve, some great, some not. But I don't regret any of them because each has revealed not only something about myself, but about men as well. Anyway, it's not what happens that matters; it's what you do with what happens.

Brown Sugar 2 celebrates great one-night stands because the beauty of a momentous one-time encounter is that it doesn't reveal everything: the skeletons in the closet, the emotional dirty laundry, the crazy exes or the nonsense we get so caught up in that we forget to have fun. With a one-night stand all you have is each other in the here and now. Steeped in the present you can ignore the imperfections, the human frailties and insecurities. Safely coddled in the moment, you are to each other perfect in that instant.

That memory stays with you untarnished and glittering, wrapped in a ribbon of remembrance, unsullied by the day-to-day. A one-night stand is not about the unremarkable, the practical, or the mundane. It's about the fantasy of what could be though we know it will not be, and the beauty of not caring. Either way, it feels good to be bad, that's probably why we do it.

A Trip in the Sack

Sometimes doing something so out of the ordinary, so unlike yourself is just what you need to put things back in perspective. I can testify. Not long ago I was out of my mind. I'd been caught up with a trifling so-and-so who'd first rocked my world, then wrecked it. He'd done a slow fade out of my life and took my heart with him. Since I was already dead I took to my bed and was never gonna get out of it. I was gonna lie there forever listening to *The Best of Al Green* on a continuous loop: "I'm so tired of being alone, I'm so tired of being alone . . ." Hair uncombed, face a mess. Pathetic. I'd shuffle from the bathroom to my bed, hysterical. I'd start laughing, then burst into tears, then go back to manic laughter, then back to sobs again. Can you spell PMS? Oh, the drama.

It's probably too late to make a long story short but a friend came over, let herself in with her key. Fed my cats, opened the drapes and the windows, then dragged me from the bed and out of the house. We went out, we talked, we laughed, and I met someone. My thoughts as I gazed at his strapping six-feet-two, 200-pound frame and the downy peach fuzz of his baby-soft brown skin, are too private to share, even for me. But, as India.Arie so eloquently put it, he made me want to "Hershey's Kiss his licorice."

His name was Kevin. He was twenty-two. I was not, and I felt like a dirty old man. I hung my head in shame but I took him home anyway. Had to, Baby Boy lived in Queens; *Jamaica*, Queens, the *last* stop on the F train. That's almost as far as Colorado when you're coming from downtown Manhattan. Either way, he lived with his moms. Yes, he did. I could almost blush with shame, and I'm pretty shameless. But I digress. Though I knew it wasn't forever, it was okay for today. Did the trick. You feeling me? He was definitely a trip in the sack, that Kevin. I threw him down and sexed him up. Yep, the pep was back in my step. And, it's true: Sometimes the best way to get over someone is to get under someone. Now I'm not saying you should give it up to everybody who asks; Lord, you'd never get off your back. And I know as well as the next sister that if you lie down with "dogs," you'll get dirty. What I *am* saying is that sometimes it's okay to give Mr. Right Now a chance until you find Mr. Right.

The Beauty of Being Black

Since publishing *Brown Sugar: A Collection of Erotic Black Fiction*, I've been talking a lot about sex and it feels good. I'm meeting a lot of wonderfully evolved black men and women who've found many things to relate to in the stories because we truly represented what makes us tick sexually and emotionally. *Brown Sugar* became a best-seller because the stories were not just about sex; they were sexy stories about black life, in all its myriad forms. That's the beauty of being black, our diversity. And though we don't know it, our diversity is also our greatest strength.

I am a black woman born in Jamaica, who grew up in Brooklyn, reading Harlequin romances, Machiavelli, C. S. Lewis, Iceberg Slim and Sun Tzu. I am as comfortable in an auction house as I am in a rib joint. You may have been born in the North, or South, or uptown or down. You may come from the Caribbean or England, or the Caribbean via England. You may hail from the East Coast or the West, or from somewhere in the middle of America. Though you are black, you may also be French, Asian, Italian, Jewish or a mix of all of them. So to lump black people under one category called Black People is as limiting and ignorant as crediting blacks with Ebonics but not with influencing everything in America, from literature, art, dance, music and fashion to language, culture and policy. As black people, we have shaped many things about America and we have many things that have shaped us into the people we are. Those things are called our experiences, sexual and otherwise. And there are a wealth of these experiences in *Brown Sugar* and now in *Brown Sugar 2*.

Be My Almond Joy, I'll Be Your Sugar Daddy

In *Brown Sugar 2* you'll find best-selling authors, whom you already know and love, writing *outside* of their genre but *in* their own particular style about characters you'll recognize in places you'll know: Zane, Tananarive Due, Bernice L. McFadden, Sandra Kitt, Shay Youngblood, Yolanda Joe, Jenoyne Adams, Nelson George, Timmothy B. McCann, Michael A. Gonzales, and Willie Perdomo among them. What their stories give you are glimpses into the many different worlds that make up Black America.

In here you'll find the erotic elevated to the everyday, for it is always around us. The warm scent of cocoa butter on the nut brown woman sitting next to you on the train. The dewy peach fuzz of hair on the back of her neck prickling as she feels your gaze meets it and then holds it. Or the way that brother's bald head glistens with sweat as he drives for the basket, his shorts barely hanging on around the curve of his gorgeous ass. That look he gives you when he sees you watching from the sidewalk that says: Be my Almond Joy, I'll be your Sugar Daddy.

In Our Own Words

Like so many things, we've had our sexuality placed upon us, then repackaged and sold back to us. The little we see of black sex or sexuality on TV, in movies or videos, is either too little or all wrong. In *Brown Sugar 2*, we represent the full range of our sexuality, emotionality, and physicality.

Here is black life in our own words as seen through our own eyes: beautiful black brothers, who are articulate and steadfast, tender and caring, who love their black women. Strong, outspoken black women who know who they are and what they want but are also loving and giving, caring and nurturing. *Brown Sugar 2* celebrates the big and the beautiful as well as the dark and the lovely. Many of the stories here give props to foxy sisters with big hips, big lips, untamed hair and gorgeous dark brown skin, who are tough and tender, professional and street, sexy and smart.

Sexy and smart are not mutually exclusive in my world. I know I'm as smart as I am sexy and vice versa. If you're reading this book, you probably are, too. There's nothing wrong with it. As a woman it's as important to claim your sexuality as it is to claim your intellect; if you don't, someone will claim it for you. And then where will you be? Back on the plantation, for sure.

So yes, it's time for some positive black sexual imagery and sexuality, and *Brown Sugar 2* has them in spades. These stories celebrate the beauty of black people in all their myriad forms, colors, tones and shades, from the blue-black of ebony to the nutmeg freckles sprinkled across *café con leche* skin. From the pimp roll on a chocolate-coated hottie to the sexy high-heeled sway of a sweet young thang as she sweeps her braids across her shoulders. From the high yellow attitude of a Bourgie Brownstone Princess to the clipped academic tones of an uppity Affirmative Action Baby. You know who you are.

Even with the Blindfold, Gagged and Bound

We're about due for a revolution, maybe even overdue, so why not a sexual one? We're all having sex, if we're lucky. Men and women are talking about sex separately; why not talk about it together? Better yet, why not talk about it together in bed? Why can't we fuck *and* talk? Or better yet, talk *then* fuck. We might actually learn something about each other. Lemme testify again. I knew my lover was the one when I jokingly asked him, in the moment, what did he want to do to me and he said, in all seriousness, "I'll do anything you want." And he did; even with the blindfold, gagged and bound. And I've returned the favor, again and again.

I wouldn't have known if I hadn't asked him. Luckily he was man enough to tell me and then man enough to do it. I'm lucky I stumbled across him, because I wasn't looking for *him,* you see, he wasn't my "type." How wrong I was. When I tell him to "Give me some sugar, Daddy," he knows just what I mean. I now marvel at how someone so seemingly straight can be so wonderfully bent.

Knowing Is Half the Battle

In your twenties it's trial and error. In your thirties and forties it's trial and error, followed by disaster and devastation, remorse and finally regret. Hey, I know, at thirty-five I've been there, a few times, even. I've lived those crazy-ass, four-minute "relationships" full of nothing but fucking, then bullshit, lies, bullshit, lies, bullshit, bullshit, lies,

lies, lies. So no, I wouldn't be twenty-two again if you promised me peace on earth and good will to all men. I'm glad to be where I am. Hindsight is crystal; I know that now. But it's okay 'cause every morning I wake up and I'm glad I'm a little farther along in the journey toward myself. I'm just now understanding how to play the field. And you know what? To the victor go the spoils.

Hey, don't sweat me. I don't want it all, just most of it. You should too. We should all be fascinated by the depths that experience can show us or the heights to which knowledge can take us. That's the only way we'll know what we want or what we don't want. And it's good to know what you want, 'cause knowing is half the battle.

Now, halfway through my life, I've learned a lot, and I'm just beginning to retain it and—surprise—learn from it. I used to spend all my time yearning for the fucking, and when I was close to getting it I'd spend all my time worrying about what so-and-so is going to think. Does he look right and make enough money? Is he the right color, or the right race? Or whether we were forever or not. What is forever, anyway? I was with someone for ten years, and though I don't regret one moment of a second of that time, it was not forever and I'm glad. If you're smart you'll live in the here and now and maybe give someone, who you might not think is "right" for you, some play. He might surprise you.

I've been surprised. The men who've made the best love to me are the ones I didn't expect would. The ones who'd had to talk me out of my clothes and into their bed. The ones with whom I thought I'd had nothing to lose. The ones I could lose myself with because I knew we were not forever. These are the lessons age and experience have taught me: You often have to give it up to get it back. Sometimes you have to lose yourself to find someone else. And that, funnily enough, as I can attest, often Mr. Right has been there all along.

Let me share a story with you.

Don't Block the Blessing

We'd been friends for years, can't even remember how we met. Don't know how many times I'd answered the question, "You sure you two aren't dating?" To be quickly followed by, "Then you won't mind setting me up with him, right, girl?" And I hadn't. He was a great guy. Good-looking, straightforward, often single. But to me none of that meant anything. To me he was just Darryl; my boy "D." My friend from way back.

We'd grown up together in Brooklyn. Done everything together. We'd gone roller-skating every Saturday at Utica Roller Skating Rink, then strolled up Eastern Parkway after—hot, sweaty and funky—to eat dinner at either his house or mine. He'd let me win at handball on Sundays, and fetched all the balls I hit over the fence. I'd help him dress to get the girls most other times. Tell you the truth, homeboy's moms was dressing him in rejects and high-waters before I came on the scene. He owed me big-time and he's paid it off with interest.

* * *

As we grew older he started to cock-block me. Now I know why I could never get a date; all the guys thought I was going out

with him or that we were fucking. Meanwhile, all the girls—
friends or not—flocked to him regardless. But I can't blame
them. I can see now that he is quite beautiful. Dark and sweet,
tall and manly. Long-lashed almond eyes and deep black skin.
Lips you want to run your tongue across. That chip in his tooth.
Cheekbones sharp across his face and a head as bald and smooth
as amber glass.

He looked good bald. I'm glad he listened to me and shaved
his head when his hairline started to recede. I can't stand when
those brothers be bald on top with all these dreadlocks in the
back. Perpetrators, you ask me. I wasn't gonna have D. going out
like that. Made me go with him to the barbershop, in fact. Held
his hand the whole time the barber shaved his locks. Then later I
held him while he cried. Rubbing his head cradled in my tear-
soaked lap I'd told him my tits'll sag and my ass'll drop. I'll get
lines and no one'll have me 'cause you'll have cock-blocked 'em
all. Meanwhile, you'll be a bald black Adonis when you turn forty.

And I was right.

But not only that: D. was sweet and kind, funny and smart,
brave and outspoken. And from what Loretta had told me, he was
a damn good kisser, great in the sack and had a big dick to boot.
Lucky, lucky, Loretta. But that didn't last. She was too bourgie for
him. I knew it from jump. She was a high-yellow Brooklyn
princess and though that hair she kept flipping at him had
entranced him, it didn't last. D. liked to get dirty, like me. He
liked to run and jump and drink and cuss and carry on and
Loretta was a princess and I was not. I was his girl. And that's why
D. and I had been friends forever.

* * *

I'm not even sure how it happened. We'd gone to an opening. He'd brought that new girl with the big tits he was seeing. I had on a new clingy black halter dress made of some shiny material that hung down the front in folds, then fell to the floor after skimming my hips and thighs. In the back it was open almost to my ass, actually, to my ass, as D. had been kind enough to point out. I liked it because I was comfortable in it but mostly because it made me look like I had cleavage. God bless it. I'd brought David, this new guy I'd met who D. took to calling "Corporate Man," and running him down whenever he was out of earshot: his shoes were too shiny, his shirt was too shiny, his hair was too shiny. But I knew the real reason: David was light-skinned, had green eyes and a full head of curly hair.

D. hated light-skinned boys; they'd always used to mess with him when we were kids, calling him tar baby and black boy. I thought he'd gotten over it. David had nothing on him. D. was beautiful, dark and lovely. Unrefined. Every girl in the place wanted him. I knew 'cause I could tell. Even that silly new girl was hanging on him like a cheap suit, shoving her tits in his face. I'd dated light-skinned boys before so I didn't know what was up with D. Whatever. Homeboy had a J-O-B. And I liked David enough to tell D. Usually we were cool like that, D. and I, but tonight was different.

I don't know, one minute we're standing around pretending to look at the art—David had gone to get me a drink and D. was whispering bullshit in my ear, making me laugh, riffing on people, talking shit. All of a sudden Tits throws a fit; she actually stomped her foot, no joke. She stomps her foot, turns to D. and yells, "Why don't you two just fuck and get it over with." Then she storms off. I turned to D. and was about to laugh. But when I saw him standing there in his dark suit, his white shirt opened halfway down his chest, one hand in his pocket, and that look in his eye, I thought, *hmmm*.

* * *

We split after that. D. told David he'd take me home. Like my father or something. Cock-blocked again. We went to my place and were hanging out, doing who knows what. Listening to music, gossiping, bullshitting.

"Yeah, D., another one crossed off the list. This fool was like, 'Yeah, well I want out of this relationship.' I was like, '*Relationship*, we ain't *in* no relationship. We just fucking. Negro, *please*.' As if he could *have* a relationship." I sucked my teeth. "Homeboy had no cards but he insisted on trying to play me." I shook my head.

D. wasn't laughing. "Why you be dating them uppity half-white boys, girl? They be dogging you."

"Man, y'all *all* some trifling niggahs." I said, surprised, struggling to sit up, mad at D. for no reason. "Look, I can get any guy. He's just gotta be a guy worth getting. Why you so color-struck anyway? It's not something I *try* to do, it's just something that happens. Dark brothers like you don't date me. Y'all too busy running down them high-yellow sisters like Loretta. Too scared to step to me 'cause I got a brain. 'Cause you got to talk to me, and not just fuck me. 'Cause you can't run your trifling games on me."

D. lifted his head from my lap and turned to face me.

"Yeah, right. They don't talk to you 'cause you're stuck-up, girl. All y'all Jamaicans are. And you know I'm right. Walking around like your shit don't stink. Like you better than everybody else. So don't talk this bullshit with me. You know it's true. You would never get with a *real* niggah 'cause we'd turn you out. Rip your clothes, muss your hair. Make you moan and sweat and come so hard you'd have to give it up then. Right? And that's *not* what you want, right? 'Cause you a control freak. And with a niggah like me you'd be outta control."

We just sat there looking at each other, breathing hard like we'd run a race. I didn't know what to say so I got up, stormed off to the bathroom and slammed the door. I yanked off my clothes, cussing the whole time. Then I stepped under the shower, letting the hot water run over my head and course down my body. I don't know how long I stayed in there, probably hoping D. would be gone when I was done. When I came out with a jar of shea butter in my hand, he was sitting on my bed listening to music. He sat up when I came in, looked at me, shook his head, then motioned me over.

"Come," he said, gesturing with his head, "sit here." I padded over in my towel and bare feet and sat on the floor between his knees, my back to his crotch. He opened his legs wide and settled his hands on my shoulders, rubbing the butter in small tight circles across my back and neck, easing away the tension and the knots.

"Better?"

"Yes."

He then started rubbing the butter into my close-cropped hair, still damp from the shower, massaging my head as he did so. I settled my knees in closer with my feet on the floor and felt the tension flow out of my body. We fought all the time, D. and I, but never like that. When he was finished, we just sat like that for a while, the scent of vanilla heavy in the air, D'Angelo playing softly in the background: *I love your smile, your mouth, your laughter. Never ran into your kind before or after.* . . .

"I'm sorry," I mumbled, more to my knees than him.

"I know. I'm sorry, too, baby."

Then he reached down and lifted me up onto his lap and held me there. I didn't even care that the towel had stayed behind on the floor.

*   *   *

This is how I found my best friend between my legs, his mouth on my clit, one of his fingers in my mouth, two others deep inside me. He looked good enough to eat. I apparently was.

"Mmmm. How's that?" he asked, sucking harder.

"Yeah, that's good." I moaned. "Just like that, baby. Just like that. . . . Oh, yes . . . Just like that . . ."

"Yeah, that's it," he urged, "come for me, baby, come for me."

And I did.

*   *   *

Hard to believe that at thirty-five, this was the first time I'd ever really talked to the man between my legs. Not just "yeah, yeah, harder, harder," but told him how I felt, what I wanted. Usually we were both too embarrassed or too busy in our own heads to pay attention to each other. But with D. it was different. I trusted him.

As I looked down at him in the V between my thighs, I loved everything about him. His bald head. The curve of his long brown back. His sweet ass and his long legs. The strong curve of his hips and his shoulders, his arms under my hips lifting me up to meet his mouth. His long-lashed eyes intent on me, unflagging under my gaze, even his lisp. It was even more apparent when I'd sucked him off and he'd come, moaning, "yeth, yeth, yeth." I'd almost laughed then, but I'd come just from watching him: his head thrown back, eyes closed, mouth open, his hips bucking up off the bed. Imagine, as much work as it takes for me to come and I had at just the sight of him.

* * *

"So what are you thinking?" he asked, propping up on one elbow and finding my nipple with his finger, first licking it, then rubbing his finger across the tip.

I moaned, then smiled. "I was thinking that Loretta was right."

"Loretta" he frowned. "What about?"

"Well, you do have a big dick and as a plus you seem to love to eat pussy."

"Damn," he laughed, slapping himself on the forehead and falling back on the bed. "She told you that?"

Now it was my turn to prop up on an elbow.

"Of course. She tells me everything; she's my friend." Then I smiled. "Plus she has a big mouth."

At that he let out a deep booming laugh, his mouth wide open in a way he never let it be because of his chipped front tooth, and I remembered how we met.

* * *

It was in Brooklyn, outside of P.S. 189. I was walking home from school and saw him on his bike at the corner. I recognized him as one of a group of older boys in my class, though he had to have been at least four years older than I. He'd been left back twice and I'd been skipped twice. As I stood near him waiting for the light to change, I heard him say, "Yo, whassup, Coconut? How'd you get to America, swim?"

It was the seventies; Jamaicans were not yet popular. I ignored him. I already knew he was stupid.

"Is it true you Coconuts eat goats?"

I continued to ignore him. When the light changed I stepped off the curb and started across the street.

"Yo, Coconut, your moms wanna come clean my house?"

I stopped, turned around and looked at him. He didn't look like much. Barely looked like anything really, just another skinny black American boy. I walked back toward him.

"What you said?"

"You heard me, Coconut."

"Oh," I responded. Then I kicked his bike with all my might and watched as he fell to the curb, landing tangled in a heap, stunned.

I shook my head and called him an idiot. Then I turned and started back across the street. I was halfway across when I looked back at him. He was still tangled up in his spokes, with the wheels on the sidewalk, and him in the street. He looked pathetic.

I turned and walked over to him. I don't know why. I stood over him as he struggled to untangle himself and watched the blood from a gash in his lip, made when he'd cracked his tooth on the handlebar, soak crimson into his T-shirt. I dropped my bag, grabbed his arm and untangled him from the bike, thinking to myself that American boys are dumb. Then I sat him on the curb, poured the bottle of water I held over the cut, and used the tissues in my bag to clean it up. Then I stood up and walked away. As I did I heard him mumble.

"I'm thorry."

* * *

In the morning I was gonna put him out and tell him it can't continue. I love him too much to chance it. Passion comes and goes but we were going to be friends forever. But that was tomorrow. We still had tonight.

We had been blessed and I would not block it.

The Souls of Black Folk

These stories set the stage for seduction with a distinctly new flavor, and they are as insightful as they are sexy. If you fellas want to know what the sisters talk about when they get together, then read Zane's story. If you've read her before she might surprise you with her narrator's aching vulnerability when she finally finds

"Mr. Good Lay." Or try to figure out the surprise ending in Yolanda Joe's outrageously funny "Don't Stop 2 You Get Enuf"; when a woman gets more than she bargained for from a lover half her age. Let Shay Youngblood take you somewhere else entirely, in her subtly sexy, beautifully depicted story, "Lula Mae." Though blind from birth, she is now able to "see" what she really wants and needs and can now finally leave her cheating, abusive husband. Journey with Bernice L. McFadden in "Sit," as she shows you her Barbados, its lush and sensuous beauty and its even more sensuous men wanting to tempt the American women who flock to their shores. Or be "Transplanted" by Tananarive Due to the other side by the spiritual love "letter" left to a newly widowed young woman who finds that she can be with her husband one last time. Her story is alternately passionate and poignant, sad and uplifting. Take a trip with Sandra Kitt as we are stranded with her feisty professional heroine, who must somehow put all her trust in the mechanic of the town she's "Passing Through" after she is forced to stay the night.

In Jenoyne Adams's lyrical and luscious "Next Time Take Flesh," sit in with a group of poets whose game of Truth or Dare takes a decidedly sexy turn. In Shawne Johnson's provocative and quietly sensual "Counting Days," a young woman regrets a decision that may have cost her the man she loves until she remembers that she has to love herself first. Leone Ross's gorgeously sexy story, "Art, for Fuck's Sake," is set in Jamaica, where we find out that black men are not "dogs," that they can be friends as well as lovers, if we'd let them. In "Letters & Remembrances," Kathleen E. Morris brilliantly reunites two lovers who find out that the more things change, the more they stay the same. "Mr. Man" is a candid and sweetly introspective story about the head games of color and class that we blacks play against each other. Rebecca Carroll, herself biracial, explores the meaning of black, white, other, with a man at the other end of the color spectrum who "could lift her skirt with just his breath alone." Then find out in Nicole Bailey-Williams's funny and surprisingly sad "Zoe" what a woman means when she says, "she's not feeling brothers right now." Though I think we all know the answer.

If you ladies want to know what the brothers are up to, then let Nelson George escort you through a night in the city, as he shows why "It's Never Too Late in New York." His bold and successful brothers alternate between poignancy and posturing, desire and dominance, strength and submission. You may never look at a brother the same way again. Then spend the night with Michael A. Gonzales as he takes you through the same city but light-years away. His New York is one of moody blues, haunting music and aging honeys still sweet and tempting. Pay attention as he shows you what he thinks is "Simply Beautiful" in a black woman; you might learn something. If you've read Timmothy B. McCann before, he's going to surprise you with his white-hot story of sweet revenge and righteous redemption, which will have anyone who was less than perfect in high school cheering. His "The Most Beautiful Thing" is not what you think. When you're done, trip with Willie Perdomo through his Nuevo York as he sweet-talks his way into the arms of "Ella by Starlight"; his tongue as sweet as his prose is sharp. If you liked Preston L. Allen's story "Nadine's Husband" in *Brown Sugar*, you're going to love "If He Only Knew," the continuation of that story. This time that philandering "'ol' water head" Christopher gets what's coming to him. And it's not what you'd think. Then, sit back and let Reginald Harris take you to a whole different place, show you a whole different scene. In *Brown Sugar,* his "The Dream" was all hot and horny imagery, but here he's gonna surprise you as he takes you to a place you'll find more familiar than not in "Prelude To . . ."

Fantastic stories all. These are the real souls of black folk, and these stories will take you there in many more ways than one. Just be careful, you might get more than your mind blown.

If, as Prince says, there are twenty-three positions in a one-night stand, then imagine the possibilities open to you. In *Brown Sugar 2* you'll find eighteen singularly sexy situations in various combinations and variations. So if you're ready, let's explore and revel in all the rich and varied dimensions of sexuality and sensuality in every color and hue—in fact, the whole nine. In *Brown Sugar 2* is something for everyone. And you never know, you might learn something, because you and your honey are gonna love each other a little more because of it.

So come with me now, 'cause it's time again to come correct.

Brown Sugar 2

LEONE ROSS

Art, for Fuck's Sake

I had been celibate for a year before a pair of lions happened along. Well, they weren't lions, but the kind of men who make you think of lions, with their tumbling shades of brown and their big soft paws.

I thought men were dogs. Panting, impatient things that looked at you with irresistible eyes, then wagged their tails at the very next bitch. When I was fifteen, I met a young man with a mantra. His mother taught it to him: "There is only one way to handle women. Fool them, fuck them and forget them." Two can play that game. I'd chosen to forget. My best friend, Amba, fucked them. She specialized in one-night stands where the talking went wrong the sex went right. But I couldn't imagine a careless grind and a stranger in my bed the next morning. I'd never done anything like that, and I never intended to.

* * *

I sit on Amba's sofa two hours after I finish my third novel. I haven't seen her for months, but she is used to me coming out of post-novel hibernation. That kind of work does things to you, loses you in a world of one. My eyes are bloodshot and my weave needs emergency treatment; I feel ugly. Amba looks at me in friendly disgust.

"Girl," she says, "you need some sex."

"You always think that sex is the answer to everything," I say.

She sticks out her breasts and wriggles suggestively. "Sex is good for you, Simone. You know how much man I check since you disappear into that novel? Me nearly call you the other night to come out and party, but then me remember you don't business wid crotches when you ah write."

She tells me about her latest exploits: a man at a local bar with three golden teeth and an oral technique that made her praise God; another who leaned against her car while she was having her nails done ("The man waited for me two hours when him see me go in there, girl!"). I let the details wash over me. Crickets sing through the burglar bars that frame her French doors. I love that sound. Whatever changes in Jamaica, the sound of crickets at night is constant.

The night before I finished the novel, I dreamed crickets and dreamed a man. Just a nice man. Someone who did what he said he would do, and knew that when he touched a woman he made a promise. To cherish her, to love her. To be there. And then we made love: skin and arms and moans among the sounds of crickets calling for a mate. I woke up aching, knowing I'd never find him. There had been too many broken promises. Too many goodbyes.

Amba touches my arm. "You all right?"

I shake myself. "Yeah. Sorry. That sounds good."

"You not listening at all." She laughs and smacks me lightly on the knee. "Stop pretending."

I turn to face her. "Why you do it, Amba? Why you sleep with so much man? Why you make them use you so?"

She screws up her face. "I don't feel used."

"How can you *not* feel used?"

She stretches out for her wineglass, sips delicately. I think that she looks fragile under the lamp. Perhaps that is why men come to her; perhaps they need to bed something they think they can break. "Is just the vibe," she says. Her lips dip into a smile I don't recognize. "You meet them, you don't *know*. And they don't *know*. And then you're there, screaming. With a stranger. Letting go. It . . . makes me feel alive. And I think they feel alive, too. If it's using, me using them, too."

I struggle with this idea. When I began this latest novel, I tried to base one of my characters on Amba, but I couldn't. There are things about her life that I can't imagine. "So, it's the abandon?"

"Yeah, I s'pose so."

"I'm trying to understand. You don't feel like you're just filling a void?"

She laughs. "Don't try make me into some sad bitch!" She pats me. "Is all right if you don't understand. But me? Me will drink to abandon, girl! And to finding you a man!" She raises her glass.

I drink, not believing. I feel sorry for her.

*   *   *

Two weeks later, in time-honored middle-class Jamaicanness, my hair is a sleek waterfall down my back and my nails are scarlet.

My manuscript is off to my American editor and I am well into what Amba calls Operation Run Down Man. We party. It isn't that I can't party. Or flirt. Or laugh. I can do all those things. But I find myself in the middle of bars and on the front steps of houses sweating into my frock, wondering if everyone can see how dead I feel inside. I don't want to do this. *Waste of time,* I think, as men buy me drinks, leer down my cleavage, present their crotches for me to dance with. *Love isn't this superficial. And love is what I want.*

It is Joshua who calls, one morning, as I down strong coffee and hold my head. I grab the phone.

"Hello?" I say, hating whomever it is.

"Is this Simone Jacobs?" Warmth floods through the receiver. I have to smile. It is the kind of voice that makes you want to smile.

"Yeah, that's me."

He is very professional. He tells me that he is a musician, tells me about gigs he's played and contacts we have in common. A friend introduced him to my novels; now they have a proposal for work.

"Tell me more about the project." I'm not curious about the job yet. I just like how the growl in his voice wakes me up.

"We don't have a name for it. We've been calling it Project X." Multimedia, he explains. He'll do the music; his friend Che will create the central piece, a sculpture. And they want me to think about words. A series of short stories, perhaps.

"Is there a theme?" I ask.

"Passion," he says.

I nearly laugh.

* * *

I meet them in a wine bar off Hope Road. They rise to their feet when I enter. I recognize Joshua's voice. He is shorter than Che, but bigger, darker. Barrel chest, rock face. Che bounces on his heels, smiling. A yellow man. His hair is an explosion of soft, black flames.

We order pasta, bread, crisp salads. They tell me about Project X, interrupting each other, joking, occasionally dropping into the kind of code reserved for old friends. It is nice to watch.

"Blame everything on Che," says Joshua, mock-serious. "I wanted to explore the implications of twenty-first-century post-modernism in Jamaican politics, but *he* wants to get into slack-ness!"

Che is always bouncing, like he can't keep still. He coughs over his Red Stripe. "Me? You see how you making the woman think is foolishness we trying to do? Passion is everything—not just sex." His hands are rough, a sculptor's hands. He touches his own face, puts his fingers into his mouth, crosses his arms as if he doesn't know what to do with them.

"When did you first meet?" I ask.

Che rolls his eyes. "Dis bwoy was looking *friend* and followed me around school till me talk to him. And I still can't get rid of him."

Joshua smiles around his wineglass. "I like your work," he says to me. "You care about everything you write."

"I . . . can't do it unless I care about it."

"Like playing God, eh?" he says.

"What do you mean?"

"You get to make everything turn out right."

"Well . . . it's not as simple as that."

Che pats me on the arm. "Yeah man. Of course it is."

They are right. They are speaking my language, and it feels scary and good at the same time. I've never met anyone who could do this. I have never let myself be part of a shared creative space.

Hours go by easily. A huge vase of flowers wilts on the table. We pass each other cheese and black pepper, and cover our hands with dying pollen, bright yellow against our palms. Joshua has longer, more delicate hands, strange on a man of his stature. His hands are like butterflies. He knocks things over, but he is not clumsy; it is as if his energy is too big for his skin, like it keeps pouring over the edges of him. They talk to me, showing each other off. They don't seem to notice the pollen, the golden cloud across the tablecloth. But something about it promises union all the same.

"Yes," I say. "I'll do it."

They don't turn me on. They aren't chatting me up. I like that.

* * *

We have funding for four months of work. The deadline is non-negotiable, but they tell me we can do it. I am shy, sometimes. They have worked together before and it takes me time to fall into the rhythm. But slowly, I relax. For three weeks I go to Che's apartment every Monday, Wednesday and Friday. Fans buzz overhead. His home is messy: tarps cover works in progress; odd, painful paintings are askew on the walls. Books teeter and the fridge smells bad. I ball up at the edge of a sofa, tucking my edges in. These daylong sessions take on a life of their own: we bitch, discuss, then move to our own little bubbles of space in the room. I sit scribbling ideas on a pad and then transferring them to my laptop. Joshua plays questioning chords, pats a big, fat drum, hums. He is creating sound, but his is the quietest corner. Che dances around weird buckets and makes sketches on pieces of paper. Sometimes there is only the sound of our breathing and our thoughts. It is always Che who gets bored first.

One day when I arrive they grab me at the door and haul me back to my car, laughing.

"Give me the keys," says Joshua.

"You mad? Give you the keys to my baby?"

Che snorts and taps my battered VW bug. "Baby? Look like a big, hard-back man to me."

"Where are we going?"

"Manning Cup match."

"What?"

Joshua tuts. "Manning Cup, woman. You know football, right?"

"Of course, but—"

"JC's playing Campion," says Che. "We have to go watch our team bruk up dem rass!"

I roll my eyes, but I do want to laugh. "You guys not over this high school rivalry yet?"

"Never!" they chorus.

* * *

We worm our way into bleacher seats while above us jittering young boys beat drums and cheer before anything starts. We're covered with moisture and hot wind. People call out to Joshua and Che, and the journey to our seats takes a long time, as they swap stories and memories. They introduce me to everybody; I begin to see friends of my own, make my own introductions. Men probe me with their eyes.

"JC!" Che and Joshua yell as loud as they can. Which is loud. They're in blue, the color of their team. Che has wrapped an old school tie around his head. He looks ridiculous, and it's wonderful.

"Campion!" roar the rivals.

I watch an old man selling peanuts in the crowd. I have not been to a Manning Cup match for ten years, but this is the same old man who sold me peanuts when I was sixteen. His back is bent into a question mark; the wrinkles that cover his face are an elaborate pattern. He is calling his wares into the crowd; this is how I recognize him. I've never been able to understand what he's saying. I pluck at Joshua.

"You know what the peanut man is saying?"

"Who, Burt? He's been here from time."

"What's he saying?"

"You don't have ears?"

I'm irritated. "Joshua, if I could hear him, I wouldn't have to ask you."

He reaches for my face, closes my eyes under his palms. "Listen."

The peanut seller's voice is clear and beautiful under the roars.

"Peee-nuts!" Then something I can't make out. I open my eyes. "Joshua, I can't—

"*Listen.*"

I close my eyes. His skin smells like this day—of hot nuts and laughter.

"Peeee-nuts! Peee-nuts! If you cyaan crack dem, mumble dem!"

I want to giggle. "*Mumble* them?"

Joshua takes his hands away. Points at the man. "See? He has no teeth. If you cyaan crack the peanuts, mumble them. Mumble them between your gums."

We giggle. It is so Jamaican. I grab my notebook and scribble a description of the old man as the teams run onto the pitch and the crowd rises to its feet.

Later, I dance. We all dance, as rhyming insults run back and forth between the teams. Our side mashes their rivals into the ground and we dance. Someone pours a bottle of beer down the back of my T-shirt and I break a nail. I don't care. I dance. Che picks me up and puts me on his shoulders. I worry that people will complain that they can't see, but no one does, so I dance there, too.

"Boy, you feel all hot and sweaty," Che says.

I drum my fists on the top of his head. And when Campion equalizes, I pray, for the first time in a long time. I pray for the winning goal, and it comes, with twenty-five seconds to spare.

*   *   *

We work around each other in circles. We peel each other's layers. I sit in Hope Gardens with Joshua telling me about his divorce three years ago. I know that Che has loved only one woman in his life. I know that Joshua has a three-year-old child and sinus problems. I know that Che likes bad sci-fi.

Finally, I tell them I'm celibate. They think that this is funny. They ask me how I'm managing. I am prim. I tell them it is a choice. That there are no good men; they're all married or gay, or worthless. The old excuses.

"Is true!" yells Che. "Talk it, sister! Man ah dawg!" He hits Joshua. "You ah dawg?" They howl and bark and I try to be angry. But I can't.

We get stoned a lot. It seems to help the work. They praise me, like the big brothers I never had. They pat me all the time, on the butt, on my shoulders. They ruffle my hair. They toss me back and forth between them. I am writing well. Images are smooth; narrative seems effortless.

One night we get drunk. Joshua and I play-fight with Che's cushions. I am laughing so hard I keep falling down. Joshua is sweet and awkward, his chuckles are gentle. We end up on the floor, panting. My legs are plaited through his. They're like iron bars. His face is inches from mine.

"Where *is* your libido, these days?" he says.

I giggle. "Nowhere. It took a trip on a sailing ship."

Che grabs me under the arms, slides me from underneath his friend. "*What* you say you libido doing?"

I blow him a kiss. My head is swimming. "I hear it's having a nice time in some drunk jungle. But those are only rumors."

Che shakes me. "Girl, you need a grind."

I stick my tongue out at him. "Typical male response."

"I know what Simone is like in bed . . ." he says, singsong. The comment is directed at his friend, like I'm not there. Joshua smiles indulgently.

"She's the kind of woman who takes hours . . ." says Che.

I sit cross-legged and keep my face expressionless.

"She's not the kind of woman you can check for five minutes," he explains. "She likes foreplay—"

"Oh, shut up you mouth. Every woman likes that," I say.

He ignores me. "She'd cover you in scented oil, rub you down, feed you stuff. Take a bath, suck you, back off again. Tease."

Inside me, something is turning over, burning. He is talking about the way I would like to be. If someone loved me, I could be that way.

"She'd want to drive you crazy, keep you waiting. And just when you can't take any more, she lets you in. And you just settle down in the plushness, fall into it." He sighs, theatrically.

We laugh at him. I laugh because I am embarrassed. I don't know why Joshua is laughing. I know that his knee is brushing mine. It is a small thing; it might even be an accident. He has one hand around the stem of his beer bottle, rubbing it up and down. The movement of his hand seems languorous, lazy but purposeful. I stare at the hand, trying to remember what it reminds me of. I drag my eyes to his face. Through the sunlight I can suddenly see the little boy behind the man's countenance. I want to tell the child that everything is all right.

"What?" he says.

"Nothing," I say.

Che goes back to his work, his body set in concentration. He is molding a woman's hips from what looks like Play-Doh. In the background, Joshua begins to drum. I write.

*   *   *

And then one night, problems come. I get to the house and find Joshua prowling around the door, banging. He looks as if he wants to cry.

"What is it?" For some reason my heart is beating too fast.

"Che won't answer the door."

"So maybe he's not there."

He glares at me. "He's there."

He pounds. "Che! Answer the bloodclaaht door!"

Silence.

"Joshua, what is the matter?"

"Him sick, all right?"

"What do you mean?"

He pounds.

"Joshua!"

There is a slight crack of the door and we see Che's face.

He is nearly unrecognizable. His hair has gone dull. His eyes are dull. Joshua puts a foot in the crack and shoves. Che scuttles back and sits in a corner.

Later, I try to describe it to Amba. I try to tell her about this most passionate of men, swollen with apathy. I try to tell her about the scratches on his face and his hands, where he'd been trying to distract himself from the pain. I never knew that the one woman Che loved died. Stabbed with an ice pick on a bus. For a gold chain and a purse with fifty dollars.

"So what did you do?" Amba asks.

"It was all Joshua. He talked to him; he treated him like he was him pickney. Then he put him to bed. He's there now. He says this happens every couple months. Depression. He's manic-depressive."

She frowns. "But the man have to get over this, girl. Is how long since him woman dead?"

"Three years."

"Isn't that when Joshua wife lef' him?"

"Yeah. They brought each other through."

"Rahtid," says Amba. Her voice is soft. She hugs me. "Boy, Simone, I love you. But if my man dead, and you marriage mash up, I don't know whether I could—"

I try to smile. "So you planning to give up you slack ways and get a man?"

"If you can find me one like dem two. But not the mad one."

"Amba!"

"Just jokin', baby."

We hug.

"I'm scared," I say.

"Why?"

"I want him to be better."

"And . . . ?"

I bury my face in her shoulder. I feel so guilty. "I want us to finish. I've never done anything like this. We've got thirteen days left. I've never written like this and I want him to be better."

"But you can always publish it—"

"No. It's *ours*. It has to be all of us."

* * *

Three days pass. I know that I should be helping, but I can't think of a way to help. And then Che arrives on my doorstep. He's carrying a bucket. I hug him at the door and give him lemonade. I am awkward. I don't know what to say. I watch for the bounce. It is there, small, but present.

"So how you feel?" he asks.

"Me? How *you* feel?"

He looks around my apartment. "This place feels like you."

I sigh inwardly. It's a lie, this place. It is cream and orderly. Just like my mother would like it. Sometimes I want to be untidy, but I can't.

"No it doesn't," I say.

He smiles. "But it does, y' know. Not the fancy sofa or the colors, but look." He gets up and moves around, touching things. A bottle of oil on the side table. He opens it and sniffs. "Cinnamon oil. You rub your face with it at night. I can smell it on you." The wind chimes at the window. He tickles them. "You play with these when you're lonely. And—" He sits on the sofa again and reaches underneath. I watch him, disbelieving, as he pulls out a sheaf of paper. "Yeah man, me did know. Poetry. All about man, right? Man that leave you."

My mouth is open. "How the hell—"

He laughs. "Do me a favor." Pushes the bucket forward. "Stick your hand in this."

"What?"

He reaches for me. "Your hand. Come play in the plaster."

He covers my hand, the one I write with, in something that

feels like Vaseline. His touch is quiet and efficient; I can almost feel him rubbing the jelly into my pores, into each crease and crevice. Then I am up to my forearm in coolness. After a while he signals for me to pull out. When it is dry, he pulls it off. We regard the disembodied hand in silence. Its fingers are spread, long, frozen in a caress. The wind chimes tinkle. He places the hand on my side table. I didn't know my hand looked like that. Capable. Powerful.

"That's for you," he says. "I'll finish it and then you can have it."

We order pizza and call Joshua. We've begun again.

*   *   *

I give them three stories and they take them away. They tell me they want to surprise me. I don't see them for two weeks, and it is strangely unbearable. I prowl my house. I write and write and write: I am astonished that another novel is coming, with two protagonists. One with disheveled hair and sad eyes, one with skin like jet rock. But there is space for other things, too. I masturbate idly, call old friends. I am writing and I am not hiding. It's not necessary.

"Didn't even *one* of them make a move?" asks Amba.

"Don't be stupid," I say.

She ignores me. "Which one of them do you prefer?"

"It's not like that," I say. My head hurts. "Neither."

"I woulda grab at least *one* grind offa them," she says, grimly.

"That's you," I say.

I think about the first time we all met, and the golden pollen that spilled across the tablecloth, and our hands.

* * *

They call me, finally. It's finished.

The drive takes so long.

Joshua meets me at the door. If he were Che, he would be dancing from one foot to the other. Because he is Joshua, he is still and mysterious. He carries a blindfold.

"May I?" he says.

I let him tie me blind. I let him put a hand in the small of my back, another on my shoulder. I let him lead me.

In the room, there is silence, and then the sound of drums. They fill me up. I want to reach for the sound, to grab it, to pull it to me. It is sound that could be felt, that could be loved. It is just like Joshua: solid, unmistakable. But there is a new vibe, something I didn't know about him before. The sound of mischief conquering rationale. It is a gorgeous surrender of his masks. It is vulnerable. I pull back against him. "It's beautiful, Joshua."

"Of course it is. It would have to be."

"You so full of yourself."

He laughs. "You don't understand. Listen."

I listen. Then I realize. It's not the sound of him. It's the sound of us. The roar of a crowd. Dipping down into drug-laden laughter. A dark piano chord for Che.

"It's us," I breathe.

"Yes," he says. "But with you at the center. Hear it?"

A guitar wails through. Passion.

I want to cry. "That's me?"

"If you were sound, that would be you, girl."

And I know what they have done. "Let me see the sculpture."

He unties the blindfold and light creeps into the room. Trickles of blue smoke. I stare.

The sculpture is eight feet tall. It smiles out of the gloom. Che has crafted her of soapstone, apricot soapstone. Behind her, my stories climb across the wall, in oranges, yellows, reds, against the blue. The sculpture's eyes are blurred and beautiful, as if she is looking at forever. She is naked. Edges tucked in. Hands soft in her lap. Fingers wreathed in golden dust. Pollen. They saw what I saw.

She's me, too.

* * *

I think it will be Che, with his wild-child hair and his bruised-cherry skin, coming from behind the sculpture, dancing up to us, so proud, looking at me for pleasure. I am wet-eyed. But it is Joshua who brings it to a beginning.

"Look at how beautiful you are," he says.

He puts his hand between my legs, and I realize that more than my eyes are wet. I am amazed that what he does is okay, that a kiss was not what I needed first. He is stroking me through my thin leggings, and his hand knows me. Like his fingertips have been watching me for these months, waiting. I don't think of protest, implications, even how it will be. I just sink into Joshua as Che stands behind me, waiting his turn.

Joshua is slow. Slower than I ever could have imagined. The drums have not stopped, and he winds the music through my hair as he places tiny kisses along me. His breath is hot.

Somewhere a woman's sounds of pleasure are echoing in my brain. I'm moaning their names like a string of silver curses, like their names make one name.

Joshua gives me to Che. He sits on the floor and watches his friend pull my T-shirt over my head. I watch him watching us. Che picks me up, leans against the wall, pulls my legs around his waist, my heels in the small of his back. He pulls off his shirt, lifts my breasts until our nipples are dancing together. I look into his face, so serious.

"You're a clever man," I say. My throat hurts. We're sweating, and the rub of his skin against mine makes me want to scream.

"Scream, baby," he says. He always knows. I throw my head back and scream. Che is rubbing me into him, masturbating me against his waist and groin. His legs are trembling with the effort. I look back at Joshua. He has his dick in his hand, rubbing and rubbing. I want it in my mouth. I slide off Che, kneel in front of Joshua, run my tongue around his balls, tickle the underside, listen to him groan.

They have no coordination. It doesn't matter. They pull my clothes off, ripping fabric, pull my panties off. We are all laughing like children. I am on the floor, blue music and blue smoke and blue arms cradling me in the queer light. Joshua spreads my legs and dips his head into me, licking me thoughtfully. I push my hips into his face. He slips his fingers inside me and rubs the moisture across my lips. Che leans over me, sucking cream off my mouth. He groans against my cheek. He is naked, too. His cock is shorter than Joshua's, but thicker, and he pushes his erection away from his belly again and again, an odd urgency. I reach for him, wanting to feel him, but he pins my hands back to the floor.

"You work too hard," he whispers into my hair.

I can't disagree; I can't concentrate. Joshua's tongue is so thick, inside me, up and down my thighs, circles around my clit, which gets harder and harder. I want to grab his head, I want to fuck his mouth, but I can't move. Che is kissing me upside down, his teeth are in my neck, his palms spread on mine, letting a pulse reach through his skin into my bloodstream. I arch my back. I am sobbing, running up the rungs of a ladder, pussy wetter and wetter, insistent, like drums.

"Tell him to do it faster," I beg.

"Faster . . ." Che whispers to his friend.

Joshua is humming into my crotch. He is tossing his head side to side. No one has eaten me like this before. I'm up the ladder. I am at the top of the fucking ladder; I am falling over the ladder. I can hear myself: *oh-god-oh-god-oh-god-oh-god.* I sound insane.

They have no mercy. None at all. I come in Joshua's mouth and Che is over me, sliding into me, one sure movement, *bam,* like a fireball. I cling to his back as he rides me, like a man in the sea. I can feel them turning me. My body is being manipulated. Like a sculpture. Like music. Joshua is rubbing oil into me, up and down my back, I've been turned onto Che, I am riding him now, rubbing my clit, just slow and easy, like a Sunday afternoon. I can feel warm oil dripping down me, down the crack of my ass, and I know what Joshua means to do. My shoulders freeze.

"Let me," he breathes against my spine. He's twisting his thumb into my ass.

"But . . . but . . ." I have an absurd fear about cleanliness. Did I wash properly? Do I smell good? Che is bucking inside me, throbbing.

"Just let me, Simone . . ." Joshua murmurs. "Stop thinking."

I push my ass back into him and he begins to slide into me. I breathe. I think good thoughts, hot thoughts. I will myself to relax, as more inches invade me.

Che stops, abruptly. He grabs my hips, stills them. Confused, frustrated, I look down into his face. Joshua has stopped, too. Fear swirls in me. They are regretting it, regretting me.

Then I understand.

They can feel each other. They can feel each other's cocks. There is only a thin layer of me between them.

There is a strange kind of confusion in Che's eyes. I wait. I cannot bear the moment; my body is crying for movement. But I wait. They have never gone this far; there is no male plot. They have never thought of going this far, and because of this, they are afraid. Of what it shows them. Of what it shows me.

Che has let go of my hips. His hands are spread out, away from the sides of his body. Joshua's hands are on my shoulders. We are all very still. The music has stopped. There is only the sound of us breathing.

Joshua's hand slides down to the floor as Che's hand comes up from the ground. They touch palms, fingers lingering.

I watch, fascinated, aching. It is so brief.

Che begins. He pushes up inside me, just a small movement. My pussy grabs him, hard.

Joshua sighs. "You like what he's doing to you?"

"Oh yes . . ." I moan.

Joshua pulls his penis out of me, halfway out. Then back into me again, so slowly, so gently, I can only gulp air.

Che smiles up at me as his friend sinks home.

"You like how he feels?" he says.

My hips make circles.

They double-fuck me as if they have been doing it all their lives. I am lost in a world of purring. They are pulling and pushing me along the length of both of them and in the minutes it takes, in the strange hours it takes, in the years that we all fuck and love each other, it seems as if one cock is inside me. It feels as if a million hands are in my hair, a thousand lips on my skin, as if we are all dancing in a lake of mingled sweat. I am speaking in tongues, screaming, begging, I can hear the slap of thighs, I am calling out that old plea, the only thing I can moan in this moment. I thaw out. I give in. I demand.

"Fuck me, fuck me, *fuck* me!" I say.

Oh, and they do. And in some part of them, they fuck each other, too.

*   *   *

They dress me in the blue light, as if I am a child, pulling my panties up my legs, scattering kisses along my back as they hook my bra, smoothing my skin, Che soothing my ass with little sighs, Joshua stroking every pubic hair into place.

We sit on the floor, look at Project X and smile at each other through the darkness. And suddenly, I see. They are not dogs. They are lions. I hold up my head in the face of their grace and their beauty. I can't wait to tell Amba.

For I am a lion, too.

"Art," I say. "They're going to love it."

We hold hands, all of us.

PRESTON L. ALLEN

If He Only Knew

When Maleek's wife, Hortensia, died, he took off nearly a month and then announced he had gotten over it.

He came back to school as his old happy, helpful self. Life is for the living, he told us. But we noticed that his pants were now often unpressed, his socks mismatched. He gave foolish advice to the kids like, "So what if you cut classes? If school is not for you, school is not for you." He made a rule that no one, absolutely no one, could use the office copier without his permission because he was tired of all the waste. Then he was never in his office to give permission, instead roaming the halls in a cloud of cigarette smoke. It set a bad example for the kids, watching their principal fall to pieces like that.

But I knew how he was hurting. I understood his pain.

I felt it was my place to help him because I alone knew that Hortensia was the first woman Maleek had ever been intimate with: his first love, if you will, though not his only love, not by any stretch.

Big, bald, and beautiful, Maleek was an angular-faced brother with rich, basket-brown skin, a cleft in his chin, and soul-searching, long-lashed eyes. Maleek had quite a sense of style for a middle-school principal. He liked jeans and high-top work boots, and turtlenecks that delineated his sculpted torso and arms. You'd see him in loose-fitting suits and jackets once in a while, but rarely in ties. Under his suit coats, he preferred stylish clerical collars or shirts with shapely lapels. Maleek was a musician, an athlete, a scholar, a poet, and he attracted women like wildlife to an oasis. But he was a good man, and I would not call him a dog even though he had strayed with that substitute from Michigan, two of his three secretaries, and Dr. Dillard from the school board.

After each affair had taken what it could from him, he would crawl back to me, his old buddy, and say, "I'm a naughty, foolish boy. Vonda, why am I so blind?"

And I would say, "I'm ashamed of you. Hortensia is a good woman."

"It's not about her."

"She's a good wife to you. She loves you."

"Oh, Vonda, I love her, too, but you know how it is with us men."

"Just keep your dick in your pants, Mr. Man." Then I would smack him playfully in the middle of his forehead with the meat of my palm. I was the only one could do that to him. We had been buddies since middle school, and Maleek didn't see me as a woman so much as two friendly, familiar arms he could fall into when things went bad.

If he only knew.

If he only knew he was not alone in his pain at the loss of a lover.

Maleek's wife was dead. My man treated me like I was dead. Like my eyes could no longer see. Like I was some kind of fool, which I am not. The new cologne. The flashy jewelry on his wrists and his neck. The pierced ear. His body hard and tight again from three nights a week in the gym. Like I didn't know what that was all about. Christopher said he was doing it all for me, but I suspected he was hitting it with that little waitress of his. Last month I saw her at the Hospitality Management Fundraiser, a skinny sister with relaxed hair and bright skin. The slick way he lit her cigarette. The slick way she took it from him. The slick way she smiled at me. The mouse already ate the cheese.

When we got home that night, he had denied.

I scratched and bit.

Tore the tie right off his neck trying to strangle him.

His skin was very fair, like a peach sprinkled with nutmeg, and he was sensitive about his appearance. He cursed at the red marks I left and hit me, and the boys ran to get the phone to call 911 like we had taught them to do in emergencies. Christopher grabbed the phone and took them into their room, where I heard cooing first, then talking. He came out and didn't say a word to me. I watched him pack a bag. I watched him go to the door.

He stopped and turned to me. "I don't know what this is about."

"It's about that damned waitress!" I fired back.

He slammed the door.

Good riddance, asshole.

* * *

If Maleek only knew.

There was a time when I had really loved him. Way back. When we were children, the last year of middle school. He was in the band room after school helping Mr. Gleason inventory the instruments. I was fooling around on the piano playing "Endless Love," and Maleek plopped down next to me and sang the lyrics in a tenor surprisingly beautiful for a boy with such fat cheeks. I smacked his forehead with the meat of my palm and said, "You can sing? Not you."

"Ouch," he said, rubbing his forehead. "Yes, I can."

I fell in love with him then—a trip to the movies in his mother's station wagon, phone calls that went beyond midnight, some fumbling around in the empty auditorium after school (his hand on my nipples, my hand on his zipper), the frequent and public forehead smacks, our little game—but it quickly passed. I dumped him, you see. I think I know why, but sometimes I'm not sure. He hurt me, of that I am sure. He would look at them, the fair girls, and call them pretty. He would look at me, and, well, I knew what he was thinking. Dark. Even back then my legs were long and sexy. My breasts heavier than the other girls. But I was dark. I remember how hard I cried, mostly because he didn't even realize he had done it. I fell in love with Christopher after that, the first chair clarinet. Maleek grew up and chiseled his extra pounds into an athlete's physique, broad chest, narrow waist, powerful arms, and for a while dreamt of a career in professional sports. I watched him get more handsome as he got older. Sometimes I wondered what might have been.

Now I was a music teacher and director of the chorus at our old middle school, and Maleek, the principal, was my boss. We ate lunch together every day. Sometimes we talked about the old times. Christopher wasn't the least bit jealous because we were all friends from way back. More important, Maleek kept me out of Christopher's hair, and Christopher had a lot of hair—waitresses, I mean—at the restaurant he managed.

But Maleek was still coming to work in mismatched socks, cloaked in cigarette smoke.

Today at lunch he had said, "Maybe I want to do something else with my life. I used to be a good singer. I'm tired of this job. The children are stupid."

"Don't say that," I chastised. He was a good principal; he had achieved so much so young. A singer? "You don't mean that."

But he was looking the other way, at his degrees hanging on the wall. Like he hadn't heard me, like he hadn't heard himself, maybe. When he turned back to me, he said, "I'm taking half a day. I'm too tired to do this."

He finished his hot dog and milk, wiped his hands with a napkin, collected his briefcase, and was gone. It was left to me to explain his whereabouts to the secretary, Phyllis, who, like everyone else, was growing tired of this new Maleek. We all liked the old Maleek, who was so together and could solve all of our problems with a funny story or a song.

Blue-haired Phyllis typed Maleek's sick leave form in a huff, eyeing me through the upper half of tinted bifocals. "You're his friend. I think you should know there's a petition going around about this copier policy of his," she said. She whipped the sick leave form out of the typewriter and handed it to me. I took it and signed it for Maleek.

"He's going through a hard time." I sighed.

"The school has to be run right," Phyllis said. She was the secretary Maleek had not flirted with. "You have any idea how many days he's missed already?"

"You know Maleek. He'll work through it."

"There is talk," warned Phyllis, who had been the old secretary even back when Maleek and I were students here. "There are rules, and rules need to be followed. This copier thing is driving us all crazy."

*   *   *

I called Maleek several times that day and kept getting his machine. After school, I had an impulse to drive over to his house, but I had to get home to help Christopher clean up the place for our big night. This was his second week back home, and we were trying hard to work it out.

When I got home, Christopher had already dropped the boys off at his mother's. He had set the table with flowers, jasmine-scented candles, and champagne. I vacuumed, straightened up the room, changed the sheets on the bed, then took a shower. He had the music playing loud in the living room. "I'm Your Baby Tonight." I liked Whitney Houston. He hated Whitney Houston. He was doing it for my benefit. As the water washed over my body, I couldn't help but think, *The bitch dumped him. The bitch dumped him real good.*

But I was glad to have him back. He was my man. He was a

good provider. A good father to Thad and Deion. Even in college, when he was wild and things between us were real rocky, I had always taken him back, no matter what. No matter who.

I turned off the water, put on the dress he loved me in, the short, white Versace that left most of my upper thighs uncovered. Then I went into the dining room, where the lights were dimmed and the candles glowing.

He held my hand under the table as we ate. He rubbed the insides of my thighs. His pot roast was delicious. We smiled a lot. We didn't talk at all.

After dinner, he came up behind me while I was at the sink and said, "You don't have to wash those." His breath warmed my ear the way I liked, and my body fell against his in our old familiar rhythm. Apart from his flaws, Christopher could be very romantic when he wanted to be. He had to know that I still carried the pain from the affair, which he still hadn't admitted to. He kissed me patiently around my neck and ears, giving me time to think about it all, time to forgive and move on. He pushed the dress up to my neck and sucked each nipple languidly, then we fell to the floor by the sink like two teenagers. He was doing everything right tonight, making no mistakes. I felt inside his pants and he was not wearing any underwear. I took his dick in my hands, one hand gently tugging the pulsing shaft, the other tickling the balls. I rolled over him. He was on his back now, and I was on top, my breasts hanging out of the Versace, but he stopped me. "In the bedroom," he said. "The floor's too cold."

"Okay," I said, my breathing shallow.

He lifted me up with a triumphant shout. In the bedroom,

there was a wrapped box on the bed. I opened it, and he told me to put on the lacy things I found inside. They fit funny. They were the size I had been before his affair, before I had started overeating as therapy. The other woman, Miss Sexy Waitress Bitch, had the perfect body. She was all curves and booty and perky tits. My breasts were better, bigger. I had show-off breasts. And I had a prettier face, doe-like brown eyes, a cute little punch of a nose, and luscious lips. But what's a face when you're dark? I was tensing up, becoming angry.

Christopher laid me down and positioned himself over me. I tried thinking happy thoughts to get the heat back, thinking about the time he had covered my body in whipped cream. I had been six months pregnant with our second boy, Deion, my stomach was out to here, and Christopher had licked it all off. All of it. Bathed me with his skillful tongue. I remembered how wet he made me. I was wet again. But now Christopher couldn't get it up.

I said, "It's okay, baby," and stroked his smooth face. He turned away from me and began talking into the darkness. There was something boiling inside him. I had been married to him long enough to know this. I listened quietly as he talked about the bills, where the boys would go to college, his plans to buy a new house when he got his own franchise. I touched his earring, the double-pearl stud. He did look good with an earring. It worked well with his exotic features, which less perceptive people had described as odd. Thin lips, wide-spaced eyes, prominent forehead accented by slanting eyebrows. The earring made him look harder. More like a regular brother. This is the best my man had ever looked. I went to hug him, but he jumped out of bed.

I cried softly as he stepped into his pants and wrapped himself in his shirt. "What did I do? What did I do?"

"I don't even feel like a man around you. You nag me and bring me down."

I got up and put my arms around him. "What did I do, baby? Let's talk about it."

He pushed me off. "You think I have another woman. Why shouldn't I, the way you treat me, like I'm not even a man."

My whole world was falling apart. "I don't understand, Christopher. What are you saying?"

"I can't do this anymore. I can't do this," he said. Twelve years. Two children. Five affairs that I knew of. Now six. And *he* couldn't do it anymore. I was still wearing the lacy things that would have fit better two months ago. They were bright white things. I felt fat, ugly. My man said, "I love somebody else."

I said through tears, "That waitress? Nadine?"

I was falling apart, and he was strangely composed. "It's not a question of who, Vonda," he said. "The problem is with us."

He took a suitcase this time.

When Christopher left, I cried some more, and then the crying stopped like someone had turned off the faucet. I thought I would have cried longer. Perhaps I should have. Something had come over me, but I didn't know exactly what it was.

It drew me to the piano. I played scales, which was what I always did whenever he hurt me, or hit me; or I would go some-where with Maleek, a movie maybe, something awful that we could make fun of, and Maleek would make me feel better.

My fingers hammered out scale after scale. The pain was still there, like a heavy thing in my stomach, but I didn't feel sorry for myself. I felt sorry for Maleek, who was still coming to work in mismatched socks. Maleek, whose career was in jeopardy.

"Poor Maleek. Poor Maleek." I played scales, but "Endless Love" played in my head. I hadn't heard Maleek sing in so long, and that was a shame. He had such a beautiful voice. And he was in such pain. I was in such pain. I packed an overnight bag, leaving behind Christopher's tight, lacy things, called my mother-in-law to pick up the boys, and then I drove to Maleek's house.

* * *

I had been to his house many times before, every house he'd ever had, many times, even spent a week on his couch after Christopher hit me the first time. This was while I was pregnant with Deion, and Maleek and Hortensia had only just gotten married. All I had wanted was just to lie in a dark place and die. But Maleek had comforted me, and Hortensia, a green-eyed Cuban with pale skin and raven hair, had made me eat breakfast and drink a potent coffee that required no cream.

They had been a good team, Hortensia and Maleek.

I was beginning to understand his loss now. She had been good to him. He had been a rogue. So he couldn't help feeling that he had taken her for granted, and now that she was gone it was too late to make amends. This was how Christopher was going to feel when he tried to come back to me, as he always did, and he found out that I had someone else, someone I should have been with all along.

I had been to Maleek's house many times, many times, but I had never been in his bedroom.

If Maleek only knew what I had felt all those nights on his couch. I had been ashamed to even think it. Did he even have a bed? What kind? If I asked him, would he take me back?

There was a reason I had put on my best panties and bra tonight.

* * *

He opened the door wearing the same shirt and pants and mismatched socks that he had worn that day in his office. There was only one light on in the house, in the living room, where a basketball game played on the TV. I went into the living room and sat on the couch. He asked if I wanted anything to drink. I said, yes, a Coke, or juice, or water, anything. When he brought back the glass of cranberry juice, I took a swallow and told him that I wanted to sleep with him, how about it?

Something under his skin jumped. "Just like that?" he said. "Vonda, you kidding me, right? Did Christopher hit you? I swear I'll kick his narrow, yellow ass."

"I don't want to talk about Christopher," I said, finishing my cranberry juice. I put the glass down, opened my blouse, and unfastened my good bra. The way Maleek looked at my breasts made me feel good. I'm sure he had always wondered at them. Most men do. Yes, they were a perfect D cup. He sat there, just looking, for how long I don't know. Then he came over and kissed me on the mouth. It was our first kiss since we were fourteen. It was a good kiss. I lay back on the couch, and his hands went down to my breasts, my stomach, then lower. He pushed aside my soaked panties. I pulled him on top of me, the man I had wanted for so long. I parted my legs.

He said, "Give me a second now. Just give me a second." Then he got up and disappeared into the bathroom.

I went into his bedroom and sat down on his bed; he had a bed, a firm bed. I heard the shower running, twenty minutes. Then the toilet flushed. Twice. What was he flushing? Maleek came into the bedroom in a silly silk thing, Japanese print, with trees and a mountain on it. Beneath the stud he had grown into, I spied the soft, chubby Maleek who had sung to me as a child. It felt so good, so right. He sat next to me and we picked up where we had left off on the couch. His mouth on my mouth, his hand on my tender breasts, his fingers between the slick, fat lips of my pussy. It was a great disappointment when Maleek couldn't get it up, either.

"Jesus, I'm sorry, Vonda."

"Don't be."

"I can't believe this." He put his head between his hands. "I've wanted you for so long."

"Not as long as I've wanted you."

He stretched his big, naked body out on the bed. His sex was a fat, flat invertebrate sleeping peacefully on his stomach. He groaned and closed his eyes. He sounded like the kid I used to know. "I can't believe this."

"Would it help if I . . . kissed him?"

He gave me that look. "Oh, Vonda."

So I rested my head on his stomach and placed my hands on

his thighs. I began with light kisses, from his almost hairless sac to the slit in the top of the proud head, and yes, it helped. By the time I had kissed my way down to the sac again, the flat worm was gone and I was holding a sturdy, brown-veined club in my hand. Its curve and size were magnificent. I slicked the purple head with spit. He liked that, and groaned. I put him in my mouth and worked my tongue around and down the proud thing. He put his hands on my head and began a slow in-and-out motion, his smooth hips lifting up off the bed with each gentle thrust.

"Okay, baby," he said. "I'm ready. I'm ready."

After that, Maleek made love to me like he wanted to prove something, win something. It hurt a little, but I would make myself enjoy it. I shifted my hips just so, then he leaned back a little. It felt much better this way with my legs around his waist. My skin was tingling the way it does when my man is slapping it real good. I thought, *How weird, this is me and Maleek. Me and Maleek are finally making love.* How weird, because sometimes when sex with Christopher wasn't going so good I would think about having sex with Maleek, and I would get hot and wet. I ground up now into Maleek while fantasizing about *Maleek,* and kept thinking, *How weird.* Then I noticed the photographs of Hortensia placed all around the room. She reminded me of a swan, large eyes, long neck, pale.

Thank God, Maleek turned me over, and I couldn't see the photographs anymore. But now I could smell the sheets he hadn't changed since—*Oh God, no, are these her hairs on the sheet? This is her house. She died here.* I pictured Hortensia the way Maleek had found her, one hand clawing her face.

Now he licked my ear, which I usually liked, but my flesh was cold as death. Maleek grunted and pushed against me hard, twice, three times, grunted, then rolled over onto his back.

"Wow," he said, without looking at me.

"We finally did it," I said, but thought I screamed in my head, *Look at me, Maleek. We need each other. Look at me.* When he did look at me, I pulled Hortensia's sheets over my breasts, which were fat and swinging free.

"You were great," he said.

I touched my breasts. My show-off breasts.

"Great," Maleek said.

"Liar," I said, raising my hand. I had made it worse coming here, doing this. I brought the meat of my hand down on his forehead. "You liar!"

"Ouch!"

"I love you, Maleek, but this was bad. Bad!"

He pleaded with his eyes, like he was grieving again.

I couldn't take this, I couldn't take any more of this big baby. I got up and went out to the couch in the living room where the basketball game had been replaced by the *Tonight Show.* I sat with my feet up on the couch and my face pressed against my knees. When he came out, I wasn't crying anymore, but my nose was stuffy and dry. He sat down next to me on the couch and put a hand on one of my feet. His beautiful eyes glittered in the colored light of the television. He was wearing his silly Japanese robe again. "Come back in the room," he said.

"What for?"

"I love you. I've always loved you."

"It's no use."

"What happened was—"

"I'm not blaming you," I said. "It's probably me. I've been married to Christopher too long. I'm too used to him. I know what to expect with him. It's too hard to start over with someone new."

"I'm not new," he said, massaging my foot, my toes. He was using both hands now.

"You know what I mean," I said. "I had this fantasy of what it would be like. To be with the man I always wanted. All my problems would go away."

He huffed. "The man you always wanted." He took his hands off my feet. "The man you dumped."

I pulled my body in tighter. "The way you treated me, what the hell did you expect?"

He was so surprised by my answer that he went into the black man's falsetto and responded in soprano. "The way I treated you?" he almost shrieked. "I was good to you. I was a good boyfriend, but then along comes old waterhead Christopher."

"Stop calling him that! He hates that." I pointed a finger at him. "And you remember it all wrong."

"Remember what?" And still in falsetto: "What did I do?"

Oh, he was all innocent, poor baby. They were always all innocent. Him and Christopher both. "I'm the wrong color. I'm the wrong color for you, the wrong color for Christopher." He was quiet now as I spoke. "I used to watch the way you talked to them, then the way you talked to me. And Kathy Walsh, the way you talked to her. She was my best friend."

"I only dated her after we broke up. After you dumped me, girl. You got your memory hat on backwards."

"You only dated white girls after that, too. And then married one."

"Hortensia was Cuban."

"Whiter than me," I said. "You and Christopher both. You like them light. I don't blame you for your taste. I'm just saying that there's nothing left for the rest of us sisters."

He sucked his tongue. "And yet you married a man so light, he could pass for white. Sitting in this room right now with only this TV on, you couldn't tell whether Christopher was black or white. How about that, my sister? What flavor do you like?"

"I like chocolate."

"Shit. White chocolate," he said. "But please understand me, that's not the way I play it. I like people, black or white, and women who are fine, women who turn me on, women who are good to me. I love people, dark or light, who are good to me. That's why I loved Hortensia. She was good to me. That's why I love you, even though you're talking mucho shit right now."

"You don't love me, and don't be using that Spanish with me," I said. "No speaka de Spanish. I am African American with the emphasis on the American."

He shook his head, laughing. "See? Again you're choosing the lighter side."

"With emphasis on the African, then."

"Too late to take it back now," he teased. Then he nodded his head. "And I do love you. Always have, always will. Because I know you care about me. That's why you came here tonight. You're my true friend."

"True dat." But a friend had to tell a friend the truth. "You're going to lose your job if you don't watch your back."

"Ain't nobody gonna take my job. I got it under control."

"Wearing them mismatched socks."

Falsetto again: "Sister, don't you be so cruel!" His beautiful smile spread across his face. "Sometimes a brother be rushing in the morning."

"I just care about you, is all. I'm your buddy."

"And I thank you, buddy." He nodded slyly. "Humph. But the rest of my buddies don't be sitting their fine, naked asses up on my couch showing me all their pussy hair."

"I'll go put my clothes on."

"Good." He had his hand on my foot again, massaging.

"I'll sleep here on the couch."

"Great." He had both hands on my feet now. Grinning.

"And we'll be friends forever and pretend this night never happened. Mmmm."

"Excellent idea. Pal." His hands were on my feet again, but way, way high up on my feet, like deep, deep in my wet sex and on top of my clit.

"Mmmm, Maleek."

"That fool Christopher don't know half what he got. You are so beautiful. You are so damned fine."

I lay back on the couch and let his fingers light the fires inside me. Maleek was on his knees before the couch now. My feet danced on his shoulders. His tongue had replaced his fingers.

This time the anxiety, or whatever it had been, was gone out of him, and he was eating me leisurely, patiently, the way I like it, so that I can enjoy the good feelings through eyes half closed with pleasure. I enjoyed watching his face as my womb expanded and contracted under the attention of his mouth. His eyes never left mine. It's like we were still kissing. He was kissing me with his eyes. He was kissing my mouth through my pussy with his eyes. My tongue lolled outside of my mouth. I was kissing him back. I was breathing through my nose again. He was in control of me now.

"Here it comes!" I shouted. "I'm coming!"

My orgasm was his. I pressed against his face when I came. I grabbed his beautiful, bald head and pressed so hard I thought my womb would swallow his face. I wanted to see his face, but I kept pressing against it, mashing it hard, back and forth and then in a circular motion around his nose, his eyes, his chin. When he looked up, his smiling face was glazed with my juice.

He flung off the silly Japanese robe and kissed his way up my body. He brought his sweet, pussy breath to my lips and said, "God, I love you." He sucked my lips. His tongue slipped into my mouth. I was juicing all over his couch. I ran my hands up and down his tight, muscular ass. He was magnificently hairless and glossed over in sweat. His smell was a sharp mix of soap, expensive cologne, and pure lust. He said to me, "Let's go back in the bedroom," and he began to lift me.

"No," I growled. I was not going to argue with him. I was not going to break his groove. I would explain it to him later, if necessary. But I was not going back into *her* room. "Hell no, baby.

Let's do it right here. Right here." *Right here on the couch where I had dreamt about you so many nights.*

With a shrug, he complied. The couch was not big enough for the two of us to lie on, so he turned my body, shaped me like a spoon, and got behind me. I felt one of his legs against my thigh. The other, I assumed, was on the floor. He kept one arm under me so that I would not be pressed into the back of the couch. He entered me, and the slick, electric pleasure made me raise the top leg higher and cry out. He fucked me from behind like that, and I reached out and held on to the back of the couch. His big dick slid into me. I pushed back as best I could with my ass. I wanted to open wider. He reached around and found my clit with his fingers.

"Oh, Jesus, Maleek! Yes!"

He leaned over my shoulder and took my tongue into his mouth. My face was wet with tears. I sucked on his darting tongue, and I yielded to the pleasures of my finally liberated flesh. I was so happy, so happy to be with the one man I loved. I kept on crying all through my orgasms.

When his orgasm came, it was a mighty thing, with contractions, and sharp thrustings, and a deep groan from his belly. He pulled me down onto the carpet with him and he held me there, kissing me.

I fell asleep there, my tongue in his mouth, kissing him.

* * *

I awoke to the sound of a phone ringing. The TV was off, and I was covered in a cool sheet. As I sat up, I checked it surreptitiously for signs of Hortensia.

Maleek was watching me from the couch. He was wearing a kente cloth wrap around his waist and drinking cranberry juice from a crystal glass.

"Want some?" he said, offering me the glass.

I shook my head, and stretched my body, which had been properly loved for the first time in a long time. But now I was beginning to remember that I had another life. A job to go to tomorrow. Two children at my mother-in-law's house. A husband, for what he was worth, out somewhere with a suitcase and another woman. "What time is it?"

"After three," he said.

The phone was still ringing. "How many times did he call?"

"This one makes five." As if on cue, the phone stopped ringing and the machine picked up the latest message. Maleek turned it up so I could hear: "Maleek? Me again. It's after three. I know she's there. I know she's safe with you. Tell her I put the boys to bed. They're sleeping like champs. I don't know if she told you what happened between us tonight, but I kind of said some things I shouldn't have. I'll explain it to you later, buddy. Stupid man shit, you know. Just have her call me so I'll know she's safe. She probably doesn't want to talk to me tonight, I understand that, but maybe you can call me and let me know what's going down. I trust you. We all go way back. Way back."

The timer cut Christopher off.

But me and Maleek weren't really paying much attention by then. We were on the floor, holding each other, rocking in each other's arms, crying, that was part of it, too—crying was a crucial part of making the most of these last few minutes before we would go to sleep and awaken to a world that would be entirely changed.

Yes, I would go back to Christopher. We both knew it.

I had to go back. I had two children.

But now I knew what it was like to be loved by someone who loved me, and that made me a very dangerous person, a selfish person. I was not going to take anybody hitting me anymore. I was not going to take anybody's sloppy seconds anymore. I hoped old Christopher knew what he was in for.

Lord, if he only knew.

TANANARIVE DUE

Transplanted

trans•plant, *v: to move from one place to another.*

*O*risa decided, at the last possible moment, not to view the body.

She could see the rose-colored casket not fifteen yards from where she stood, but suddenly her feet were rooted. She wouldn't do it. Her husband was Kevin Emory Bryant, the second of three brothers, thirty-four years old, gifted actor, poet, and even more gifted lover, hopelessly addicted to both football and dancing (especially funk, reggae, and—since he'd met her—salsa), world's worst on the free-throw line but heaven on Rollerblades, politically inclined toward the radical, too softhearted to ignore a beggar, and the most sterling soul she had ever known. *That* was Kevin Emory Bryant. The thing in the casket was not Kevin, and never would be.

"I'm going to sit down," Orisa said, to no one in particular.

Hands were grabbing her, cupping her elbows and propping her underarms, trying to pull her up. Maybe she had lost touch with herself for a moment, Orisa realized, because for some rea-

son she was sitting with her legs in a V on the cold church floor.
If Kevin could see her now, he was laughing his ass off.

As she was brought to her feet and led to the pew beside her
mother, Orisa was suddenly very glad of the arrangement she and
Kevin had made. She hadn't thought much of it at the time—
she'd only agreed to humor him—but now she was very glad
indeed. The videotape was all she could think about during the
funeral, even over the singing and wailing and remembering.

Orisa couldn't wait to get home to her husband.

*   *   *

"I think she's taking too many of those pills."

"Her doctor prescribed them, *Mami,* so stop acting like she's
some kind of junkie. She needs them. I've never seen her like
this. I'm worried."

Marisol and her mother sounded like they were trying to keep
their voices down as they spoke in Spanish in her bedroom, but
they weren't trying hard enough. Orisa guessed that they were
standing close to the wall, in her closet. She heard rearranging, so
she assumed her mother was trying to push Kevin's clothes out of
sight, as if hiding his belongings would mean he had never been
there. She wanted to scream at them to get out of their fucking
bedroom because she needed to see Kevin, but she just waited in
silence. They meant well, she told herself. Her mother had been
forced to leave *Papi* in Havana when he arranged for their passage
to Miami when Orisa was eight, and it had taken *Mami* another
eight years to be able to say his name in their presence again. Her
mother expected Orisa to want to forget right away, when noth-

ing could be less true. Orisa didn't want to forget a single thing.

"Let's leave this alone until tomorrow, *Mami*. Orisa might not like you doing that, and she needs to go to bed. She said she wants to sleep in here tonight."

Her mother clucked. "She's not in her right mind. She hasn't cried."

"You didn't cry when we came over," Marisol said.

"That's how I know she's not in her right mind," *Mami* said.

*   *   *

Despite her resolve, and her *need*, it took Orisa two hours to open her nightstand drawer to pull out the videotape marked KEVIN. Then, it took her another fifteen minutes to finally walk to the VCR on their bookshelf, slide the tape inside, and push PLAY. Her heart was pounding so hard, her knees were nearly useless. She wobbled where she stood, waiting for Kevin's gift. He'd known she would need it before she did.

As snow played on the beginning of the tape, Orisa gave up her battle to remain standing. She sat at the foot of the bed.

When Kev's face suddenly appeared on the television screen, nearly twenty-six inches tall, it made her breath freeze in her throat. His shaved brown head gleamed faintly from a muted light somewhere near him. There was only a white wall behind him, a stark contrast to the richness of his dark skin. The camera was focused so close to his face, she could see all of its nuances; his laughlines, his pink-tinged bottom lip, those carved cheekbones that seemed to bespeak royalty. And his almond eyes—that was the eeriest part of all. His brown eyes were shining, gazing at her intently. Studying her. When he smiled a small, sympathetic smile and his eyes seemed to talk to her, Orisa felt shivers of mingled grief and joy travel through her, colliding. She clutched the edge of the bed.

"Hey, Boo," he said, after a short time.

"Hey, Kev."

He leaned slightly closer. "This is hard, isn't it?"

Orisa nodded, not speaking at first. "Yes," she tried to say, but the single word was so large that it nearly choked her. She couldn't make a sound.

His brow furrowed. "I'm sorry it's so hard."

"Me, too," she said, but he had already gone ahead to say the next thing: "We talked about this, Orisa. Don't do it if you don't think it will help. I'm only trying to bring you joy, babe. That's all. Don't do it if you're not ready to visit with me yet."

Despite everything, Orisa felt a flash of anger. He was always second-guessing her! But Orisa's anger struck her as absurd, and then it was buried by a sudden sadness that made her panicky. Maybe she wasn't ready. Maybe this would only make it worse, if such a thing were possible. But she could not take her eyes away from him.

"I think you're ready, or you wouldn't be watching," Kev said, his words rolling out gently. "You know your own mind. You keep telling me that."

Slowly, Orisa nodded.

His smile grew broad, even eager. He licked his lips. "Then turn off the lights," he said. "Light some candles like we do when I'm out of town, when I light mine and you light yours and we stare at the flame and meditate together. That's all we'll be doing, like before. And put on some drumming music, maybe the Mongo Santamaria you bought me. That brother jams."

"I don't know where you put it," she said, feeling the panic bubbling up again. They had five shelves of CDs, most of them Kev's. There must be hundreds. She felt lost and small, a sudden stranger in her own home.

"It's on the third shelf, under S. I alphabetize them, remember?" Kev said patiently, barely giving her time to speak. "Next to Santana."

"Yes," she said, remembering. Her relief electrified her.

"Not too loud, though. Put the music on very, very softly. Let's do this right. Let's try to make this better somehow. Just a little. I want you to feel my touch again. I think that's what you need right now. Light those candles, and let's get that music going. And know what you're gonna do next?"

She did not. She didn't have the foggiest idea.

"You're going into the bathroom, let the water in the sink get good and hot, then fill it up. Fill up the sink with hot water and put your little friend in there. Your toy."

Orisa stared at the television screen, wondering if she was hallucinating. *What* had he just said?

Kev's eyes twinkled, and he motioned with his arm. "Go on, girl. You heard me. And put the little bottle of baby oil in there, too. Let it heat up. Do everything just like you showed me. Just the same. The baby oil, the hot water. Everything. Please trust me on this one, Boo. I think we should do this. I want to do this for you." His eyes locked with hers. "Go on. Get the candles. Turn down the lights. Heat everything up. This is how we'll be together again. I'll wait for you. Just go do it. Please?"

She never could resist him when he pleaded. Without any further argument, and with barely a thought, Orisa began to follow her dead husband's instructions.

*   *   *

He had laid it on her the very first night they met, as they'd walked on the South Beach sand after a reggae band finished its first set at the Paradise Bar, back before Paradise changed owners and went to shit. He told her right from jump.

The friends who were supposed to have met her at Paradise after work had never shown up, and she'd been thinking about leaving when she saw Kevin walking toward her, a mirage in an open white linen shirt and matching slacks. She didn't recognize him, so she had no idea that he got sacks of fan mail for his role on a daytime soap opera, or that he'd played Wesley's younger brother in a movie she'd missed earlier that year, but she did know that he was one of the most striking men she had ever seen up close. His teeth could have been pearls, if only pearls were whiter. His dark skin looked smooth enough to melt from his broad-chested frame. This man was *muy, muy guapo.*

"I love your dreads, sister. Are you Jamaican?"

"Cuban," she said. "My family took a long boat-ride when I was little." She didn't know why she'd told him that. She almost never told anyone that.

He dropped his head to one side, ready to listen. "Were you sorry to leave?"

She blinked, glancing away from his eyes for a moment. When she glanced back at his face, she felt overcome by its rigid-jawed beauty yet again. "Of course I was sorry. It was all I knew. We had to leave my father there. I never saw him again."

"I'm sorry about your father. I really, really am," he said. "I don't want to play down that loss, and I hope you can forgive me saying this, but you know what? I'm not sorry you're here. Way back when, the slavers dropped your folks off on that island and dropped mine off a few miles down the way. And if you were still there, I wouldn't have met you tonight. And I couldn't have told you how miraculous I think you look. Or that I can see your intelligence in your eyes, and how it makes me want to know you. We wouldn't even speak the same language. That would be a crying shame."

For a long moment, Orisa couldn't even think to say thank you. "That's the second time I've heard that line tonight," she said finally, holding her face steady, trying not to show how dazzled she was. "That poetry and courage and honesty are so played out. Is that all you've got?"

He smiled a winking smile. " 'Fraid so, sister. That's all I've got."

It was all she needed. They decided to leave before the next set and walk on the beach instead, wading in the scent of the placid ocean. They had been talking for only twenty minutes, barely past revealing their respective occupations, when he said suddenly, "I hope this won't freak you out, but I'm a direct kind of guy. My time's too precious for games. I treat everything in my life the way I treat my work: I don't play. I'm twenty-seven, and I always knew I would have to make it in my business by the time I was thirty. I won't live long past that. That's almost a bet."

He'd said it so casually, for a moment she thought he was speaking in metaphors. Then, she noticed his gaze intensifying, waiting for her response.

"What does that mean?"

"That means I was never supposed to live this long. I was born with a heart defect, and I got a transplant two years ago. Only half of heart transplant patients survive five years. Those kind of stats really put life in perspective."

Orisa nearly stopped walking, slowing. "Why did you just tell me that?" she asked after a very long silence, when even her mind had been mute.

"Damned if I know," he said.

They walked without speaking for several minutes. He was giving her the chance to make a graceful exit, she realized, and she thought it might be smart to do just that. Instead, Orisa decided to say something brave. "What's it like to get a new heart?"

"It beats faster than my other one, mainly. High gear. That's the big difference."

"Is there anything you can't do?" she said.

"Besides grow old?" he mused, rubbing his chin playfully. "Nothing I can think of. The rest of me works pretty damned good. Some parts of me work great." As he said that, he deftly wrapped himself around her from behind, slipping his arm around her waist and nestling his solidness against the small of her back. He swayed, boldly pressing his erection to her. She wanted to feel indignant that he was being so forward, but the spot on her back where his crotch touched her burned, radiating up her spine.

Kev sighed into her ear. "I really like you, Orisa," he said, "but I'm not good at the casual sex thing."

She felt her heart jog. "What are you good at, then?"

"I'm good at taking things sorta slow. I'm good at getting to know the spirit beneath the face, and I'm good at seeing through people who ain't looking to see what's beneath mine. I'm good at talking, going to movies, eating Chinese takeout. That kinda thing. I'm not good at puzzles. I've put away childish things, I guess you could say."

She'd been in love with him before she had a chance to think better of it. And by the time she did think better of it, after she'd had time to research Kev's transplant and realize that he hadn't been exaggerating about his future, it was too late. Their spirits had known each other by then; their spirits had built a house of brick and put up wallpaper and planted a rose garden before she and Kev had spent their first night together. To her, it had some-how seemed like a fair trade: Kev was a true-life prince, every bit as smart and spiritual and sexy as she'd wanted her man to be, and the only price for his love was that she didn't know how long she could have him. *But isn't that true for everybody?* she'd asked herself, lying about what it really meant. She lived her days won-dering if Kev would live to be forty, or fifty, or if she would just wake up any old morning and discover he'd died in his sleep beside her, that his flesh was cold as stone.

In the end, it had been nothing like that. He'd gone to his doctor for his regular cardiac exam, and he'd gotten bad news. Three subsequent appointments and a new specialist had turned bad news to really bad news. Kev's dying had taken a month, from beginning to end. There had been no miracle telephone call proclaiming the discovery of a new heart donor. Neither of them had ever really expected there would be. They'd made a joke about it during a Hail Mary pass on *Monday Night Football*, the last time she'd held Kev's hand, in the hospital room they both knew he would never leave.

That night, she'd actually caught herself feeling relieved. After seven tense years of wondering, at least she finally knew when Kev was going to go.

*   *   *

"I hope you let the water get good and hot," she heard Kev's voice say from the bedroom, and the suddenness of his presence after the videotape's long silence startled her. Orisa was in the master bathroom, tending the steaming sink. She was making the preparations exactly as she'd been told, as she'd shown Kev last year when he'd opened the bottom drawer in the bathroom and accidentally found her toy. *Show me what you do when you're alone, Orisa,* he'd said. And so she had.

"You about ready, Boo?" Kev called out from the television set. "If not, maybe you better hit PAUSE. I'm about to start."

"I'm coming!" she said, but she was immediately sorry she'd said it so loudly. If *Mami* or Marisol heard her talking to Kev, they would come knocking on her door and ruin everything. They wouldn't understand. *Mami,* too bad for her, had never had a videotape from *Papi*. She'd gotten letters at first, but only a few.

When Orisa got back to the bedroom, her hands dripping with warm water from the items she carried, she noticed that the video's image had changed. Kev had adjusted the camera, pulling back the frame so she could see the contours of his baby-smooth chest as well as his face. He wasn't wearing a shirt. She hadn't noticed that before.

The room flickered with yellow-tinged candlelight, and Mongo's drums were racing, praising Chango, giving thanks to the ancestors. She felt as if she had stepped into a new world, a dreaming place.

"Don't be nervous, Boo. You'll be all right," he said. "Try to turn off the part of your head that feels fear, or sadness, or anything else right now. I'm not here for your head. I'm here for your heart and every other part of you."

"Are you really here, Kev?" she whispered.

But Kev did not answer. Instead, he stared hard at her, his lips peeling back into a smile, liberating his luminescent teeth. "Are you ready?"

"Yes," she said.

"I want you to be naked. But not too quickly, not like you're undressing after a long day at work. Take your clothes off for me, like a dance. Dance for the drums. Do it slowly. Let me watch you."

Orisa felt her hips shifting slowly back and forth, obeying Kev's words of their own accord. She allowed the bottle of baby oil and her toy to fall to the mattress, for now. Then, she felt the

drumming seduce her muscles. Her hips' motion widened, circling, and she began to pull her blouse over her head.

"That's it, Boo. Nice and slow. Free yourself, baby. Let it all go."

Orisa felt her heart quickening. Her heartbeat was tied to the
Mongo's congas, and the fire of the drums engulfed her. Her skirt
was off next, an improvised shimmy. Next, her breasts were freed
to bob with their own rhythms, separate from the rest of her.

She began to twirl, her hips swinging, propelling her.

"Let me tell you how much I love your body, Orisa," Kev said
in a husky whisper. "I love the curve of your abdomen, and I love
running my hand over those ham hocks you call an ass. Girl,
sometimes at parties I see you from behind and think, 'Who's
that?' and it always turns out to be you. And can I tell you about
your breasts? There's a purple sweater you wear that could make
a brother have a car accident. And if I look at your face too long,
I think I might fall into it and lose myself somewhere in there.
Your face makes me feel shy. I love all of it, Orisa. Even your little
toe with the fucked-up nail. I love all of it. I love your workout
funk and the dirty soles of your feet. I love all those little hairs on
your chinny chin-chin. I love the endless corridors of your mind.
I love the sexy dimples just above the crack of your ass. I love all
of it. All of it. *All* of it."

Kev's whispers washed over her. Orisa was perspiring lightly
now as she danced, and her skin was radiating heat. Her face
was hot.

"Thank you for sharing yourself with me, baby," Kev said. "Let
me take care of you. I can take care of you and your body. I
promise, Boo."

Orisa believed him. She lay down nude across their bed, ready.

"First, take that warm baby oil and drip it all over you. Drip it on your chest. Drip it between your legs and let it find its way. Just close your eyes and feel it seep to all your secret places. Feel your body waking up wherever it touches you. That baby oil is the wetness from my mouth, Orisa. From my tongue. That wetness you feel is from all the places I'm kissing you. All the places my tongue is bathing you."

Orisa squirmed, feeling the warm sensation of the slick oil making its way across her breasts, creeping through the forest of her pubic hair until it met her waiting skin. She was almost certain she could feel Kev's tongue making little quick-fire darts between her thighs, teasing her. Yes, she really could.

"Now, feel the palms of my hands rubbing your nipples, but not hard—barely touching them. A whisper. Feel the meat of my palms there, baby. Feel me making little circles. Feel my calluses on you. Do you feel me, Orisa? Do you feel your nipples singing? Are your thighs sliding together, pressing tight so the temple between your legs can return the song? Press your thighs tight and then pull them apart. Do it again. Do you feel the call-and-response?"

Orisa arched her body, her mouth falling open with a tiny whimper. When she opened her eyes, she saw Kev's face staring back at her, his lips slightly puckered, his eyes slitted the way they always were when he wanted her. Seeing his face, a river seemed to gush from her. All of her insides were seeping out, exposed.

"Feel my index finger tracing a line exactly down your center, Orisa, starting at your navel and gently through the curly hair I love to taste. Feel my finger tracing that map to your gold. Gently,

gently, girl. Feel my finger touching you lightly, with little butter-fly pats. Don't do anything else until I ask you to."

Orisa gasped. With each pat of Kev's finger, she felt a near-spasm. Her vagina felt swollen, grasping. Her body yearned for pressure, for penetration.

"Not yet, baby. Not yet. I'm massaging your nipple with one of my palms while my finger explores this valley. Let my finger get wet with the oil. Now, feel my finger making tiny circles—start high, and then move lower. But slow, do it slow. I'm making cir-cles, savoring that gentle rosebud, feeling it bloom. I can feel you opening up to me. I can feel those hard thighs of yours tensing up, then rolling open. I can feel how much you want me, Orisa. Do you want me?"

"Yes," Orisa gasped, her eyes closed. Her face was aflame from all the blood beating its way through her body.

"Now, this is where I'll need your help, Boo. Get the toy you brought, the big brown one you said reminds you of me. That's *my* yearning. That's my manhood. It should still be warm from the sink. It should still be wet. Let it tease you where your finger used to be, touching you lightly with the tip, little flicks. Can you help me do that, Orisa? Let me touch you."

The dildo from the bathroom drawer was no longer synthetic, no longer a toy made of lifelike rubber. It was warm and vibrant and living. Its slick, firm aliveness startled Orisa when she first felt it touch her.

"Kev," she said, amazed.

"Yes, baby, it's me. It's me. Let me touch you. Let me tease you. Let me stir you up until you can't stand the stirring. Let me make you forget what and who and where you are. Let me make you forget up and down and day and night."

Orisa felt her body buck, impatient. Kev was teasing her, pressing here, lightly bumping there, and with each contact she felt her insides screaming at her. Her insides wanted him. She wanted him.

"Shhhhh. Not yet, baby. Not quite yet. Hold back," Kev said, and Orisa moaned as if she were in pain. She wriggled, and her thighs clamped around Kev, hoarding the warm weight of his flesh nestled across her clitoris. It seemed to her that she spent a near-eternity that way, struggling not to cry out amid waves of mini-climaxes.

"I love you, Orisa," Kev said. "I want to be inside of you. Let me go inside."

And she felt him gently, gently nudging himself past her folds, filling her up, planting himself inside of her. Her chest sighed, unlocking.

"Let me go in a little ways, pull back a tiny bit, then push in again," Kev said. "Let me love you, Orisa. Let me make love to you. Let me find your Spot."

Orisa was floating out of the room, oblivious to everything except the powerful waves of pleasure that had possessed her. When she closed her legs tightly, trapping Kevin inside of her, her body writhed and danced. Mongo's congas were still playing on the CD player, and now her body had adopted his rhythms as its own.

"I love you, Orisa. I'll always love you," Kev said.

Orisa screamed. She was so absorbed in pleasure, she didn't hear her own choking sobs. She didn't notice her tears. She didn't feel the railroad stake that had plunged into her chest the instant the nurse came to her and said, *I'm sorry, Mrs. Bryant.*

"Yes, baby, feel my love. *Feel* me," Kevin said.

When Orisa screamed again, her pleasure popped like an over-filled balloon. Instead, she felt something big and awful waiting to be born from inside of her, a kind of hard knowledge that was final and confusing and sad. It reminded her of staring back at the hazy shoreline from a wildly bobbing boat, in the false comfort of her mother's embrace, trying to see *Papi* waving out to them from the beach with his white handkerchief in the early-morning light. But he'd been too far away. Too far. When she couldn't see *Papi,* she had started screaming. She wanted to jump into the water and go back to him, even if she drowned like so many people had drowned in the stories their widows and orphans had told *Mami* when they warned her not to get on the boat. *Don't look, negra,* her mother had said, stroking her hair. *Don't look.* So, Orisa hadn't looked.

But this time, Orisa opened her eyes, and she did look. *Mami* had never been able to grieve, but Orisa would. It was hard to see through the long-absent tears that were stinging her cheeks with their salts, but Kev was still on her television screen, smiling at her in the gift of himself he had left behind. She missed him. *Dios Dios Dios,* she missed him. Orisa heard an animal's warble coming to life in her throat, fighting itself free from the wall Orisa had erected with all of her energy. Her wall was crumbling. She was going to cry many hours tonight, she realized. She might cry for days on end.

"I'm here, baby," her dead husband said. "I'm here."

And even though Orisa knew he really *wasn't* here, in a way she hadn't allowed herself to know it before. Somehow, yes, he was.

BERNICE L. McFADDEN

Sit

*H*e was hearing talk. Whispers that sounded like palm tree leaves brushing against each other. He'd grown up hearing this type of talk. When he was a boy the women talked over and around him. Now those same women spoke directly to him and eyed him with interest, wondering if he was the same type of lover his father had been.

His mother's friends, some cousins, not so distant, his brother's wife, his sister's classmates and the women who walked the beach offering to braid the white people's hair for two dollars a plait.

There were others. Many, many others.

He'd been back only a day and a half. His skin was still pale from the cold German winter he'd spent making love to a rich white widow.

He hadn't wanted to go; he hated the European winters and the bright sunshine that lent no warmth at all.

But he went anyway because she'd promised him her dead husband's brand new BMW if he'd come and stay through the New Year.

Now he was back, a little heavier from the rich foods he'd eaten during the two months he was gone, but still solid, still, according to what he was hearing, desirable.

"He back on the island."

"Nah, man! That ain't true!"

"How you meaning? I saw him myself, in town near the stop post!"

"He look just the same, you know! A little bigger, but—"

"But?"

"But still sweet as hell!"

Butler laughed to himself. They all wanted an invitation to sit, but he was particular and so there were only two or three from the island who had experienced it.

He jumped into his car and started down Highway One, beeping his horn and waving his hand in greeting when people stared wide-eyed at the slick black car and then, recognizing the license plate number, yelled out to him.

The news would spread quickly about his return and the new car. There would be plenty of jealousy and malice. But Butler was used to that and mentally prepared himself to deal with it.

He took the right turn sharply and screeched onto Spring Garden Highway; Square One's "Faluma" pounded out from the car speakers.

Turquoise water to his left, brightly colored wall houses, palm trees and uniform-clad schoolchildren to his right, he smiled at the beauty of his surroundings. Barbados was more than an island to him; it was a beautiful woman, full of lush, deep valleys and salty curves.

"Barbados is the only place for me," he thought as he came to a stop in front of Bombas Beach Bar & Restaurant.

The lunchtime crowd filled every table and stool in the place.

Butler stood at the end of the bar closest to the doorway, perus-
ing the crowd. There were so many different ethnic groups
there that the chattering voices sounded like a conference at
the UN.

A group of German men, their skin seared red by the sun, sat
ogling three English girls Butler was sure were all under the age of
eighteen. A family of Italians sat nearby, their waitress sucking
her teeth as she explained to them for the third time that she
could not take lire as payment. Across from them two Frenchmen
sat quietly smoking cigarette after cigarette while sipping wine,
openly amused by everything going on around them.

The rest of the people were locals, except for a golden brown
Yankee girl seated at a table closest to the railing. She had her feet
propped up in a chair, her head moving between the blue ocean
before her and the open magazine that lay in her lap.

The sea breeze was teasing the colorful material of her wrap,
flipping it back and forth, allowing Butler to see that her thighs
were thick.

Butler tilted his head to try to see what the rest of her looked
like.

"Lemme have a Banks," Butler called out to the bartender for
the national beer.

"Well, look who's back."

The voice was soft and he recognized it immediately. Still, he
was annoyed at the interruption and took his time moving his
attention between women.

She looked good, even better than before he'd left. Her dark
skin was smooth; her eyes large round and clear with long eye-

lashes that feathered out. She was short, thick and tight with a behind so broad you could almost sit a plate on it.

"What you saying, Sandra?" Butler reached out for her, but she stepped away.

"Can't shout. And you?" She gave him a wicked smile.

"I all right, you know."

There were no more words between them for a long time. Butler could see the remnants of her disappointment still clinging beneath her eyes. Could tell by the sharp cut of her jaw that she had cussed him plenty of times over the few months he had been gone. He had decided that he would invite her to sit, but she had spoiled it and all the desire he felt for her had slipped away.

She had needed a lift from the supermarket and Butler had obliged. It was safe; he knew his cousin, her husband, was away.

She told him he should stay awhile, that she was going to make coo-coo and steamed fish and he was more than welcome to some.

"Some of what?" he'd asked, allowing his eyes to move from her face to her breasts and then down to her center.

Sandra had smiled, shook her head and walked into the kitchen.

They'd known each other since first form and he'd always yearned for her, but back then he was small, shy and unsure of himself. By the time they were grown, his cousin Ian had her and Butler had put his desire for her away. But things had begun to change between Sandra and Ian, and often whenever Butler found himself in her company, their eyes wandered over each other and old familiar feelings began bubbling to the surface again.

Butler strolled through the small living room looking at the framed photographs on the wall and end tables. Wedding pictures, Ian looking scared, Sandra glowing and jubilant. A family portrait, a pregnant Sandra, a sober Ian and their grinning one-year-old daughter, Fay, between them.

"You need help?" he called from the living room as he straightened the lace doily on the arm of the chair.

"No, I'm fine."

The sky was darkening and thunder sounded in the distance. The rain, even the thought of rain, made him horny. He moved to the doorway of the kitchen and watched as Sandra bent over to retrieve the frying pan from the cabinet. Butler smiled and took a seat at the table.

Sandra dumped the okra into a pot of boiling water and began to stir.

"Work all right?" she asked, her voice wavering a bit. She could feel Butler's eyes on her.

"Yeah, man." Butler's response was slow, his words thick. Sandra felt a stirring in her belly.

Five minutes passed and no words moved between them. Sandra wiped at the perspiration on her forehead and then dumped the cornmeal into the pot.

Butler was enjoying watching Sandra turn the coo-coo, her strong arms working the cornmeal and okra together, her hips moving in rhythm with her limbs. She was nervous and excited; he could tell by the way she kept shifting her weight from foot to foot and the small hisses of air she released after every fourth breath. Butler stood and made his way toward her. The tiny wall house vibrated beneath his footfalls.

She kept stirring.

His hands were on her hips, pulling her backward against him.

She kept stirring.

He kissed her neck and moved his hands over her thick belly.

She kept stirring.

He took the heavy wooden spoon from her hand and turned her around to face him. The coo-coo bubbled behind her and she felt the heat of the flame on her backside.

He pulled her to him and Sandra's breath quickened; she could feel him hard against her. Butler softly kissed her eyelids, her cheeks and the tip of her nose. Sandra felt dizzy and reached over to grab hold of the counter.

Butler ran his tongue slowly across her lips and then down her chin, before bending his head to kiss the space above her breasts.

Sandra could no longer contain herself and flung her arms around his neck, she showered his head and face with kisses before finally finding his mouth and swallowing his tongue.

She felt hungry and primitive in a way Ian had never made her feel.

Butler moved away from her; it was Sandra's turn to reach out for him, but he gently pushed her hands away.

His eyes never left hers as he slowly unzipped his pants. Sandra's breath caught in her throat when he reached in and pulled out his penis.

It was large and long and Sandra thought she'd never seen a

6

Bernice L. McFadden

more beautiful piece of flesh in her life. "Mercy," she whispered when her breath returned.

Butler stepped forward and took her hand; it was shaking. "Touch me," he whispered.

Sandra placed her trembling fingers on him.

His eyes still held hers, urging her on, and she obeyed, wrapping her hand around it and closing her eyes as the flesh pulsed against her palm.

Butler smiled; he had decided he would extend her the invitation to sit.

"Come," Butler started, but Sandra had dropped to her knees, she wanted him in her mouth, she wanted to taste him.

Butler looked down on her as she gently kissed the tip of his penis, it jerked and Butler let out a groan. "I love you," Sandra whispered.

The invitation came to a halt on the tip of his tongue.

He pushed her away.

Sandra, confused, looked up into eyes that had grown as dark as the sky.

Butler zipped up his pants and looked over at the stove. "The coo-coo is sticking," he said as if she hadn't just had him in her mouth.

"When Ian coming back?" he said as he walked over to the table and sat back down.

Sandra was still on her knees, her eyes searching the tile floor for answers.

"Next two days." Her response was quiet and filled with shame.

"Where he gone again . . . Canada?"

"No. Miami."

She stood, dragged her hands across her face and turned off the stove.

"All right, then." That was Butler's way of saying good-bye. He slapped the table and jumped up from the chair.

"Yeah, man," Sandra said, still unable to look at him.

She heard the door slam shut, the car engine turn over and the rattle of gravel as Butler sped away.

Sandra had not forgotten that embarrassment and now standing there before him again, her face flushed with the memory of it.

"Ian all right?" Butler asked before tilting the beer to his mouth.

Sandra looked at Butler for a long time before responding. "Yeah," she said, her voice dripping with disgust.

"Kids good?"

Sandra didn't answer. She just turned and walked away.

*   *   *

Butler shook his head and drained the contents of the bottle. Women always put their hearts in situations they didn't belong. Sandra was still hurt and confused, but Butler knew she wouldn't always feel that way. *She'll get over it,* he thought, just as the basket weavers, fish women and silver peddlers who used Bombas as a shortcut to the road, came up the steps that led from the beach.

Butler looked at the women and smiled. They were gray-haired, but their skin was still as smooth as silk, their legs and arms, muscular.

"He look like his daddy spit 'em out, ya know!"

"Pretty, smooth and dark like chocolate."

"Lips like pillows!"

"Dem eyes! You could lose yourself in dem, ya know!"

"Jes like 'em father!"

"Hmmmm . . . Wonder if he hung the same, too?"

"Ya too old for that nonsense, Judy!"

A flurry of giggles surrounded him and he turned to face five brown, smiling women who no longer looked at him as a child. Their eyes moved over his body slowly, seductively drinking in every inch of him. The women breathed him in and then moved away. Butler looked at their retreating wide hips and round bottoms, before calling for another beer.

Butler's father, Errol, was a seaman. He was shorter than Butler, stocky, with rugged good looks and a passion for rum and women. Errol bragged about having had more than three hundred women in his lifetime and Butler, who idolized his father, set out at a very young age to accomplish the same.

"It sweet, eh?" the fish woman shouted over her shoulder at him before stepping out onto the road.

Butler felt sure she wasn't referring to the basket of fish she balanced on top of her head.

The lunch crowd began to thin as people returned to their hotel rooms for a midday nap, or back to their beach chairs and books. But the stranger remained and so did Butler.

"What the lady drinking?" Butler asked Peter the bartender while nodding toward her table.

Peter was tall, dark and lanky with a pleasant smile. The customers loved him and after a few of his special rum punches, almost always ended up revealing their deepest, darkest secrets to him.

"She?" Peter pulled at his chin while his eyes moved slowly from Butler to the woman. "Well, she don't talk much. 'Hello, afternoon, night.' That's all I hear from her and this the third day she been in here."

"Uh," Butler said, pulling at his own chin.

"She look good, though. Thick, nice eyes. Gray, I think. Maybe contacts, I don't know."

Butler tilted his head once again in order to try to get a better look at the woman. There was something about the way she held her head and the rigid line of her back told him that she had not been touched for a very long time.

Butler was entranced; it was rare to stumble upon a woman like that. It would be, he thought, almost like having a virgin.

"Well, what she drinking?" Butler asked again, reaching for his wallet.

"She drinking some of everything. She call for something different each time and only take a sip or two from it. She waste it, the ice melt down and the waitress take it away," Peter said, and then dropped his voice and leaned closer to Butler. "I don't think she really a drinker."

They grinned together. They both knew that a woman alone on an island was either running from something or looking to run into something.

"Well, send over a bottle of champagne, then," Butler said, and placed a hundred-dollar bill on the counter.

Peter's eyes widened. This type of behavior from Butler was usually reserved for the white women he was trying to pick up. This would be the only money he would spend. After the champagne, the talk and the sex, they all but handed him their credit cards.

The beach boys didn't usually try to hustle black women, especially American black women; those women had a thing about spending money on a man.

"Ya sure?" Peter asked, looking down at the money and then at the woman.

There was no indication that she had money; she wore no jewelry, she paid her bills with a credit card that wasn't platinum or even gold.

"Yeah, man." Butler said, "Very sure."

*   *   *

Haydree watched the surf roll and a sense of calm washed over her. This trip was everything she never knew she needed. Barbados and its gentle breezes, crystal-clear waters and star-filled nights seemed to be the perfect tonic for all that ailed her.

She could live here, she thought, as a smiling Rastafarian waved at her from the beach. Haydree nodded her head and then looked down at her magazine.

She did not want to encourage conversation, even though every night since her arrival she'd been stricken with a heavy sense of loneliness. It was a temporary dilemma; her fiancé, Griffin, was back at home in Brooklyn, waiting for her.

"You want to go away?" Griffin asked her for the fifth time. "A month before we get married, you want to take a trip to an island without me?" He was confused for the first few days and then angry the closer it came to her departure date.

"I just need to do something totally for me, Griffin. I can't make you understand. Just accept it," Haydree had said as she stroked his hand.

Griffin did just that—he accepted it, just as he accepted their sexless relationship.

Griffin hadn't pressed her about it. They were, after all, both in the Church. He understood, he said, even when their kissing moved to heavy petting and Griffin would push her back into the couch, climb on top of her and begin a slow grind that made his already stiff member larger and harder, so hard she thought it would cut through his jeans and the soft silk skirts she'd taken to wearing whenever she knew they would be together.

She'd allowed that as well as his hands beneath her blouse, but not beneath her bra. He could cup her Victoria's Secret–clad breasts, kiss the lace material, even the soft mounds of flesh the bra did not cover, but nothing else.

Anything else would definitely lead to sex, and they were, after all, both in the Church.

Griffin always said he understood, even after Haydree finally pushed him off.

She would clear her throat, nod at the clock and then the door. He'd grimace, reach out for her again, she'd laugh and slap his hands away before moving from the couch to the wing chair on the other side of the room.

They'd meet up again at the front door to exchange good-byes and small kisses while Griffin checked to make sure his shirt was buttoned right, tie was straight and worked to adjust his still stiff penis to a comfortable and unnoticeable position in his pants.

Haydree had decided when she met Griffin at the church social eight months earlier that she would not give herself over to him, not before he said he loved her, not before the engagement ring and not before she walked down the aisle and said I do.

If she'd learned nothing else from her relationship with Curtis Anderson—the incident, as she referred to him—she'd learned restraint.

Curtis was a hard two years ago. She was only twenty-four, working part-time at Macy's and going to school full-time to finish her degree in Fashion Merchandising. Curtis was thirty-two and worlds ahead of her on every level. She was taken with him immediately; he was so different from the men her age she'd dated. He was suave and debonair, like the men she'd read about in the Arabesque romance novels that were piled high alongside her bed. She told him she loved him after their second date and two months later he invited her to move in with him.

She'd expected that living together would be sweet and sticky-good like the chocolate ice cream they'd shared after the first time they'd made love. She'd expected long sweaty nights with him between her thighs, the headboard thumping rhythmically against the wall while he called her name over and over again until he climaxed and moaned, "B-b-baby."

After lovemaking they took long hot showers, him bathing her breasts and the small pointed flesh between her legs with the sponge and soon after, with his tongue. Her fingers would grip his shoulders for a moment, her nails boring into his tight brown skin and then when the orgasms began to rip through her and she could feel her body slipping against the tile, her hands would find his head, her fingers becoming entwined in the dreadlocks she had encouraged him to grow as she screamed, "Yes, yes, yes!"

It had been that way all through the summer, lusty and wild, Haydree showing up at work without panties and calling him from the stockroom to tell him so, hiding behind boxes and touching herself as she cooed to him over the phone.

When she'd told him the color green made her horny he took her to Central Park, where there were hundreds of shades of green. They spread a blanket out on the grass near the lake but far enough away from the sun-worshiping, thin white women with their large breasts in tiny bikini tops.

When the sun dipped and the droves of people thinned, Curtis guided her to an out-of-the-way bench and had her straddle him there.

Curtis kissed her chin, her eyelids and then deeply on the mouth. His hands held her behind, guiding her in a slow grind against his hips. Haydree shuddered and her panties went damp.

He slipped his hands beneath her short sundress and pulled her thong to the left, while his right hand cupped her vagina. "Ooh," Haydree squealed. "No, Curtis, no," she exclaimed, becoming more excited. She was panting by the time he slipped himself free of his sweat pants and moved inside of her.

He did nothing for a long time, he just held on tight to Haydree's waist as she rolled her hips against him. Her eyes were closed and her head thrown back as she sucked hard on her bottom lip to keep from screaming. A dog howled off in the distance and for a brief moment Haydree felt ashamed of herself. Her hips slowed to a stop.

"No, baby, please," Curtis panted before arching himself upward and easing himself deeper inside of her.

Haydree felt a rush of pleasure rip through her, everything around her began to spin and meld, she felt pain and joy all at once, and for a split second her mind danced on death and then heaven. When she cried out his name, the birds fluttered from the treetops and Haydree's body went limp against him. She sobbed into his neck, and wailed like she'd lost her best friend instead of having finally found the orgasm she'd spent years reading about.

Yes, she thought living with Curtis would always be like that and it had been, for a while, but then September came along and the nights grew cool and so did Curtis.

He didn't look at her the same; most times he didn't look at her at all. Their lovemaking, when he did decide to touch her, was mundane. He would climb on top of her, peck her once on the lips, shove himself inside of her and ride her for three minutes before rolling off and going to sleep.

Curtis said it was work, said she needed to understand that his job was demanding and that it drained him mentally, emotionally and physically.

Haydree bit her tongue and tried to understand.

Fall moved to winter, allowing night to creep in at five, Curtis followed at ten, sometimes eleven. An indecent hour for a married man, Haydree's mother, Doris B, had said. "But not for a man who is getting the milk without having purchased the cow."

Haydree knew that her mother really wanted to say: "He got another woman, fool." But all Doris B. did was roll her eyes and suck her teeth in that signature Bajan way.

Haydree just folded her lips and looked down at her thighs, which had grown thick with satisfaction. Happy weight, is what she called it, those extra pounds a woman always seemed to pile on when she was enthralled in a relationship that had her grinning like a fool all day long. Now she supposed the misery that was growing inside of her would soon melt it all away.

There were business dinners, client socials and even a ski trip that wives and significant others were not allowed to attend. "Sorry, baby," Curtis said, and pecked her on the cheek as he packed the new Shetland sweater she'd bought him for Christmas.

When she shared these things with Doris B., her mother huffed, gave Haydree a narrow look, then finally said, "Wake up, child, he got another woman."

"I said ya should have never moved in with him. A good man, a decent man would have asked you to marry him, not shack up with him," Doris B. said as she sliced a thick wedge from the mango she held.

Haydree just looked down at her thighs, which were growing thinner by the week.

* * *

Reality came tumbling in when she found the hair. She had touched it to make sure she was seeing right. She slid her pinkie across the length of it to make sure it wasn't a streak of soap or a piece of thread clinging to the tile. After touching it and being sure, she felt dirty and turned the hot water on high, shoving her hand beneath the steady rush of it and scrubbing her hand until it was raw.

*   *   *

"You're imagining things," Curtis said as he moved about the bedroom trying his best to avoid Haydree.

"Do you see them?" Haydree screamed as she held up eight strands of blond hair between her thumb and forefinger. She'd gone searching, finding two more in the bathroom, three on the couch, one on the floor in the kitchen and two on her pillow.

"Yeah, I see it, Haydree, but I don't know where they came from."

Curtis's composure was breaking down, his voice was beginning to waver and there were small beads of sweat forming around his hairline.

"The bitch is white and going bald!" Haydree screamed and rushed at Curtis, smashing all eight hairs into his face.

"Bastard." She spat and walked out of the house.

*   *   *

That was two years ago, but she still carried around that hurt and even though Griffin was a good man, she knew he would never have her the way Curtis did; her bruised heart wouldn't allow it.

"This is good," Doris B. exclaimed after Haydree showed her the two-carat diamond ring. "Yes, yes, this is good, this is the right way to do things!"

Haydree didn't know about all of that, but she did know that Griffin loved her more than she loved him and that was a good thing, a safety thing.

So what was she doing just a month from becoming Mrs. Griffin James, on a romantic island all alone?

She was here to give herself her own little private bachelorette party, a final stupendous send-off from single life. She was here to get her groove back, take it home and share it with Griffin on their wedding night.

But she was already three days in and no one had tickled her fancy. She had received a lot of attention. Island men could do wonders for a woman with low self-esteem. They showered you with compliments and looked at you like you were the most beautiful woman they had ever seen.

Haydree was waiting for a sign, something inside of her that would let her know *he* was the one.

"From the gentleman at the bar." Peter set the silver bucket down on the table, smiled and walked away.

Haydree stared at the foiled neck of the champagne bottle. She'd had beer and cocktails sent over to her, someone even had Peter bring over a branch of hibiscus blooms—but champagne, this was a first.

Haydree turned to meet the dark, smoky eyes of the stranger who smiled casually and saluted her with his beer bottle.

He was good-looking, not pretty, but striking in a way that made you want to look at him longer than would be considered appropriate. His dark skin glowed and his teeth stood out bright and clean against his complexion. His chest was wide and

Haydree could see the sharp curves of his well-developed chest through the thin material of his tank top.

He was more than striking; he was beautiful.

Haydree smiled and mouthed Thank you.

Though the sun had started to slip from the sky, the stranger still had not approached.

Haydree thought she would have to take the champagne back to her hotel room, maybe enjoy it after dinner in her private Jacuzzi. No, champagne was meant to be shared. She would invite him to do just that.

But when she turned around, the stranger was gone. Peter was alone at the bar, arms folded and grinning.

Haydree's mouth dropped open.

"His name is Butler. I think he wants to invite you to sit, but you never heard that from me," Peter sang out to her, and then began to wipe at the wet spots on the bar.

Haydree just stared at him. What the hell did that mean?

Two days passed and Butler had not made an appearance. Haydree found herself staring into every dark male face that walked into Bombas. She squinted her eyes against the bright sun in order to make out the dark figures moving up and down the beach. She even strolled over to investigate a group of men congregating beneath a coconut tree, allowing her eyes to move slowly over the faces that looked back at her.

"Nice lady."

"Beautiful!"

"You alone, can I come?"

Haydree felt like a fiend in need of a fix, but her preferred dealer had disappeared and soon she might have to settle for something less.

She had even dreamed about him and had touched herself while sleeping.

What did he sound like, how did he feel, what would he smell like? Haydree had one more day and night left; she had to know.

"So where is your friend?"

Peter's eyes went wide with surprise as he looked quickly over his shoulder to make sure she was speaking to him.

Haydree dropped her beach bag down to the ground and settled herself on a stool.

Peter smiled knowingly. "Uhm, who would that be? I have lots of friends, pretty lady."

Oh, it was a game, Haydree thought. She would play along.

"The man who sent over the champagne the other night."

Peter scratched at his chin and looked up into the sky. "Champagne?"

"C'mon." Haydree laughed.

"Ah yes, Butler! Well, I don't know where's he's at. Why, are you looking for him?" Peter grinned.

"Well, yes, I guess I am. I mean, a bottle of champagne . . . well, that was very nice of him. I'd really like to thank him."

"Yes, it was, he's a very nice man." Peter's tone was playful, teasing. "If I see him, who shall I say is looking for him?"

"Haydree Sanders," Haydree said, thinking she sounded a little too eager.

"Uh-huh, the pretty Haydree Sanders. The American, Haydree Sanders?"

Haydree didn't know where this was going, but she would continue to play along. "My parents were born here."

"Oh, a Yankee Bajan."

"I guess," Haydree said, shrugging her shoulders.

"And where would the pretty lady be staying?"

"Why?" Haydree's New York instincts kicked in.

"Just curious."

Haydree looked at him for a while, he seemed harmless. "Sandy Lane."

Peter grabbed his chest and stumbled dramatically backward. "Well, the only people that be at Sandy Lane looking like me and you get a paycheck at the end of the week."

Haydree laughed. It was true; there was one other brown guest at the hotel and Haydree suspected he was Iranian.

Peter rubbed his thumb and forefinger together. "Expensive," he said.

"Yes it is, but I'm worth it." Haydree was surprised at the boldness of her response.

"Well, it looks as if you are," Peter said, nodding his head in agreement.

*   *   *

Haydree had to make a decision. Butler had not returned to Bombas and she was leaving the island in the morning. There was the doorman, the pool guy and the front desk manager. All of them appealed to her and they had made it known that she was quite appealing to them, but she still couldn't get Butler out of her mind.

Maybe it just wasn't meant to be, she thought, as she swung open the French doors and stepped out onto the marble balcony.

She had just showered, her body wrapped in a thick white towel that barely contained her wide hips and broad behind. The foliage around the balcony was thick, so Haydree was not concerned with a strolling guest or hotel employee seeing her from the winding stone path below.

The air was warm and languid, wrapping her in the sweet scent of hibiscus. Haydree's body swayed to the gentle sounds of the steel band as she sipped champagne from a crystal flute.

She was debating whether or not to order dinner up to her room or join the forty or so couples in the main dining room. The captain was always very gracious to her, and he was good-looking, too. She had noticed a few lustful looks sent her way.

"Maybe him," she said aloud just as she heard soft tapping at the door.

It was seven-thirty. That would be Claudia the maid, there to turn the bed down, fluff her pillows and don them with chocolate mints.

Haydree didn't ask who, just flung the door open.

"Good night."

Haydree took two steps backward and then her hands flew up to her mouth. She didn't know if she was going to scream for help or shout for joy.

Butler stepped in and closed the door.

"We say good night here; I know in America you say good evening."

Haydree could neither speak nor take her eyes off him: the

smooth black skin, thick arched eyebrows and those lips, she could live for days off those lips.

"How did you get up here?" Haydree said when she was finally able to speak.

"I took the stairs, of course." Butler grinned.

Haydree cleared her throat and took another step backward. She was more than happy to see him, but at eight hundred dollars a night she thought security should be a little more scrupulous.

Butler read her mind. "Everyone knows Butler." He purred and Haydree felt her knees begin to knock.

"I hear you were looking for me," Butler said as he walked past Haydree and out onto the balcony.

Haydree was stunned at his boldness, but found herself following him like a cat in heat.

"Well, I uhm, yes, I wanted to thank you for the champagne. That was very nice of you."

Butler leaned over the balcony. "You could make love right here and no one could see." He turned to face Haydree; his eyes danced over her body, reminding Haydree of her attire. "They would hear, though," he added, and ran his tongue slowly across his top lip.

Haydree felt her skin begin to heat.

"Are you a screamer?"

Haydree's face flushed. "I think you should leave." She supposed that was the right thing to say, something a decent woman would demand.

You didn't come here to be decent, did you, Haydree? the little voice in her head reminded her as she tugged the towel tightly around herself.

"Okay." Butler began to move toward her. She could smell the sweet, subtle scent of his cologne.

"I mean, you come here unannounced, you say these things . . . what am I supposed to do?"

The words fell from her mouth like rainwater. She didn't want him to go; she wanted him to stay. She wanted those lips on her body.

Butler stopped in front of her and placed his hands on her bare shoulders, they were hot and Haydree thought that she would melt beneath them. He looked deeply into her eyes. "I have something you need. I know this because I see it missing from your eyes."

He bent and kissed her. He kissed her passionately, as though they were longtime lovers and just like that Haydree began to melt.

The towel fell to the floor and Butler stepped back to admire her. "Lovely," he said as he slid his hands down her hips and then her thighs. Haydree was shaking. Butler walked around her like she was a statue in a museum, commenting on the beauty of her backside, the arch of her back and the small mole on her shoulder blade.

When he came face-to-face with her again, his shirt was off. Haydree had never seen a more perfect chest; his nipples were ebony against his mahogany skin.

Butler cupped her breasts, tilting his head so he could lick each nipple with the tip of his tongue before sucking it into his soft, warm mouth.

He guided her through the French doors and toward the bed. There he eased her downward, kissing her as she went. He stood over her, slowly removing his watch, sandals and pants.

"Don't be afraid," he said when Haydree's eyes widened. She had never seen a penis so large in all her life—well, not up close and personal. She wanted to tell him that it wouldn't fit, no way, no how!

Butler slowly parted her knees and then pushed her legs apart. Haydree turned her head away with shame. The lights were on and bright. "Hmmmm," he crooned as he ran his index finger between her legs. "You are so wet."

Haydree moaned. He hadn't even penetrated her and already there was a wet spot spreading beneath her.

Haydree reached out and took his penis in her hand. It pulsed in her hand like the beat of a heart and like dozens of other women Butler had had, she too thought it was beautiful.

"I don't need sex," he said as he positioned himself beside her.

Haydree turned to look at him. "What?"

"I don't need sex," he said again.

Haydree felt a tinge of fear rip through her. If not sex, what did he want?

Butler stroked her hair and then moved his hands over her breast and down between her legs. His eyes held hers even as he slipped his index finger inside of her and began moving his thumb rhythmically back and forth across her clit.

Haydree's mind began to bend.

"I want to invite you to sit," Butler breathed into her ear before pulling her earlobe into his mouth.

"Yes, yes," Haydree groaned. She didn't know what she was saying yes to but the good feeling he was creating between her legs didn't let her care.

She was almost there, almost there, her back began to arch just as Butler pulled his hand away.

Haydree shot straight up.

Butler just laughed and rolled over onto his back.

Haydree jumped up from the bed, looked down on him for a moment and then went out onto the balcony for her towel and a bit of sobering air.

"What the hell am I doing?" she whispered to herself as her senses slowly returned to her.

"Haydree, come, sit." Butler's voice floated out to her.

Haydree spun around. The lights were off, but she could make out Butler, his body bathed in the cool blue moonlight. He was sprawled out on the bed, his cock stiff and reaching for the night sky. Haydree's mouth went dry.

"Shit," she said as she dropped the towel and headed back to him.

"Come." He urged her over.

"Condom?" Haydree asked, wondering if he had any or was she going to have to go for the pack she had hidden in her tampon box.

"No need. I told you I don't want sex."

"What?" Haydree was really confused now.

"Come, woman. Come and sit."

Haydree eased closer and closer, like small child unsure if she should accept the candy that was being offered from a stranger.

Their knees touched.

"C'mon." Butler indicated his stomach.

Haydree straddled his legs, and slid forward, hoisting herself high enough to clear Butler's towering penis, before coming to rest on his stomach.

He grabbed her behind and began pushing her forward, forward until his chin rested in the short hairs that covered her vagina.

Haydree understood now.

She had been loved that way before, but never in this position of power, of total control.

Butler inhaled her and then eased his hands beneath her and suspended her.

He raised his head and kissed her in the place that no man had seen or touched in two years. He took her clit between his lips and rolled his tongue across its pointed tip. Haydree's body shook. "Oh God yes," she moaned as a searing jolt of pleasure moved through her.

Just when she didn't think she could take any more and her throat was almost raw from screaming, Butler eased his head away from her and the invitation rolled from his mouth.

"Sit."

Haydree took a deep breath, eased herself down and felt her body explode into a million pieces as Butler slid his tongue deep inside and swallowed her.

*   *   *

Haydree gazed out onto the blue Caribbean waters as the jetliner climbed away from the island. Her body jerked every so often at the memory of it all. She would try hard to put those thoughts away before she landed, but she had four hours to replay the whole scene over and over in her head and that's exactly what she'd planned on doing.

"S'cuse me?"

Haydree turned to see an attractive white woman looking down at her. "I was wondering if this seat is being used, I hate sitting so close to the flight deck. Would you mind?"

Haydree shook her head no and moved her pocketbook from the seat. "Come, sit," Haydree said, and didn't know why she'd phrased it that way or even used that tone, his tone.

Haydree's eyes locked with the woman's and she knew from the expression on her face that she had been extended the invitation, too.

The woman nodded her head knowingly. Haydree just grinned.

*TIMMOTHY B. M*c*CANN*

The Most Beautiful Thing

Whats the most beautiful sound you've ever heard? You think about that, rub your fingers over your lips and her scent reminds you. It's the sound of her saying, "Good Morning."

"The Reunion"

You walk out of the South Bend Swanson Hotel Grand Ballroom with its arched alabaster ceiling and exquisitely wrought chandeliers. You spent the weekend reading name badges and repeating the same sentences. "So nice to see you again. Did you get married? So what are you doing nowadays?" You repeat the lines so many times you wish you could just link the sentences on a recorder and play back the phrases at the appropriate moment. But you continue to listen to the songs from the year you graduated, shake hands, show your smile and think about how disappointing the past three days have been. Not because of the faces you saw, but because of the one person whose name badge remained on the sign-in desk.

"The Departure"

As the elevator door opens several other members of your class file out, mostly drunk, all speaking loudly. "Wussup, Peri-Dick-le!" Johnny Hayes shouts. "Perry-Perry-Mo-Berry-Banana Fanna-Mo-*Ferry.*" And then like the Pips his cohorts chime in, "Fe-Fi-Mo-Narry. PER-RY!"

Johnny and his cronies hold their bellies, which hang over their belts, and walk away as if they are still in high school. You hear Johnny shout, "He's still a punk."

Since the third grade Johnny has been your nemesis. He poured water on you from the second floor when it was below zero outside. He pulled down your gym shorts in front of the girls' soccer team and gave you the nickname you knew you would never outlive during high school.

You enter the elevator, which smells of cheap whiskey and urine, and you slide your room key into the slot to gain access to the top floor. The doors slide closed. As you see yourself in the mirrored doors you feel stupid. You paid more for the suite than you paid for your first car. It was equipped with a fully stocked bar, a massage chair, and a Jacuzzi. In your mind you'd fanta-sized about finding the right moment and saying to everyone, "Hey, let's take this back to my suite!" But it's Sunday night; almost time to pack your bags for the two-hour flight east and the three Trojans in your wallet are still intact. Although you thought they'd applaud your success, you still feel like the buck-toothed, high-water-pants-wearing nerd who graduated two years early.

They made fun of your last name then, and they did it tonight. The jocks back then are the jocks tonight. In spite of your accomplishments, you are the same outsider you were ten years ago. As you return to your room you wonder why you attended the gathering. You thought their acceptance would give you closure, but instead their rejection opened old wounds.

You went to Stanford after high school and put on a muscular fifty pounds she'd never seen. In college you got rid of the glasses, the braces, and buried the ache. You knew that the new and improved Fredderick could walk into the room unafraid and Tandee would see you like you saw her every single day you went to high school. She'd be captivated by your touch. She would take you home in a pocket of her mind, lay you on the bed and fuck you until you died. Much like you did her every single night for years after high school.

The red digital numbers at the top of the elevator door reach your floor and the elevator whispers to a stop. "What a waste," you say, but instead of going to your room, you go to the balcony and look over. You see them. They're laughing, joking, drinking and flirting under the banner that says THE GOOD OLD DAYS NEVER LEFT! You return to your door and just like in the good old days, you feel ostracized by a group that continues to reject you.

"The Call"

Your phone rings and you say, "Who knows this number?" The previous night a few former members of The Mighty Metaphysics Club called you to join them for cocktails but you declined. Outside of that, the only sound in the suite was from your Bob Marley CD.

The phone rings again as you hurriedly slide your key card back and forth in the tiny slot without success. You try repeatedly as the phone rings a third time, then a fourth. Then you bite your bottom lip, close your eyes, and you hear the lock slide open. You enter your jasmine-scented room and snatch up the phone.

"Hello?"

"Yes, I'm looking for Fredderick Periwinkle."

You know the voice. You had no idea if the fingers of time had changed her attitude, spirit, or body, but it had yet to touch her voice.

"Yes, this is me, I mean he. I mean—let me start again. This is Fred Periwinkle. Whom may I say is calling?" With the heel of your palm you whack your forehead. *Damn, now I sound like a receptionist.*

"Hello, Fredderick. I don't know if you remember me or not but I'm"—you resist the temptation to say her name since you screwed up with your own—"Tandee."

You are speechless.

"I was in your senior class?"

An awkward pause tumbles into the conversation and you feel your heart thump around your chest like a pinball.

"Tandee Evans? I was in Calculus with you and my brother used to play forward for the basketball team."

You close your eyes, unable to wrap your thought around the idea that Tandee was on the other end of the phone *and* she remembered you. "Oh yeah," you say and sit at the foot of the bed. "I kinda remember you now. It's been so long."

"I know. In fact, I'm just getting into town myself and trying to meet everyone before they pull out tonight and tomorrow. I was on a business trip in Denver and I was *supposed* to fly out Friday but got snowed in. I'm an accountant now and Sydney Earle told me that you were with Price Waterhouse. Is that correct?"

You see her angle and clear your throat. "Yes, I've been with them seven years now." As you tell her about the company, you're contemplating ways to maneuver her into talking about this over coffee. Possibly finishing the conversation over breakfast. You've never been the assertive type but even the discussion of 401k benefits with her seems erotic and sends blood to your dick. You can feel him wake and stretch.

"I'm happy for you. I've been trying to get with them for the longest. I'm moving to Chicago and I've had difficulties getting an interview. I was wondering if I could leave my résumé and cover letter at the front desk and have you intercede for me?"

"Better than that. Why don't you just bring it to my suite."

Earth-shattering silence.

That was so stupid, you tell yourself. *You're rushing it! Dumb, dumb, dumb.* She says something on the other end. "What did you say?"

"I asked, what floor?"

"The Panic"

After you hang up you wonder what to do next. *She'll be in my room. She'll be right here in my suite,* you think.

You pace back and forth in the room and remember the

protection stored in your wallet. Taking them out, you ask yourself, *How am I gonna do this?* You walk to the corner of the bed facing the door and slide them under the mattress. *But what if we're on . . . the other side?* You detach one and place it at the foot of the bed as well as the edge nearest the wall. *Now I'm set.*

You walk to the mirror and stop. *There's no way in the world you're fucking Tandee. Stop dreaming.* You shake your head to physically remove it from your thoughts. Still dressed in eveningwear, you wonder what first impression you will give her. Should it be the still-dressed-to-the-nines-about-to-go-out look or the disheveled I'm-about-to-watch-*Sex-in-the-City*-do-you-want-to-join-me look. *Stop dreaming.* You loosen your tie with your forefinger, pull up your belt so she can better admire your trim physique and you look at your package. *This is Tandee Denise Evans. Who are you kidding?* Like a woman trying on a bra you pull it up, adjust it. You turn to the side to see your dick in profile. "Damn, I can't believe she's coming up here." For some odd reason you fill with confidence. "We're fucking tonight," you say out loud. "I know we are. I don't know what the hell I'm going to say but I know one way or another, we're fucking."

You sit on the edge of the bed again, reach for the remote and turn up the soft sounds of reggae. As Bob Marley pleads, "No Woman No Cry," you walk over to the bar and make sure whatever she wants to drink will be— You hear the faint knock. *Don't blow it!* You want to be cool and allow her to knock again but before she can your hand is twisting the brass knob.

"The Hello"

"So, how are you," she says with a girlish smile and chocolate eyes. Her jet-black skin has a pinkish undertone and her generous lips are seductively curved and painted with chestnut-brown lipstick. Her hair is close-cropped and she looks even more beautiful than the day she signed your yearbook:

To the smartest kid in our senior class.
Tandee E.

You smell her perfume and try to steal a glance at her body without being too obvious. Her scent is sweet and spicy. Her fingers flutter to the nape of her neck. The résumé is pinched under her arm against her breast as she blushes into ten different shades of sepia.

"I'm fine," you reply.

"Do you remember me now?"

You want to scream, "ARE YOU KIDDING ME?" but end up muttering, "Yeah, you look familiar."

"I used to be a cheerleader? Was in the pep-club and—well anyway," Tandee says, "here's my résumé. Fortunately I had one in my car, but if you could have it forwarded with possibly a letter of recommendation to the head of personnel, I'd appreciate it. That's if I'm not asking too much."

"Sure," you say. So far you notice she has acted like a professional and has not shown a bit of interest in anything but advancing her career.

"You look a lot different," Tandee says, and allows her body to relax from its corporate posture. "Looks like you've grown at least three or four inches since Kennedy High."

"Six, to be exact. I just hit this growth spurt around eighteen for some reason and shot up." You step to the side and like Billy D., you say, "I'm being rude. Why don't you come in . . . and tell me more about what you're looking for?"

Tandee looks into the room at the bubbling Jacuzzi and says, "No, I'm really pressed for time. I just got in and there're so many people I want to see." Though her lips say no, her eyes steal a peek below and you are glad you checked your profile before she knocked.

Please don't go. "Are you sure?"

"No, I better not, but whatever you can do to help me would be appreciated. I'm living in Gary now but I think there are more opportunities in the Chicago area."

"Okay," you say, at a loss. You want to pull her into the room with just the right words, the right phrase. But instead you get a last scent of her perfume and you say, "Good night."

"The Regret"

As you return alone to your oversized bed, shoulders rounded with disappointment, you kick yourself repeatedly. A thousand lines you could have said tease you, taunt you. The hundred different ways you could have gotten her inside the room. At least fifty ways you could have maneuvered her against the wall. Ten ways you could have made her scream your name. But none of them were there when you needed them.

"Fuck!" you say aloud. A part of you would like to walk downstairs, grab her by the arm and drag her to your room in front of your former classmates. That would heal the wounds. But you know you won't. No matter how much you feel like Billy D., inside you're still Peri-Dick-le.

"The Second Chance"

There's a knock at the door.

"Yeah—I mean, hello?"

"It's me, Fredderick. I forgot to give you my card."

You open the door with enough force to create a breeze. "Hey, back so soon?" *Damn, is that the best shit I could come up with?*

"Yeah," she smiles. "Here's my card. If you know of or *hear* of an opening in the Chicago area, please let me know. They told me you're in Philly but I'm trying to cover all my bases."

"No problem." *What do I say?* you ask yourself. You have a second chance and in your heart you know there will not be a third. "I'll umm, give it to this friend of mine who's in corporate." *Think, dammit.* "She owes me a favor. I'm sure she'll have some, some, some," your words get stuck like a scratched 45. She sweeps a glance across your body one last time, her eyes pause below your belt and that's all it takes. You grab her by the slender portion of her forearm.

"Oh, no," she says with a smile, "I can't come in, I need to—"

Before Tandee can finish she's plastered by your body to the wall and you're looking into her eyes. The sound of her quickening breath turns you on. Your dick hiccups and swells to half-mast as you bring your lips just inches from her mouth. You feel the heat of her breath on your skin. Her body splash smells like rain and you can't wait to get wet. "Tandee, you don't know how long I've wanted to do this."

"I thought," she said, closing her eyes, "you'd forgotten my name?"

"How could I forget someone who's always on my mind?"

"The First Kiss"

"Fredderick," she whispers, and you feel the brush of her eyelash on your chin as she opens her eyes. "How in the *hell* did you get so fine?"

Your dick stands like a bent bow with twice the tension and begs to be touched.

You kiss the corners of her lips at the crease. You gently roll her head back with your fist and suck the pulsating hollow at the base of her throat. Your tongue touches her skin like a ghost in the dark and you feel her body quiver and shake. Your mouth slides along her jawline and grazes her earlobe.

"Gushsshs," she moans. "Don't-don't do that. I can't *stand*—"

You bury your tongue in her ear as her body slides up and down the wall.

"Baby," you whisper in your nastiest voice, "nothing will happen tonight, you don't want to happen. Okay?"

Tandee nods and you cover her lips with a kiss. Blood leaps from your heart to pound in your brain as you lace your fingers with hers and pin her harder against the wall. You want to taste her words. You want to taste her thoughts. You want to make love, but she returns the kiss with such reckless abandonment that you know she wants to fuck.

The kiss is sensually devouring as your tongues intertwine and you grind your now rock-hard dick on her stomach. You know she likes it by the way she wraps her leg around your thigh. She's so hot you can feel her heat radiate through your clothes.

"Baby, I just want to—"

Tandee covers your mouth and says, "Just fuck me, Fredderick. Just fuck me."

"The Seduction"

You lead Tandee to the bed, where she sits seductively and crosses her long legs. You have not been with a woman in months. You kick off your Cristoforo loafers, take off your cuff links and fling them across the room. You hear the gulp as one of them sinks into the Jacuzzi. You unbuckle your pants, allowing the belt to slither to the floor. You watch Tandee as she uncrosses her legs, gives you a peek at her white panties and moistens her lips. "I can't believe this is happening," she whispers. "I can't believe we're doing this."

You pull off your shirt, your pants slide to the floor and you stand before her in just your bulging bikini briefs. You slide your hands into the waistband and wrap your hand around your dick as if it's a heavy black rope, letting her get an idea of its thickness.

Unhurriedly you walk to Tandee and stand beyond her reach. Your abs are rock-hard, your arms firmly chiseled. You step closer and watch her eyes slide over your body from the bulge of thigh muscle just above the knee, to the nipples on your well-defined chest. She looks in your eyes and says, "Fredderick, your dick is so——"

"Don't tell me, baby," you say and walk close enough for her to touch it. "Show me."

Tandee brings both of her hands to the outside of your thighs and pulls your underwear down in one slow, steady motion. You watch the expression on her face. "Damn," she whispers.

"You like it like that, baby?"

"The Second Kiss"

She holds it like a microphone and kisses it like a long-lost friend. She rubs your fat dick over her lips, over her chin, under her neck. You grind your hips as you feel the slippery warmth of her mouth even as she parts her lips. Slowly her tongue encircles the mushrooming head and your eyes close. You rub her cheeks with the back of your curled fingers and you can tell she knows she's in control. She allows your body to enter her mouth. You feel the soft skin of her lips, the smooth surface of her teeth. You feel the soft folds of flesh inside her cheek and you watch her mouth expand as she swallows you into the back of her throat. Your hands close into fists.

Tandee looks up at you and eases you out of the silky warmth of her mouth. She takes her hands from your dick, allowing it to stand up and to the side. She looks at the veins that break like a river. She looks at the mahogany cord running on the underside that looks like a half-buried cable. Tandee smiles and kisses the tip once again and you can see by the look in her eyes that she wants you inside of her.

You pull back but she recaptures you in her mouth. Your toes curl into the carpet. Her lips slide wetly over the soft skin on your dick. Somehow you manage to reverse positions and find yourself on the bed and she follows you, wanting another taste. You ease back onto your elbows, close your eyes and your head falls back. Never in your dreams did you think it would it be like this.

"Baby, you taste so good," she says, and then runs her lips over your dick. She growls, "I even love the *smell* of you." Tandee slides her sweet, juicy lips up and down the outside of your shaft and you move her head farther back as you fight the first temptation to lose control.

You want to stop her but you know she's in command now of even the air you breathe. You grind your teeth and your back arches. You look at this amazing woman as she undresses with you still in her mouth. She slips out of her dress and panties, then takes off her bra. Her breasts are no more than a handful, just the way you like them. Her nipples are hard and you lick your lips at the sight of them.

"Baby?"

You answer in a little more then a groan. "Yes?"

"I don't know, um—I don't know how to ask but do you—"

You move so fast you scratch your knuckles pushing your fingers under the mattress to retrieve the condom from the foot of the bed. You bring it to your teeth to unwrap it as she smiles.

"Damn. Well I guess you thought of everything, huh? Or was that for someone else?" She doesn't wait for an answer.

Tandee takes the blue square from you, slips it into her mouth, then slides her mouth over your dick, slipping the condom around you. *Oh my god.*

"The Passion"

Tandee straddles your leg and you approach the eighth heaven. You can feel the heat from her pussy and you want to feel her wetness. As if reading your thoughts, she guides your finger into her pussy.

She sucks you and allows you to slide in and out of her sweltering love. So many nights you'd dreamt of being with her. So many nights you watched her scream and beg for more.

Her eyes shimmer from the moonlight coming through the window and she says, "Fredderick?"

"Yes," you reply with strength you didn't know you still possessed.

"I was hoping you'd show up. I ran I don't know how many red lights from the airport to get here."

"Are you serious?"

"I know they gave you a rough time in school and I should have said something, but I was too caught up in the popularity thing that I could not—I could not . . . Fredderick?"

"Yes?"

In a breathy tone she says, "I want you to fuck me."

"Just tell me which wall you wanna climb, love."

"Any one you want me to," she replies.

You sit up and sweep your eyes over her body. Over her soft curves and the hairless mound you can't wait to enter. You stand, allow her to lie on the bed and then you slowly cover her body with yours.

In your fantasies you cover her with kisses. So you start at her lips but then inch down to her collarbone and her nipples. They are as black as an Oreo and sweeter than the creamy middle. Your lips circle them slowly and you know you have hit a sensitive spot by the way she runs her fingers over the back of your head. By the way her body jerks, and her mouth opens. Although you hear her breathing quicken you're not done with her and your mouth slides farther down.

You slide your tongue in and out of her navel and she whispers your name. Your kiss slides down a little lower.

You smell her arousal, pulling you farther south. You kiss her softly above her sweet cherry. Then your tongue slides over her swollen clit.

The first time you lick it slowly. The next time a little faster and then back and forth as fast as you can. You lock her thighs over your shoulders because you know her hips are going to try and squirm out of your grasp and this is a ride you know she'll never forget. Then you look up and say, "Tandee?"

"Yes," she pants.

"Put your hands around my head?"

"What?" You know she's confused but you repeat it and she does it, and in one motion, you lift her from the bed, and she rides your shoulders to a corner of the room. You plant her like a flag against the wall with her feet kicking back and forth as if she is in a swing and you open her up with your tongue. The deeper you lick, the faster she grinds until you feel her thighs stiffen and you know she's about to come.

"Baby?" Tandee says.

"Yes?"

She screams louder, "Baby!"

"Yes!" you answer.

"BABY!"

This time you can't reply. She grabs your hair, yanks your head back, her thighs grip you like a vice, and she pushes herself away from the wall and you both fall onto the bed.

Tandee's breathing is shallow and ragged. She reaches up and grabs the headboard and arches her back. Bringing your hands up, you pull her lips apart and slide your tongue in deeper than it had ever been before. Just the salty sweet taste of her body makes your dick throb even more. But you control yourself because the best is yet to come.

* * *

Flipping Tandee over and onto her back you look down and for the first time she smiles. There's a glow in her face.

But you don't return her smile. Instead you pull her hips toward your dick. You rub it down her inner thigh and you see the contrast of her jet-black skin, your chocolate brown dick and her pure pink pussy. As you tease her flesh Tandee says, "Fredderick?"

"Yes, baby."

Her eyes roll upward. "Make me come, make me come hard."

"Is that what you want?"

"I—I haven't come *hard*—in years."

You ease her legs apart and watch her love open to your body. As you part her lips, her mouth opens and then one by one you wrap her legs around your waist like a belt. Her body is as wet as your dick is hard. You guide yourself inside of her without using your hand. Her eyes open and she looks at you in surprise. You grab the headboard and give her the first two inches and her teeth clench. She's so tight you can feel your dick stretching her.

"Oh!" she says, breathing heavily. You give her another inch, and she says, "Fuck me!" as if she is speaking with her last breath.

You slide another three inches inside her and feel her body shake. You feel the fleshy portion of her calves squeeze your waist. You hold on to the headboard and push inside her love nest a little deeper. And then you guide your dick to touch places inside her body you are sure have not been touched before.

You close your eyes as she says, "Baby, *fuck* me harder." You smile; you know now she is ready to go anywhere you want to take her.

You arch your back to thrust harder and you put her legs over your shoulders and feel her feet lock behind your head. The deeper you stroke the more she moans. Then Tandee opens her thighs wider and looks hard at you. The beginning of a smile is tempting the edges of her lips and her pupils look like shards of black glass. As you move inside of her, you notice a tear form and then slide down her cheek as she moans in the rhythm of your strokes.

You plunge in deeper. Tandee grabs your ass as you push inside her. Her mouth opens, her eyes close and you feel her nails on your back. You feel the muscles inside her vagina walls grabbing you and you know she's about to flow.

"Baby . . . Baby."

You want to make this a night she will always remember so you lean away from her body, grab her knees and push them back so that her hips raise to meet your strokes.

Her eyes close, her fingers relax, her mouth falls open as you stroke deeply inside of her. You want to come so bad but you're determined to wait until she does. You can feel her pussy quivering. You can tell by the emptiness in her eyes that she's about to come.

"Bring it for me, baby! Bring it for me, baby," you say.

"I am—I am."

"I want to feel your pussy gush," you say.

"I am—I am."

You thrust faster, harder, deeper and you say between clenched teeth, "I want this pussy to *drown* me. I want you to come so fucking hard, baby."

"I am—damn, baby. I—I—I . . ." Tandee's voice trails off.

You feel her pussy pulsing. You feel the hard thrust of her hips and her muscle contraction feels like fingers milking your dick. Then you slam your hips deeper into her as your own orgasm overpowers you. Everything in your world is pitch black and then you feel Tandee bite you on the chest. Your toes curl and the feel of her teeth firmly planted in your flesh makes your orgasm even more intense. You feel like a hose with a thumb inside of it. You want to scream but only air comes out. Your eyes are open, but you can't see a thing. Then she releases her hold on your flesh and your body returns to earth.

"The Aftermath"

Once you regain your composure you look down at Tandee. By the jerk of her body you can tell she is still coming. Between convulsions, she sobs softly. You whisper her name.

She's quiet.

You're both soaked in sweat. You look at the window with the overlooking view of South Bend and it's foggy. You look at Tandee. "Baby," you sigh, "I have never wanted a woman in my entire *life* the way I've wanted you. From the moment I saw you in the ninth grade, I've wanted you. I've waited for this night my whole life."

She stops crying. "And I wanted to be with you, too. It was just so hard to do it back then. You know?"

You allow her shaking legs to slide from your grasp and you kiss. A soft kiss of affection and you know of all the things the two of you have done, the kiss would be the most cherished.

"The Most Beautiful Thing"

The next morning you wake up but are afraid to open your eyes. You still feel her beside you and know it was not a dream. As you lie amid the rumpled sheets, she moans from your featherlike touch down her spine. You nestle her into your body, her ass to your crotch, knee between her thighs.

"Question?" you murmur into her ear.

"Yes?"

Smelling her hair, you kiss her neck and say, "I never thought to ask you before, but how did you get up to this floor? You need a room key for the elevator."

Tandee turns to you and kisses you again. "It's all about who you know."

Your hand slides down her stomach and pauses below her navel. "So, you flirted with a bellman and he let you up?"

"No."

"You rode up with someone coming to this floor?"

Shaking her head she says, "Sorry."

"Then how did you get up here?"

"Well," Tandee says as she pulls your fingers over her mound and grinds it stiffly. "My fiancé is the accountant for the hotel."

"You kidding me."

"Don't worry. He's more than likely drunk out of his mind. Actually, you may remember him." Tandee eases your fingertips over her clit and moves it slowly.

"What's his name?" you groan.

As she slides your forefinger past her swollen lips into her pussy she says, "He was in our class, a wrestler? Johnny Hayes."

You smile, kiss the back of her ear and say, "Nope, never heard of him."

You know she knows you're lying and she opens her mouth to speak, but instead she slides on top of you, kisses you on the mouth, then says, "Oh, good morning."

And then you think of those simple words and ask yourself, what's the most beautiful sound you ever heard?

SHAY YOUNGBLOOD

Lula Mae

*D*oc Romer say he didn't feel sorry for me because I was blind or like me because I was pretty. He said it was the shy way I had of laughing behind my hand and lowering my eyes that made him want to protect me. I had big breasts then. He called them his babies. I think he wanted to protect that part of me with his soft, small, easygoing hands.

Doc was the pharmacist at Coffee's Drugstore, which sat on the corner of Eighth Street and Railroad Avenue. That was where I got my heart medication, hard lemon candies and horehound lozenges for my throat. Once a month I walked half a mile down a dirt path following the railroad tracks in back of my house to get to the store. From the day I started going in there Doc Romer waited on me like I was a special customer. When I come in, even if other people were lined up, he would stop what he was doing to come over and ask me if I wanted something cool to drink while I waited. He knew I liked lemon drops, so when I only had enough money for my medicine I would get home to find he had put a little something extra in my bag. After a while he stop charging me for anything, even the expensive creams and cocoa butter I took to using for the bruises my husband made on my arms and neck. Doc brought out the shy in me whereas my husband brought out the evil and the shame.

Wasn't always that way between me and Wallace. He used to bring me presents and comb my hair. The way he made me feel on top of my clothes before we were married wasn't nothing compared to after we became man and wife, the way he'd stand me up naked against a wall and make over my body. Then he would turn me around and I'd almost scratch the wallpaper off the wall. When Wallace was loving me, it felt like I could see. Every morning, every night after supper and on the weekends I couldn't get nothing done for him worrying me about being naked. The man didn't want me to wear clothes in the house and I grew to like the way the air felt against my skin. Then he started to cut up my clothes so I couldn't go out of the house if I wanted to. When he lost his job he started drinking and when he found another one it was harder work with less pay and he started treating me like I was the one fired him and cut his wage. After that first year there wasn't no more little presents.

God as my witness I didn't like Doc because of the things he gave me, I liked him because he was nice to me, and I hadn't ever had that kind of nice from a man. When I told my best girlfriend Martha, she say, "Lula Mae, that man want you. He got it bad." I just kept shelling peas and listening to them *ping* as they fell into the big enamel pan that fit in the lap of my housedress.

"I don't want nobody to feel sorry for me," I snapped at her.

"I mean he like you special." Martha's voice got soft and whispery. She walked around my kitchen snatching open cabinet doors like she was looking for something.

"Doc Romer?!" I laughed long and loud. "You know that man is married."

"Married to the stingiest, most hateful woman God could have made from a turd."

Martha banged a big soup pot down into the sink and opened the taps wide. I wished she wouldn't talk so much or so loud. She acted like I was hard of hearing, but I don't say nothing because I'm used to her country ways. She made the days go by fast.

"Why he marry somebody like that? He seemed to me like the kind of man would marry for love."

"Truth be told, Romer married her because she play like she was pregnant. She ain't had no baby to this day. Only thing she do have is a constant case of indigestion. That be her breaking wind all through church service, playing like she sleep. Her daddy sent Romer to school and give him the job at the drugstore. It's thirty years later and she still ain't had that baby. Come to find out she can't even have babies. That like to broke Romer's heart. All she do is sit up in that big old house on Grant Street eating whole hams and waddling around switching her soap operas on and off."

"I don't know nothing about all that and you know I ain't one to gossip, Martha. I'm a Christian woman." I put the pan of peas on the table and got up to look for the strainer because Wallace was always moving things around.

"Lula Mae, I got just as much religion as you, but truth be told, that woman crazy and that man want you bad as a dog want a bone."

"Martha, watch your mouth." I reached out and smacked her on the hip.

It was almost time for Wallace to come home. Martha had to leave. My husband never liked none of my friends, especially Martha, because she would tell him to his face what she think of him and that wasn't much. After she left I ironed a pile of shirts and pants, cotton sheets and big cotton handkerchiefs. I cleaned up in the kitchen and put the dinner on. I ran a bath for my husband and when it was way past time for him to come home I put his food in a tin plate, covered it with foil and put it in the stove. When he finally came home late in the night smelling of whiskey and cigarettes, I took his food out the stove and sit at the table listening to him eat. He didn't say much except to ask me where his socks or have I seen his pocket watch or to tell me to put more starch in his shirts.

I never imagined married life to be as miserable as this. Some people been in prison say they wouldn't know what they wanted if they could have it, but I know what I'd do with my freedom. If I had it the way I wanted it, my man would come home every evening in a good mood, leave some money on the table, his bad attitude at the door and we'd make love in the bathtub with the water running. I prayed every day for a sign of change. I'd been blind all my life, but some things I could see with my heart. I wasn't completely without my suspicions about Wallace running around. I just tried harder to make him want to be a good husband to me. I wasn't worried about other women; I believed what my mama used to say, "If she can beat me rocking, she can have my chair."

The next time I went to the drugstore Martha made up her mind to go with me. She and Doc joke around. They had gone to high school together and had some friends in common who they talked about for a while. When we left the store Martha put her arm in mine to guide me down the steps and whispered to me, "Lula Mae, that man want you." I laughed and slapped her big, wide butt with my walking stick. About a week later Martha say Doc tell her he want to meet me. She say we can meet at her house on the day she take her mama to visit her sister over in the next county. I don't know what to say at first. I feel funny because we was both married, but I wasn't happy at all and Martha said he wasn't, either. The thought of Doc liking me made me feel kind of light inside, like a little girl being given a present for being good. For the first time I wondered what he looked like. His voice was soft and cultured, like his hands. With nothing else in front of me, I wanted him, too.

My husband didn't get off work till six or seven o'clock at night, sometimes he didn't come home at all. He was mean when he drank, and he drank every weekend. He would cuss or throw things at me I couldn't see coming or put things in my way so I'd fall. Sometimes he would lock up all the food in the house so I had to go to the neighbors or over to Martha's house for something to ease my hunger. Most evenings I spent ironing his shirts and pants and keeping house by myself. That man was mean and miserly and that helped me make up my mind to meet Doc Romer at Martha's house.

The first time me and the Doc meet outside of the drugstore, I'm waiting for him in Martha's parlor dressed in the one good dress my husband hadn't cut up in one of his rages. I hope I don't have a run in my stockings or sleep in my eyes. Doc Romer bring me a big box of chocolate candy and a sweet-smelling flower he put in my hair. It was quiet at first. He sit at one end of the thick, lumpy sofa and I sit at the other. I felt kinda funny. I was thirty years old and he was at least fifty according to Martha, but I felt like we was both sixteen that evening. He said he liked me, that he wanted me to be his special friend. He made a big speech about how he was married and even though his wife was crazy he couldn't leave her, she needed him. How he know I didn't need him more? He say he know I'm married, he seen the bruises on my arms and neck and sometimes on my face. He say he want to be nice to me.

"Do you like me, Lula Mae?" His voice had a tremble in it.

I don't say nothing right away. I first have to choke back some tears of joy. I reached out till I found his hand resting on the distance between us and I held it up to my face and wash his fingers over my eyes and smelled the clean and Old Spice smell of him. He pressed the flat of his hand against my mouth and I kissed it. He handled my chin and neck like it was a bottle that would break. His hand read my face. My hand followed his over my breastbone, between the buttons on my dress. Every other evening while she was visiting her mama, me and Doc, we sit together on Martha's couch and I let him learn a new part of me until he was ready to love me whole. It seemed I'd found some peace at last.

A few weeks later we went to a hotel. He had to pick up some medical supplies in Savannah; I told my husband I was going to see my mama down in Macon. Doc picked me up in his car at a bus stop at the end of the People Street bus line. We had a fine time. All the way to Savannah he described the things I'd see if I could. When I smelled the ocean I wished I could swim clean to the other side. Dip my body in the salt water and float right out of my life. Doc had a beautiful way of showing me the world. His voice was deep and rich, baritone; his words had color and tone like he was singing a song and there was a feeling he wanted me to have, and I got it.

When we get to the hotel, he checked us in as Mr. & Mrs. I blushed like a new bride. The hotel room had a thick carpet and smelled like cedar leaves and tea roses. There was a big, cold brass bed, soft, thick towels in the bathroom, a radio next to the bed. He showed me where the dresser drawers were and the bathroom. He turned on the radio to a country music station. I didn't care for that kind of music—I liked the blues—but before I could say one word he was kissing me and unbuttoning my blouse. I forgot all about that music and couldn't hear nothing but his heart beating next to mine. My mouth was thirsty for his kisses, my body give in to him. He started out so gentle and sweet. His hands worked my body like it was bread. Kneading and leaning into, and smoothing out my flesh, patting out a song to part my thighs, while his mouth milked my breasts first one, then the other, then both at once. He seemed to be praying over them and I didn't ever want him to stop.

"You all right?" he whispered. All I could do was make a noise and use my hands to tell him I was better than all right. When he moved to put his head between my knees I prayed Holy Jesus.

"I'll make you feel good, Lula Mae," he said like he meant it, and he did.

I was scared to death when I first felt his lips on my private parts. I heard that if a man put his mouth on you down there he could suck out your womb. But I trusted him and tried to loosen up. I was rewarded for his patience. I came out of my skin and hollered out once, though I could have screamed for hours. Only after he satisfied me did he let me give him comfort. He lay back like he was tired, but we was just getting started. I had years of love to make up for. I made love to him with my mouth, my hands, my feet, on the floor, up against the closet and in the bathtub with the water running. I caught up to my nature and I let it ride, ride, ride.

The next day Doc took me to a fancy dress shop and bought me a blue flowered dress with lace at the neck. His favorite color was blue. I found out a lot of things about him I didn't know before. That he had a sister who was a dressmaker in Ohio and a brother who was a eye doctor in Tennessee. He missed his mama, who had big breasts like mine. He slept naked, talked in his sleep and kept his arm around my waist all night long. That one night was sunset, sunrise, twilight and dusk, all at once, in colors my skin could see.

Two days after my night with Doc, I found out my husband hadn't been paying the rent and we was about to be evicted. That didn't surprise me; he was always drinking up the rent money and I was always borrowing from Martha or my mama. But this time Martha sat me down in her kitchen and told me about my husband's other woman. Said she'd seen them together. I made her take me to where the woman lived. Me and Martha stood on the front porch of a shotgun house not a mile from where I ironed my husband's shirts, cooked food for him and kept his house clean. I stood out there in the moonlight listening to my husband making love to another woman. If I'd had a gun I'd have killed him dead. He was supposed to love me. Martha said the only reason she wanted me to know this for myself because she know I don't believe nothing I hear unless it's firsthand. She'd wanted me to leave him for a long time and because she my friend she knew the one thing I'd break over. I cried all the way home holding on to Martha like a prayer in a storm.

I didn't have nothing but ice water in my eyes when my husband come home that night.

"Where you been?" I asked casual, standing by the window where I'd been waiting all evening. He answered me by knocking me down on the floor. Then he sat in his chair, took a drink of whiskey from the pint in his pocket and started listening to a ball game on the radio.

"Bring me some ice for my hand," he said. I got up from the floor, went into the kitchen and filled a plastic bowl to the top with ice. I didn't want him to hit me again. I sat in the rocking chair next to him thinking about how I used to love him like he was my salvation. I rocked and I raged. He took me out of my mama's house, loved my body like it was something holy and I was grateful for that, but he also promised to give me babies, be a family man and to love and honor me. He didn't do a single one of them things and I knew in those final hours that he never would.

'Round about midnight he stumbled into the bedroom and fell out on the bed, dead drunk. I sat there next to him remembering all the times I had lived on soda crackers and tap water while he was taking care of another woman. I remembered all the beatings and the cussings and all the times he called my mama out of her name. I rocked and I raged. I went to the linen closet and took a bedsheet from the top shelf. I snapped it up, out and over my husband's body. I pushed and pulled and tucked at the sheets until he was wrapped up good and tight, then I knotted the ends. I felt around for his mouth and stuck a balled-up freshly ironed and starched handkerchief in his mouth, then taped his lips shut. He started to wake up but he was drunk and hog-tied and all hope was gone.

I dragged a kitchen chair into the bedroom next to the bed. I went into the hall closet and I got out the brand-new iron my mama sent me and I plugged it into a socket behind the ice box. I used all my strength to drag him into the kitchen. I tied him to a chair with a piece of rope. When the iron got real hot, and hissed from the touch of spit on the end of my finger, I pressed the steaming hot metal to the back of his neck. I slid the iron across the creases in the sheet and made sure not a wrinkle remained. I ironed his butt good. He bucked and moaned like a witch was riding him, but I didn't stop and them sheets didn't come undone until he was pressed. I could feel the sweat on his forehead and tears rolling down his face. I was so hard-hearted I ironed his tears. The smell of smoking flesh made me nauseous. I threw up into the bathroom sink, then called Doc Romer to come pick me up. Doc took me and my two cardboard boxes to the bus station so I could go home to my mama.

For the next six months I slept with a shotgun by the door in case my husband come looking for me. Martha called to tell me about the patch Wallace wore over his dead eye and how pitiful he was, sleeping on street corners because his other woman put him out when he lost his job at the mill. She told me how the light was gone out of Doc Romer's eyes, but I didn't want to share nothing supposed to be mine. I set my sights on a full-time, round-the-clock kind of love and I told Doc that nothing less would do.

ZANE

Mr. Good Lay

Y̶ou know you need to hang out with us, girl!" Leigh exclaimed before biting into another freshly baked chocolate chip cookie.

"Sistahgurl, you ain't never lied!" Anita said, giving Leigh a high five. "Twyla never goes out this freakin' house."

I stood there holding another batch of cookies with an oven mitt. "I'm not interested in going anyplace. I go to work and come home. That's enough excitement for me."

"Excitement?" Anita asked sarcastically. "Puleeze! When's the last time you had a man?"

"That doesn't matter because men don't define me," I answered coyly. "Just because men define both of you doesn't mean I have to jump on that train to nowhere. I'm doing great all by myself."

It grew silent enough in my kitchen to hear a pin drop. I knew it was only a matter of time before one or both of them copped an attitude. Leigh was the first to prove me right.

"Um, Twyla, so what are you tryin' to say?"

"I'm not trying to say anything. I'm saying it." I set the pan down on the counter to cool off and joined them at my glass-top table. "All I ever hear from the two of you is how hellified your sex lives are, how many big dick brothers you know, and how many times you can come in one night. That's really more information than I need."

"Aw, you're just jealous," Anita stated accusingly. "I guess being celibate isn't as wonderful as you make it out to be."

"I've never made celibacy out to be wonderful. It's just my choice at this point in time. I came to a crossroads in my life and made a decision: continue letting men use up my temple for their own benefit or hold out for Mr. Good Lay and get something out of it my damn self. I chose the logical solution."

Anita and Leigh locked eyes and fell out laughing.

Leigh almost choked on her glass of milk. "Twyla, you sure are hard on the brothers."

"I'm just keeping it real, Leigh. I mean, think about it. How many times does a child have to play with matches before they figure out they can get burnt?"

"So you're saying that you've never had a decent fuck?" Leigh asked in disbelief. "Not ever?"

I shrugged. "There were a couple of men that broke me off with a little something interesting but none of them were as interesting as my fingers or my personal toys."

Anita giggled. "Personal toys? Dang, Twyla, you're a freak."

"Why's it considered freaky for me to play with myself but it's perfectly acceptable for me to fondle all over some man. Lawd knows where these men have been."

Leigh waved her hands in the air like she was testifying in church. "Amen to that! I was reading this article in the *Post* the other day about the number of undercover men in this area."

"Undercover?" Anita questioned.

"Yeah, mad undercover. They did an article about the amount of bisexual men that go to these clubs in D.C., do their dirt, and then go home to their wives and girlfriends."

"That's just straight-up nasty," I said. "It doesn't surprise me, though. Look at all these people on talk shows. They're passing their privates around like tubs of popcorn."

Leigh slapped me gently on the arm. "Twyla, you seriously need to ease up. It's not that serious. You can't go without sex for the rest of your life."

"Why can't I?"

Leigh pondered the question for a moment, searching for an answer.

"Why can't I?" I asked again.

"Because that's practically criminal. I don't think sex controls me but it helps me relieve stress, get through the day, and it makes me feel wanted."

"There was a time when I yearned to be wanted," I admitted. "I opened myself up and let my emotions lead me around like a sick puppy only to get disrespected, humiliated, or kicked to the curb like yesterday's garbage."

Anita shook her finger in my face. "Watch. One of these days that Mr. Good Lay you were talking about is going to walk into your life and blow your mind."

It was my turn to laugh. "I seriously doubt that."

"Keep on doubting," Anita replied, waving toward my countertop. "And while you're doubting, grab that other batch of cookies. These things are slammin'."

* * *

After Leigh and Anita had decided to head to a jazz club without me, I lay in my bed that night and thought back over our conversation. It had been three long years since I'd been held in a man's arms. Three years full of dedication to my work, which had seriously paid off since I was now the CFO at the bank. The youngest person to ever hold the position and without question, the only African-American female to ever occupy the spacious corner office on the tenth floor.

While I was completely satisfied with my career, my home, and just about everything else, having someone warm to cuddle up with at night would've been the icing on the cake. But I was determined not to settle. I'd seen far too many women settle just so they could lay claim on a man that more than likely had two or three other women claiming him as well.

I'd told myself that allowing one year to pass without intimacy would clear my head, give me some new direction as far as what it was I should look for. Sadly, one year had turned into three and I still didn't know what I needed. I just knew I needed someone, even though hell would freeze over before I confessed that to my girlfriends.

Part of my problem was watching too many late-night talk shows when I should've been doing something more constructive. Every time they showed a man who was a cheater, it restored my faith in keeping my temple sacred. I took good care of myself and looking good at all times was definitely a must for me. I often wore my shoulder-length auburn hair in a bun because it was conservative enough for my job and easy to maneuver during my rushed morning exits. I was blessed to be born with my mother's smooth ebony skin and almond eyes. Being short, five feet exactly, it was imperative that I kept my weight evenly proportioned, so I worked out in my home gym four nights a week. I knew I looked good and wasn't about to give anything away.

I grew restless from staring at my ceiling and there were thirty more minutes of bad news to suffer through before my first talk show came on. I got up and went into my bathroom to look into the mirror.

"You do look good, girl," I said to my reflection. "So why can everyone else find someone to love them and you can't find shit?"

I stood there, half expecting an answer. When the woman in the mirror said nothing, I opened my medicine cabinet and pulled out the bottle of men's cologne that Jeff had left behind when I kicked his sorry ass out three years ago. Jeff was the last man I'd ever been with, the one who'd left me with a broken heart, nearly left me for dead. Yes, I was the one who'd formally broken it off, but how could I stay with him after finding out he'd gotten another woman pregnant.

Shelly, that was her name. I didn't believe her at first when she called me to issue threats about staying away from "her man." It amazed me that she could call my house, the house Jeff and I lived in together, and address him as "her man."

Anyway, I assumed she was some woman sweating Jeff, since he claimed that sisters were always coming on to him. To hear him tell it, he ignored them all. Well, apparently, he didn't ignore Shelly because she described his birthmark to a T. Considering it was on his dick, she would've had to have been one hell of a psychic to know that unless she was doing him.

After accepting Shelly's invitation to visit her apartment across town to view hard evidence, I practically lost it when she produced pictures of them together doing things Jeff had promised to do with me: taking in a play in the park, touring the botanical gardens, posing in front of the gigantic hand statue down at Haines Point. I was sick and grew even sicker when she grabbed a pregnancy test off the coffee table, marched into the bathroom and returned moments later with a positive reading.

Jeff was history that night and, unfortunately, so was my sex life.

*   *   *

"Earth to Twyla! Earth to Twyla!"

Glendon was banging lightly on the conference table to get my attention.

"I'm sorry," I said, snapping back into the present. My daydreams were becoming more frequent and the crazy thing was that I'd never really know what or whom I was daydreaming about. "Please forgive me, Glendon."

Glendon flashed his cinematic smile at me and said, "No big deal. I just hope I wasn't boring you to death."

"Never that."

"Good."

Glendon was an account executive based out of our Tokyo office. Extremely good-looking with a pleasant personality to boot, I was immediately attracted to him when we met two years ago. That is, until I found out he lived across the ocean. I'd never believed in long-distance relationships, even if the distance was just two or three states away, so Japan was definitely out of the question. However, I did enjoy working closely with him when he came to town for brainstorming sessions four to five times a year. He was well over six feet, slender but muscular, the color of honey, with these deep dimples that made me want to slip my tongue into them. Damn shame the only brother I'd been remotely attracted to since Jeff, lived so far away. I felt myself slipping into another daydream and shook my head to clear it.

Glendon got up from the table and stretched his legs. "We probably need to call it a day anyway. It's after six," he said, glancing at his watch.

I felt bad about my lack of concentration so I replied, "No, I'm good. Since you have to hop a plane in the morning, it's best that we go ahead and finish up."

"We've covered most of the important stuff. The rest can easily be handled by fax."

I got up to stretch my legs. We'd been sitting in the same positions for nearly four hours. "You're so sweet, Glendon."

Glendon frowned. "Oh, come on. You should know better."

"Better than what?"

"To call a brother sweet. Call me kind, generous, bighearted but never sweet."

"Why?"

"Because that's a feminine term, Twyla."

"But if you're comfortable with your masculinity, nothing should offend you," I challenged.

Glendon adjusted the lapels of his double-breasted suit and stuck out his chest. "Trust me, my masculinity is fully intact."

I laughed at his body language. "I just bet it is."

"Listen, what are you doing tonight for dinner?" he asked suddenly.

"I don't have any plans," I responded, caught a bit off guard. Then I decided to lie so my social life wouldn't appear as pitiful as it truly was. It was Friday night and women in their thirties like myself, the so-called prime of life, were expected to have plans. "Well, I had some but my companion had to cancel at the last minute."

"I see." Glendon started putting his paperwork into his briefcase. "How about joining me for dinner?"

"Oh, um. . . ." I stuttered, searching for an excuse.

"Twyla, I've been coming back and forth from the Tokyo office for two years and you've never shown me the least bit of hospitality outside this office building. Didn't your mother teach you better?"

"Oh, no, not the guilt trip," I said sarcastically. "Don't even go there. We've done quite a few business dinners."

"Yes, with five or ten other people around. I'm talking about a man and a woman sharing a meal together and enjoying each other's company."

Was he flirting with me?

"Unless, of course, you have a man waiting at home who might object."

"No, that's not an issue," I admitted honestly.

"Great!" Glendon exclaimed, slamming his briefcase and locking it. "What time shall I pick you up or would you rather just leave straight from here?"

"I haven't even accepted yet," I reminded him.

"Then accept already," he persisted.

"I really should go straight home and continue going over these papers but I'll understand if you want to break it off here."

Glendon wasn't going to let me off the hook that easily.

"When's the last time you've been out on a date?"

"That's personal," I said with mock disdain.

"That long, huh?"

Okay, I was officially uncomfortable. "Why do men always assume things?"

"Why do women always beat around the bush and answer questions with questions?"

I laughed. "Touché."

Glendon came around the table and picked a piece of lint off my suit.

"So are we hanging out tonight or not?"

I contemplated another Friday night spent watching talk shows and decided, spending it with a fine man—and more important, a safe man, since he lived so far away from me—was more enticing.

"Sure, why not. We might as well leave straight from here unless my dress is inappropriate for what you have in mind."

Glendon flashed that beautiful smile and dimples at me again. "I don't have anything in mind. I live life on the edge. That way it's more adventurous."

I shrugged and started tossing papers into my own briefcase. "If you say so."

"This is what I propose. We go outside, catch a cab, head north, and stop at the fifteenth restaurant we come across on either side."

"That's silly. What if it's horrid?"

"Then we have a horrid dinner and go someplace else for dessert."

I bit my bottom lip and thought about it. "Well . . ."

"Is it a go?"

"My horoscope today did say that I need to do something out of character to reinforce my sense of adventure."

"See, this is fate," Glendon said, obviously pleased. "Didn't I just use the term 'adventurous' a minute ago?"

"True enough. Just give me a moment to gather my things."

*   *   *

"Amazing!"

"What's that?" Glendon asked as we walked into The Dragon House Restaurant.

"That the fifteenth restaurant we came across happened to be a sushi bar."

"Fascinating, isn't it?"

I playfully punched him on the arm. "Either it's fascinating or you set me up."

"Who, me?" He tried to look angelic but it wasn't working. "I'm completely innocent."

"I bet you love sushi, don't you?" I asked as we were directed to a table.

"I do eat it from time to time in Tokyo."

"How often is from time to time?"

"Daily, for lunch." Glendon held my chair for me while I sat down and then he took the seat across from me. "How about you? Are you a sushi lover as well?"

"How about no." I shook my head. "I've never had it before in my life."

"Then you're in for a treat."

I picked up my menu and then looked around at the other diners plopping pieces of raw fish and rice into their mouths. It was totally unappealing to me. "Don't they have anything else here? Some normal food?"

"Normal food . . . like?"

"Fried chicken, a hamburger, something cooked?" I replied. I was hoping it would be one of those restaurants that specialized in one type of food but still offered other dishes.

"No, you won't find that on their menu, but the sushi here is incredible."

"See, I knew it." I took my menu, reached across the table, and tapped Glendon on the head with it. "You knew we were headed here from jump."

"Okay, I confess." He unfolded his napkin and placed it on his lap. Glendon had such good manners during business meetings and dinners that I'd often wondered if he'd gone to charm school as a child. Unfortunately, my parents had forced me to attend and I'd hated it.

"If you're truly not into it, we can go someplace else. While sushi is my favorite, I'm originally from the Dirty South, so I can

get down with soul food just like the next brother. I heard there's
an awesome soul food place a few blocks away."

I grinned, thinking about the macaroni and cheese, greens,
and yams at the restaurant he was referring to. "I know it well."

"You go there a lot?"

"Daily, for lunch."

We looked at each other and started laughing.

There were dozens of items listed on the menu and I was clue-
less about what they were. "So, what do you recommend?" I
asked, determined not to put anything unidentified into my
mouth.

I'd gone to a friend's surprise birthday party at a Jamaican
restaurant in Georgetown and after devouring half a platter of
what I thought were scallops, I located a menu to figure out the
name of the dish. When I discovered that scallops weren't even
on the menu, I asked the owner about the food on the platter and
he told me it was shark. I almost brought it all back up right then
and there.

"Let's see. I can give you a quick rundown. Kani is crab, ika is
squid, hirame is flounder, sake is salmon, maguro is tuna, anago
is eel, mekajiki is—"

"Hold up," I stated in dismay. "Did you just say eel?"

"Yes, that's actually delicious. You should try it."

"Um, no thanks. I think I'll go for the tuna."

"The maguro?"

"Yes, whatever." I smirked. "Tuna is usually relatively safe."

"If you say so, but that's not being very daring."

"It's daring enough for me."

Glendon and I had a lovely dinner. I discovered so much about him that I never knew. He'd indeed grown up in the Dirty South, less than an hour from my hometown of Spartanburg, South Carolina. We even had a couple of mutual friends.

"So, how in the world did you end up in Tokyo?" I asked him over a pot of green tea. "I thought I was being bold by leaving home and moving to D.C., but Japan? That seems like a world away."

"It is a world away from here. Why don't you pay the Tokyo office a visit? I'm sure the company would foot the bill."

"I'm sure they would, but long flights are not for me. I have a four-hour limit in the sky."

"With a four-hour limit, you'll never see much of the planet."

"Maybe not, but I can see both coasts and that's good enough for me."

"I'll just have to see about convincing you to increase that limit."

"You'd have to do a hell of a lot of convincing."

"I'm up for the challenge."

There it was again: he was flirting.

Glendon took his napkin off his lap, waved down the waiter, and mouthed the word "check." "What's next on our agenda?"

"Next?"

"Of course. It's Friday night in the city. Surely you don't plan on heading home before ten o'clock? Things are just getting started."

"Glendon, I've really enjoyed the dinner but I'm kind of worn out."

"Then let's go for a quick jog around the block and rejuvenate ourselves."

Was he serious? I pictured us jogging around the block in our business suits, hard-soled shoes, and briefcases.

"I'm joking, Twyla."

I grabbed my chest. "Whew, you had me worried for a minute there."

We both chuckled.

"Can I ask you a question that you promise not to answer with another question?"

I rolled my eyes. He really was under the assumption that women avoid too many questions. "Go for it."

"Do you love your life?"

"Do I love my life?"

"Yes, do you love your life? Do you wake up in the morning and feel like doing cartwheels because you've been blessed with another day? Another opportunity to do something incredible."

"I wouldn't go so far as to say I love it, but I enjoy life," I replied honestly. I had never really thought about it in such terms before. I usually woke up with my list of things to do already embedded in my brain.

"So you don't ever run around your house naked and jump up and down on the furniture or fill your tub with whipped cream and swirl your butt around in it?"

Embarrassed by the mere thought, I crossed my hands on my chest. "No, I definitely don't do that."

"Then you're missing out. Those are the best things in life."

"If you say so."

"I do, and I'll tell you what else. I've been watching you over the years and the fact that you're lonely sticks out like a sore thumb."

I was immediately offended. *How dare he?* I thought.

"You don't know me like that so don't go there," I started angrily.

"I may not have a right to go there, but I'm going." The waiter brought the check and Glendon whipped out his corporate card, gave it to the waiter, then continued. "Let me tell you how I see you."

I shook my head. "This should be enlightening."

"You're beautiful, successful, intelligent, and probably have the ability to make any man's toes curl in bed if given the space and opportunity."

I almost choked on my tea. "You're hilarious."

"I'm glad you're enjoying yourself."

The waiter returned with the credit card slip. Glendon added a generous tip and signed it.

"Shall we?" he asked, getting up from the table. Once I stood up, he whispered in my ear. "For the record, I happen to be handsome, successful, intelligent, and I definitely have the ability to make any woman's toes curl in bed." He bent down and brushed his lips gently across my forehead. "Given the space and opportunity."

Either that green tea had made me high or Glendon's flirting was beginning to pay off. I suddenly felt liberated and giddy, possibly even horny.

We were chilled by the night air when we stepped out onto the street.

Glendon put an arm around me and hailed a cab. One pulled up immediately. He held the door open for me.

"Where are we going?" I asked suspiciously. The way he was talking, he was ready to take me home or back to his hotel room to engage in some toe-curling experiments. While I wasn't totally against it, I wasn't quite ready just yet. Breaking a three-year cycle of celibacy was not a minor thing. Then again, it wasn't like I was collecting dividends on my pussy.

"I've got an idea. One that is full of adventure. You game?"

I grinned at him mischievously. "Sure, why not?"

* * *

When the cab came to a halt in front of The Pink Flamingo, I thought I was seeing things. The Pink Flamingo was a strip club in Northwest that many of my boyfriends had gone to over the years. While I'd never stepped foot in the place, I was mad at each and every last hoochie mama up in there for shaking what their mamas gave them in front of my men for cash.

"Glendon, this is a strip club," I announced, like he didn't already know that.

He chuckled. "I'm quite aware of that. Let's go in."

"I'm not getting out of this cab," I said angrily. "I'm a woman."

Glendon ran his fingers through my hair. "I'm quite aware of that, too. Remember your horoscope. If you don't go in this place tonight, is there a chance in hell that you'll ever go in?"

"Not a chance in two hells."

"Then, go in there with me, kick back a few drinks, experience something different."

"This is different, all right." I got out of the cab. Oh, what the hell! Glendon and I were business associates and it wasn't like we saw each other every day. Besides, in order to squeal on me, he'd have to squeal on himself and those were pretty good odds he'd keep quiet.

Glendon paid the cover charge and I was nervous the second we stepped inside. I'd seen strip club scenes in movies but nothing could've prepared me for the real deal. A thick sister with enough breasts for herself, me, and about three or four other women was on the stage doing splits around a pole and letting men look at every entry hole on her body. She wasn't just topless. She was as naked as naked could get.

The place was packed and we struggled through the crowd before locating a table in the corner. I felt a lot of male eyes on me and I didn't like nor appreciate it. They were probably making all sorts of assumptions about me. Once we sat down, I took a survey of the room and noticed there were several other females scattered around at tables enjoying the show. One woman was even getting a lap dance from a stripper over by the bar.

Glendon yelled into my ear over the loud music. "What'll you have?"

"Something extremely strong!" I yelled back at him.

He ordered us Orgasms, of all things. I started to object but realized if I couldn't get a decent orgasm from a man one way, maybe I could get one another way, even if he had to buy it for me.

As much as I hated to admit it, the strip club was fun and arousing. Despite the thick smoke clogging the air and men yelling out the most disgusting things I'd ever heard, by the time I'd finished my second drink, I was of another mind-set. I was drunk, I was relaxed, and I was mad horny. Glendon was fine before we got there but now he was looking like a sex machine.

"Want a lap dance?" he asked, kissing me on the forehead.

I slapped him on the hand. "How about no, but you feel free to get one if you wish."

"Don't mind if I do?"

I shook my head. "No. Your life, your money, your dick. Do what you want to do."

"Ooh, you said the 'D' word! You must be loosening up some."

We shared a laugh. Glendon stood up and directed a tall, caramel-coated sister over to our table with his finger.

"How much for a lap dance?"

"For you or for her?" the sister asked, eyeing me in a manner that instantly made me feel uncomfortable again.

"For me," Glendon replied.

"Oh, too bad," she said coolly. "For you, it's fifty bucks."

"Let me guess. If I'd said it was for her, you would've given me a discount."

"Brother, as fine as that woman is beside you, I would've done her for free."

I was shocked. I'd never had a woman come on to me before.

"Well, after she witnesses what you do to me, maybe she'll change her mind," Glendon said jokingly.

"Then I better do you right." She licked her lips at me while Glendon reached into his pocket to get the money. "I'd love to play around with her a little."

I was speechless. I didn't know whether to politely reject her offer or cuss her ass out. Before I could decide, she was on Glendon's lap gyrating her hips to the rhythm of the music. He wasn't looking at her, though. He was watching me.

He found my hand and pulled me closer to him. "Twyla, you see what she's doing to me?"

"How could I miss it?"

He let go of my wrist and shook his head. "Question with a question."

I giggled. "Sorry. Bad habits are hard to break. Yes, I see what she's doing to you."

The woman's back was so close to us, I could smell the cocoa butter on her skin.

"I want you to do it to me, tonight, back in my hotel room."

Something came over me. What it was, I have no idea, but the next second I was running my tongue up Glendon's right dimple and chiding him. "Why don't you just say what you really mean?"

"Fine." Glendon pulled me in even closer. "I want to fuck you, Twyla, tonight, back in my hotel room."

I slipped my tongue into his mouth and kissed him roughly. The dancer on his lap got off, turned around, and dropped to her knees. She caressed his thighs and then found the mound sticking up in between them.

"Why don't all three of us go back to your hotel room and fuck each other?" she suggested, having overheard our conversation.

Glendon stopped kissing me and let me go. "Sorry, this is a private party," he replied, pushing her gently off him. "Thanks for the dance." He reached into his pocket and pulled out a ten. "A little bonus, for helping a brother out." Then he turned to me. "Let's get out of here."

*   *   *

Things got way out of hand in the cab. Let's just say the driver should've been paying us. We were all over each other. Normally, I don't even like to hold hands in front of other people. But I'd already tongued Glendon down in a raunchy strip joint and was now leaning back and lifting my hips so he could take my white lace panties off in the backseat of a cab.

Glendon started inching his fingers in between my thighs but suddenly hesitated.

"What's wrong?" I inquired, seriously feeling those Orgasms from the club. Now that he'd gotten me started, I didn't want to stop.

He removed his hand and whispered, "Do something adventurous."

"Um, I'm drunk and in a cab with no panties on. I'd call that adventurous."

"True, but do something more adventurous."

"Like what?"

"Play with yourself."

I would've laughed it off but he was serious.

"You want me to play with myself? Right here? Now?"

Glendon nodded, smiling. "There's not that much light in here. Just enough for me to see."

I pointed to the driver, who almost ran up on a curb from trying to watch us and the road at the same time. "What about him?"

"What about him?" Glendon retorted. "A minute ago you let

me take off your panties and were ready to let me do something kinky to you in front of him. What's the difference?"

I let my head fall back and saw the street lamps flashing past as we cruised along Constitution Avenue. I couldn't believe I'd allowed myself to be placed in such a compromising situation. Then again, it felt kind of nice. All my life I'd been taught that "good girls" don't do certain things. They don't sleep with a man on the first date. They don't masturbate. They don't have oral sex. They don't have anal sex. They also don't have any fun and I wanted to have some fun, if only for one night.

I sat up and looked Glendon in the eyes. "Okay, I'll do it, on one condition."

Glendon's left eyebrow rose with interest. "What's the condition?"

"If I do it, you do it, too."

"You want me to jerk off after you're done?"

I shook my head. "No, we do it together or not at all. I'll jill off while you jack off."

Glendon was so excited about my suggestion that he had his belt unbuckled and his pants unzipped within seconds.

Glendon glanced at the driver again. "If you drive us around until we're done, I'll give you the tip of the century."

The driver laughed. "Consider it done."

"What's your name?" I blurted out. If I was going to masturbate in front of a complete stranger, I felt entitled to at least his name.

"My name's Albert," he responded, pointing to an identification badge adhered to the dashboard that I couldn't possibly make out in the lighting.

"Nice to meet you, Albert."

"Same here."

I pulled Glendon's legs closer to me so I could place mine over his and position my feet on both sides of his hips. "Shall we begin?"

He released his dick from his boxers and it was absolutely scrumptious. Long, thick, juicy, and so smooth that it looked like chocolate that would melt in my mouth.

I slid my index finger down between my legs, ran it over my clit, and then offered it to his lips. He licked my fingertip.

"How do I taste?"

"Like heaven."

I took the same finger and glided it into my pussy walls, letting my finger get completely coated with my nectar. I pulled it out and offered it to him again. He sucked it down to the knuckle.

"Now how do I taste?"

"Like heaven and hell."

I giggled. "Heaven and hell?"

"Yes, heaven because you taste so sweet and hell because you're a very dangerous woman."

"Oh, so now I'm dangerous?"

"You might be."

"How so?"

"Because I'm supposed to be going back to Tokyo in the morning and if a night with you is half as good as I suspect it will be, I'm not going to want to leave."

Even though I was still a bit drunk and dazed, I was flattered by what he was telling me. I'd always been attracted to Glendon but distance kept me from pursuing him. Might he possibly ask for a transfer to be with me?

He seemed like he was waiting on a response so I gave him one. "Glendon, if this becomes something, I'd like that, but if it ends up being just about tonight, I'm cool with that, too."

I wriggled out of my blazer and unbuttoned the three top buttons of my blouse. Then I unfastened the front clasp of my bra and let my breasts fall freely. I closed my eyes and pretended I was alone in my bed. I rubbed my nipples between my thumbs and forefingers, becoming aroused by their hardness. I pushed my left breast up to my mouth and flicked my tongue across my nipple.

I could hear Glendon moaning and the sound of his hand sliding up and down the shaft of his dick. I used my right hand to begin fingering myself again, spreading my pussy lips with two fingers and moving a third in and out. Albert suddenly slammed on the brakes. Several cars blew their horns but I kept my eyes clamped shut. I sensed that Glendon was watching me, though. I started praying that we didn't end up in a car wreck. Talk about being caught with your hand in the cookie jar.

My pussy grew more moist by the second and soon my entire hand was covered with my juices. When I felt Glendon grip onto my right thigh, I opened my eyes. He was panting and sweat covered his brow. He moved my hand from my pussy and replaced it with his.

"Now let's do each other, Twyla."

The way his dick was glistening in the dim lighting was so appealing that he didn't have to ask me twice. I wrapped my hand around him, ran the tip of my finger over the head of his dick, and rubbed his cum over it. I worked his shaft like a master, even though it had been three years since I'd even seen an actual dick.

We came after more than ten minutes of getting to know each other's private parts. I screamed out in ecstasy, Glendon screamed out in ecstasy, and Albert screamed out in ecstasy. Lawd only knows what he'd been doing in the front seat the entire time.

*   *   *

Glendon gave Albert the fare plus a fifty-dollar tip when we got back to the Hilton, where he was staying. We surely looked a mess, not to mention guilty as sin, as we rushed through the lobby for the bank of elevators. No sooner had the doors shut on elevator three than we were groping all over each other and kissing passionately. I wrapped my arms around his neck as Glendon palmed my ass cheeks and lifted me up so I could straddle his waist. When we got to the twenty-first floor, Glendon had to put me down so we could get our briefcases. We'd been lugging them around with us all night while we did our dirt. Absolutely wicked.

We got into Glendon's room and started ripping each other's clothes off by the door. After Glendon's chest was bare, I pushed his back against the door and sucked on his neck until I was positive I'd left a hickey and then licked a trail down the middle of his chest to his belly button. I undid his zipper while I dipped my tongue into his belly button, blew on it to dry it, and then dipped it in again.

Glendon pulled the pins out of my hair and ran his fingers through it. "Damn, Twyla, you're something else."

I looked up at him as I pulled his pants down to his ankles. "Want to know a secret?"

"Sure."

"It's been three years for me."

He hesitated before letting out a low whistle. "Are you serious?"

"Yes. You asked me earlier when was the last time I'd been out on a date. Well, now I'm telling you. It's been three years since I've been out on a date, been interested in a man, or been fucked. What do you think of that?"

Glendon tightened his grip. "I think it's turning me on."

"Good." I sucked on the head of his dick for a few seconds and then let it go. "Then what I'm about to do to you should really turn you on."

I caressed Glendon's balls with one hand and held the base of his dick with the other one. Then I lapped my tongue over the underside of his dick and traced the tip of it along each vein. I relaxed my throat and placed my full lips around his shaft and took him in and out of my mouth, slowly at first, before picking up the pace. I'd forgotten how great it felt to suck a man's dick. It's the ultimate high because women are never more powerful than when they have a man under control sexually. Nothing makes a man succumb faster than good head.

Glendon caught onto my rhythm and moved his hips in unison with my mouth. I sensed he was about to come and since he'd already had an orgasm in the cab, I didn't want to risk him climaxing again without actually fucking me. While not an expert, I realize most men have limitations and everyone knows that the second erection often has more staying power than the first.

I was honest and told him as I released him, "I don't want you to come yet." I got up and sauntered backward toward the bed, removing the rest of my clothing along the way. "Come to bed," I beckoned.

Glendon attempted to walk with his pants around his ankles but gave up after five or six steps. He then kicked his shoes off and stepped out of his pants.

"Hurry up," I said insistently, pulling back the bedspread and sliding down between the sheets. Glendon was reaching for me when I got my priorities back in check. "Please tell me you have a condom."

Glendon grinned and walked back over to his pants, picked them up from the floor and retrieved a condom from his wallet. After he sat down on the bed beside me, I ripped the packet open with my teeth, placed the condom in my mouth and put it on him.

Glendon moaned. "I've heard about women doing that but I've never had it done before."

I winked at him. "See, you underestimated me. You assumed you'd get me here and turn my ass out but for all you know, it might end up the other way around."

He chuckled. "Actually, I was banking on us turning each other out."

"Umm, then let the games begin," I said, pulling him between my thighs.

His entry was smooth, like a jet making a perfect landing on a runway.

"Mmmm, you're tight." Glendon moaned, grabbing my hips and pulling me closer to the edge of the bed.

"I told you it's been three years."

"I guess I'm the luckiest man in the world tonight."

"Just shut up and fuck me." I laughed. He felt so good inside me, so right.

I locked my legs behind Glendon's back and dug my fingernails into his ass. The room was humid and droplets of sweat started gathering between our bodies as we moved together in harmonious bliss. The alcohol had worn off and my head was perfectly clear, which was a good thing because I wanted to remember every second of my night with Mr. Good Lay. I'd finally found him. He had been right in front of me the entire time. This was the kind of sex Leigh and Anita were always bragging about. This was what I'd searched for my entire life. Glendon was hitting all the right spots, in and out of my body and after he slid a finger into my ass, I completely lost it. I shifted my legs from around his back and clamped them around his neck. Good dick can make the stiffest, most out-of-shape woman a contortionist, and I damn sure was turning into one that night.

Glendon pulled out after a few moments and told me to turn around. He entered me from behind and started sliding in and out of me until I felt the head of his dick in my stomach and his balls slapping up against the back of my thighs. I was dripping, my juices sliding down my thighs onto the sheets.

"Stop," I whispered to him.

He didn't stop but asked, "What's wrong?"

"Nothing," I replied. "I just want to take you for a ride."

Glendon started laughing and pulled out. "Mmmm, I like the way that sounds."

I got up, pushed him onto his back and straddled his thighs. Then I leaned over and gave him a long kiss. "Now let's see if you like the way it feels."

I pushed myself down on his dick and once I grew accustomed to the position, I dug my fingernails into his chest and used my vaginal muscles to bring us both much pleasure. He ran his fingers up and down my spine, causing a tingling sensation, and the look on his face was one for the books. It might've been a while since I did the wild thing, but Glendon was enjoying my comeback.

Glendon pressed my breasts together and pulled them toward his mouth. I gripped the headboard with both hands and rode him harder. Then Glendon finally lost that second erection and came with a vengeance. Exhausted, we fell asleep, Glendon's head nestled on my chest.

*　*　*

After Glendon's wake-up call at nine, we showered together. Then he packed his things, called the front desk to check out and we dashed off in a cab to the airport.

Since Glendon made it to the gate as the plane was boarding, we had only a moment to say good-bye.

"So, do you regret it?" he asked, kissing me on the forehead.

I put my arms around his waist. "No, do you?"

"Absolutely not. My only regret is that I can't take you back to Tokyo with me."

"When are you coming back?"

"Two, three months. Sooner if I can make up an excuse."

"Why do you need an excuse?"

"Why do you need one?"

I laughed. "Good point. I'd like to come visit you, Glendon, but you know how I feel about long flights."

"It's doesn't matter how you feel about long flights. It only matters how you feel about me."

We gazed silently at each other as they made the announcement for final boarding.

I let go of him. "You'd better go."

"Just like that?" He pouted. "Don't I at least get a kiss?"

I looked around the terminal. "In front of all these people?"

"You weren't worried about all that in front of Albert."

I blushed, embarrassed, but I didn't regret it. I gave Glendon a long, wet kiss and then pushed him away from me. "You're going to miss the plane."

He started for the gate, looking back at me over his shoulder. "So what are you going to do once I'm gone?"

I smiled before replying. "Maybe I'll go home, run around my house naked, fill my tub with whipped cream and then swirl my butt around in it."

Glendon smiled back at me. "Sounds like a plan."

"Then I might get up in the morning and do cartwheels because I'm still alive and because I love my life."

"You love your life?"

"Yes, I love my life!" I yelled, drawing stares but not caring. Glendon had changed something in me, my complete outlook on life and on men, and I wanted him to know it.

"I love my life, too," he responded. He was handing his ticket to the attendant when he added, "And, for the record, I love you."

I was speechless. Then again, I didn't think I really needed to state the obvious.

"I'll call you, Twyla," were his last words before he disappeared into the plane.

"You'd better call me, Mr. Good Lay," I said aloud. "I'll be waiting."

JENOYNE ADAMS

Next Time Take Flesh

The situation could have occurred with any game—spades, bones, Monopoly. It's never the game, it's always who's playing. Tonight it was Jenga and as always, it was the poets and their appetites in the home of someone who knew exactly what to expect. If everything would have flowed according to plan, the gathering would have been held in Loren and Reggie's living room around a large blond oak coffee table. When Loren's newborn nephew ended up in the hospital with a hundred-and-four-degree fever, the locale got switched to Arisa's place because everyone knew that Arisa's house was always clean.

And it was. The two-bedroom, one-and-a-half-bathroom house got scrubbed and poked twice weekly. Cleanliness was one of the squares in her life. So were the six years she'd been serving on the police force. So was the man she'd liked fairly well, dated for eight and a half years and almost married. She was aware of the squares in her life. She needed more circles. The poets were circles. Enough roundness to make her reach through her numbness and dress her five-feet-two, one-hundred-and-fifty-seven-pound body in black knickers with beaded fringe and a hot pink halter top with NAUGHTY written across her braless breasts.

She'd ended her shift early that evening to prepare for guests she'd seen almost every third Friday of each month for the last year of her life. She deposited lit vanilla incense in the soil of each of the four hanging plants in her living room, amber-colored candles on the two coffee tables and lavender in the bathrooms. Venus Musk burned unattended on her bedroom nightstand.

As she set out plates for the veggie greens, barbecued tofu chicken twists, and baked potato wedges sprinkled with onion-curry powder she'd gotten from the local black bookstore and soul food kitchen, she thought about the roundness of her body. She'd never been an extravagant eater or drinker. She was a nibbler, a water sipper, a bona fide leg and wing girl before she'd given up meat. And right before the doorbell rang, she got to thinking that maybe her roundness was a square, a safety net to protect her from attracting what she wanted most.

"I'm first, huh?" Hootie said, as he crossed the threshold into Arisa's vanilla-scented air.

She smiled and took the four pack of Mike's Hard Lemonade from his hand.

"Technically, I'm first brotha."

He hugged her and they rubbed cheeks in consummate poet tradition. Arisa noticed the cat in herself more around the poets than in any other group. Poets loved to brush their scents onto each other's skin.

"Sistah, as long as I don't have to pay the pot fee anymore, I'm straight."

Arisa watched him bend at the waist to peel his brown loafers from his feet and place his shoes on the cedar shoe rack.

"You only have to pay the pot when you're late," she reminded him.

"Right, right," he said, heading over to the couch to make himself comfortable. "You mind if I spin a tree, sistah?"

Arisa rolled her eyes as she walked back toward the kitchen. *Dammit.* She hated having that mess in her house—funk that punctuated air and breath—that compromised her station. She was a police officer, after all, not a security guard at Wal-Mart. She reached up into the cabinet over the refrigerator and knocked the paper cups into her arms with the tip of her spatula.

"Go ahead, Hootie. Just don't drop any seeds on my carpet."

"Right, right," he responded.

Arisa took the silverware from the drawer closest to the stove. "I'm a poet first," she said under her breath. "Remember that."

She *was* a poet first. A good one. She'd be an even better one if she trusted herself enough to let go. Reality was, she wasn't sure if she could afford that kind of freedom in her life. Most of the time she wondered if letting go would cost her the order that had kept her going all these years. Other times she didn't care about the cost and just wanted to taste the other side of living. That's what attracted her to Ten.

By the time she had set out the hummus and salted corn chips, the only person who hadn't arrived was Ten. He—like everyone else in the group—had relied on Hootie to pay the pot. Hootie had paid the pot five out of the last eight meetings. Twenty dollars a pop. There was only one rule of their group: the last one to arrive late paid twenty on the spot. It was their *Stop CPT Rule.*

Arisa was getting nervous. Ten was the underlying reason for every poem she'd written in the last year. He was the purple plum liquor she licked from cupped hands of longing, the bareback brown ass rising on the summersault of her tongue. He was everything she wanted him to be on moist evenings of self-fingered deliverance.

*   *   *

By the time Ten arrived, everyone had relaxed into their spots for the evening. Hootie sat next to Shonteal on the couch. His navy blue jogging suit a shade darker than the JUST DO IT motif written across Shonteal's baseball cap. Blizzy massaged his bald, almost brown head as he sat next to Arisa on the love seat, his twelve-inch-long, blue-cotton-ribbed feet resting on Electric's size-six rayon-skirted lap. Ten rolled in smooth like he normally did. After he'd unlaced his boots, he walked over to the breakfast bar and placed a glass dish of skinned mango slices on the counter. Then he strolled casually into the living room, and flicked the twenty-dollar bill next to the Jenga box sitting atop the round, beveled glass coffee table.

"You know you've missed out on your lovin' tonight, right?" Electric said, taking a break from licking the last barbecue sauce from under the tips of her hot pink acrylic nails. "We're full now; can't nobody get up to hug your late ass."

"Give me a pound, then," he said to Electric, as he leaned down to give Shonteal a kiss on the cheek.

"Brotha no," Electric spouted back.

Ten locked hands with Hootie and gave him dap.

"What's up, Hootie Mack?"

"Chillin' man, 'bout to get lifted off of this tree, man."

As Ten moved across the floor, Arisa watched the hem of his jeans skim the fuzz of the beige carpet. Despite their bagginess, she could almost see his bowleggedness. He reached over and knocked fists with Blizzy.

"You gonna give me some or what?" He held out his arms and gave Arisa a look. She pushed up off the couch and went to him. The top of her head rested against the middle of his chest. When he bent to kiss her cheek, his dreads brushed a peppermint scent across her face.

"What kind of shampoo do you use?" she said, smelling his locks, feeling apple martini relaxation soaking into her spine.

"You know I make my stuff. A little tea tree, a little peppermint, nettle, sage, this and that. You want some?"

"Umm-hunh," she said, bringing one of his locks to her nose, her face cocked up toward his.

"I'm going to hook you up this time," he said, "but don't start trying to take advantage of a brotha, all right?"

He smiled. *Damn. He shouldn't have smiled,* she thought. Not all big and bright and fresh in her face like that. With a gold cap on the third tooth from center she would have hated on any other man, but loved on him. He let go of her shoulders and two seconds later she loosened the grip of her left hand on his waist.

"Come on, girl."

He pulled Electric up by the hand.

"Let me lick some of the Q sauce from your sexy-ass fingers."

He took her pinkie into his mouth and sucked lightly; Electric brushed her lips against his ear.

"Don't make me shit my pants," she said, then they both broke out into laughter.

Arisa cringed. "Okay y'all, it's Jenga time or we ain't gonna get to our poetry tonight."

"We *is* poetry," said Blizzy, reaching across the table to pinch the spliff from Hootie's fingers, "look at my socks." He pointed the spliff toward his toes. Each toe was individually mitted like a hand of gloved fingers. He wiggled.

"Shut up," Shonteal said, laughing like everyone else in the room, including Blizzy.

"Okay." Arisa knelt on her pink-and-blue-beaded knees and began to erect the Jenga blocks into a high-rise form. "Tonight is Truth or Dare. The questions are carved into the blocks. Red is dare, black is truth, and the beige ones are blank."

The fact that the questions had sexual undertones only increased the natural sexual tension of the group. A red block deemed that Ten had to sit on the lap of the person to the right of him until his next turn. While Ten was sitting on Shonteal's lap, Shonteal had to blow a raspberry on the stomach of someone in the group. She chose Hootie so she didn't have to get up. He leaned over her on the couch, bringing his thin, muscular stomach to her lips. Electric pulled a black block from the structure and had to tell her most embarrassing moment. She said it was when she was having sex in the men's rest room of a movie theater and after she and her man had climaxed a voice chimed "good show" over the rest room loudspeaker. Blizzy knocked the structure over twice trying to pull impossible blocks from the unstable base of the leaning Jenga tower. Both times he had to super-freak the TV set, which was playing *In Living Color* reruns.

By the fourth rotation, two spliffs, one pitcher of margaritas and another of apple martinis, the beige blank blocks had become offensive to the forthrightness of the night. Electric declared that whoever pulled a beige block would have to take a dare and that the last person dared would create the dare for the next person who pulled one, and so forth.

Arisa had a system: pull beige; when beige is not possible, pull black for truth; lastly, pull dare. Her system had worked fairly successfully the whole evening and she'd been able to play it safe. With the rules changed, by her third time around, she had to pull red. The block read in white letters: TAKE OFF ONE ITEM OF CLOTHING. Arisa slapped the red block onto the glass. Her bra was out because she wasn't wearing one. All that was left were her pants, blouse or panties.

"Take it off, naughty," Ten said, a big smile on his face, Shonteal now resting on his lap.

"And no changing in the bathroom," Electric added.

Arisa stood up, unzipped the zipper in the back of her pants and stepped out of both legs. Hot pink micro-briefs covered her pubic hair and most of her ass. She sat back down on the couch, placing a burnt-orange pillow over her crotch. Surprisingly, she felt liberated by the act of undressing, like taking off her clothes in front of the poets softened her lines and made her a little bit more circular.

The chemistry in the air had changed. Everyone could feel the sexual charge. The pace of the game sped up. Electric gave Ten a lap dance and Hootie was dared to give Shonteal a passionate kiss, during which tongues touched—several times. By the time Blizzy sucked Arisa's big toe, gold toe-ring and all, forbidden had captured reality and, for hours, none of them would catch up to the weight of what the evening meant.

* * *

After the game, the room scrambled for their journals and Arisa walked into the kitchen in her panties to retrieve extra pens and the wicker basket she had left on the chopping board.

"The theme for tonight," she said, taking her seat next to Blizzy, "is 'Touching.' We want to capture the emotions and feelings of touch, first in our bodies, and then transfer the experience into word." She scooted to the edge of the couch and reached into the basket. "Inside here is an assortment of oils—from olive and almond to flavored piña colada spice. Each partner gets fifteen minutes. You may apply more than one oil. At the end of thirty minutes each of us will record our experience by attempting the first fifteen lines of a poem." Arisa checked all the faces in the circle to make sure everyone understood. "Okay. Choose a partner, and not the same one you had last month."

The exercises were always intimate. Last month's theme had been "Hurt." They had paired up in different corners of Shonteal's apartment and exchanged the one experience in their lives that had hurt each of them the most. Everyone cried, even Hootie. Everyone had written a poem about a mother, or father, sister, or lover that struck a chord of deep connection among the members of the group. They knew about almost every area of each others' lives: Blizzy's divorce at twenty-seven, Shonteal's abusive ex-boyfriend, how Electric had dated twin brothers at the same time, and also had dated Ten. The games facilitated this special kind of bonding they'd grown accustomed to. They all knew that the games were the entrance point of trust. Whether the host chose bid whist or tic-tac-toe didn't matter, the goal was that they played until the chemistry of openness took over.

Ten chose Arisa to be his partner. The two of them faced each other in the dimness of the room, sitting Indian-style on the carpet, the back of the couch shielding them from the other paired-off poets. Ten pulled his sweater over his head, then his white T-shirt, sending a whiff of frankincense to Arisa's nose. She had dreamed of this moment. The way his pecs formed ripe nutmeg mounds against the backdrop of tight muscled arms and moist black-man skin. Arisa poured sweet almond oil into her curved palm, rubbed her hands together and touched him with the flat of both palms and all five fingers. She felt pinpricks of heat surface between her breasts. Her hands shook the tiniest bit. Ten inched his body closer to hers and framed her Indian-styled legs with his own. Her hands still on his chest, Ten pressed his hands around the outside of hers and slid them down the length of his stomach.

"Touch me here," he said with his eyes, piercing her with the urgency of his request. The vibration was strong. She needed a man to want her this way. She unbuttoned his jeans over the muted moments of the other poets. He stared at her as she watched him growing in the sweet almond of her fingers. Sight, touch, and smell collided against her consciousness. She knew for the first time what communion felt like. The heartbeat of his dick synchronized with the pulsing between her thighs. Arisa leaned into him. The moistness of her breath collected in the locks draping his shoulder. She wanted him like she wanted breath. Maybe more. As he moved the cotton crotch of her panties to the side of her pubic hair, Arisa gasped. Her hand still around the brown of him, the pinkest part of her baptized his bare fingers with its juices. They wrote themselves into each other, pasted need under the skin. Not for the sake of marriage or long-term love, but for the sake of knowing what it was like to be stained by touch.

"I won't open you here," he said, locking both thumbs together like a doughnut twist, then pulling them out of her. "But I'm telling you the truth, I can fuck you and pray inside you at the same time. I want you tonight."

"Time!" Arisa said, feeling the nude roughness of her voice. She slid her panties from the side of her crotch back over her vagina and made her way quickly to the love seat. Pray and fuck at the same time—shit. She was stunned by her reaction. This is what she'd been waiting for. She shook her head. This man scared her. Now more than ever. What if she let go with him and didn't know how to make it back to sanity. "Nuh-unh . . . *Nuh-unhh,*" she said aloud. He could take her places she'd never been before and she knew it.

"You all right?" Electric said, as she took Blizzy's old spot. Arisa sat catty-cornered on the love seat, her left leg angled like a chicken wing on the cushion, her left foot locked under the back of her right knee. Electric stroked the inside of Arisa's thigh to comfort her.

"Umm-hunh. Just fine."

"Girl," Electric leaned into Arisa, the warmth of her breath collecting around Arisa's earlobe, "he used to make me feel that way too when I first met him. It's like he undresses your spirit and exposes what you want most."

Arisa nodded, not caring that Electric understood what she was experiencing. She was overwhelmed. How was she supposed to write a poem feeling like this?

Blizzy took his writing pad from the coffee table and lay on his stomach on the carpet. Hootie poured himself another margarita and set up his iBook on the breakfast bar in the kitchen. Shonteal sat facing the wall with her notebook on her knees. Ten stayed behind the couch.

Under the click of keys and scratch of pen against paper, Arisa could hear his breath. It was deep and controlled, just like it had been when she'd touched him. Even with her hands massaging oil onto his penis, he didn't miss a normal breath. He didn't get excited. Just stared at her, concentration embedding him into her pelvic walls. He was still inside her. And all at once, she realized that he had opened her, whether he had intended to or not.

"You gonna read yours, Arisa?" Electric glanced down to read Arisa's page, then started grinning.

Next time take flesh, not my heart sat at the top center of the sheet.

Arisa closed the notebook. "No," she said, feigning control, "my poem hasn't come yet."

"It came all right; you just mistook it for something else." Electric smiled and tapped Arisa's leg again.

"Get out of her business, Electric, and let me read my stuff."

As the group gathered again to critique Shonteal's poem, Arisa promised herself that she would ignore Electric. Ignoring Ten was the hard part, even though he seemed to be ignoring her just fine. He was business as normal. Giving Shonteal feedback, making jokes, leaning forward on the armrest when he was listening hard. Arisa watched his lips move and each thought of him sent a liquid jolt through her body.

As Ten read his own poem, Arisa became embarrassed by the wetness between her legs. She wondered if he wanted her like he wanted the woman in his poem—if he would spit-shine her uterus and split her like a single pomegranate seed. Arisa had to separate herself. She leaned back with the burnt-orange pillow hugged to her body and took comfort in the fact that he hadn't looked her square in the eye for almost an hour. She laughed to herself and thought this beautiful-ass Negro is bluffing—bluffing big-time. Arisa slowly eased herself into the critique of the last two poets, completely ignoring Ten's sexy, bowed-leg stance and coarse black hairs resting against his fully developed bare chest. She ignored the way the ridges between his stomach muscles intensified with each breath. By the end of the night, she had completely relaxed and distanced herself from what had happened behind the couch, almost like it was something she had fantasized about, but never experienced.

After another twenty minutes the poets started their departure ritual: taking plates and cups back into the kitchen, stuffing notebooks back into bags and putting on shoes. Arisa busied herself in the kitchen, covering up the leftovers with tinfoil at the stove.

Ten helped by bringing glasses and bottles into the kitchen.

"Okay, girl, thanks for having this at your place last minute." Shonteal gave Arisa a hug and a kiss on the cheek.

"No problem," Arisa said, gripping the roll of tinfoil tightly in her hand.

"You walking out with us, bruh?" Blizzy asked Ten.

"Naw, man, I'm gonna be here for a while."

They gave each other a pound on the fist.

"See you, girl," Electric said, smiling as she walked onto the porch. Ten flicked the light switch off, then closed the door behind them.

"Give me that," he said to Arisa, taking the foil from her hand and dropping it to the floor.

She couldn't say anything, just nodded the slightest bit.

Ten grabbed the dish of sliced mango and led her behind the couch. They faced each other Indian-style.

"I wanted you to relax; that's why I didn't look at you," he said, scooping the whole of her breast into his mouth. The pink fibers of her tank top moistened with each slow suck.

"How do you want me, Arisa?" he said, switching breasts.

He sucked. She held her breath. He sucked harder. She gasped.

"How do you want me?"

Arisa recognized the strength in his stare.

"I want . . ." she paused, "like the woman in your poem."

The full brown flesh of his lips pressed against hers. He kissed her with his tongue, teeth and breath all at the same time. She kissed him back with equal commitment.

The candlelight in the room coated their skin. Ten raised

Arisa's arms above her head and pulled her tank top over the length of her arms.

"Keep them up," he said.

He stared at her. His eyes on her body made beads of sweat form between her ample breasts. The approval in his gaze let her know that he liked her ripe thighs and thick curves. Arisa, arms still raised, closed her eyes and began to move to the slow winding music in her head. She gyrated her waist smoothly and rolled her shoulders and hips. She was his own personal belly dancer.

Ten inched forward and slipped a sliver of mango into her mouth. The warm fruit melted on her tongue. He sucked his fingers, then fed her another slice. As she chewed, Ten licked the sweet juice from her lips. The taste and smell of the mango made Arisa sink deeper into her winding groove. Ten, with a sliver of the yellowish-orange fruit in his own mouth, uncrossed her legs and started to lick the sweetness between her thighs. Arisa leaned back onto her elbows, her legs spread somewhere between a V and full split. His dreadlocks danced across her stomach and breasts; Arisa gripped his hair and relaxed into the cool feeling of mango and tongue against her clitoris.

Ten stood up, pulled off his socks, then stood gap-legged as he tugged apart the button-fly of his jeans. Arisa stared at the purple-brown of his dick. She watched a butterfly spread on his back as his shoulders broadened and his waist tightened when he bent to remove the bunched pant legs from around his ankles. She wanted to know what the tight black hair around his dick smelled like.

"Stand up."

Ten held Arisa by both sides of the waist and folded her upper body over the back of the couch. Her legs spread, Ten knelt between them. He opened the lips of her vagina again. This time he slid his dreaded head onto her clit.

"Ride me," he said.

Arisa moved her pelvis in slow circles, absorbing the shock of her softness against the round cords of his locks. Ten grasped her waist and pulled her down harder onto his dreads. They settled into a counterclockwise grind, then a staccato rhythm. Arisa couldn't hold back any longer. She groped a handful of his hair and let her body release against him. She felt a quaking surge from her vagina into her stomach. Ten maneuvered himself into her opening. He knew the right spot without searching for it. She could feel his head expand against the sweet knot in her body. She rode him in wild convulsing movements. He rode her back, untaming her with each stroke.

As he dressed, Arisa lay on the couch under the blanket Ten had gotten from the cedar chest at the end of her bed. He pulled his T-shirt back over his head; she thought of her scent mixing with the peppermint of his hair. He placed his boots back onto his feet; she thought of the thick roundness of his dick.

"Don't get up."

He held the sides of her face and kissed away doubt. At least for now, she had no questions. She didn't need to know if this was the first and last time. If it never happened again, she would be satisfied. Arisa lay there, his smell tattooed onto her body—complete in her instant of touching.

* * *

When the doorbell rang, she figured Ten had forgotten something. Arisa wrapped the blanket around her body and let the fringe drag as she walked to the door. He'd placed the lined page under the brass knocker:

For Arisa

She seeps through the hollow of my dick
I split her like a single pomegranate seed
Suck her red from my bottom lip
Spit-shine her uterus with my tongue
She is opened by my longing
I exit her womb ancestor
Birth her into mother
of man I want to be next time

Ten

KATHLEEN E. MORRIS

Letters & Remembrances

LYNDA:

I almost didn't recognize you—waiting at the gate. Your hair, once a riotous mass of black curls, was now a sparkling halo of silver stars. Your eyes, which I remembered flashing lightning on a stormy sea, had calmed—now a quiet pool in a secret inlet. Even your smile, your precious smile had changed. The angry, proud grin of the warrior had mellowed to a sad, thoughtful turn at the corners of your mouth.

Who is this middle-aged woman? I wondered as I moved toward you, this woman, looking so tired and worn, lost and confused in the ocean of bodies swirling around her.

You were at once familiar and strange. I wanted to hold you, feel your heart, smell your hair, but I was suddenly afraid of what I might find in the embrace of the shadow form before me. I stopped and waited, instead, for a sign from you. For you to rush to me, strong and sure, smile large and welcoming. I waited for that weary facade to wash away, revealing my Sea Goddess— powerful enough to slay my dragons and free me from the chaotic, fractured life I was trying to run away from. I would step away from those chains, and we would enter into our secret place, our sacred space—you and me and Florida, like we used to do, once upon a time.

But you didn't rush to me. There was fear, uncertainty in those tired, middle-aged eyes. I realized that my Sea Goddess had returned to her ocean, leaving me to battle my demons alone with only this weary stranger, who didn't look as if she could save herself.

NIKKI:

My heart was pounding in my throat as I watched you push through the crowds. I'd never seen you like that, still dressed in your office clothes, so . . . New York. No flowing drummer pants, no jangling gypsy earrings. Your beautiful lips, once soft and inviting, were tense, tightly pressed. Your eyes, once clear and laughing with the wonders of discovery, flashed with irritation at slower moving people, someone bumping into you. Your eyes brushed over me as you scanned the crowd impatiently. And then your gaze fell on me again—at first uncertain, and then recognizing. You smiled . . . well, your mouth smiled. Your eyes were disappointed. I saw that. My heart grew heavy as I moved toward you.

We stood there in the crowded terminal—awkward, uncomfortable—and allowed the moment of embrace to pass, unfulfilled. My eyes burned with threatened tears as we made our way to the baggage claim. We stood there, waiting. Silent. Separate. Until you pointed toward yours, and I moved forward to claim it, ever, I thought, your strong hero. You brushed me aside like crumbs from your lap, tossing me your smaller bag. Rebuffed and diminished, I watched you carry your suitcase to the exit. You'd made it clear. You didn't need me anymore.

LYNDA:

We drove past the apartment of our youth. There was a dingy FOR RENT sign in a window once decorated with tiny white lights. "Too busy saving the world for housework!" you'd laughed so long ago.

I closed my eyes, forcing back tears, and remembered the last time we loved there . . . amid plaster dust and cans of soaking brushes, a paint-spattered rag draping the lampshade, dimming the room in faded kaleidoscopic colors. Your volumes on Frida Kahlo leaned haphazardly in a dusty stack beneath dried yellow roses and that seagull's wing you'd insisted on picking up on the highway one afternoon. . . .

Your new space was neat, ordered. You had settled . . . down. Gone was your defiant clutter. The art supplies of yesterday's dreamer were neatly stored away, books of revolution still in boxes. Your altar, your tribute to the Mother . . . your celebration of women and women's power . . . had been reduced to milk crates filled with bits of incense and chipped, smoke-blackened statues, hidden in a cabinet with doors not closed completely, but difficult to open. Lesson plans and assorted papers of your work as a teacher of children were scattered over a table once crammed with candles and oils, crystals and flowers . . . your work as a teacher of women, forgotten.

NIKKI:

I wanted to say something that would reach you; find some way to break down the wall you'd built between us. I struggled to find my voice, but my words could not force their way through my tightening throat. The car filled with our strangeness. Your disappointment. My frustration.

I thought to turn down the street of our yesterday, hoping to spark in you a remembrance of our connection. I watched you take in the trees, the building where we last shared our lives. I saw your rejection and felt your disillusionment. Even my new home, which I'd spent hours readying in honor of your arrival, registered nothing more than resentment. I had failed again. You wanted yesterday. I had only today to give.

LYNDA:

I dreamed we were walking on the beach. It was dark, the black sky dotted with points of light. We sat at the water's edge, holding sparklers. We lit them and watched as they danced on that dark stage, sputtered on the evening breeze. Finally, as the lights flickered and died, we kissed. Your lips were sweet, giving. Your tongue dipped into me and I shivered, goose bumps rising on skin, warm. My hands touched you, held your shoulders, pulled you closer. Your nipples touched mine, your full breasts pressed hard against mine. I felt your breath brushing across my ear.

The waves splashed against our feet as we lay back in the pale sand. I looked up at you, gazed into eyes wide and black, loving and hungry. Your lips found mine again and my body welcomed yours again. We darkened the sands beneath us with our passion.

* * *

I awoke, tears still damp on my cheek, to glowing morning light. Not the bright grayness of a New York City dawn, but orange, reds, dazzling—March in Florida. You lay beside me, your hair curling on the pillow. I studied your face. Lined, soft around the edges, heavier than my memory. Your long, dark eyelashes brushed your pale, olive skin.

I don't know this woman, I thought. And suddenly, I longed to be back at home—in my own space, with people I knew and loved. I knew you once upon a time, and loved you then. But now?

I wanted to destroy the woman sleeping beside me—older, calmer, afraid of the world. I prayed that you wouldn't wake up. I didn't want to hear the resignation in your voice, or see the fire of revolution dimmed in your hazel eyes.

I slipped from the bed, moving quietly through your rooms, searching for some—*thing* . . . some memory that would link our yesterday to today. I found a plaster bird, half-painted, as it was the last time I saw you.

I moved to the window, looked out, finding yesterday. I saw you—young, militant, woman-centered. You taught me rituals, history—how to celebrate my Mother power, to move through the world with pride and entitlement. Books, art, lectures, you shared all of that with me. You shaped me, made me strong. That is who you *were.* It is now who I *am.* And we are left worlds apart. I think, too far to travel.

NIKKI:

I dreamed the room was filled with candles, smoky with incense, fragrant with our spent passion. We lay together, talking theory, weaving dreams. Your face is open, happy, content. Your eyes see me—know me—love me. My heart is full as I reach out my hand to brush your cheek. I awaken to a pillow already grown cold.

I feel the emptiness as a deep ache. Reluctantly, I push away the memory of our lazy mornings—of your stroking me to wakefulness, of listening to our favorite radio show over steaming cups of caffe.

I know what you wanted—I have always seen into you—but it was not within my power to transport us back in time. I know that we are, both of us, very different people today, our lives have taken us in different directions. Still, I had hoped we hadn't lost our love, our friendship. I know I hadn't. Why couldn't you remember the ease, the trust that had never been betrayed?

I listened to your wary stillness in the other room and wondered if you believed I had betrayed you by giving in to the years? Had I betrayed you by growing older?

LYNDA:

I heard you waking; the rustle of covers, your bare feet on the floor. My eyes filled with tears. There were so many changes happening in my life. Love ending, wanderlust beginning, a new career—even, I feared, a new me, someone alien, unknown to my experience. I felt lost, afraid. So, I traveled back to you seeking— I don't know. Maybe I had hoped to find the Me of yesterday, the Me who was happy, carefree, excited about life's possibilities. I wanted back my fresh new eyes, my skin—pores open to the sensations of sun and wind and water. I didn't know when or where I'd lost them; I had hoped that I'd left them with you. But *my you*, the you I had in my heart, was packed away in a box marked FRAGILE and DO NOT DISTURB, pushed back into a shadowy corner.

The you I found was only a shell, the final echo of a voice that once climbed mountains to shout its existence to the world. You had faded to a specter without form or substance. Slipped through my outstretched hands, taking with you my joy—and hope.

Gone. My foundation. My touchstone. I hated you for allowing time to wear you away—leaving me alone and adrift and lost.

NIKKI:

I watched you for a few moments, looking out at . . . nothing. Or rather, you are lost somewhere inside of you, in a place where I was once welcomed, but am now forbidden. Your back says "go away," your shoulders, square and tense, shut me out. You know I am here, but you don't want me near you. My heart aches with the truth in your shoulders.

When had it changed? I struggle to recall our late-night calls— at first, daily, long whispered promises closing the miles between us. Later, weekly calls, hurried. Complaints about work, stories of people I would never meet. Uncomfortable laughter at my mention of love, or of meeting again. And then, occasional calls. Birthdays. Holidays. "Just touching base." Insincere returns of my "I love you."

And too, my growing silences. Too long to explain people and places, better to skip to us. Only there was no "us." Not anymore, was there? Our lives had spiraled out of each other's orbits. Too busy to visit, you were. Too broke to come, I. Days passed when I didn't even think of you and then fear of that forgetfulness dialed your number.

It was your idea, this visit. I heard old tears in your voice when you called, and knew that it would be our last chance to salvage us. Even if you didn't know it then, you had done your crying. You were prepared to let us go, to release even the memory of the special link we once shared.

I study your back. Is it too late? Have you really, finally, gone from me? I inch slowly toward you, half afraid that your image will dissolve into the light streaming through the window if I dare touch you. But I need to touch you. I need to know.

LYNDA:

You touch me softly and then wrap your arms around my waist. Your cheek rests tentatively on my shoulder, your breasts press lightly against my back. I feel your heart beating against me, uncertain of my acceptance, afraid that I will pull away. I see our reflections dimly in the window and recall that antique mirror we used to stand before—naked. We stood before that antique mirror in the before or after of love, in the hours between night and day, in that passion-fragranced, darkened room, gently lit by candles and little white lights.

I take your hands in mine, lifting us both up to my breasts. I study the differences, the sameness—as we used to do in those nights in front of that mirror. Your thick, squared fingertips entwine with my smaller, rounded ones; my winter beige skin and scarlet red, manicured hands remain a delicious contrast to your short, unpainted nails. I note that there is no trace of ink stains from printing presses and silk screens, no blue or green or red ridges of dried paint beneath your nails. Your skin is almost as smooth and soft as mine.

I turn our hands, palms up, and slide my fingers over your flesh, remembering when they had a rougher texture—proof of an artist's life impulsively led by the senses. I remember the paint tattoos, yes, but carpentry and plaster molds, clays and stone, burns from candlemaking, cuts and scrapes from your long hours chopping, cutting and cooking for that restaurant around the corner of that little apartment, had all left stories here, too. Your pale, olive hands were golden then.

They give off heat, your hands. I feel the heat of them through my shirt, feel my skin glowing beneath your fingers, remembering magic. I had forgotten the heat—or rather, having not felt it in the hands or passions of the lovers who had filled the years since, I had come to believe that I'd created that memory to warm and comfort me on cold, lonely nights.

But I feel it now. It is real. I feel it spreading out from those rosy points; traveling remembered pathways through my body. I feel my ice melting . . . *remember that winter night, together in New York?*

I look up at the window, search for our reflections, but they are gone, burned away by the sunlight. I am getting hot. . . . I feel myself burning. . . . *There is only us, only now,* you whispered to me once upon a time, and your hands glide over me . . . as you covered my mouth with yours. *Only now, only us.* I repeat the mantra in short, whispered gasps. . . . Our lips meet again. . . . The world beyond our bodies, our pleasures, our needs, disappears.

Only us, only now. My body is warm, the ice inside melts and I am liquid. Your body presses closer to me, your square, artist's fingers spread slowly out, mold my breasts, bringing me back to this sun-filled room. Your lips bring me back to us. Your teeth graze my back, melting my final shard of ice. I feel it. Ice to water, water heating as it travels down . . . from my breasts . . . down . . . steam pulsing a rhythm of call and response to my throbbing cunt.

I lean back into you, and you press into me; your mound, cushioned by long black hair, moistened by . . . You press softly, but urgently against my ass—and I respond. We grind together in a dance never forgotten.

Your hands squeeze possession of my breasts, my nipples pressing hard under your palm, aching tender with the pain of want. *There is only us, only now.* Yes. I turn to you, fill your mouth with my tongue as my hands slip the robe from your body. *There is only us, only now.*

I want you to to know who I am, this Woman, this Warrior. I want. I want you.

My skin is burning as we strip the clothes from our bodies, silk and cotton thin cushion for two women writhing on a wood-planked floor. We don't speak; no words are necessary. Our bodies know each other. There are no calendars to mark time in passion's place. *There is only us. Only now.*

And I am hungry. My tongue tastes salt on your neck. You pull me closer and I bite, then suck, leaving a mark. I intend to mark you, your shoulders, your breasts, belly, thighs. Later, you will ache, remembering that your nipples were so hard, became harder still, as my tongue captured them, secured them between my teeth. I roll them around inside my mouth. *Ahhhh . . .* Your body tenses.

Your body arches into me; pleasure and pain. My teeth scrape your skin, my lips offer soft kisses to your belly. My hand slips beneath you, lifts you up to me.

I feel your heart pumping—hard; I taste your body flushing as the blood rushes to the surface of your skin. As plants offer themselves up to a sky that promises rain, you offer yourself up to me; give yourself over to my hunger. A trail of strawberry bruises mark the trail I blaze, foretell where I will go.

Earth and sea blend with ripe fruit—citrus. I bathe my face in your scent; I taste you on my tongue. My mouth rides with the gentle rise and fall of your hips. Moving my mouth over plump flesh, my fingers part you, my tongue slips inside. . . . *Oh . . .* I taste your excitement, pungent cream on my tongue. More. I want more. Slipping into your wetness, I am wild with lust. Your thighs hold me willing captive; I wet my face with your fragrant welcome.

I feel your heat rising up with your swelling clit and take that sweet, hard berry into my mouth, juicing it slowly. *I know how to juice your berry, baby.* I wash my face in a torrent of liquid fire. I suck greedily. *Yes. I want that. I . . . want . . . that.*

My tongue slips into its place, my lips close around your hood and thus trapped, my tongue is relentless. I am relentless. I will have this. Your body thrashes against my face, but my tongue is a dagger, flesh point jabbing hard against your raw, swollen clit. I feel, just beneath the surface of your skin, an orgasm welling up, straining, wanting to burst through.

Ah . . . Please . . . please . . . take it. Your hands grip my head; your hips rise up—steady, deliberate motion.

I soften my tongue; wrap it around your burning tip and thrash it—deliberate torture. *Yes . . . I* will *take it. But not yet . . . not yet . . .*

There is only now. . . .

I want . . .

Only us . . .

I want . . .

My hand cups your mound firmly, wet hair curled around my fingers. Back. I pull back your furred protection, push back the hood that conceals my prize and claim it. I claim you. I suck you in . . . out . . . in . . .

Yes. . . .

Yes. . . .

Your whole body trembles in anticipation of the storm that cums. Mist soaks my face. I want it all.

Rain down on me.

I tremble in anticipation of your storm. Your body flashes lightning. I slip my finger inside. Thunder rolls in the distance. I roll my hand down your thigh, my fingers burning red lines into your flesh, scorching new memories.

You open yourself more . . . more. . . .

The water rises. I want more. . . .

I want . . .

My fingers dive in, into your roiling surf and are lost in the foam and spray. You open more for me and my hand is consumed by your sweet stickiness. I feel you giving yourself up.

I am in you, your walls pulsing around my hand as I pump you slowly. I lay my tongue down on your clit and pulse slowly, synchronizing the dance.

Rain down on me. . . .

I feel the cloud bursting. . . .

Your orgasm is a tidal wave that takes me with it. I close my eyes and ride . . . ride the wave. I am still deep inside you. I stroke you gently, slowly, until I can slip my fingers from you. So released, I kiss your mound and then rest my wet cheek against it.

Love and spring are not the same thing, I know.

We lay there quietly, the sun shining brightly on our nakedness. I was slipping into a satisfied daze, when I felt your body shake with quiet laughter. I opened my eyes and looked up at you.

Only now.

I smile, wistfully.

I would not find the girl I came in search of. Neither she nor my Sea Goddess lives in this place. Their story is done.

I turn the page and find two women, with history, with memory. Here is where a new story might begin.

NELSON GEORGE

It's Never Too Late in New York

*T*here's a part of me that's always envied my good buddy Walter Gibbs, so whenever we played ball, I always came hard. An elbow in the lower back, a kick toward his groin on a jumper, a move to inflict a bit of pain and give me an edge. After all, Walter was a better athlete than I was. I was taller and had longer arms but Walter had strong legs that gave him more hops than a rabbit. I know that if I let up on Walter for even a moment, he'd win.

So whenever we were matched against each other, I found that if I beat on him enough, Walter would fold. I'd use my legs to cut off his drives. My elbows to push him off the parameter. My whole body to keep him from spots near the basket when he posted me up. If I brought it like that, Walter would give in. Not quit exactly but just not care as much as I did. So on this Super Bowl Sunday afternoon, I beat Walter in three games of one-on-one, not by outshooting or even outplaying him, but by making one or two hustle plays—getting my own rebound on a missed shot, knocking a ball off his leg, anything that gave me an edge. I never won by much—one point, two points tops. But it meant something to me every time.

Later, as we sat in the steam room, Walter, in his humble way, remarked, "Niggah, you ain't shit."

"Then why did I win the trifecta today?"

"You won three games because my mind was on ass. I was holding back for tonight."

"Since when do you have to marshal your strength to get busy, Walter?"

"I have a special treat coming my way, that's why."

"I take it you're not talking about going to Andy's for the game?"

"Nah. But you know what, Dwayne? I'm gonna put you down."

"You mean 'in-there-like-swimwear'?"

"You know you're really showing your age right now, niggah. You sound like a Heavy D. record. This is the twenty-first century. It's time for some new slang. Word?" I laughed at that. Walter was getting as old school as I was. So for effect he capped his riff with, "Yes, home slice, word."

* * *

In a cab downtown Walter gave me the details of his post-game strategy.

"Her name is Medina."

"As in 'Funky Cold'?"

"Yes, yes, and you don't stop. Met her at the Paradise Strip Club. Right as she rubbed her pussy against my dick she realized she'd seen my picture in *Vibe.*"

"Wait a minute, I met this girl. Her real name's Beatrice. Remember, we all went to the movies together?"

"Oh yeah. Beatrice. I like Medina better myself. When'd she tell you her real name?"

"I think when you went to get popcorn."

"Okay, good," he said, not really sounding pleased. "She must have liked you."

"I guess so."

* * *

It was about two months back. He'd just wrapped production on a movie and was chillin' in town. He'd met me at the Sony on Sixty-eighth Street with Medina aka Beatrice. She was petite with skin the color of a ripe tangerine. She wore outrageously high black platform boots—the kind Japanese tourists usually sport—and a flimsy beige dress under a snazzy leather coat. In her hair were two decorative beige barrettes. Her eyes were slanted and framed with dark eyeliner. Her lips, moistened by red lipstick, seemed to go on forever. Though probably twenty-six, she radiated a baby-doll sexiness I liked. That night she eyed me carefully, pulling me in with her gaze. *Desire me,* her eyes ordered, and I obeyed.

Somehow Beatrice ended up sitting between Walter and me. The protocol for your man and his date is that he sits in the middle. At first that didn't seem important. Not until Walter got a page on his two-way and left to make a call in the lobby. Nothing should have happened. I was attracted to her but I wasn't gonna kick it to my man's date. All I did was lean over and say something innocuous to her about "too many commercials and not enough trailers." She responded by brushing my knee with her hand and then letting it rest there. I covered it with mine and then, impulsively, brought them to my lips and kissed her fingers. She took her hand out of mine and, using both hands, held my face.

Wordlessly, we tongued each other as images of coming block-busters flicked across our faces. I hadn't known this girl more than ten minutes and we'd made this quick, curious connection. Maybe it was because we both knew that Walter had a high pro-file girlfriend. Maybe we just felt like being naughty. I wondered what the people behind us were thinking.

By the time Walter came back with his arms full of bottled water and a huge bag of buttered popcorn our lips had parted. But, despite Walter's presence in the darkened theater, I still let a hand rest on her thigh and she'd brush it even as Walter chuckled at Eddie Murphy's latest. When he went to the rest room, about halfway through the movie Beatrice whispered her real name to me along with her number but, alas, all I could recall later was her warm breath on my ear.

After the movie Walter, not an unperceptive man, gave me a hug and then whisked her away in a taxi while I went home with a very hard dick.

*   *   *

"So, you're meeting her, huh?" I said, feeling jealous. "Sounds like fun to me."

"Oh, Dwayne, that's not all. She's bringing her lover to meet me."

"Who, based on your grin, is a female."

"Yes, niggah. And because of your fine performance on the hardwood I'm gonna give you an opportunity to express your hard wood. You feel me?"

"Oh shit."

"Yes, niggah. Oh shit."

Walter and I had been friends some fifteen years and I'd watched (and sometimes helped) his rise from movie novice to edgy low-budget film producer, to Hollywood hack capable of making $20 million jammies with admiration and envy. Along the way Walter developed an amazing skill for orchestrating nontraditional, multipartner sex. Just as Walter had a knack for finding the right young director to give voice to black rage and humor, the man had a gift for plucking the inner freak out of otherwise seemingly conventional women. I'd seen him fuck models in Porto Sans in Bryant Park and entice the collegiate daughters of potential investors back to his crib. I'd also received a few three A.M. phone calls from my stoned friend in some posh hotel with the voices of many women groaning in the background.

As a pop music journalist now turned screenwriter, I'd bedded my share of singers, models, actresses and wanna-be stars. Yet, in all my years in the entertainment game, I'd never followed Walter's lead and indulged in orgies. There seemed something, well, unsanitary about more than one person penetrating a woman at the same time. Two dicks in the bed, in my opinion, meant two testicles too many.

A couple of girlfriends had suggested we add another woman to the mix, but I'd declined. I think of myself as a one-on-one kind of guy. Yes, I'd cheated on women—sainthood was not my destination—but to me sex demanded full concentration and abandonment into the depths of a woman's body and soul. I simply didn't believe I could split my focus and be a good lover. But, yes, of course I was curious. And I already knew I desired Beatrice and that she desired me.

"Come correct," Walter said a half-hour later as the cab stopped in the East Village in front of Bowery Bar. "I know you're new to this orgy game but it's never too late to learn. That's why I love this city. It's never too late in New York, niggah."

Inside, a huge TV screen set up in the back of the restaurant was projecting the interminable pre-game hype hard-core football fans savored. A few of the mostly male downtown hipster crowd were making wagers on the Titans versus the Rams. Thankfully, instead of sports chatter, light r&b was playing as the commentator's words ran across the bottom of the screen. However, if you looked to the right of the screen, there was a much better show under way.

Swinging her hips in a slow, seductive motion was Beatrice. She was dancing alone to the music in front of a small table where an attractive thirtyish woman sat sipping wine. She had a oval face with hooded eyes, slim lips and skin the color of a harvest moon. Her breasts were full and, from what I could see under the table, she had thick, shapely legs. To the envy of many at Bowery Bar, Walter strolled over and kissed Beatrice as I stood anxiously behind him.

"You remember my man, right?"

Beatrice received me with a light kiss and a long hug. Then she said, "This is Sonja—the friend I told you about."

"She talks a lot about you, Walter," Sonja said, locking eyes with him.

"Likewise," he replied, and then sat down next to her. After I was introduced I squeezed in on the other side of Sonja as Beatrice went back to her dancing. Sonja and Walter traded endearments and then gazed at Beatrice, the lovely link between them. I watched Sonja laugh, then softly touch Walter's lips. "Yeah, sweetness," he murmured. "Yeah."

Walter's two-way buzzed. He checked the message and grinned. "I'll be right back," he said. "Why don't you two lovely people make friends." And so we did. I went first: ex-full-time music critic; author of the critically acclaimed black music history, *The Relentless Beat;* single; childless; writing a screenplay for Walter's Idea Factory Productions called *One Special Moment.* I told my story neatly with an emphasis on my professional résumé.

Sonja, in contrast, took time with all the details, especially the personal ones: Trini immigrant family; raised in Hempstead; Cornell undergrad: New York Law; a day job at Universal Records in business affairs; an IBM executive boyfriend with a crib in Jersey; and a nightlife that had nothing to do with contracts and depositions.

"My boyfriend," she said at one point, "would love this big-screen TV and this conversation. He's always watching documentaries on jazz and blues and all that. He probably knows your work."

"Really," I replied, not knowing how to respond. "It's a shame he's not here."

She smiled and turned her gaze from me to Beatrice. "Now that's not what you really think, is it?"

"No, counselor, it isn't."

"The truth is always a good thing. How long have you and Walter been friends?"

"Known him fifteen years or so. Way back before his first music videos."

"So you must have a lot in common."

This was an encouraging line of questioning.

"As much as good friends do. As much as you and your good friend have in common," I answered.

"Well, it's only been two months but we already share so much." She had more to say but Walter walked up to the table.

"Let's go, team," he said, gesturing for us to stand. "I have a new recruit."

Walter led Beatrice by the hand while I guided Sonja behind them, my hand resting in the soft curve of her waist. We moved around the chairs of envious men to the bar where a barely post-college chocolate brown cutie awaited us. Her name was Robinette and she was dressed in seventies' retro style—plain hip-hugger slacks, a beige turtleneck, a brown leather jacket, black platform shoes and yellow tinted shades. A woolly natural silhouetted her baby face.

"Walter," she whined, "I'm supposed to be meeting some friends."

He took her by the hand like a father would his child. "No, Robinette, that's dead. You're coming with us." She didn't resist, but wore a petulant scowl as we headed for the door. A bouncer looked at me and joked, "Y'all planning your own personal Super Bowl party, huh?" I nodded like it was my game plan and headed out the door.

Outside we commandeered two taxis. Walter got into the first one with Robinette. "Let me get her head straight," he whispered and then instructed me to jump in the second cab with the other two women. As we drove west across the Village to Moomba, Beatrice nestled in between Sonja and me, turned and began kissing her friend. As their tongues tied I at first watched like an intruder until, timidly, I started rubbing the insides of Beatrice's legs. I then progressed to kissing her neck. She opened her gams wider in encouragement. By the time we reached Moomba my fingers had traced some delightful geometric patterns inside her panties.

Up on Moomba's second floor we dined on seafood, artfully arranged vegetables and a medley of alcoholic beverages. The seating was strategic: Sonja and Beatrice sat next to each other, nuzzling like deer. Walter sat at the head of the table, beaming and pouring Moët like water, Robinette and I sat to his right. Robinette stared, mesmerized by Beatrice and Sonja, while Walter and I soothed, cajoled, and whispered to her about the joys of being sexually open. Robinette's eyes looked a bit glazed and it hit me that "getting her head right" probably involved drugs. Walter was an old hand at this game, so I just noted it and said nothing.

Initially I'd just followed Walter's lead in seducing Robinette. But, as the evening's possibilities became apparent, I grew more animated. I softly rubbed her legs, gazed deep into her brown eyes and listened empathetically to her frustrations with the fashion game. "Yes, I worked at Condé Nast two years before I got to go on a shoot," she complained. As I nodded that I understood her frustration, mentally I was licking my lips.

Unlike Sonja, a seemingly practical girl with an extravagant inner life, Robinette was obsessed with the surface. It was clear why she fancied Walter—he represented power, opportunity and mobility. Still I wasn't sure we would pull Robinette in until she bragged about her close relationship with a Eurasian model and her white photographer hubby. At this couple's mention Walter's eyes widened.

"Have you been out to their house in East Hampton, Robinette?" He leaned in close to her.

"Yes," she said haughtily. "They were kind enough to ask me out."

"And did you stay the weekend?

"Of course, Walter. I wouldn't go out for just one day."

"No doubt. Now," he said matter-of-factly, "who ate your pussy first—him or her?"

Her reply was a guilty giggle. So now it was on. All our predatory eyes gazed hungrily at young Robinette. Walter pressed on.

"Did you enjoy more eating or being eaten? C'mon, darling. Everybody at this table likes the taste of pussy."

Walter's frankness must have melted Robinette as a dreamy look replaced her earlier self-absorption and it was now clear she had officially joined our party.

"Let's go," Walter announced, the check disappearing under the weight of his black AmEx card.

Robinette asked, "Where are we going?"

"My place," Walter answered. "After all, it's Super Bowl Sunday."

*   *   *

Outside Moomba we snared a cab. Now the rules of the New York taxi industry preclude carrying more than four passengers at a time. Sonja, the attorney, sweet-talked Pierre, the Haitian cabbie, into taking us. Walter, Beatrice, Sonja and Robinette squeezed snugly into the backseat and I, the fifth wheel, sat up next to the driver. The taxi's two sides were separated by a bulletproof partition. There was a wide hole in the center for exchanging money. Soon after we pulled off I glanced into the back and saw the most remarkable things.

From left to right sat Sonja, Walter, Robinette and Beatrice, as tightly packed as the dot on an *i*.

Walter kissed Beatrice by leaning across the body of a very uncomfortable Robinette. With his left hand he reached back toward Sonja, who began sucking his fingers. Beatrice reached down and across Robinette to unzip Walter's pants. Then she bent down and placed her mouth around his dick. Sonja and Walter locked lips as Robinette sat motionless and the taxi's windows began to fog.

And then, as if someone gave a signal, Sonja, Beatrice and Walter descended on young Robinette. Walter unbuttoned her blouse. Beatrice unzipped her slacks. Sonja reached over and pulled down Robinette's leopard bra, revealing her tiny, hard black nipples. Her matching leopard panties showcased a flat, smooth stomach and a thin wisp of carefully shaved pubic hair. Her moans filled the now steamy car as I stuck my hand through the opening in the bulletproof glass, stretching my fingers to touch Robinette's soft, slender legs. But that was all I could really do aside from peer at the proceedings like a poor child outside a bakery. Pierre, our very focused driver, didn't flinch, slow down, complain or even seem to care. He just rolled up unconcerned to Walter's apartment in a smooth, efficient manner. As we drove I could hear the Super Bowl starting lineups being announced on the radio.

Outside of very well-cast porn videos I'd never seen anything like this. I was involved but then not really. What could be worse than being three feet away from an orgy? I was just a horny-ass voyeur, separated from the action by steel and plastic and leather.

When we stopped at Walter's building on West Thirty-fourth Street, I paid Pierre as the lord of the manor and his three concubines sauntered inside. I have no idea how much money I gave Pierre 'cause I was not getting left behind again. I had never been in an orgy before—hadn't even had a threesome. Now I was ready to lose my "virginity."

Walter was reserved in the lobby, speaking politely to the doorman, before checking his mail even though it was Sunday. Even in the elevator, when a glassy-eyed Robinette tried to smother him with kisses, he seemed more interested in the security camera than her.

Ah, but once he closed the door to his apartment, he dropped the mask and returned to his true lecherous nature, doling out orders as if he were a drill sergeant.

"Ladies, there are two guest bathrooms. Why don't you make any necessary stops while Dwayne and I get refreshments."

The women, dutifully, retreated to the bathrooms, which were located along the apartment's long central corridor adjacent to two guest bedrooms. Walter's main bedroom was at one end of the corridor next to his gym. Beyond that was the kitchen. At the opposite end of the hall was the entry to the living room and dining area. Walter locked the door to the master bedroom and opened the door to one of the guest rooms.

He then turned to me and spoke with great seriousness. "If anyone asks, you spent the night here. Unknown to me you took advantage of my generosity and brought some ass up here. You with that?"

"Of course."

Walter then dropped down to the carpeted floor and began furiously doing push-ups. I laughed. "Laugh now, niggah. In twenty minutes you'll be singing my praise," he huffed between sets.

I went back into the hall. One of the bathroom doors was open. In Walter's gym, Robinette stood staring at herself in the floor-to-ceiling mirrors. I came up behind her, placing my hands on her hips and my lips on her long brown neck. She moaned as I nibbled softly, but never took her eyes off her image. She ran her hands up her body, finally stopping at her chest. Then she cupped her breast through her blouse. My hands followed her trail and then blazed new territory by sliding inside her blouse and under her bra. Together we slipped out one breast and then the other. My groin pressed between her small buns and my hands pinched her nipples. Slowly, like we were dancing to an old school jam, I turned her around until we were in profile in the mirror. Watching the spectacle of my hands on Robinette's girlish body and shining ebony skin, I felt like a vampire preparing for the first bite.

But I knew that for Robinette I was just a tool being employed to achieve pleasure—a pleasure that her hazy eyes suggested wasn't necessarily dependent on me. This moment was more about her mind, her fantasy, than me. I went down to my knees, pushing aside her leopard panties, savoring her taste with my mouth. As I slipped my tongue under the crotch of her panties she opened her mouth and a moan escaped from the back of her throat, a beautiful sound I remembered from the taxi. But now I was the reason she made it.

As Robinette rocked in my mouth an animal sound came from down the hall. It was primordial. It came from deep inside someone; from down where the larynx meets the lungs.

For the first time since Moomba, Robinette's eyes seemed focused. "What was that?" she asked, her voice hushed.

"Sounded like either Sonja or Beatrice?"

"Who?"

Now I was pulled out of the moment. This woman—a girl, really—didn't know anyone here except Walter. Not even the guy who was currently eating her pussy.

This was really crazy.

"Let's find Walter," I said, pulling her clothes up around her as I stood up. We walked down the hall, drawn by the heaving of bedsprings. We entered the guest bedroom and stood there staring at the bed. Walter was on the bottom. Sonja was above him, her pussy enveloping his dick. Beatrice was behind Sonja humping her ass with a black strap-on dildo. As Sonja was penetrated from below and behind shock waves of pleasure moved through her fleshy body. Walter smiled as he saw our faces and motioned Robinette over. When she reached the bed he pointed at Sonja. An obedient Robinette then leaned forward and began fondling Sonja's breasts and kissing her neck.

At that moment I vowed, "This is not gonna be the mother-fucking cab all over again!" After ripping open a packet of my favorite green-and-white Trojans and doffing my coat, I placed myself behind Beatrice's active little ass and found her sweet spot.

The other four bodies had to adjust to my presence and, for an awkward moment, I felt like an intruder, like a DJ playing Bach at a down-home blues joint.

But then we found our collective rhythm. Beatrice adjusted her stroke to mine, Sonja arched her back higher, Walter thrust his pelvis differently, and Robinette, well, she didn't do anything but close her eyes even tighter. For a time we were all in harmony.

After a while it felt like I was standing outside the pile, just marveling at the beauty of these five undulating brown bodies. It was gorgeous in the way of some erotic African wood carving—the kind they keep under wraps at the Metropolitan Museum of Art. My mind took mental snapshots of this moment, moving around the bed like the camera in *The Matrix*. It was sex but not sex as I'd experienced it in my previous thirty-plus years. It wasn't just fucking—it was a full-fledged-never-to-be-forgotten-freaky-deekey-funkadelic-jam. I was already nostalgic for it and the night wasn't even over.

It was like a sequence of edits in a film as we shifted from person to person, position to position. It seemed like I spent most of my time with Sonja, doing a duet that was deep and funky, while Walter somehow handled Beatrice and Robinette in a balancing act involving fingers, mouth and penis.

Things took an even stranger turn when I became aware I was kissing a leg that was a touch hairier than it should have been. I looked up to see it belonged to Walter. "Go ahead," urged Beatrice as she returned my lips to his leg. "Lick it," she ordered. "Now kiss it and use your tongue."

And so I did, as the three ladies murmured their approval. Walter sniggered and said, "Don't be a trick, Dwayne."

"Shut up," Sonja said.

"And," Walter responded, "what does he get for licking me, ladies?"

"Yeah, what do I get?" I chimed in.

"Sonja, go help him," Beatrice commanded.

And, like magic, a soft hand took control of my dick and a mouth engulfed its head. I tongued Walter's leg right up his knee, and then asked, "Is that all I get?"

No, it wasn't. Robinette took one nipple and Beatrice began licking the other, and I was caught up in a series of new, joyously weird sensations. My mouth opened and body wiggled and I could feel blood twirling inside me as I licked Walter and was licked by the ladies. The feeling was of total abandon. I don't know that I'd ever felt so free, yet so passive. I was a vessel, a cup that pleasure was being poured into. And, happily, I was overflowing.

* * *

I didn't sleep for long. Maybe a half hour. But there had never been a sleep like that in my life because I'd never had a night like this before. So satisfied, so calm. I opened my eyes slowly. It was quiet. To my right was Robinette. I saw her swallow a little black pill and follow it with wine.

"Are you all right?"

"Ah-huh," she replied.

"Where'd they go?"

"The girls said they were hungry."

"No doubt."

"But they told me to stay here."

"Really?"

"Yeah. That Beatrice girl is so bossy, but it's all right. I'll have my time with Walter, too."

I rolled onto my back and took inventory. Had I already had my Super Bowl? Was I out of the game? After that experience, what did I have left? Not much, it seemed. Yet Walter was somewhere in the house still getting busy with two women. Again I was envious of Walter, but I guess that's why he was a mogul and I wasn't. There was a certain hunger for conquest in Walter I just didn't possess.

I rose gingerly off the mattress and felt dizzy when I stood up. I'd come so hard my head was still spinning

Down the hallway, past the two bathrooms and into the gym I stumbled toward the strange, sexual sound coming from the kitchen. It was different from the moaning and grunting from before. It was a man's voice. Not a moan or groan, but a weirdly contented whimper. Didn't even know that such a sound existed.

I stepped into the kitchen doorway and, for the third time tonight, witnessed sex as I'd never seen it before. My eyes widened. I almost stopped breathing. Sonja was sitting on a chair with her legs around Walter's neck. So far, so good. Walter was on his hands and knees, jerking himself off with one hand. No surprise there. The tricky, heart-stopping, world-wrecking part was Beatrice, who was bent over Walter's back, slowly humping his ass with that black strap-on dildo. In and out she stroked, moving as expertly as she had with Sonja, but with a more leisurely, almost luxurious stroke. Not only hadn't I ever seen anything like this, I'd never even imagined it was possible. I guess I was more innocent than I wanted to admit.

Beatrice saw me standing there, smiled and then bent her finger in a "Come here" gesture. Before I had been stunned. Now I was horrified. I stepped backward, turned and almost ran back down the hallway.

The guest bedroom was a mess of rumpled sheets, wet spots and condom packages. In the air hung the aroma of sweat, perfume and sex. Robinette had disappeared into a bathroom. I slipped on my pants and T-shirt and sat on the bed feeling numb. I decided to do something normal. I went into the living room, sat down and messed around with the remote, hoping to find the Super Bowl and try to blank out what I'd just seen. It was the fourth quarter and the Titans were mounting a comeback led by quarterback Steve McNair. It was shaping up to be a memorable effort; commentators predicted this could be one of the greatest endings of all time. But, obviously, the game, no matter who won, wouldn't be what I'd remember about tonight.

To my surprise Beatrice, in panties and an open robe, walked in and sat down on the sofa beside me. She wanted to know the score.

"The Rams are winning but the Titans are making a game of it," I said. "You like football?"

"A little. I watch it at the club with customers. It gives men something to talk about. But I find it too violent."

"Sometimes," I suggested, "a little violence is good?"

"A little pain, yes," she replied. "But not violence."

"Okay," I said, and then took a moment to really study her. Her face was moist and her eyes tired. Still, if I didn't know what she'd just done, nothing about her manner would have revealed it. She looked like someone's flirtatious girlfriend. We pass people every day on the street, people who have done the most unusual things. We think they are just ordinary people but we don't know who they really are or what they're truly capable of. I thought I knew who Beatrice was. A freak. A stripper. She's still both. But on this Sunday it was clear the lady was also one hell of a head coach.

She said, "You know, I think you're cute."

"Are you being sarcastic?"

"No, Dwayne. Don't be so insecure."

"Did Walter ask you to do that to him?"

"Do what?" She wanted me to say it.

"You know. What you did in the kitchen?"

"No," she said slyly. "I asked him and he agreed. I've done a lot for him. Things you don't know about. It was something he owed me. A little returned favor, you know?"

"A little favor. Wow. You sure move through the world differently."

"I don't know. Everything's about exchange. If we get closer, Dwayne, I may ask a favor of you, too."

"You already had me kissing Walter's hairy-ass leg. Isn't that favor enough?"

"And that wasn't so bad, was it?"

"I was, you know, distracted."

"That's how it starts, baby. One distraction leads to another."

*   *   *

On the TV McNair was driving the Titans. The clock was ticking. A field goal wouldn't do. A touchdown was the Titans' only shot. Walter ambled in and sat next to me, requesting an update on the game. Sonja appeared next, seating herself partly on Beatrice's lap and partly on mine. We sat there and, for a funny moment, we were just any close American family watching the big game.

Sonja asked for the phone—something about calling her boyfriend. I suppressed a chuckle and watched her ass bounce as she exited. A moment later Beatrice left, too. When they were gone Walter leaned over and said, "Soon as the game's over you say you're going home and take all the freaks with you. I gotta call Daria."

Daria Dinkins, black ingenue, decent actress, all-around cutie, was shooting a sci-fi/martial arts flick in Thailand. She was "the black girl" in a multiculti cast.

Whatever "favor" Walter felt obliged to do for his bisexual gal pal was in the past. The bass was back in his voice and he'd reverted to mack mode. But now, of course, I would never, ever, see Walter Gibbs the same way again.

Still he sounded, looked and acted like the Walter I'd always known; like the guy I'd played ball with that afternoon; like the man who'd seen more ass than a toilet. Besides, wasn't I the one who'd been licking his leg not too long ago? Yes, I had been "distracted." But then again, licking a man's leg and being ass-fucked by a stripper is not exactly the same thing.

"Mums the word on this, right?" I said.

"Niggah, we shouldn't even have to have that convo. But you got a big mouth, which is one reason I never put you down before."

"Like I can't be trusted."

"Like you're CNN. I only tell you shit I want known. In this situation I expect you to tell lots of niggahs everything. Shit, I expect you to be a big man in every gym or bar in the Apple. Just leave my motherfucking name out of it. Aiight."

"No doubt. By the way, that girl Robinette is talking like she expects to stay."

"Yo Dwayne, you got to take her. She wants to be my girl. Now, she's talented for her age—"

"Which is?"

Walter ignored my question and just said, "I just don't wanna be alone with her right now. That girl's trying to get ahead in life. You never know what ideas she might get about how to do that. Tonight was cool. Two weeks later I'm in the motherfucking *Post*.

As long as you guys are all in it with me, I'm safe. You feel me?"

"I got you, dog. You have the most to lose."

"And you have the most to gain, so keep my name out of it and we'll be stacking paper for a long time to come." He held out his fist and I met it with mine.

We looked up and saw that a Titans wide receiver was being tackled by the Rams linebacker one yard short of the goal line. The gun sounded. The Super Bowl was over and bettors all around the nation were scrambling for their phones. Back in the bedroom I began searching for my shoes and socks, all the while keeping an eye on Robinette, who had emerged from the bathroom and was sprawled lethargically across the bed.

"Robinette," I said, shaking her. "Robinette."

"Yes," she said in a sleepy voice.

"We're all getting ready to leave."

"Oh."

No movement, not even an effort. Sonja and Beatrice, now dressed, walked in. Beatrice placed her slender hands on her hips and surveyed the situation. "Why don't you take a quick shower?" she suggested. "I got this."

The water rolled over places of my pain—a bite on my left forearm, scratches on my back, a sore right shoulder, a rawness of the left side of my dick from someone's teeth. I put my clothes on gingerly, like a running back after a 100-yard game. In the mirror my eyes were red and my face flushed. I craved my empty bed.

By the time I was dressed the ladies were gathered in the living room. Robinette, now fully dressed, sipped apple juice. Walter was nowhere to be found. Beatrice stood by Robinette and clearly had our young friend under control. Perhaps the godmomma of decadence had found a fine young disciple. Meanwhile, Sonja's demeanor had changed. I could see the well-bred, highly motivated, ambitious Buppie in her had now reemerged. She'd freaked enough for the week. I guess it was time to put her mask back on.

"I just spoke to my boyfriend and he does know who you are," Sonja said excitedly. "He saw you on something on A&E about Prince."

"That's what I used to do," I said. "I was a talking head for years."

"Well, I need to get an autographed book for him."

"Not a problem," I replied, as if we'd just met at a book signing.

* * *

In a perfect world I would have met Sonja at a conference on African-American something or other. Maybe at a dinner party via a mutual friend. There we would have talked about our families, our careers, our past lovers and what we liked for dessert. We would have gone to the movies. Some theater perhaps. Had sex on the third or fourth date and vacationed in Cancún or Negril. But this wasn't a book signing.

* * *

As we stood on Thirty-fourth Street hailing cabs, I mused that Sonja was outwardly the type of sister any man would aspire to marry. Her shape, her gig, her complexion were a black man's ideal. But then Sonja was no stereotype of upwardly mobile accomplishment. There were other shades to the lady. And then there was that boyfriend.

As if reading my mind, Sonja asked if I had a card. I didn't but I wrote my digits on the back of hers and put another one into my pocket. Beatrice watched without comment, though there was a twinkle in her baby browns. The ladies hopped into the backseat but I didn't get in.

"You're not going with us?" Beatrice wondered.

"No, ladies, I'm gonna stop and grab some food and then take the subway home."

"See you soon," Beatrice said warmly.

"Call me," Sonja commanded. "I want an autographed book for my boyfriend."

Robinette offered a listless "Bye" and then sank into the backseat as the cab pulled off.

I stood on the curb watching the departing cab and then slid out my celli. By the time I was in Mickey D's I'd raised Walter.

"Yo niggah, I'm still on the phone with my girl."

"Just wanted to say that was unbelievable, my man."

"No doubt."

"No doubt, indeed."

At this point in the conversation I tossed a fry into my mouth and wondered if I should mention what I'd seen in the kitchen. Should I bring up the fact that my longtime friend and current employer had just an hour ago been looking like a *Man Date* magazine cover boy? Eventually I would ask him. I would. Just not on Super Bowl Sunday.

Instead I mumbled, "Okay Walter, I'll let you go."

"Aiiight. My niggah."

"Yeah. Peace."

I sat there, munching on my fries, remembering the pleasure and trying to forget that damn dildo. A brother came in wearing a Tennessee Titans snorkel, "Tough, my man," I said to him.

"Naw, dog. Nothing like being in the Super Bowl. Don't know when you'll be back. Getting in the game is all you can ask, you know?"

He held out his knuckles. I met them with mine. Then I stood up luxuriating in how sore my whole body was and smiling at how it got that way.

SHAWNE JOHNSON

Counting Days

*F*ive months and still counting days since my uterus was scraped out by young man in white coat with nurses standing close like my spread legs sang some sad song, told some sad story with words, rhythm, and beat. Five months and still counting days since I woke up in bed next to Miles, sun moving across his glowing brown skin, pouring down on the perfect shape of his pretty bald head, and everything inside me tense, burning like the pink flesh of my insides being scraped out.

Miles drove me to towering, shining building downtown. Morning rush hour traffic over and done with on Kelly Drive. Early fall and Philadelphia beautiful with leaves changing color, falling like expensive carpet scattered on the sidewalk and grass. People already out on the river, rowers with muscles flexing and faces tight with concentration, small fishing boats with fishing rods swaying from the sides. Men and women in bright jogging suits running or power walking, ducks wandering in the grass and belly flopping into dirty water. I stared out the window at the river, tried not to think about where and why we were going.

Miles's hands at the wheel but his eyes on me, making me feel smaller and smaller, as if sucked in by the cool leather of the seat.

"Umi, I'm not . . . I know we talked about it and I know you feel this is the best possible thing, but can we just think about it a little more before . . . ?"

My head heavy on my neck, no way I could turn all of that weight from the window toward him. Outside, the golden, red and orange leaves picked up and thrown by speeding cars. "I'm not ready to be anyone's mother. I'm just not ready. Are you ready for a baby?"

"I don't know. I just want more time to think it through."

Miles's answer was not good enough and no more time. One more month and no choice, just tied to another person for as long as until. "I don't have time to give you. I'm sorry if you feel like I'm not being fair or not thinking about you, but I don't know what else to do."

We arrived at towering, shining building downtown. Miles, well dressed and smelling like something expensive, had to be back at work by early afternoon. He signed me in, smiled politely at all the women dressed in white. Then sat down with head cradled in hands when they took me away. He was still sitting like that when I came back from white table and white lights and feet in stirrups.

He smiled at me, teeth slightly crooked, beautiful.

"Everything fine?" Hand at the small of my back, pressure heavy, reshaping the pain crawling about the middle of my body even though women in white gave pain medication and pretty smiles.

My legs unsteady, mouth dry and tongue scraping against teeth. Damp and wetness between my thighs. I just stared at him, the room too bright and my head falling like something rotten from my neck.

"Let's get you home in bed and all better." His hands holding my hands, guiding me down the hallway into the elevator and out to his car. I thought about the first time he smiled at me, the first time at someone's poetry spot. I blushed over the charm in his smile, blushed over his pleading, everything inside me seeping open and hot. First time Miles touched me, beating heart and pumping blood went still. His tongue against the spot right beneath my chin, moving up and over my jaw line, beneath the underside of my breasts, then lapping at my inner elbow and the back of my knee. His hands lifting up the fall of my locks, wrapping my locks around my neck, around his wrists.

Miles took me home, fetched me glasses of juice and water, then left for work. He woke me up when he came home late, crawling into bed, his hand on my belly.

My breath warm against his neck as I went over all the reasons why. "We weren't ready. You know we weren't ready. I have to finish school. We're not married, never discussed marriage. I'm not saying that I wouldn't marry you, we just haven't gotten to that point yet. That's all. I know this is hard, but we did what was best."

I thought about home, the small island of St. Lucia, where no one walked barefoot on the beach because the sand was too hot, and people's eyes permanently strained from staring at the sun's reflection off the sea all day. Men working hard to support families and women pregnant, their older children playing in the dirt in front of their houses. Women left with no choices outside of being mamas and wives.

Miles lay still, my voice something obscene between us. My legs thrown over his muscular thighs and arms around his waist, my head buried under his neck just above his collarbone. His hands tangled in the long fall of my locks, slowly twisting and reshaping. My insides clenched raw and bloody. I wanted him to wrap his arms around me, stroke my cheek and back like I stroked him sometimes in the middle of the night when the city lay quiet like some small town in Middle America.

*   *   *

Something about the language of skin against skin that lets old hurts heal, something about touch like rebirth making everything new. Five months and still counting days and child who almost was kicking and screaming all the time in our heads. We held each other cautiously, his head at my breast, my fingers slow dancing up and down his back, his sides, his pretty bald head. Before insides scraped out all my time spent waiting for him bathed and perfumed, long locks piled on top of my head, my mouth painted moist red.

I missed nights spent with the covers and sheets pulled off the bed and his mouth lingering at the back of my knees and inner ankles. I missed the mess of sex, getting up from the couch or floor with sweat between my shoulders, his cum running down my thighs.

Miles no longer touched me like he used to touch me, no longer bent down to whisper in my ear, "God, I want to make love to you," while we were out.

I lost weight, I lived on fruit and vegetables and bread. The sight of bloody meat reminding me of death and the morning Miles drove me home from towering, shining building downtown. I watched him and learned regret sits along the lines and hollows of a person's face, changes the shape of a smile and the feel of a good-night kiss.

Listening to the throb and the want of my body, I tried reaching out to him in the morning before he went to work, my hands playing against his skin, my mouth settled on his collarbone. "When are we going to be better?"

His hands at his side, beautiful skin pulled tight over muscle and beating blood. "Don't know what you're talking about, Umi."

His arm around me, the weight heavy with obligation.

"Don't do that. You do know what I'm talking about. You barely look at me, you won't touch me—"

"I'm touching you right now."

Something hot and desperate eating at my insides. I loved him, I wanted to stay with him.

"I can't do this with you. It's like you're punishing me and I didn't do anything to deserve it. I'm sorry, I'm so sorry that you're feeling however you're feeling about me and us now. I need things to be better. I can't do it alone, Miles."

He pulled his arm away, got up from the bed. He stood, staring down at me, so much sadness in him that I wanted to curl up and weep.

"Umi, I'm really trying, but the more I think about it . . . I know I wanted our child. You didn't give us any time, you didn't even really talk to me. You told me what you were going to do and I loved you and wanted you to be okay, so I didn't say no."

Miles sighed, went into the bathroom. I listened as he turned on the shower. When I was certain that he couldn't hear I pulled the sheet over my waist and hips, hugged my pillow like it was him, cried.

*   *   *

End of spring semester and the English department feeling free and crazy and giving out tickets to a jazz concert at the Arts League. Miles away for a weekend seminar. Without him our huge apartment pressed down on me.

I took my time dressing for the concert, my reflection in the mirror seemed on the verge of being erased so I added color and sparkle to fill in all the blank spaces. I had a lavender skirt set that Miles said looked lovely against my dark brown skin. Skirt long and tight at the hips then flowing down, dancing about my feet. Blouse fitted and dipping into a deep V at my breasts, sleeves stopping just below my elbows.

In University City early Saturday evening the streets crowded, most people with somewhere to go. I walked from my apartment to the Arts League, side stepping men with their lingering glances, crude comments and sweet smiles. I passed neighborhood men sitting on stoops, beers held like children in their hands.

A block from the Arts League and the beat coming from the building carving out a looseness in my thighs, coaxing a stretch and arch in my lower back, persuading tense shoulders and neck to relax. Old couples dancing the salsa as easily as walking, spun each other around and around. Men in full suits and women in loose skirts, their hems flying like bright tropical birds.

I was pulled into the dance by friendly hands and a coaxing smile. It took me a minute, body ignored for so long that moving my feet felt difficult, hips stiff and face tight.

Drummer on stage with Afro full and thick, skin dark and smooth. He was drumming hard, face relaxed, hands flying with precision. The stage crowded with other musicians, men playing horns, plucking at guitars. Dressed in suits, dark shoes polished and catching what little light was in the room. I stared at the drummer until he looked up at me, startled. He was the complete opposite of Miles. He was slender, almost fragile. Miles was broad across the shoulders, slim at the waist, and strong.

The stretch and arch coaxed out of my lower back became deeper and my thighs looser as I watched his body sway with the beat. He was sitting down; I thought about his hips rolling on his stool, about the sweat and heat coming off his body. I wondered if his chest was covered with nappy curls or smooth like Miles's. His eyes on me and dancing bodies at my back and the stretch running up and down my body lengthening and widening, almost reaching for the sky, spine pulled in so tight almost touching my belly. I swayed with the beat, kept time with shoes lightly kissing the floor.

I never sat down, danced for him until my feet were numb in my high heels. People all around me, pushing up against me, and some man's hands always at my back or around my waist. My skin was soaked, my perfume a moist mist around me and I knew the drummer on stage could smell me, almost taste me. The floor beneath my feet vibrating with stomping feet and the energy in the room like a man with good hands touching me. I didn't leave, didn't realize my body was waiting for him.

Dancing done and people looking for coats and purses and high heels kicked off at the edges of the dance floor. The drummer came toward me like he was already familiar with me, the music between us all that we needed. He was so different from Miles. Miles gone and he was here. Miles no longer touching me and this drummer thinking about nothing else.

He wore light slacks and short-sleeve dress shirt. His dark skin wet like my skin wet, the smell of his sweat and cologne reaching out to me.

"Hey. How you doing? I'm Jabril." His voice soft, not like his drumming.

The bright lights making his dark skin prettier.

"Hi, I'm Umi. I enjoyed the band."

"Thank you. I haven't played that well in a long time because I haven't had someone who listens as hard as you do." He leaned into me, his breath sweet-smelling and warm against my forehead. "I know it's getting late and all that. And I normally wouldn't even do this, but I don't want to let you leave without talking to you a little bit first. There's a nice little coffee shop around the corner. Do you have a minute?"

He was nervous, a part of him still on stage beating at drums, his music between us. "I have a minute for you."

His hand at the small of my back leading me away from the stage. My lavender skirt set soft against me. Moist skin tingling with anticipation over the possibility standing next to me. I didn't want to think about consequences and feelings hurt and Miles all the time turning away from me, didn't want to think about the little face like mine lost forever.

We went outside. Early spring air cool against my face and light breeze chasing the hem of my skirt. "I'll wait out here for you."

"I'll be right back. Just give me a minute."

The steps cool beneath my ass like no fabric between skin and worn concrete. I thought about how I looked, how a man might see me. My skin glowing with makeup but dull underneath. My eyes sad.

Jabril came back, long legs in front of me and his hand reaching down to pull me from the steps.

Walking in rhythm, my steps measured to his and night air like a child's kisses moving across our faces. His fingers wrapped around mine, his touch enough to keep me wanting. Five months, two weeks and three days since the last time I was aware of my body as something to be loved, not just for conceiving babies, keeping or getting rid of babies.

Jabril made idle conversation, asked yes or no questions. I thought about Miles refusing to touch me, my open arms and open legs reminding him of things long gone. Jabril next to me, hand in my hand, eyes on my face and breasts and the curve of my waist. I loved Miles but needed to be touched.

I gathered courage, stopped him by lightly squeezing his hand. Jabril looked down at me, smiling.

"I don't want to go to a coffee shop."

"Okay. Where you want to go, then?"

The want pounding beneath skin and muscle. "I want to go home with you. I want you to take me home."

He stared at me, surprised, excited. "You sure?"

"I'm sure."

We started walking, his hand pressing more firmly into my lower back, head bent and the wildness of his hair brushing against my forehead. "You doing fine?"

My body waiting and wanting, my skin so sensitive the night air felt like a man's open mouth against my flesh. Five months and still counting days since Miles drove me downtown and the sadness about everything still there. Jabril walking next to me, his hand at my back, reminding me that my whole life not over and done if Miles never touched me again. "I'll be fine."

*   *   *

His apartment something thrown together, chairs found on the sidewalk, sofa and coffee table picked up from yard sales. A futon close to the floor, propped up by a sturdy wooden frame. Walls white and bare. Only decorations the word magnets scattered about his fridge. The hardwood floor cool beneath bare feet. The lights on because I liked to watch, liked to see want and pleasure in a man's face when he touched me. His hands in my hair and his mouth at my breast, pulling on the nipple through top of lavender blouse and vibrant blue bra. His mouth on me and my hands tangled in the thickness of his hair.

I tried to hold myself still, my insides singing the rhythmic play of his tongue on my nipples, his hands along my back and the sides of my breasts. I had been dying inside waiting for Miles to touch me, shriveling up with the guilt of his feelings. Jabril's hands pulling back dead layers of skin.

His hands lifting up the length of my skirt, hands running over bare legs and thighs. His palms callused, my body warmed by friction and heat. I spread my legs wide, grabbed at his hair until his head arched back and the skin around his eyes pulled tight. His head turning, tongue licking at the pulse thudding at my wrist, mouth opening wide and tender patch of skin sucked and bitten.

Jabril wasn't who I really wanted, wasn't who I dreamed about touching at night, wasn't the man I wanted to love me. Hard not to fantasize he was Miles while he was touching me, hard not to close my eyes and take everything I needed without offering anything in return. I wasn't that selfish, let my hands roam the bare skin of his back and arms and neck, squeezing and shaping skin and muscle, making him moan softly.

My skirt dragged down my hips, down my spread thighs and he was on his knees, his tongue slow dancing across my hipbones, my inner thighs, the curved length of my legs. Jabril's wide hands cradling my ass, his arms spreading my thighs. His tongue, his hot breath touching me through vibrant blue panties. I stared down at him, at his face between my legs, glimpses of his tongue stroking me.

I shuddered and he laughed. His hands frantically rolling panties down my hips and his tongue inside me. His tongue so deep inside me I couldn't stand, my body gave out. He eased me onto the futon. Music coming from somewhere outside. Music loud like the pounding of my insides, blood racing and crashing throughout my body, skin flushed and wet.

Jabril's mouth on me and staring down at him, trying not to think of Miles, trying hard not to see Miles's face, not to feel

Miles's mouth and Miles's body. Jabril's touch like the pounding of his drums, loud and hard, soft and fast. Miles's touch a brass horn, seamless and indefinite, endings and beginnings blurred.

Jabril's mouth wide, pulling all of me inside hot heat. I wanted to wait, hold off, but the rumbling deep in my belly racing up my spine. I raised my arms over my head, listened in my head to Jabril pounding his drums and Miles blowing his horn, two men making love to me. Miles on the futon with us, Miles kissing my stomach and the undersides of my breasts while Jabril reached for a condom. Miles stroking my hair away from my face and tongue tracing my eyebrows and the arch of my nose while Jabril made space between my thighs. Miles and Jabril inside me, like some kind of song, my hips circling, humming out the melody, my fingers clutching at damp sheets.

I left Jabril in the morning, left him sleeping on the damp sheets of his futon. I didn't leave a note, no address, no phone number. I knew who and what I wanted, ready now to shape our present, anxious to hold on to our future. I went home, relaxed and easy in my skin, to face Miles.

WILLIE PERDOMO

Ella by Starlight

Ella. Not Ella like Ella Fitzgerald, pero Ella like Eh-ya. Yeah. I met her at a contemporary art exhibit in the West Village. She helped me cure a cold I'd caught while on a location shoot in Amsterdam for *Tribes* magazine. I was assigned to shoot a portrait of MC Haarlem, a French Antillean brother who was somehow spitting fierce rhymes in that fucked-up, hock-spit Nederlander language. *Tribes* used a shot of him standing in the middle of Liedesplein and a break-dancer in mid head-spin behind him. MC Haarlem gave me a hard-rock stare with eyes heavily glazed by a selection of coffee-shop ganja he'd just blazed, as shards of river light bounced off the moon and onto the street.

Most fucks after art openings are filled with rhetoric on isms until you get to spit your ism wherever she wants it. Then you exchange business cards and make plans to have a few tuna avocado rolls at Satori's, but you never meet again. Out of those eight million New York stories, there is always one that follows you wherever you go and however far you try to get away from it. You can be walking down some block in Uzbekistan, and boom, there she is, a reflection of her, a ghost dashing into a boutique with the same caramel-colored hair that makes you think about that one night you spent together.

I saw her standing in front of an *Untitled* Basquiat, checking out his crossed-out text and acrylic nod strokes. I was partial to Basquiat's work, having known him briefly before his star fell from the sky. We had shared a taste for ten-dollar bags of poppy powder—especially when it was time to fuck. I remember Tony Rome telling me once you a catch a chick with a dope dick—it's over. Put a black eye on that pussy, boy. Make her come so much she almost vomiting. She can be married for fifty years and on occasion, during a hot midnight shower, she'll use a soap bar like it's got your name on it instead of Ivory. But I stopped sniffing those bags because I ain't have room for a monkey—let alone a girlfriend—on my back.

* * *

Rain pellets struck against the galley window like a microwave bag of popcorn. That cool-ass Chet Baker sound—once in the summertime of his James Dean prime—surrounded the revolving saucers of shrimp skewers, smoked salmon, mini chunks of what looked like plantains, chunks of wealthy cheese and beams of Moët. She was checking out the art like a Sotheby's inspector: all up on the canvas, diagonal, vertical, from the side, checking the consistency of the paint, the authenticity of Jean-Michel's signature. She was a brunette with *tamarindo* highlights; no doubt it was blown out in the morning because she had that Boricua curl consistency at the ends. She was wrapped in a confident, Dijon-mustard, two-piece leather suit—jacket, skirt—and a black silk shirt, its two top buttons undone. Her *tetas* were chillin' comfortably in her push-ups while her calves, shapely and commanding, were stylishly holding down the fort in a pair of shiny, knee-high, black Manolos.

Looking at art is an art in itself. There are a few people in this world who can make love to one of de Kooning's women, ugly as them bitches can be. A few who can catch the rhythm of a drip in Pollock's wheat fields even though my mother said that it looked like something she did in second grade finger-painting class. I catch mad recreation watching *blanquitos* look at art. I've seen many a *gringo* get beat for what they thought was the real thing. It's like watching a dope fiend buy a bag of saccharine with his last ten dollars.

*   *   *

I walked to the open bar, grabbed a sweaty Heineken, casually passing a Keith Haring South African baby tied to a neon leash and looked for a familiar face or a professional contact. The object was to leave the gallery with at least one phone number; some piece of information that was going to advance my vision, or get me my next photo assignment. I saw Deacon Stiles from *The Root,* on the prowl for young, fresh bodies to gloss over his hip-hop gossip rag. Naomi Safy, a hot Hindu supermodel, was in a far corner, synchronizing sips of champagne with drags from her cigarette. The masks that people wore repulsed me, but I also knew that I was part of the parade. My attention gravitated to the Basquiat gazer. She was drinking a Heineken. I operate on Chris Rock's theory that women usually know within the first five minutes if they are going to give you some, so I try not to say anything stupid within the first five. She was standing in front of *Riding with Death*.

"Man got to see himself dying before he can paint like that." I said, casually slipping in behind her.

"More like fucked-up and he needed to get his ass into rehab. You can hear him screaming for help," she said like she gave orders for a living. She had a no-nonsense timbre. A translation could've been: *You just got your answer—now bounce.*

"He was screaming for help, but every time someone gave him a hand he bit it."

"You talk like you know him." She finally turned to me. Her front matched her back. Definite bon-bon curves. Faint caramelized freckles were sprinkled at the beginning of her *café con leche* cleavage. She could almost be called bowlegged with enough hips to make me consider getting into fake *Playboy*-photographer mode.

"I did," I said, recalling the nights I use to hang out at Jean-Michel's studio.

"Really?"

People see you differently when they know that you hung out with genius.

"How did you know him?" She sipped from her Heineken and sized me up from my Kenneth Coles to the Cuban-link tucked inside my shirt.

"I photographed him for a magazine after he sold his first major painting."

"After the P.S. 1 show?" She knew her Basquiat.

"No, after he started getting picked up by the downtown dealers and Warhol started dreaming about his cock. I also shot Jean spray-painting his poetry on SoHo walls. Are you an artist? You look like you own the gallery."

"I do," she said, with a hint of flirt.

"Say word to everything you love."

"Word to everything I love." She replied with thuglike reflex. There was ghetto in her pedigree.

"*Vaya!* That's hot. That's hot," I said.

Her laugh was tinged with mischief, as if I needed a map to follow.

"I'm only kidding. I don't own the gallery, but I do collect art," she said.

"From what period?"

"Whatever period my heart is feeling."

"Well, shit, it's all good if your pockets can follow."

This time her laugh was soft, more like a hum, and curious.

"You do the corporate thing, huh?"

"Something like that. I'm a senior production manager for a start-up." She handed me a business card.

"Telenovela.com. What's that about . . . Ella?" I asked, reading her card. It was a cute light-blue card with a sky motif, bubble lettering, and her contact information printed in a black font. "Ella. I like that name. Like Ella Fitzgerald."

"Yeah, but my mother calls me 'Eh-ya' like 'her.'"

"I know what 'ella' means. Boricua, baby. One hundred per-cent," I said, letting her know.

"Of what? African? Taino? Cuban?"

"You ain't getting me into that conversation," I said, avoiding the indigenous people of the world, Pan-Africans-unite riff. "Let's just say Boricua from Bushwick by way of Big Pun's Bronx. Cheverenski minski? Okay? Can you live with that?" I asked.

"I can live with that," she said, her lips twisted into a faint smile.

"Here. I'm a photographer," I said, pulling out my business card and handing it to her.

"I like your card. It's artsy without being cheesy. You do portraits?"

"I do it all. But I like street photography and gritty city landscapes. Weegee, Diane Arbus–type shit. I also do hip-hop album covers so I can buy film. So what's Telenovela.com?"

"We follow the novelas on television. The Spanish language soap opera stars, gossip, story summaries from past episodes, E-mail access for all the novelas on Univision and Telemundo."

"Like *Marielena, Buscandote,* and *Besame el Culo,* I mean, *Mucho?*" I said, listing my mother's favorite novelas. She almost choked on a sip of beer. Making a woman laugh was like building a bridge out of LEGOs. Soon you get the right colors, then you fit the right pieces, and before you know it you got it just the way you want it.

"Exactly. Are you a fan?" she asked.

"Hell, yeah, when I go visit my mother, I follow the drama with her. And then *Mami* talks to the television, 'She's not lying, *canto de pendejo. Ella te quiere.* She loves you, stupid!'" I finished.

"Exacto. My mother is hitting Telenovela.com every ten minutes," she said, putting my card into her pocketbook. Her laugh, man . . . *sonrisa* sweet.

I could feel my cough starting to crack in my chest, making its way up to my throat. The cold was trying to kick my ass back to bed, but I never took a day off from living, or making a living, for that matter. I had been taking everything, trying to beat it in time for my next assignment. But I wasn't helping the cure by smoking blunts with my next door neighbor, Che, a Panamanian conga player, who every day would present another argument in favor of weed's medicinal value. He said pot was being used to cure AIDS, deconstructing cannabis's chemical properties, comparing the damage done by protease inhibitors to a good drag of chocolate Thai.

"Here. Good for colds. Break a lot of that phlegm up," he said, passing me the joint and me nodding.

I turned my head, a cough almost doubling me over.

"Uh, damn. Excuse me. Caught a cold in Amsterdam. I was doing a shoot for *Tribes*," I said between coughs.

"Are you okay? You sound terrible. You should be in bed, with some blankets, and tea, not in an art gallery."

I sneezed again and blew my nose with a cocktail napkin. Then I apologized.

"No need to apologize. As long as you're okay. You should get that checked out," she said with a frown.

"Only time I want to see a doctor is when I'm dead. Doctors got a way of making me sick," I said, as if Tony Rome was chilling on my right shoulder, feeding me dialogue.

"And that's why so many of you brothers are always dying young. My brother was the same way. He got a permanent view of the trees of Raymond's."

"In The Bronx?"

"Yeah, The Bronx," she said, sharply.

She was from the Bronx. *Damn,* I thought. I liked her more for it.

"I'm okay. Didn't mean to be insensitive." I said, putting Tony Rome into my pocket. "It's just a cold. I didn't know about your brother, I'm sorry. I got myself checked out a month ago. It was mandatory to get my traveling papers for a shoot in Africa, and the only thing my doctor told me was to stay away from those damn *chuletas* or I'd be able to cook with my arteries if I keep eating fried pork chops. I ain't trying to lose an opportunity to know you because of an innocent cough," I said, copping a plea.

"What are you taking for the cough?" she said, concern in her voice. Her eyes spoke about a few trips around the block, maybe a fling with a big drug dealer at some point. She definitely had some ghetto in her, but she knew how to mix it with the *Sunday Times.*

"A cough drop cocktail. Vitamin C tablets with cherry Halls," I answered.

"You're taking candy for a cold?"

"Mixed with chocolate Thai," I said, smiling.

She shook her head.

Honesty was at a high premium, even if it was raw, from the curb, and uncensored. Better that than someone stepping to you with fake ID and an envelope full of dreams with no return address.

*   *   *

We walked to an Antonio Mendez photograph. It was a Gursky-like image of a bodega, enlarged and nightmarish with spurts of bright orange, red, and green lettering. A pregnant negrita was sitting in front of the bodega, on a milk crate, looking toward a corner, as if she were waiting for the Brooklyn-track number to be announced or holding the spot down for her husband, who was doing a Sing-Sing bid.

"You should try herbs, fruit, natural remedies," she suggested.

"I've tried eating those damn veggie burgers and those shits taste like cardboard and ca-ca."

Her laugh kept getting sweeter. She looked at Mendez's bodega while I looked at her.

"When I leave here I'm going to get a good ol' Vicks rubdown from *Mami*," I said, sure that one of my mother's rubdowns would vaporize the cough syrup cocktails.

"That's the secret to life in the barrio, right? Vicks," she said, knowing the power of Vicks in a mother's palms. It was true, though. Pimple on your nose? Vicks. Blister on your lip? Vicks. Having trouble breathing? Vicks in your nostril. Scab on the knee? Vicks. My mother should have been a stockholder, she used Vicks for everything.

The opening was coming to an end. The Buena Vista Social Club now playing on the speakers. The guitar licks in "Chan-Chan." Hot like a strong burst of chicken and garlic soup. Ella took a deep breath as if she felt it, too.

I was always searching for the right light, perfect positioning, when I looked through my viewfinder. Ella had excused herself and walked across the gallery. I admired the way her hair bounced off her shoulders when she turned her head. Her neck was exposed. I took mental snapshots of me under her hair, biting her on the shoulder, *con gusto.* The few people left watched the way she walked across the floor, her strong thighs wrapped in silk stockings. Back around the way, she would walk by, and a brother on the corner would say, "God bless you, Ma." I knew why I liked her laugh so much. I could hear a moan under it. I could hear her getting into a hot bath after a long day. I could see me sitting on the edge of the tub.

*   *   *

Ibrahim Ferrer was playing on the speakers. I caught Ella looking back at me and thought, *that's right, Ibrahim,* gardenias para ella. Gardenias for her. A surge of electricity shot down to my loins. I wanted Ella to appraise me with full liposuction *besos.* Fuck the erotic poems with all that mango juice metaphor. I wanted the bittersweet after-sex funk of her sweat and pleasure. She knew I wanted it, too. I could feel her watching me when I wasn't watching her. She came over to me as though I'd called to her.

"Can I get you another beer?" I asked, smoothing a crease on the shoulder of her jacket.

"No, thanks. It's time to go home."

"Where's home?" I asked.

"Broadway and Prince."

Broadway and Prince. I'm not sure she was kidding about not owning the gallery. Maybe she was lying so I wouldn't be distracted by her status. Broadway and Prince was Mark Anthony neighborhood. Schnabel, Clemente, cats with mad dough.

"Do you mind if I walk with you? My train station is right on Houston."

"In the rain?"

"The rain is gone. C'mon. I want to see what Ella by starlight looks like."

"Ain't you smooth? Ella by starlight," she said.

"I just want to walk you home, baby. That's all."

She looked at me, one eyebrow arched. "That 'baby' said a lot more than just a walk," she said.

"You feelin' me?" I asked.

"I'm not sure yet. I ain't trying to catch no feelings," she said, serious.

"Don't worry. I'm a member of that club. So can we get to stepping and celebrate our membership?"

"C'mon." The smile at the end said it all. I was in. A few more blocks were being put into the foundation. A few more blocks left to go. I didn't even have to worry about knocking it down. No feelings.

I remembered one summer when my *Mami* punished me for riding my new Apollo five-speed outside of the neighborhood. I was under house arrest for one week. One afternoon as I day-dreamed through my cracked bedroom window, I spotted Tony Rome romancing two women sitting with him. He had one leg propped on the bench, his arms resting on his thigh in true Don Juan style. The women were on each side of his leg, their eyes braced on him, mesmerized. I wanted access to Tony's flow. I wanted that abracadabra phrase, those melodic links of sentences, that rhapsodic line that would make a woman open her mind, unlock her heart and unzip her pants.

As we turned east down Prince, I gently put my hand on her hip as if we were at the Copacabana, and guided her to the inside of the curb. Next to the dope-dick secrets, this was something else I learned from Tony Rome. You always walk with a woman on the inside of the street. Otherwise you're telling the world that you are giving her away; that she's for sale.

"Oh, you're from the old school," she said, impressed.

"It's probably the best thing I learned all the years I spent standing on the corner."

"I like that. I do. I do. How much time did you spend standing on the corner?" she asked, matching my stride.

"Enough to know that the world is one big hustle. That I had to find something that was going to get me off the corner."

"I know that's right." The *morena* in her came out. She was a cosmopolitan chameleon. She could rock a corporate conference call, a *casita bombaso, and* a Baptist revival meeting. "So you found a camera," she said, adding one plus one.

"Well, I was always seeing weird, interesting shit standing on the corner, so I figured I might as well start taking pictures of it."

Her cell phone rang a tango beat.

"Hi, baby."

Baby?

"I'm walking home right now. Noooo, I'm not by myself. He's a photographer I met at the gallery. No. No. No," she said, laughing. "Did your finish your paper? I told Jimmy that you could only watch an hour of television."

Jimmy?

"I know he's your father but I call him Jimmy. Did you eat? Good. Call me in the morning, okay?"

She blew a kiss, then turned off the phone.

"Sometimes my daughter can be like a husband."

"And the husband can be like . . . ?"

"Not there."

"At home?"

"Not there at all. We're legally separated."

"Is that like being a giant midget?"

"You digging kinda deep for somebody who ain't got no feelings." She looked at me. It reminded me of the way gangsters look at you when they're trying to figure out how much you know.

"Just ain't trying to get tangled up in no one else's loose ends. Next thing you know they reading about me in the *Post*. 'PHOTOGRAPHER FOUND OVEREXPOSED IN SOHO CAN,'" I said, framing my words with air quotes.

"It ain't like that. He wanted to keep standing on the corner. So I moved on without him."

"I hear you," I said, supporting her decision.

"My daughter is staying with her father for the weekend, so she needed to check in with me." I heard a note of invitation in her voice.

* * *

The mist was clearing as a breeze wafted up Houston. Her building was the type of nondescript place you walk by every day without knowing that there are two-million-dollar living spaces above.

"Okay . . ." she said, trying to hear my thoughts.

"Okay what?" I asked, looking back at her.

"Just okay."

"Oh, I thought you said, 'Okay, come up and see my art collection.' Or, 'Okay, why don't you come up because I have something better than Vicks.'"

"Your girlfriend might not approve." She was digging, and not trying to hide it.

"Like I said, no loose ends. Heartbreak is not one of my favorite sports."

"That's real. You just a pick-up artist who takes a few photos on the side."

"Just a photographer who picks up a woman here and there, and sometimes takes a few photos of them," I said.

"Get outta here."

"No joke. Some women like to see themselves in pleasure. Self-love, baby."

"I hope you ain't no Puerto-Rican psycho."

"Psycho for you, Ma." I smiled. "Seriously, it would be a shame if we left all this to a tap kiss and I had to take the train home thinking about what it would be like to have held you tight, talked to you, told you everything I knew to be real and true for just one night." I leaned in close enough to see the peach fuzz on her cheeks. "I can tell you still carrying a few emotional bags and you want to lighten up your load. I know you tired of those dot comers who ain't comin' right. Asking you to trade pussy for stock options. Those so-called single brothers who end up being Al Bundy. I could tell you a strong woman, not too far removed from the 'hood, don't want for anything, and if by chance it got to getting it, there wouldn't be any respect lost." I was now close enough to smell the coconut in her shampoo.

"I don't want anything you ain't ready to give. I live alone and pay my own rent. You alone and you probably like it that way. Fine as you are, unescorted to a major exhibit? Shit. I *know* you like it that way." I laughed. "Look, I'm not taking anything away from your independence, because you have that in spades. But I know how it feels to get into a king-size bed with a twin-size body."

Two taxicab drivers stopped short in front of each other and resumed an argument that seemed to have started a block away. One argued in Arabic, the other in Spanish. The Arabic brother went to his cab and pulled out a baseball bat from under the driver's seat. A gay couple walked by, and the man of the two called 911 on his cell. The Mexican ran back into his taxi. "*Cabrón!*" was all I heard above the car horns.

"C'mon." She took my hand. "Let's see if we can find a cure for that cold."

I'd forgotten all about my cold. We walked into the freight elevator.

Ella was quietly watching each floor pass by in the elevator porthole. She smiled wryly.

"What?" I asked.

"Nothing," she answered.

"Oh, please don't start that 'nothing' shit. Please. I hate when people do that."

"No, nothing. I mean I just can't believe the way you just read me. I do hate getting into bed by myself. And I appreciate that you're straightforward. No guessing games, no poetry, no deflectors. I just want you to know that this is not my——"

"Don't even go there." I put my hand on her arm. "I just want to hear you laugh. I want to know you before you became you. I know we have to put on mad fronts in the name of business. Let's not do that here. Chances are I probably won't ever see you again, and part of me don't ever want to see you again. That's my shit and I don't want you falling into it. I want you to be that memory I have when I'm in a rainy-ass city, waiting for a plane, listening to my Walkman and thinking about tonight. If the cards call for us to see each other again, I'm sure it'll happen."

"Damn, you don't hold back." She laughed, incredulous.

"No time for holdin' back, baby."

She didn't take my hand off her arm. I smiled.

* * *

The elevator bell rang, then opened into a loft space. The living room was a quarter of a football field long with a spiral staircase at the rear, and floor-to-ceiling windows overlooking Broadway. The red and white of a police siren was flashing at the window. We laughed at the shared joke. I walked over to the window and saw the Yemeni cabbie cuffed to his taxi while the cops questioned the Mexican, who was holding a towel over his head.

"Yep. Somebody is going through the system tonight," I said.

"What can I get you?" she asked.

She walked toward an open kitchen in a corner of the loft. Everything had a silver sheen to it.

"A beer if you have any," I said.

"No beer. Tea. I'm going to make you some tea from a home-made remedy that my mother taught me."

"I hope you not putting a spoonful of Vicks in it."

"No. Just some raw ginger and herbal tea."

"Cool."

The loft's brick walls had just been stripped and finished. The hardwood floors were buffed and her feng shui wealth corner was set up perfectly. Her place was part New Mexico with red clays and rust trimmings, and part El Barrio tenement, with a clean corner saved for an altar with El Divino Niño Christo and a bottle of lavender Mistolin chilling by the bottom of the sink. Her art collection ranged from de la Vega's street art aphorisms, to a few original Basquiats, an authentic photo portrait of a smiling Sarah Vaughan (I knew I had seen Ella's smile before) and a Mapplethorpe photo. She was careful and sentimental in her collection.

* * *

The scent of patchouli and champa left to burn in the morning had finally settled in to her spirit corners. A beaded curtain with a portrait of the singer La Lupé led to her bedroom.

"You have nice place here." I said, looking.

"Thank you. Put on some music."

Ella was like her music: some Mahalia Jackson, some Aretha, some Fania All-Stars, some Frankie Ruiz, some Biggie, even some Cat Stevens. I set up her CD player with Al Green's *Call Me*, Hector Lavoe's *La Voz*, The Fania All-Stars *Live from Yankee*

Stadium, The Notorious B.I.G.'s *Ready to Die,* and capped it off with Mary's *Share My World.* I pushed PLAY and Al Green crooned. *Call me . . . Call me . . . What a beautiful time we haaad together . . .*

"Good choice," she said. "Al is the man. D'Angelo, Musiq, Safiq, Tariq, none of them can hold a mic to Al."

I walked into the kitchen and stood behind her, helping her stir the ginger until we squeezed the juices out of it, letting the steam and aroma make circles of mist on the refrigerator. I put my arm around her hips and started a turn-off-the-lights slow grind to Al's rhythm, whispering the lyrics into her ear. I pressed her against me, so she could feel my potential. She moaned and arched her back.

"You not gonna drink your tea?" she asked, softly.

"You are my tea, Ma," I said, running my fingers through her curls, exposing her neck, and placing my lips softly on her skin. Her perfume had a green, earthy smell. She was the perfect emollient to rub on a feverish body. I closed my eyes and inhaled deeply for memory.

"Mmm . . ." She tilted her head to one side, exposing her neck, just like I had seen it during the fantasy shot I snapped of her in the gallery. She invited me to taste. I bit on her shoulder, slowly, deliberately.

"Ohhhh, shit," she moaned through clenched teeth.

"*Asi, Mami?*" I whispered.

"*Asi, Papi. Asi.* Yes, baby, just like that." She groaned.

If *Glamour* magazine polled me to see what I liked most about having sex with a woman it would have been the way Ella called me *"Papi."* That shit made me crazy. Ella was ahead of me. She turned off the stove, then she took my hand and pulled me toward the bedroom. I stopped her.

"Let's stay right here." I said.

"I just want to make sure you use—"

"We not there yet. Just stand here with me."

I saw her let go after I said that. Give it up. She took a deep breath. She now had permission to take candy from a stranger. If my fingers had tongues, her skin would have melted inside my lifelines. I turned her toward me for a playful, teasing exchange of lips. She unbuttoned her silk shirt and let it fall. We watched it float down to the bright hardwood floor.

"*Ai, Papiii. Como tu mé toca. . . .* I love the way you touch me," she whispered against my ear.

Like poems, sex was better in Spanish. Faint whispers of hair fell down her back to the curve of that beautiful bonbon. I unsnapped her bra and I put her *tetas*, trembling, into my warm, cupped hands. She moaned and tried to unzip my pants. I gently moved her hands away, and put them on the counter.

"No. Not yet. It's about you right now, Ma." I said.

I turned her around and sat her on the counter. Hector Lavoe started singing *"Mi Gente."* I removed her Manolos, one by one, and then her silk stockings. My tongue traced lines, made pathways from her Achilles tendon, roller-coasting on her healthy calves, sliding down to the inside of her thighs. I could smell the earthy scent that she'd sprayed into her stocking that morning. Her legs found rest on my shoulders. Tony Rome said this was mandatory. This is where you get the real money. You could be carrying John Holmes's cock, but if you ain't ready to go to the

Keys, you might as well not even start the trip. *A-la-la-lalalala. . . .
Que canta mi. . . .* Her labia were trembling, *bemba coloras.* She bit
her lip in anticipation. She had a diamond of pubic *pelitos* right
above her hard *habichuelita,* which I teased with my tongue.
Georgia O'Keeffe could not have painted it better. Edward Weston
would not have done it justice.

The mix of pink and brown skin tones was perfect. Two big
lips smiling on top of two smaller ones. I opened them softly to
expose her *habichuelita.* My tongue scooped it up and I saw her
bembas contract. She moaned, "Ohhhh shit, *coño.*" *A-la-la-la-
laaaaa,* libidinous, looking for it, got it, until *she* got it by the time
Lavoe was praising Chango y Yemaya. She'd dug her fingernails
into my neck and pulled off the rest of her petals. Nothing
sagged, man. Josephine Baker, circa Paris, France, 1925 redux.
She undressed me and started playing my *songoro cosongo* and
I thanked the gods that she knew how to play the bass *and*
the drums.

*   *   *

The crash of her curtain beads turned into a mellow wave by the
time we were on the bed and I had on my raincoat, preparing for
the storm. The moan under her laugh came out, "Oh, shit.
Aiiii . . . toito, Papi. Give it to me. All of it." It was all hers. We tried
169 positions for a dollar, and then took it near the wealth corner
to get tantric. Marble balls rubbing against each other with patterned breathing straight through the closing number of Congo
Bongo. *Duro,* man. Hard. We went through a whole decade of *y tu
loco loco pero yo,* me feeling good, *bien bien,* very, very good.

We took a thuggish turn and she took my hand so I could slap her on her bonbon, said that her gandule went *brrrrringgg* when I did that. I knew there was thug in her because she was asking for it harder and harder. First rule of thug life: If it ain't rough it ain't right. When Mary came on, Ella was loving me better, because only she could love me better. It was real, bruh. The sun came up, she was everything, I was tapping her champagne glass, and everything was she. Dreams. We were on the beach, clear water, and white sand. My mouth, filled with slices of mango, washed down with cold, spring water. She was born *café con leche*. No need for a tan. She walked into the water, thong-bikini, she kept walking until she disappeared into the foam.

*   *   *

When I woke up, a little before ten A.M., I found a nouvelle cuisine dish of sliced mangoes, a fresh apple, and a hot pot of ginger tea waiting for me on the kitchen counter. A note was under a teacup. *"This should work better than Vicks. Thanks for helping me with my bags."* I sipped the tea by the staircase that led up to her daughter's room. On the street, a bread truck was dropping off a load of fresh baguettes to Dean & Deluca. A *Daily News* truck was delivering the latest on last night's Broadway Mexican-Yemeni taxi standoff. I could feel the ginger flushing out the cold. Breathing was good. The phone rang. *Beep.* "Hey, girl. It's me. I hope you went home with that fine brother you were talking to by the Basquiat, and I hope you finally got some because your boss is acting like he ain't get none last night. Hurry up and get your butt into the office." *Beep.*

Hot shower, hair conditioned, healed. When I came out and started retrieving my clothes from the kitchen, the phone rang again. *Beep.* "Hi. It's me. It's Ella by starlight. Hope you had some of the tea. It looks like there's going to be a storm today. There's an extra umbrella in the basket by the door. You can take it if you need it; don't worry about returning it. Take care." *Beep.* I almost picked up the phone, but decided against it. I left the note under the cup.

When I stepped out the door, onto Broadway, there was a spot of dry blood by the curb. Shook my head. The Mexican caught it bad. I bought a Spanish orange, bigger than the typical supermarket Sunkist. I stood outside the train station and watched the rain start. I placed her business card on top of a phone booth, then watched it until its soggy pieces were whisked onto Broadway.

SANDRA KITT

Passing Through

After walking three quarters of a mile on the narrow shoulder of the road, I finally saw the service station about a hundred yards away.

"Thank God," I muttered, wishing I'd taken that course "Zen Car Maintenance for Women" instead of yoga.

I found one of the extra napkins I'd taken from Dunkin' Donuts about thirty miles back, and used it to dab at my forehead and chin. The July heat prickled on my scalp but at least I didn't have to worry about my hair turning. The decision to cut it short and let its natural wavy tendency do its thing was a good one. I wished I'd used the same good sense when I dressed that morning, wearing heels and trying to be too cute, as if the folks around here would even notice.

The freight truck driver, who'd stopped to tell me where the nearest station was, had misled me when he said it was "a few minutes down the road." He neglected to mention, if you were driving and not walking, inappropriately dressed for business, not a hike along the interstate. By the time I saw the station the damage had been done. I knew I probably looked the way I felt: no longer ready for prime-time. I was sweaty, wilted and funky.

I looked at my watch. It was going to be tight, but I could still make it to court on time.

By the time I reached the station my feet were burning and itchy from the heat of the blacktop. The lining of my pink linen dress was matted to my back, and I was damp between my breasts and thighs. I walked in the shade on the edge of the property, the five-degree drop in temperature a relief after my last twenty minutes, roasting like a raisin in the sun.

There was a skinny black service attendant pumping gas into the tank of an SUV, and a couple of kids filling their bike tires with air.

"Excuse me. I need some help with my car," I said to the attendant.

"'Round there." He pointed to the other end of the station.

Around the corner was a recessed service bay. There were two vehicles in stages of repair, but I didn't see anyone working on either of them. "Hello," I called out.

"Yeah," answered a disembodied voice.

I followed it to the open garage.

I saw a man bent over the open hood of an ancient Dodge wagon, his butt in the air. I noticed at once that he had strong, well-developed legs, his thighs and calves hugged by the fabric of his soiled pants. He wasn't wearing the usual blue or gray service jumpsuit of a mechanic, but a pair of well-worn jeans, construction boots, and a red T-shirt with the name DOC'S printed in white letters. There were fingerprints and grease stains on the seat of his pants.

"Excuse me," I said in my best I'm-in-a-hurry tone. "I need some help with my car."

He didn't stop his work to acknowledge me.

A wiry old white woman with wrinkled skin and the raspy voice of a smoker suddenly appeared at his side from under the hood.

"He has to finish with me, first. You ain't from around here."

I didn't want to be rude, but I wasn't interested in being chatty, either.

"No, I'm not."

"Visiting family, or are you lost?"

I looked at my watch. "I'm just passing through."

The old woman shook her head, pursing her lips as she inhaled from her cigarette. "If you're headed for the bridge-tunnel you ain't gonna make it. It's gonna rain."

I didn't respond because that's not what I wanted to hear. I'd planned to be over the Bay after my time in court this afternoon, and into Hampton by early evening. At the rate I was going, I could no longer make a good prediction. I glanced up at the bright midday sky and felt righteous. Rain seemed like an impossibility.

"Are you almost finished? I'm in a bit of a hurry," I called out.

The mechanic didn't stop his work or respond, and that annoyed me even more. I paced nervously outside the open bay, looking up and down U.S. 13. It looked the same in either direction. A narrow strip of Virginia that was the Delmarva Peninsula. With inlets and small offshore islands, it was bordered on the east by the Atlantic Ocean, and on the other coast by the Chesapeake Bay. Between the two bodies of water the land was flat and uninteresting. And it was country quiet, which was why I could hear a low rumble off in the northwest. In fact, now I could see gathering clouds begin to darken the sky. I still hoped the sun would win out.

"Sir?" I tried again.

"Doc don't like to be rushed," the old woman said. "He does real good work, though. Knows what he's doing. Best around here."

"I'm going to be late for an appointment."

"What'll happen if you don't make it?" the woman asked.

I didn't answer. It wasn't in my plans not to make it. I was always on time.

"Fran, get in and release the emergency brakes," the mechanic ordered, his voice distorted from beneath the car hood.

Fran did as she was told.

"Now turn the engine over and put her in neutral."

The Dodge sputtered, then finally started.

Suddenly the mechanic straightened and motioned the old woman out of the driver's seat. He took her place behind the wheel.

I could only see his profile and it was hard to tell very much about him because of the khaki baseball cap he wore. His skin was walnut brown. There was a small semicircle of perspiration under his armpits. I stared at it. I've only ever seen that happen to men. Probably because they don't shave there like women do. Hair holds moisture in the heat. I don't know why that fascinated me, that he sweated under his arms. There was another damp line down the middle of his back that disappeared into the waistband of his jeans. I knew where it ended. On the walk from my disabled car the sweat had trailed down my spine, and down the crack of my rear end. Like my dress, my underwear was wet. I wondered if his was, too. He didn't appear hot and bothered like I did. Must be a country thing.

I focused again when the door of the truck slammed shut. The old woman was leaving. Good.

"Fran, you're gonna have to put the old girl down and get yourself a new one."

"I ain't ready yet, Doc. She's holdin' up fine, thanks to you. Hell. Lasted longer than my three husbands and don't give me half the trouble they did."

The mechanic bid the old woman good-bye and stood aside as she backed the Dodge out of the port and turned onto the service road. Finally.

"What can I do for you?" he asked.

Nice voice, calm and smooth. He didn't sound country. Didn't look it either, despite the jeans and T-shirt. He looked kind of urban cowboy in a different setting. It was in the way he walked and the way he was checking me out. Not fresh, but thorough. Respectful. I liked that. It was hard to tell how old he was, but it was the other side of thirty-five, at least. He was stocky with thick forearms and wrists, and a broad chest. He had a fit and healthy physique, but I don't think it came from spending time in a gym. His face was square, his expression open and his gaze direct.

"I'm stuck back there. About a mile down the road. My car just stopped and—"

"When was the last time you changed the oil?"

I have to confess that I didn't have a clue. That's what I went to gas stations for. When I didn't answer he smiled faintly, and it made me feel foolish. He walked around me and headed toward the front of the station. I knew what he was thinking. Typical woman who just drives the car and doesn't know how to take care of it. Well, he was right. So sue me. I didn't become a lawyer to have to worry about stuff like that.

"Listen, I really need to get down to Cape Charles. I have to be in court and—"

"Traffic tickets?"

He was teasing me.

"I'm thinking you probably seized your engine. If that's the case you won't make it to Cape Charles. Unless you can figure out some other way to get there."

I stopped, anxiety gripping my chest. There were people waiting for me. I had responsibilities, a reputation. "Well, can't you fix it? Can't you put in a can of oil or something?" He stopped so suddenly to turn to me, I almost walked into him.

"Lady, if you've been driving without oil your engine is likely ruined. Dead. You'll need a new one."

"Fine, then do that if you have to. Only, I have to be on the road in an hour or I'll never make it."

He shook his head and walked away. As he talked to the young attendant I walked into his line of vision so he'd remember that I was waiting. But the phone rang in his office. He went in to answer it, talking patiently to whoever was on the other line. He finished, and then dialed a number.

I wanted to throw something in frustration. I realized he was watching me thoughtfully and I turned my back on him. I didn't care what he was thinking about me. I just wanted my car fixed so I could get the hell out of this place.

"Okay, let's go take a look at her," he said.

I followed him to a red tow truck with the name DOC'S on the side, along with not only a phone number, but FAX and E-mail address. I softened considerably toward him when he helped me into the high cab seat of his tow truck. There were a couple of parts manuals and local road maps on the seat between us, and a short-band radio on the dash tuned to a frequency used by police and state troopers.

"What does Doc stand for?" I asked.

"Doctor," he deadpanned.

I chuckled. He had a sense of humor, too.

"My name's Marshall Leonard," he introduced himself.

Marshall. It had a strong, no-nonsense sound to it.

The ride back to my car was less than five minutes, but it was enough time to begin to feel the power of his presence. He handled the gears easily with his large capable hands. Work hands, but not rough or callused. He drove with graceful expertise. When we reached my car I stood back and watched him look under the hood. He checked the gauges on the dashboard, tried to start the car, and listened. I prayed for good news, but knew that it wasn't going to be.

"Like I said, you've seized the engine," he confirmed.

It was like the old woman who'd informed me that it was going to rain. Now I believed them. He began to fill out a service report form. He asked to see my driver's license and registration, insurance card.

"Leslie Jameson." He murmured my name.

"It's a boy's name," I said defensively.

He glanced at me, repeating my name. He pursed his lips and nodded. "Suits you. Very classy and professional."

"Thank you." I was surprised.

Then he began to attach the pulleys from the truck to the front fender of my car. It was hoisted and carefully loaded onto the flatbed and secured in place. That took another fifteen minutes. My anxiety about making my court cases in Port Charles was creeping toward full-scale panic.

When we were headed back to his station I asked calmly, "So what are my options?"

"Forget about getting to Cape Charles this afternoon. Maybe at all tonight."

"No, no, no . . ." I shook my head. "That's unacceptable. There must be a bus or car service or train or something I can get. I mean, how far away am I?"

"Almost two hours. There is no bus or train service. The rail lines that divide Langford are used only for freight. There are no car services on the Eastern Shore."

"You're a service station. Don't you have loaner cars for your customers? You know, for when they have to leave their car to be fixed, and you loan them one to get around until the work is done."

"You're thinking of car dealerships," he said. "I'm not that kind of business."

I finally lost my cool. "This is ridiculous."

"Sorry you don't like the answer. It is what it is."

In other words, deal with it. I am going to *kill* my boss for doing this to me. Assigning me to the rotation that brought arbitrators and District Attorneys as needed to the Eastern Shore for cases waiting to go before the court. On the one hand, I guess it says something about a community that had so little crime, that there was no full-time or part-time magistrate. It was like the old West.

And I was stuck here.

We got back to the service station and the mechanic unhoisted my car. With the help of the young attendant, he pushed it into the empty spot in the service bay. He then ran my credit card for payment. A quick glance at the time and I grew desperate.

Marshall separated the white, yellow and pink pages of the service form. He handed me the yellow one.

"What am I supposed to do now?" I asked him.

He gave me a sympathetic look. "Call Cape Charles and tell them you won't make it." Then he headed back to his office.

"Look, I can pay you to drive me down there. I'm sure that when I'm through someone will drive me back. I could . . ."

"I can't take you," he interrupted me. "I also don't have a replacement engine for your car . . ."

I groaned piteously. He was unmoved.

" . . . So I'm going to have to call around. Assuming I find one, I'll have to hope the dealer will be willing to bring it here . . . or I'll have to go and get it myself. That could take the rest of the afternoon. If there's any hope of getting your car back to you in the morning, I better get started now."

I was not going to embarrass myself and throw a hissy-fit right there. It took a few minutes, but I had to accept that I was going to be stuck on U.S. 13, somewhere between Chincoteague and Cape Charles, Virginia. He was just getting off the phone again when I made my decision. He took one look at my expression and pointed to his desk.

"You can call from here, if you like."

I made the necessary calls and canceled my schedule. My colleagues were sympathetic to my dilemma, but there was no sense that the sky was going to fall if I didn't make it for the hearings. That was the thing that really got to me. They could do without me. I wasn't as important as I thought I was. So, if I wasn't needed there, what was I going to do with myself?

"All set?" he asked.

I turned around and found understanding in his eyes. I really appreciated that. "I guess. Now all I have to do is figure out what to do with myself until my car is ready."

"Stay the night," Marshall suggested.

"Stay overnight? Here?" I asked, incredulous. He smiled at me. He really did have a nice smile.

"Why not? There are a couple of good guest houses in town. Clean and inexpensive. They provide breakfast. You could do worse."

I shrugged. Why not? Everything else that could go wrong already had. At least there was someplace for me to stay the night. And the idea of being able to shower, to change clothing and not have to rush around for the rest of the day, was beginning to appeal to me.

Marshall told me the names of three places, said which one he'd recommend. That's the one I chose. He made it easy for me to stop feeling sorry for myself. I was going to be right here for the duration. I might as well make the best of it, I decided. There was a low rumble of thunder in the distance. I didn't want to be on the road in the rain anyway.

"Can I walk to the guest house?" I asked, taking my tote, laptop and overnight case from the trunk of my car.

"I'll drive you over," he offered, taking my things.

I quickly realized that Marshall Leonard was being much more attentive to me than I had any right to expect. He was certainly not like any garden-variety mechanic I'd ever encountered in the past. I followed behind him as he walked to a late-model sedan. I watched the athletic roll of his hips, and the way his sturdy torso tapered into a narrow waist. Before my attention could drop any further he glanced over his shoulder and caught me staring. My eyes boldly met his. I noticed his mouth for the first time. And then out of nowhere, I felt that telltale twist in my stomach that signaled attraction. It brought me up short. I stumbled in my heels.

"Be careful," he said.

I knew I'd be wise to heed his warning.

By now I was relaxing and enjoyed the ride as he drove me into town. I looked out the window at blocks of neat Cape houses, anything to distract myself from this sudden acute awareness of the man sitting next to me.

"Are you from here?" I asked him the same question the old woman had asked me.

"My grandparents were. I used to visit when I was a kid," he said.

I watched his profile as he drove and talked. He had a solid masculine aura about him. "So, you haven't always lived around here?"

He shook his head. "I came back to live about five years ago. Before then, I was in Atlanta." He pulled into the driveway of a beautiful Victorian house, on a small and neat piece of property. A sign read THE HOMESTEAD. "Wait here while I check to see if anyone's home."

I watched him enter the house and disappear. He came back almost immediately.

"They got family staying this week, so there's no vacancy."

"I guess that leaves the other place you mentioned." I was glad that there was another choice.

"Yep," he responded.

The second house was also Victorian. But it was bigger, on a larger piece of property. It was white with iron-gray wooden shutters, and a porch that wrapped around two sides of the house. There was wicker furniture on the porch and . . . a swing!

"Oh, this is adorable," I exclaimed. He grinned.

Again he pulled into the driveway and got out. There was no name for this house, no sign that anyone was home, and I began to fear that this place, too, would not be available. Marshall didn't bother checking with the owners to see if they had room for an overnight visitor. He retrieved my bags from the trunk and I got out of the car. He walked right in.

"There's nobody here," I said, disappointed.

"That's okay. You can still stay."

"Are you sure? I feel funny just walking into someone's house."

He walked ahead of me, up a flight of stairs to a second floor that had three bedrooms and a bath. The house was beautifully maintained with period pieces. There were braided rag rugs on the wooden floors and dark oak furniture. The chairs were covered in floral fabric. Very provincial, like it had been frozen in time. I no longer doubted anything Marshall did, and let him lead me to a front room. While he put my bags on the double bed, I peered out the window through—that's right—lace curtains. About five hundred feet or so, beyond a line of pecan trees, I could see a body of water. I began to feel not so much that I'd stepped back into time, but that time had stopped for me, and I'd been transported into an alternate universe.

"Is this okay?" he asked.

"Oh, I love it. This is perfect. Are you sure it's okay? I feel funny—" He cut me off.

"The owner will be here later," he said. "Help yourself to whatever you want. Make yourself at home."

"Thank you." I felt shy and beholden to him. Things could have gone a lot worse.

"Is there anything I can get you before I leave? I gotta get back to the station."

"You've been really nice about this whole thing. I could have ended up at some other place where no one cared."

"I doubt it. There are lots of good people on the Eastern Shore. That's why I came back. This place is real."

I didn't know what else to say. He was refreshingly honest. And so confident. There was a quiet control about him.

"Ah . . . do you want me to pay you something now for taking care of my car?"

He turned and headed to the door. "I have your credit card information. We can settle later."

"What about my stay tonight? Shouldn't I register or something?"

He laughed lightly. "That can wait, too. Get settled and relax. I'll get back to you with information about your car."

"Thank you," I called after him, as he left.

I turned around and slowly took in the room. I suddenly felt carefree, and a little guilty. I didn't have to go to court. I didn't have to deal with neighbor disputes, or claims of property damage, or domestic dysfunctions. I was on an unscheduled reprieve.

I showered and changed into fresh clothing, grateful that I'd had the forethought to include a simple yellow cotton tank dress. I took the liberty of exploring the house, which was clean and well maintained, but didn't show many signs of occupancy. There were displays of framed family photographs spanning decades in nearly every room. Total strangers smiling back at me.

There was a small porch at the back of the house, in the direction of what I took to be a lake. There was a view here, through the trees, and I sat. With nothing to do but enjoy myself, I watched the rest of the afternoon go by, and listened to the storm approach. Before long the thunder grew louder and the sky darkened, but I stayed there. The wind picked up and swirled around the ground, and thrashed through the treetops. The rain came an hour later. As prophesied by the old woman, I would *not* have made it to Cape Charles before the downpour. I felt misplaced here, but peaceful and content for the moment.

It was dark when the rain finally stopped. The air was cool and smelled of wet trees and wood, and a bit smoky. I heard a door open and I jumped. The owners had finally returned. I got up to go inside, preparing an explanation about who I was and what I was doing in their house.

"Hello," I called out, not wanting to scare anyone to death.

The living room light was on. Someone was in the kitchen.

"The mechanic in town said you rented rooms, so I hope you don't mind that he—"

I stared at Marshall Leonard like he was an apparition. And, of course, I wondered what the hell was going on. I wasn't apprehensive—it was way too late for that—just bewildered.

"Hi," he said. "How's it going?"

"What are you doing here?"

"I live here."

"Here?"

"That's right."

"But . . . but you said . . ."

"That the owner sometimes had guest rooms. I'm the owner. This was my grandparents' house."

I should have guessed. The family portraits in the photographs. "Well, why didn't you just say that this afternoon?"

He took off his cap. He had a receding hairline, and his hair was cut close to his scalp. It made him look mature. He was an average-looking man, but unexpectedly sexy and compelling to me.

"You wouldn't have accepted the offer to stay the night if I'd told you it was my house. My grandparents often let rooms to summer visitors. I do the same, but I'm very choosy."

I had to think about this. While I did, he was opening up bags and taking out food. He'd brought in dinner, too. Warm aromatic smells wafted through the kitchen. Definitely candied sweet potatoes. Honey'd ham or chicken. I could smell cinnamon.

"I'll set the table," I offered, not knowing what else to do. He pointed to a cabinet and I found the china.

"I'll go clean up."

It took only a few minutes and by the time he'd returned from a quick shower, I had everything on the table. Soon we were sitting down to a dinner of the best country food I'd had since I didn't know when. Down home food, *and* a bottle of Merlot. The man was full of surprises.

It started to rain again. It made me feel kind of soft and languid because I was warm and dry. I found Marshall more and more interesting, and attractive. He wasn't superficial, or manipulative. But he wasn't what I was used to. I felt safe with him, protected.

Marshall told me he'd found an engine for my car. It would be ready for me in the morning. He wanted to know what kind of law I practiced and if I liked what I did. I laughed and told him the jury was still out. I asked him why he'd left Atlanta, and why he was called Doc. He said he'd been a paramedic for the city's largest public hospital. After nearly twenty years he'd come to the conclusion that he didn't make a bit of difference. He got tired of gunshot victims, battered babies, and disasters of life, but mostly he'd gotten tired of death. It wasn't that he stopped wanting to help people. He didn't want to add himself to the casualties.

His confession moved me deeply. It was so revealing. I felt admiration for him and wanted to reach out to comfort him in some way.

I wondered if he'd ever been married, but I didn't ask. I didn't volunteer that I was divorced.

I felt comfortable enough to make my own confession. Being a lawyer wasn't what I thought it would be. I hated conflict but I also liked helping people. I said I was good at adapting, and accepting compromise.

"Yeah, I know," he responded.

I had a sense that Marshall understood a whole lot about me. I had a strange sense of having something in common with him. And I was enjoying myself.

Maybe it was because I noticed the arching of his brows, or the way he licked his lips over his food, or the way he openly stared at me, silence pooled around us. It pulled us into an awareness that left out the past and the future. There was just this singular moment that was an anomaly. An accident of circumstances that made anything possible. And anything *was* possible, because us being there in his house together was an act of fate.

That's why, when the lights flickered and went out, I wasn't alarmed. Neither of us moved, we just sat there in the dark listening to the pelting rain. After a moment I reached out blindly, as if I thought I was suddenly alone. I found Marshall's hand. He opened his palm and closed his fingers around mine.

It was reassuring. His hand was strong and warm, and I immediately felt a current that was so sharp I think I caught my
breath.

"Are you afraid?" he asked.

"I don't think so. Is it always like this?" I wanted to know. I felt
dreamy, detached.

"You mean, the rain?"

"No. The lights going out. It was almost like . . ."

"Magic," he finished for me.

All the while he held my hand, like we were lovers. He rubbed
his thumb slowly over my knuckles. I never knew before they
were an erogenous zone. When Marshall started to get up from
the table I didn't hesitate to do the same. My heart was racing and
for a fleeting moment common sense tried to insinuate itself into
my daydream. A clap of thunder shattered it, and I followed
Marshall up the stairs. If I was going to have a moment of mad-
ness, this was a perfect time.

We went into the big bedroom where I'd settled in for the one
night. Was it really a guestroom, or his room? I didn't care. He
instructed me to sit on the side of the bed, then knelt in front of
me between my knees. I could feel my lips open between my
legs. I hadn't known that sensation before, a yearning to be
entered and filled.

He began to kiss me with a sweet tenderness. Slow and con-
suming with passion, not lust. He took his time. His hands
slipped under my summer shift, and slid along my thighs with a
feathery caress. It sent a roiling of instant desire twisting in my
groin, releasing the juices that flowed to my sacred opening. His

hands reached my waist, explored my stomach and rib cage, seemingly fascinated with the texture of my skin. By the time his fingertips brushed against the peaks of my breasts, I could hardly breathe. He held his palms so that the nipples grazed against his hand. Then Marshall put his arms around me and replaced one of his hands with his mouth.

I groaned and leaned into him, held his head cradled against my breast. Moved my hands over the contours of his head. Kissed the crown. I tried to urge him from his knees, to lie atop me. Instead, he removed my shift and gently urged me to lie back on the bed. I took off my bra and tossed it aside. My legs hung over the side.

"Yes, now," I said to myself.

When I felt him parting my knees I sighed in relief. Only to have to suck in air when I felt his mouth and tongue touch my nether lips. I think I jumped, almost swooned with sheer pleasure. I think I almost died.

I wantonly opened myself as wide as I could, spread-eagle, with my hips raised and gyrating. I moved myself against his tongue but his hands on my inner thighs controlled the rhythm for both of us. There was a spiraling sensation starting at the tip of where Marshall's tongue stroked and I moaned in delight. As surprised and shocked as I was at this intimacy, thankfully my body remained in control and I lay supine in total surrender. The wet sensation of being licked left me helpless and practically in tears.

There is this thing that I do when I'm about to come. I pant in a one, two, three beat that gets shorter and shorter. Just before the last two beats rushed together I felt Marshall carefully insert a finger into the wet and hungry little mouth of my vagina. I reached out for something to hold on to. He again grabbed my hands and anchored me to earth.

I dissolved into bliss.

My body quivered and my senses were spinning crazily before I was released and dropped back into the dark quiet of the room. I couldn't move and couldn't help him at all when he moved me fully onto the bed. I heard Marshall finally remove his clothes, but I didn't even have breath to call to him. What could I say? Actions spoke so much louder than words.

I felt him climb behind me, my butt against his stomach and the hardened shaft of his penis. His body was cool against my hot skin. I could smell him; honey on his breath from dinner, rain and cotton, grease, and his own male essence surrounded me like perfume. I became drowsy. I loved the way he held me and cuddled, like I mattered. Then he slowly entered my still vibrating opening from behind. He began to rock against me, awakening little embers of joy still trembling from my first orgasm. I could feel Marshall sheathed inside me. He filled me. For the moment, we belonged totally to one another. For the moment this was the *only* place I wanted to be.

My heart pounded with the way he made me feel. I felt his lips, his teeth against the back of my neck. I shivered and he held me even closer as the goose bumps burst into tiny sparks of passion. The man was lethal. If we kept this up I was going to need CPR from him.

He moved with rigid, intense strokes, and in seconds I gladly suffered another meltdown. When Marshall finally let himself go his climax was quiet, controlled, peaceful, and replete.

I remember thinking it was going to be a long, long night.

*   *   *

I was not the least surprised to awaken the next morning and find myself alone. I was also not angry or upset. Deeply reflective, perhaps. Calm, and resigned. Grateful.

I got dressed and put my things together, but I took my time. I searched for fresh linens and changed the bed. I went downstairs and found the kitchen completely cleaned from the impromptu dinner of the previous night. But Marshall had left me coffee in a thermos. There was no note for me, nor did I leave one. To do so would have vanquished the magic.

I was prepared to walk back to the service station to pick up my car. I was surprised, however, to find it parked in front of his house. I repacked everything and started the new engine, which brought my car back to life. But for a long moment I sat gazing at the house, before driving away.

I was sure I would never see Marshall again, but I was okay with that. I had my memories and they were indelible. Forever.

Anyway, I was just passing through. I think we both understood that. He'd done what I'd needed him to do.

And he was a very good mechanic.

MICHAEL A. GONZALES

Simply Beautiful

M. had seen enough hotel rooms to last him a lifetime. While most people appreciated a certain freedom as they chilled in the comforting womb of their own homes, over the years M. had slowly metamorphosed into an insomniac nomad wandering the wondrous landscapes of fluorescent-lit hallways and chilly suites where one ordered bland appetizers from the late-night room service menu, paced across plush wall-to-wall carpeting, drained the fully stocked mini-bar overflowing with five-dollar Pepsis and lewdly eyeballed the adorable Mexican maids.

With their callused fingers, thick legs and heavy facial hair, these brown-skinned earth angels pulled back his soft bedspread at nightfall, leaving heavenly chocolate treats on his fluffy pillows. M. often felt as though these wide-hipped servants with their piercing eyes, buxom breasts and black oceans of hair were surrogates sent to comfort him in his time of loneliness. Seeping through the tissue-thin walls the cascading warmth of Ellington and Coltrane's exquisite "In a Sentimental Mood" made him feel as though he were lounging near a blissful shore. The gentle purring of the piano combined with the crying lion saxophone was more soothing than the soft symphonies of dolphins vibrating from the ocean.

As M. silently lay on the silky sheets, his cool green eyes gazing through the sheer white drapery, he was thrilled to notice a shooting star sweep across the sky. "At least," M. mumbled, "we're back in the New York City groove." Back in the sea of sirens, where howling horns hooted at crammed intersections. Back in the land of the crazies screaming curses at children, crackheads threatening old men with castration while the boys in blue laughed uproariously. He was back in his hometown where the buildings, the landscape and the people might change overnight, but the unsympathetic soul of the city remained the same.

*   *   *

In a matter of days his newest documentary, a ninety-minute feature that explored the haunting talisman that hovered over the crowns of the kings of rhythm and blues, would open the New York Film Festival. *Divided Souls,* a title M. had bogarted from soul scribe David Ritz's tome on Marvin Gaye, was a depressing cinematic experience that detailed the doomed lives of troubled men.

Opening with a thunderous pistol blast, then fading to the blood-splattered motel parking lot of Sam Cooke's last stand, *Divided Souls* explored Otis Redding's plane falling from the sky, the plunge that Donny Hathaway took from his fifteenth-floor Essex House window, the hot grits splashed on Al Green from a lover who would moments later commit suicide, the crippling crash of Teddy Pendergrass's that killed his transvestite companion, the freak windstorm in Brooklyn that toppled the lighting tower onto Curtis Mayfield, permanently handicapping a once

Superfly guy, and the saddening drug addiction that plagued Ike Turner, Bobby Womack, Sly Stone, David Ruffin, Ray Charles and Rick James.

Already the film had been hailed as a masterpiece by the alternative cultural critics, while the whiter collars at the *New York Times* had written that his arty Afro visions were like "a black pop Ken Burns with splashes of Spike Lee's *4 Little Girls* an obvious influence." What his cinematic soul ballad had to do with Spike's civil-rights joint about a grievous church bombing, he didn't know. But, "Black is black is black," he mumbled, shaking his bald dome. *Divided Souls* concluded with yet another pistol blast, this one echoing from the modest crib Marvin Gaye had bought for his folks in L.A. Even after countless hours tediously constructing this scene perfectly in the editing room, the deafening gunshot always caused M. to flinch.

As he sat in the private screening room at Lincoln Center, M. silently dedicated this labor of love to the haunting memory of a stunning soul sister named Norma Jean, who had, for only one night, strutted into his life.But with a clattering bang and a boom, she had shifted the axis of his cryptic universe forever.

* * *

He had once lived on the borderline where Harlem meets Washington Heights, a wild-cowboy hood where flamboyant drug dealers had shoot-outs in the middle of the afternoon while their dim underlings hawked cocaine on the stoop like it was legal. On his boisterous block, twenty-four/seven cornerboys swigged from forty-ounce bottles of Olde English while rattling dice into the night, then slinking away like alleycats at the first sign of daylight.

M. had crashed in a crowded pad with a few weeded-out new jack jazz cats who had journeyed from the fabled urban blues utopia of Chicago. They'd come to this gloomy Gotham to walk in the giant steps of their dead heroes ("What's up, Bird . . . you seen Monk or Mingus hangin' 'round?"), stalking the gritty streets of the city until they stumbled upon a swinging session of flying high masterblasters vibrating the walls of some musical playhouse.

Having graduated from New York University without a clue of his future days, M. had taken a temp gig as a foot messenger at Zoom Away Deliveries. Strolling through the rowdy bustle of the skyscrapered kingdom of midtown Manhattan, bulky manila envelopes tucked neatly under his arm, he absorbed the ethereal city. M. marveled at the refined ivory beauties lingering outside the Waldorf-Astoria, stared at their opulent diamond rings gleaming in the summer sun and envied their tuxedo-clad escorts. With their stern faces and wrinkled brows, you just knew they were V.I.P. Once, walking past the plush lobby of the celebrated Carlyle Hotel, he had peeped lounge lizard Bobby Short exchanging pleasantries with all who greeted him.

M. was in awe of these divine fortresses of glass and steel with their angelic architecture. They were grown-up playgrounds where the privileged relaxed with enchanting Cole Porter/George Gershwin soundtracks and dirty Absolut martinis. What vague affairs were hidden behind these decorative palace doors, he wondered—these inner-city châteaus where uniformed men tipped their gaudy hats, assisted with cumbersome luggage and were always able to catch a cab.

In his own stomping grounds of the Upper West Side, where wicked white cops rhythmlessly shuffled along their beat in fear that a stray bullet might cap their ass, M. noticed that most of the hotels in Harlem—since the closing of the Theresa, the renowned hotel where Sugar Ray Robinson had partied till dawn and Fidel Castro once stayed when visiting the States in 1960—were now low-budget hedonistic shacks where drunken couples did the nasty on stained sheets and p-funk junkies flocked to get a fix.

While these temples of drugged-out decadence might have once been concrete citadels of inner-city rapture, the illmatic introduction of crack in the eighties ravaged the neighborhood and robbed it of its former glory. Even the once halfway-decent uptown hotels had been reduced to crumbling castles of battered facades and rickety stairs, peeling paint walls and rusty water faucets. Unlike the luxe-deluxe downtown hotels, these haunting hovels more resembled tombs for the dead than temporary abodes for the living.

*   *   *

For M., the summer of '91 was proving to be the most angst-ridden since he was a morose child whose own mother had thought he might commit suicide before the age of thirteen. From the moment he woke up, M. had daydreams of raging riots, violent explosions and other pending disasters. After twenty-one years of striving on this earth, his world was filled with spooky symbols that contributed to his sense of dread. At night he dreamed of sweltering rooms engulfed by crimson flames and repulsive rats creeping in the shadows. In the real world, some lunatic with an extreme hatred for the city's winged wildlife had begun poisoning the neighborhood pigeons.

M.'s mind was tortured, truly believing that a black plague was imminent. Drunkenly walking from the 145th Street subway station one simmering evening after downing a few Jack Daniel's shots with his homeboys at a Irish pub in Hell's Kitchen, M. accidentally kicked a feathered corpse with the right foot of his raggedy sneaker. "Oh God," he slurred, bugging out. A dumpy Dominican dame wearing a tight T-shirt and painted-on jeans looked at the poisoned pigeon and carefully made the sign of the cross.

Bewildered, she glanced at M., her eyes intense, her voice strange. "Maybe voodoo," she whispered, then turned the corner. Her voice sent a chill through him. Before reaching his own battered building six blocks away, M. had counted more than a dozen dead birds littering the sidewalks.

*   *   *

As the only non-musician slumming in a pad swarming with Windy-City blues fusionists constantly blasting Miles Davis's *Bitches Brew*, electric Stratocaster masturbation fantasies from one of the two bedrooms or engaging in continuous jack-off jam sessions with other unemployed black rockers in need of space to shake their sonic groove things, M. had recently begun spending more free time roaming the badass boulevards of Harlem.

Soon he was seduced by the lite-brite neon of a saloon called

Nightbird's, where late-night chirping chitchat and early-morning drunken babble were the house specialty. A countrified false teeth chatterbox who looked like a bombed Bessie Smith bellowed, "Give a city gal one more for the road." Sitting gap-legged at the bar, she wore a gaudy dress and a putrid perfume that smelled like sour dandelion wine. Of course, since she rarely moved from her perch, no one knew what road she was actually talking about.

A couple of every-nighters named Shorty Doo Wop and Eightball shot a never-ending game of pool, talking trash about the bar's clientele as they gulped from chilled glasses of ale. "That bitch is in everything but a hearse," slurred Shorty, motioning to the old blues broad squatting at the bar. "But, she keep telling everybody bizness, she gonna be in one of those, too."

A tough cookie named Maggie Matthews worked the bar while whacking cheap lowlifes who refused to tip a few bucks ("Don't ya bums know a lady's salary in this joint is her tips," she barked, evil-eyeballing them) while speaking sweet as melted chocolate kisses to her preferred customers.

Nursing his fourth Barcardi & Coke, M. was somewhat surprised when he returned to his rusty stool and discovered a smooth paper napkin bearing the imprint of a kiss propped against his moist glass. Written underneath the lipstick traces in frilly penmanship, the simple note read: *love your eyes.* Gazing upward with his seductive jade peepers, M. caught the sweet silky smile of the mature black beauty who still looked like a skintight brickhouse beneath the swarthy dimness, hazy clouds of cigarette smoke and the sweet tears of intoxication. Not to be mistaken for the never-been-fine, this aging beauty was a one of a kind, blow-your-mind sort of woman. M. reasoned that this dashing gray fox was about fifty, give or take a few. But since black rarely cracks, honey still looked like Sheba the African Princess dashing through the concrete jungle.

* * *

M. had grown weary of the subterranean monkey hustle of these bar babes. With tricks worthy of Ringling Brothers, these broads often leaped through hoops of fire for a chilled cocktail. It wasn't that they didn't have any loot, but a drink seemed to taste better when someone else bought it. Yet, when Maggie set down a fresh Bacardi & Coke in front of him saying, "The lady wants you to have this," M. was hopeful. *At last, something different,* he thought, then smiled. It had been a low-key night without the blare of a DJ or a band. Since the juke was busted, Maggie put in a cassette of her favorite 8-track flashback/old-school soundtrack, *Roberta Flack & Donny Hathaway:*

M. was soon swept away by the moody dramatics of the opening track "I (Who Have Nothing)," where Flack's voice sounded possessed by a sweet exorcist as she strolled on flaming coals to be with her ebony loverman. By the time Hathaway appeared from the shadows bearing shiny diamonds and tarnished promises, the heat of the moment had become hotter than July. It was as though they were being smothered in a steamy shroud of stirring strings arranged by Arif Martin and the fierce tinkling of Donny's melancholy piano while Sister Flack touched the heavens with her blown-out Afro and searing keyboards.

"Ahhhh, take it!" an inebriated voice encouraged as the mystery woman slowly approached M. In her he recalled a foxy femme fatale from some late-night noir flick. Her sense of classic style and poetic glamour reminded M. of his mother describing a Lena Horne concert at Carnegie Hall. Her complexion was the color of cream sprinkled with a dash of nutmeg. Dressed in a sheer multicolored wrap dress, gold bangles covering her wrists and open-toed mules on pedicured feet, her wicked smile was almost pornographic.

With moves smoother than the minks she draped over her shoulders in the winter, the full-figured beauty led him to the floor and held him tightly as the slow train to Sugar Hill eased down the track. Without a wall of words to hinder their mutual erotic emotions, M. and the sensual stranger were guided by a pureness that responded to life's primal pleasures without being confused by intellect. They touched with a tenderness that some couples never experience in a decade of lovemaking. Together they reached cloudy crests, subconsciously soared from mountain tops and dangerously entered uncharted territory where moody phantoms were known to soar.

After the dance, they both felt the shiver of sensuality surging through their stimulated bodies. "Let's get out of here," she whispered, gently guiding him across the floor. Unlike his white-boy college buddies who had swooned over scrawny boyish girls with their flat stomachs and lanky legs, he preferred voluptuous women who reminded him of Sunday morning church sister's heaving their chubby cleavage toward heaven in Holy Ghost ecstasy.

M. began to feel as though he had fallen into a dream world

where seductive older women sang like nightingales in the dusk, blithely bellowing until the morning dawn: majestic Broadway mamas with honeyed tongues and inferno kisses and exquisitely decorated apartments that overlooked the Hudson River and the shimmering lights of the George Washington Bridge.

Yet, instead of the imaginary space he had conjured in his mind, the shabby gypsy cab stopped in front of an uptown hotel he had never noticed before—a grand residence with a gorgeous black awning, a crimson carpet flowing from the curb to the lobby and a striking Billy Dee Williams–looking brother slaving behind the sharp Art Deco desk. The name embroidered in yellow gold on his black uniform read The Jodeci.

M. had never been inside of a hotel before, and it amazed him that a person could actually live in one. "Good evening, Miss Lewis," greeted the doorman, sounding as though he were addressing a church matron instead of a middle-aged glamour girl. She smiled, he nodded, and M. prayed there wasn't a deranged lover lurking in the shadows like a wolverine, silently awaiting his prey. "Don't worry, baby boy, only me and Love live here," she said, as though reading his mind. "Love is my cat, so unless you're a mouse you have nothing to worry about."

One step closer to heaven, they embraced. On the elevator, under the glass eye of big brother's security camera, they kissed. A wack Muzak rendition of Earth, Wind & Fire's sensuous song "Reasons" streamed from a mono speaker in the ceiling. Observing the surveillance monitor, the doorman smirked knowingly. In the nine months since she had been renting the upper suite he had seen a few young studs swagger into the building with Miss

Lewis, then later sent sprawling on a fatal lovesick journey. Turning them out like blind puppies in the night, she seemed to take delight in their affection.

"All cock and no brains," he mumbled with superiority. "But, for an old dame, baby girl sure nuff sizzling." He was unable to suppress the hard-on that swelled in his ill-fitting pants whenever he got a chance to witness her ritual elevator mating dance, before the mirrored doors whooshed open and she exited the lift on the thirteenth floor.

Ushering M. over the threshold of her penthouse, they scorchingly smooched again in the darkened doorway. "Let me get the lights," she said, walking over to the ornate Tiffany lamp on the wood-and-glass end table. After hours of functioning in the semi-darkness of the night, M. was momentarily blinded by the sudden brightness.

In his daft mind she was an alluring black widow spider spooring across the lush carpet. When he finally focused, M. was slightly taken aback by the neat clutter of her sprawling web. The walls were painted beige and vivid blossoms in a multicolored glass vase were the centerpiece of a mahogany coffee table. There was an overstuffed paisley patterned sofa with matching pillows, while in a corner of the room was a leopard skin chaise longue. A curtained doorway led to the terrace, where an impressive garden of exotic flowers flourished.

"Your place is like a museum," exclaimed M., marveling at her extensive collection of ancient album covers that were framed on the wall, the countless two-color promotional posters advertising yesteryear rhythm and blues shows, including Screaming Jay

Hawkins emerging from a coffin on a Rockland Palace placard and a poster of a processed and possessed James Brown—"Mr. Dynamite!"—blowing up the Apollo's stage with his explosive theatrics. There were black-and-white lobby cards of sharp-suited Cadillac cats and tight skirt girls. The floor-to-ceiling bookshelves were crowded with small decorative vinyl storage boxes filled with vintage 45s from her adolescence.

* * *

Like most innocent teenage girls, Norma Jean had been in a hurry to be grown, to shed those Mouseketeer ears for diamond studs, crushes on Motown men and the sweaty mack daddy loving of a real man. But, life being life and not a Rock Hudson/Doris Day movie, it never quite worked out according to the script. The pendulum kept swinging, every movement representing a moment of passion and lust, heartbreak and childbirth, misery and love, and the million other experiences that made up her life. After her second husband had been blasted to the devil's doorway when he was caught stroking his best friend's girl, Norma Jean had begun collecting memorabilia she believed would help her recover the lost moments of her life.

On the shiny parquet floor of the sunken living room were stacks of albums: The Five Stairsteps, Little Anthony and the Imperials, Mary Wells, Stevie Wonder, The Orlons and The Supremes. Each stack had been divided by decade, but did not continue past a few Gamble & Huff platters from the seventies. M. recalled seeing a few of the Philadelphia International Records discs in his mom's collection, but he dared not mention that.

From the corner of his eye, he peeped a raggedy black blur dash from beneath the depths of the couch. The shabby feline's fur was matted, desperately in need of brushing, and its fierce eyes held a devilish intensity. Love stared silently at M. Before he could change fate, the bold kitty leaped toward his leg, its sharp claws tearing his linen pants. "What the fuck!" M. screamed, kicking toward the cat but not actually connecting. Rushing through the curtained door, Love disappeared into the jungle of the terrace.

M. caught a glimpse of the gloomy dawn nearing with its overcast heavens and weeping sky, once again feeling as though bad luck were crouching in the corner, playing with sharp razor blades. Eyeing him intently, she said, "Love must sense you don't like him or something. He doesn't usually act so wild."

"Maybe Love's just a jealous pussy," he joked, rubbing his torn pants leg. He nodded his head toward a stack of records. "Why don't you put on something to calm the savage beast."

"What do you know about this stuff, anyway?" she asked, digging out a copy of Al Green's classic *I'm Still in Love with You* and placing the smooth black vinyl on her state-of-the art stereo system. In a matter of moments the room had become an aural Jacuzzi of soul as the title track flooded the flat. The future reverend's smooth falsetto seemed to possess a lustful texture that conjured joyful images of chocolate bubble baths in spring and midnight basement parties overflowing with kissy-faced couples under the flash of a crimson strobe light. The protective shell of paranoia that usually shrouded M.'s fragile emotions had been temporarily lifted by the intoxicating tonic of brother Green's heavenly voice.

Walking into the neat kitchen, she opened the refrigerator. The simple contents included three bottles of champagne, four eggs and a can of coffee. Norma Jean pulled out a bottle of Moët, then carefully rinsed two crystal flutes. M. looked closer at the framed album covers that hung on the wall. It was then that he noticed that the photograph on Little Willie John's *Talk to Me* LP was of a radiant redbone belle standing in front of the tree; the next framed photo was the stunning image of the heavenly faced teen-dream dressed in a virginal white pants suit, lying on the floor surrounded by her record collection; the title printed on the cardboard packaging was *Records Galore*.

"Well, either I've had too much to drink or the girl on these album covers looks very familiar," he teased, lighting a cigarette. Norma Jean sauntered into the living room and kicked off her Gucci mules. Her toenails were painted the same midnight lavender as her fingernails; she wore a gold ankle bracelet that had been a gift from her slain husband. Standing next to M., she was at least two feet shorter, but felt ten feet taller. M. inquired, "This is you in these pictures, right?"

"That's me all right," she answered without a trace of bitterness, stifling a giggle. She felt that giggling was too girlish for an older woman such as herself. "Back in the day, I thought I was going to be the sepia Marilyn Monroe, taking the world by storm while jetting off to strange lands to have my picture snapped. Marilyn's real name was Norma Jean, too, you know." Then she giggled, unable to help herself.

Handing him a glass of champagne, Norma Jean was amazed that it had been over thirty years since she had switched her sass through the doorway of Ophelia Devore's modeling school, competing with the other nearly white cotillion queens with their good hair and nasty attitudes. Posing for these now-collectible album covers had been the peak of her modeling career. Norma Jean had damn near forgotten about the dusty discs stashed in her mother's brownstone basement until she had died.

"You have to realize, for me a group like New Edition is old school," confessed M. "A lot of this old soul stuff I'm not really familiar with, but it's cool. Learn something new every day, right?" As she moved closer toward him, M. noticed a few lines under her eyes that she had tried to disguise with heavy makeup. Though he knew he would never be able to introduce her to his friends, M. thought the lines on her face gave her character.

*   *   *

Norma Jean always enjoyed the innocence of the impatient man-children she seduced. Boys who still slightly smelled of sweet milk after sex, but hadn't experienced enough of the world to curdle in the sun. "Young, dumb and full of cum," was how her oldest girl-friend Myrna phrased it. "Hell, most of those young boys you fuck act as though they had never been past 125th Street. You know, like an invisible cage had been constructed on the corner of their block holding them as specimens in captivity like they were the latest social experiment sponsored by Tuskegee."

Most of the bony barboys she had bought into her apartment usually paid little mind to the framed album covers, let alone being able to recognize a thirty-year-old photograph. By this time they were usually tearing at her expensive clothes like wild animals mating for the first time. Mere minutes later they would be apologizing for their eager-beaver premature ejaculations, which either left them embarrassed, sad or a borderline combination of the two as Norma Jean lay fuming with frustration. *At last, something different,* she thought. Then she smiled.

The older the man, the more bitter he is, had become her mantra, and the scabs scarring her heart were proof enough of the fury those forever tormented beasts possessed: enchanting ghetto gigolos who once poured her fine wine, then slapped her precious face in a resentful rage, because another brother had looked lustfully at her thick legs. Many reckless eyeballs had rolled, like marbles, across grimy floors before she was able to make her great escape from that crazy circus where a sense of suspicion was the latest religion and jealousy flowed like boiling rivers of blood. Like the worst nodding Needle Park junkie, she once fiended to be loved by those trifling men with their constant lies, but never quite sure of where they were going. To paraphrase Poe's raven, "Nevermore, baby girl. Nevermore."

As Al Green vocalized about "Love and Happiness," harmonic butterflies fluttered from their cocoon inside the stereo speakers, shivering over the sweaty bodies sprawled on the living room floor. "Put your heels back on," he murmured. Standing up, Norma Jean slowly slipped off her summer dress, revealing a tanned body that was smooth as warm lotion. Gliding the golden high-heeled slippers onto her pretty feet, she felt like the fairy-tale princess her mother had raised her to be. Turning off the overhead lights, the emerging sunlight slow-danced on her perfect skin.

Caressing her sensitive dark nipples with his tongue, licking downward to the fullness of her beautiful belly, he lingered on her Kool-Aid–flavored button. He slipped his mouth down to her feet and began sweetly sucking her toes. "Fuck me," she sighed, as her river deep began to overflow. M. explored her dewy pink cashmere forest, taking time to smell the burning rosebushes and caress the sticky honeycombs and slowly nibbled from the wildflowers that blossomed between her smooth legs.

They were lost in the soulful music of the moment where passion becomes misty sunshine spraying golden violin rays and a thousand pianos begin to play under a cherry moon. Then, she moaned. Firmly grabbing her pillow-soft booty, M. was sweating. Rolling her over so that now Norma Jean was straddling him, she softly rubbed her full breasts against his baby face. With the rhythm of the music gently guiding them toward an orgasmic promised land, she rode him as though he were a wild rodeo horse. M. whimpered as she slapped his ass with her divine hands while roughly scratching his chest.

"Not so hard," he mumbled. For M. and Norma Jean, the temporary servitude of sex was more a spiritual symphony conducted by Willie Mitchell than the pagan ritual most men believed sex to be. Riding on an aphrodisiac streetcar named fire and desire, orgasmically he screamed Norma Jean's name in the morning. "Simply beautiful," crooned Brother Green, his falsetto a wild warm wind blowing across the fields of ecstasy, taking them higher.

*   *   *

Hours later the eerie black cat returned from the balcony. M. could hear its paws scratching across the floor as he lay breathing heavy and sweating, Norma Jean cradled like a child in his hairless arms. He should have felt as confident as a crowing cock at dawn, but instead the evil black shroud of dread had drifted back into the room like a spooky electric ghost. M. began to feel a tightness in his chest as he crawled inside of the womb of a dark cloud and fell a million feet into a murky abyss.

"Jesus," he shrieked, waking up from his creepy morningmare, body sore from sleeping on the floor. M. rubbed his peepers and was startled to see the dreadful kitty standing next to him, a dead pigeon clutched between his sharp teeth. Dropping the filthy bird on M.'s chest as though it were a bewitching sacrifice from the dark side, Love released an unholy screech as though speaking in tongues. Moments later, licking the bird's inky blood from his stained paws, Love watched as the frightened man slithered through the front door like a snake. "Good-bye, Norma Jean," he whispered, closing the door behind him.

NICOLE BAILEY-WILLIAMS

Zoe

Zoe is a delicate stone, a gentle lioness, a steel magnolia. Zoe will trot alone all over the country. She will walk a child home through the roughest neighborhoods. She'll walk up to the meanest-looking thug on the corner and pinch his cheeks. If he looks at her like she's lost her mind, she'll cop one of his potato chips and walk away, calling "Bye, sugar lump" over her shoulder. Yet she'll cry inconsolably if she sees a dog limping.

Zoe will give you her body unselfishly. She'll shower you with the love that you've craved from birth. She'll make you feel like you're the king of the world. Then she'll leave you without a good-bye.

Zoe, the most beautiful girl in the world, will stand alone near the wall at a party with loneliness etched in her eyes. She'll have the attention of every man in the room, but she'll run to the bathroom in tears, thinking that she's ugly. That's what she'd been doing when I saw her at a party during my junior year in college.

I'd been scoping her out because she was tight from head to toe. Zoe had an Afrocentric thing going on with her beautiful, short natural and silver cowrie shell jewelry. I'd never kicked it with a sister with a natural before, but looking at her in all of her regal beauty, I couldn't envision her any other way. Her dark brown face held high, gorgeously sculpted cheekbones. She seemed to flaunt her full, succulent lips. I had the urge to strut over to her and just suck on one.

Looking at her, it was easy to see that she was different from the other women I've known. They're cultured, but shallow. Intelligent, but unfeeling. They're groomed from the crib to socialize only in certain circles. Socially conscious and civic-minded they are, but not just any charity or any club will do. It must be the right club with the right members who have the right connections. They must wear the right clothes accessorized the right way, and they must have the right hair done in the right hairstyle so they attract the right man who will afford them the right lifestyle. Woe unto the poor brother who gets his heart up enough to step to one of these sophisticated sisters. He's shot down in a matter of seconds, and he walks away wondering what kind of brother *would* be acceptable to this type of woman. That kind of brother is me, but I'm tired of that kind of sister. I want somebody real, not somebody right, and Zoe had piqued my interest.

While I watched her, my drink began to taste bland by comparison, so I put it down, preparing to navigate through the crowd to my mother ship, but when I looked up, she was gone.

Too slow, you blow, I thought, walking toward the kitchen to get another margarita. New drink in hand, I rolled back into the living room of the frat house. I made eye contact with a cute freshman who stayed down the hall from one of the girls in my student leadership group.

"What's happening?" I asked, filling the time by filling the empty space next to her.

"Nothing," she responded, trying not to seem too interested. Then she looked at me, recognition passing over her face. "Aren't you Lisa's 'Big Brother'?"

"Yup, I'm Fred."

"Hi, Fred. I'm Tami," she said, smiling coyly into my hazel eyes. I looked down at my drink, giving her the chance to assess me. She tried to be discreet as she studied me, but I could almost hear her mentally ticking off my "assets." Light-skinned. Curly hair. Check. Solid jawbone. Straight teeth. Check. Strong hands. Tight body. Check. Nice clothes. Expensive watch. Check.

"Is Lisa here?" Tami asked, trying to recapture my attention.

"I don't know," I said, looking around. That's when I spotted her. Her face looked puffy, and her eyes were red. I wondered if she'd ventured off to smoke a spliff. She didn't seem like the type, but you never know. Whatever it was, something about her was diminished. Sadder.

She was walking toward the door. I had to catch her before she left with my heart.

"Excuse me, Tami," I interrupted her. "I have to say good-bye to somebody."

Not waiting for a response, I was off, rushing toward my destiny.

"Hey, you're not leaving already, are you?"

She turned and gave me a sweeping, assessing glance. "Yeah. There's nothing for me here."

"How would you know?"

She laughed, then said, "Believe me. I can tell."

I was trying to think of a way to buy myself some time. "You've got all of these good brothers and sisters from Temple, Penn, and Drexel. This is a network right here."

The look on her face told me that my card had been declined.

I tried to recover my fumble. "Well, let me walk you to your car."

As we walked toward the door, I motioned for Tami to chill. If my queen was leaving, I might want a backup plan.

"Why are you leaving so early?"

"I've got to get up early. Besides, it's the same old scene." She looked back around the room and shook her head.

"What scene is that?" I asked, intrigued.

"The split down the color line, especially from those uppity Negroes at Penn."

"I'm one of those uppity Negroes from Penn," I lied.

"Figures. Hurry up and get Susie or Muffie back to her dorm before she turns into a pumpkin," she said, motioning with her head toward Tami.

Damn! I thought, feeling like I'd been busted even though I had no cause to feel that way. I wanted her to see that I was different, though the evidence lumped me squarely into that category of men she was criticizing.

"She's in my student leadership group at Temple," I lied again.

"I couldn't tell that by the look she gave me, Mr. University of Pennsylvania."

Double damn. I was starting to feel like Florida Evans.

"Let me start over. My name is Fred, and I'm a junior at Temple. What's your name?"

"I'm Zoe, and I'm a senior at Temple."

"Can I call you sometime, Zoe?"

"You know," she said, opening her car door. "I'm not really feeling brothers right now, so how about if you give me your number, and maybe I'll call you."

"That's kind of harsh," I said, reaching into my pocket for some paper. I came up empty, but she had an old, balled-up receipt in her purse. I wrote my name and number on it, praying that its fate would be better than it looked.

I stood in the street, watching her drive off. *What did she mean, she wasn't feeling brothers right now?* I thought, shaking my head.

* * *

I couldn't shake Zoe from my thoughts over the next few weeks. I envisioned her chocolate skin next to my own honey-colored skin, and the contrast aroused in me a sense of adventure, like I was exploring the unknown. She was exotic. Different. She sported a hairstyle that showed her strength, making her unable to hide behind the mask of her hair like a lot of the other women I knew. Yet, even without that mask, she was still a mystery to me.

I hadn't heard from her, so I figured that I wouldn't. As much as I tried to convince myself that it was her loss, I knew I was lying. I couldn't believe how much I wanted her after only one brief meeting. I thought back to that night. Her red sleeveless turtleneck had hugged every inch of her slim frame, her black miniskirt skimming her shapely ass. Her legs were lean and sculpted. Thinking about her now was starting to make my nature rise like it had when I'd first seen her. Then, I'd had Tami to satisfy my lust, but right now, sitting at a table in the outdoor food court on Temple's campus, I was at a loss.

As I flipped through the pages of my Adolescent Psych book, waiting for my boy to relax, a sparkle in the distance caught my eye. The sparkles shone from words in glitter paint on a T-shirt that read DON'T QUOTE ME STATISTICS ABOUT MY MEN. PROVIDE SOLUTIONS."

"See something interesting, Mr. University of Pennsylvania?"

Think of the devil, and she will appear.

"Hey there, Lady Zoe. I'm surprised you remember me."

She didn't answer. Then again, she didn't have to, with her fine-ass self.

"Have a seat," I offered, clearing a space at the table.

Zoe slid into the seat and looked at me. She wasn't going to make it easy.

"So, I guess you've been busy getting ready for finals," I ventured.

"Why do you guess that?"

"Because you haven't called me."

"I didn't think you had time, you know, helping out your 'Little Sisters,'" she said with a sarcastic smile.

"Can I ask you something?" I inquired.

"Sure."

"What did you mean when you said that you aren't feeling brothers right now?"

"Well, Mr—"

"Fred. My name is Fred," I interrupted, sorry that I'd given her a reason to doubt me.

"Okay, Fred, sometimes I feel like I need a break from you guys. You're too confusing."

"Seems like the pot calling the kettle black," I joked. When she didn't laugh, I said, "I'm sorry, go on."

"You guys talk a good game, but you're not serious. You say you want us to be ourselves, but then you sweat us about not relaxing our hair. You talk about appreciating our strength, but that's not true. You just want us to sit there so you can look at us, talk at us. It's no wonder that most pretty women don't have personalities."

She paused to take a breath. As the fire in her ignited, her voice became hoarse and throaty. I was hard all over again.

"Is that right?" I said mesmerized.

"Hell yeah, that's right. Name one pretty woman you know who has a personality," she demanded, crossing her arms.

I looked at her and smiled. "You."

She looked at me with the side of her top lip curled in disbelief. Then, she smiled like a rainbow breaking through the clouds.

"Thanks, Fred."

"You're welcome, Zoe."

After an awkward pause, I said, "So tell me about this sparkly shirt," wanting to keep her near me.

She shrugged, saying, "I'm tired of hearing the stats. 'One in four black men have been in jail. One in three black men produce babies out of wedlock.' Blah-blah-blah. I hate the demonizing. So I'd prefer progressive programs that bring out the positivity of our men."

She was a contradiction, this Zoe. But my heart didn't care.

As if listening to my heart, she said, "You see, I love brothers. Brothers just don't love me."

Looking at her, I knew that I would, if given the chance.

"So what does that mean?" I asked, wanting her to tell me that I was worthy of her affection.

We were interrupted. "Sorry I'm late, Z. You ready?"

"Yup," Zoe said with a warmth in her voice that was so beautiful I wanted to cry. She put her hand on the forearm of a pretty, caramel-colored sister with sandy brown locks.

"This is Fred. Fred, this is Sydney."

We nodded to each other with mutual understanding. I couldn't believe it. I was jealous.

"It means," Zoe finished, standing up, "that I've got to protect myself."

There was so much that I wanted to say to her, but she was on her way.

"I'll catch up with you," I said, knowing hopelessly that my balls were in her court. She smiled a funny smile and walked away with Sydney.

I headed back to my dorm, frustrated. Although Sydney was fine, too, the thought of them together didn't do a thing for me. Anybody else, and I would have been choking the chicken as soon as I got into my dorm room. But the thought of Zoe with her heart in her hand, offering it to another woman, made me feel like the loneliest guy in the world.

I spent the rest of the night trying to study, but thoughts of Zoe kept creeping into my head. Feeling my erection, I looked at the clock. The red digital numbers blinked 5:30 A.M.. I rolled onto my back, slipping my hand into the waistband of my boxers. I thought of Zoe's moist, inviting lips, her long, elegant neck, her full, firm breasts, her beautiful, long legs. As I stroked myself, I imagined that my hand was Zoe's. My dick throbbed as I gripped myself tighter, visualizing myself sliding into Zoe's moist tightness. I moved in and out of her, meshing worlds, bridging gaps of years and space, becoming one with the chocolate queen of my dreams. I caught my breath as I felt myself begin to erupt. Just then, at the moment I came, her face disappeared, and I was alone again. I rolled over and I thanked God for the millionth time for not giving me a roommate. Before I could close my eyes, the phone rang. I wanted to ignore it, but for some reason I picked it up.

"Hello," I said groggily.

"I was just about to hang up," said Zoe's voice.

I was now wide awake.

"Good morning, Z."

"That's Zoe to you," she responded, not surprised that I knew her voice.

I turned to the clock. It was 6:00 A.M. I couldn't think of a better way to start my day.

"My running partner bailed on me this morning. Do you want to go with me?"

"Sure. Now, I need to warn you that they used to call me Carl—"

"Whatever," she interrupted. "Meet me outside your dorm in fifteen minutes."

I took twenty just to see if she would wait. As I walked out of the doors of Temple Towers, I was afraid that she hadn't. Then I heard a car horn, and I saw her sitting in the driver's seat of her truck. I fought the urge to run over to her. I was so happy to have her as my first vision of the day.

"So where do you run?" I asked, settling into my seat.

"Kelly Drive."

"Do you run every day?"

"I try to. It relaxes me, and Kelly Drive is peaceful, despite the fact that it can get crowded. It shouldn't be that bad at seven o'clock. I'm usually out here at six. Morning is the best time of day. Most people miss it by sleeping late."

Her eyes twinkled as she talked, holding the hope of a new day. Even early in the morning, she was gorgeous. Her flawless cocoa skin glowed in the sun's rays. Her plump lips, covered only with a light gloss, curled easily into a smile. Who was it who'd made her feel ugly? I felt like finding him and kicking his ass. Then I realized that it probably wasn't just one guy. That's why she had given up on us.

"Tell me about you," I said, studying her profile as she maneuvered the vehicle down Broad Street, avoiding manhole covers and dodging oblivious pedestrians. Her driving was controlled and safe, but I had the feeling that on an open road, she would let loose.

"I'm not sure that I'm all that interesting, Fred. I'm from New Brunswick, New Jersey, but my folks are from Georgia." She paused, looking out the window at the abandoned Met Theater that had served as a church until a few years ago. "Um, both my parents are teachers. They would love to see me settle into a traditional career like that, but I want to work in public relations."

"You don't like traditions?" I asked, leaning over to see William Penn's statue atop City Hall before we turned onto Vine Street and headed toward Kelly Drive.

"Not really. I think that most traditions are stupid, and they only remain because we're too unimaginative to invent new ways to do things. I can't follow the same old rules. I'm too creative for that," she said, sliding the truck into the gravel parking lot near Boathouse Row. "My spirit yearns to be free," she finished, turning off the engine, hopping out of the truck, then ditching her hoodie.

She began stretching, her arms reaching for the sky. I imagined that she was reaching for freedom, and I wondered if she realized that like freedom, I, too, was in her grasp. As she lunged, I fought against my impending hard-on as I watched the sleek machine that was her body. In her crimson running tights and matching bra top, her body was splendid. *Think of something else. Think of something else,* I warned myself, trying to calm down and turning away to adjust myself.

She finished warming up, and we walked up onto the running path in silence. Our paces were in sync, and we matched each other's rhythms. Her stride was controlled and cool. Looking at her upper body, I could barely tell that she was moving because her glide was so smooth. I wondered if she was that controlled in bed. Then I thought of her driving, her bridled ferocity, and I decided that she wasn't.

"Are you okay?" I asked.

"I'm fine, pretty boy. You okay?"

I looked at her, trying to gauge her tone. She was smiling, so I smiled back.

"Yep," I answered, trying to modulate my breathing. "Have you been running long?"

"Since high school," she answered, barely winded. "I never ran for school or anything, but I've always liked the feel of this. It's liberating yet disciplined. The air is clean, and every breath feels like nourishment."

Her poetic words wrapped around me, and I loved the optimism behind them. No other woman I knew would describe air so beautifully. I knew right then that I needed Zoe in my life. She would help me to see things differently.

I looked over at the Schuykill River, running alongside Kelly Drive. Crew teams from local colleges were pointing their long boats toward their docks and heading in. The thought of pointing my boat toward Zoe's harbor ran through my head, and I looked at her, imagining what could be. A few shimmering drops of sweat came together and raced down her face and onto her neck. They slid down her throat and chest until they nestled themselves between her breasts. Never in my life had I wished so hard to be something else.

"What are you thinking about?" she asked as we exited the running path.

"Do you still see Sydney?" I blurted out.

She shook her head no.

"What's that about, Zoe?"

"I'm not sure if you'll understand, but it's simply about affection. She helped me feel beautiful and cherished. At a time when everyone wanted to take from me, she gave to me. It's that simple."

Again, her simplicity amazed me, but I understood. Yet even though I grasped what she said, I didn't want her to go there again. I wanted her to turn to me for everything she needed.

"Look, Zoe," I said plainly, getting back into the truck. "I'd like to see you again, but I'm at a loss since I don't have your number. What would you do if you were me?"

"I'd stop whining and ask for the digits."

"All right. Let's have them."

As she wrote, she said, "You do realize that after finals next week, I'm graduating and leaving Philly, right?"

"I'll take what I can get," I said, feeling like I was playing myself as the words left my mouth. But not caring.

We drove back to campus in silence. The heat from our bodies was intensified by the heat of our yearning. As she pulled up in front of my dorm, she reached across the space between us and put her hand on my leg. I covered her hand with mine, and the moisture from my palm mingled with the wetness of her own. Our fingers intertwined, and I lifted her hand to my mouth and began sucking her fingers, tasting each, one by one.

"I'll call you tonight," I said.

"Have you ever heard that jazz piece 'Walk, Don't Run'?" she asked.

"Nope," I said, then hopped happily out of the truck.

I was glad to hear her laugh as I closed the door.

*　　*　　*

We saw each other every day during final exams. We hung out in my dorm room, studying, talking, and just kicking it between exams. I tried my best to stay close because some seniors, especially senior women, were known to try to "tie up loose ends" their last few days of college.

Zoe was the only reason why I was still in Philly. Everybody else had broken camp right after their last exams. Me, I hung around, taking my time, hoping . . . with a hard-on.

Zoe came to my room the day before graduation.

"How you feeling, future public relations diva?"

"I'm all right. I'm anxious, but all right."

"Good," I said, settling into a comfortable position on the bed. She found a spot on the floor.

"So," she said.

"So," I repeated. She looked divine, even in her white tank top and ripped up, faded jean shorts. She could probably make even long johns look sexy.

"Do you have any senior confessions?" I hinted.

"Like what?"

"Like the fact that you've wanted me ever since you first saw me at that party, and now that you'll never see me again, you want to give me something to remember you by."

Her laughter began slowly, then escalated.

"Frankly, I don't think it's that damn funny," I said, sulking.

The seriousness of my voice made her stop.

"Don't be such a baby," she said, coming toward me on her knees. She stroked my face, and as she leaned close to me, I could smell her Nite Queen oil. It had grown to be my favorite.

She kissed me, and it was everything that I thought it would be. Her lips were soft and succulent. I slid my tongue into her mouth, searching her sweetness. She wrapped her arms around my neck as I slid to the floor, kneeling in front of her. Her taut body melted into mine, and I wasn't ashamed of the hard-on that pressed into her concave femininity. Slowly I began the quest of lowering us to the floor, pulling her close to me.

Zoe pulled away from me, and with a tear in her eye, kissed me lightly.

"Thank you, Fred. I'm sorry, but thank you."

Then she got up and hurried out of the room, leaving my dick pointing north and my heart in my hands.

*   *   *

Five years later, I was still hanging around the City of Brotherly Love. The life that I had come to know here was more alive than Delaware, but it was close enough for me to get home to my folks if they needed me. I had begun teaching at a junior high school in North Philly after finishing my Master's at Penn. I was really digging my job, and I knew that it was my calling.

In those five years, I hadn't been able to forget Zoe. I wasn't even angry with her anymore for that last night. I had been angry for months, though. That anger had led me to delete unread every E-mail that she had sent. Then, she stopped writing. I knew that I'd blown it. Thinking back, she never said that she'd wanted to cross that line. She'd been honest from the jump. I'd been the one thinking about sex. If I ever heard from her, I vowed that I'd act like a chaste monk just to keep her in my life.

One day, like an answer to my silent prayer, I received a letter in the mail. The scent on the large cream envelope was Nite Queen. Inside was an invitation to a launch party for a new book. Zoe was doing the PR.

I walked around like a nervous punk for the next two weeks. I tried to forget about her, but my mind kept wandering back to that last day. Of course, there had been other women since then. They had willingly opened wide and let me come inside. But even then, it was Zoe's face I saw when they rode me, her scent that I smelled as I buried my face between their breasts, her voice I heard when they screamed my name as they came.

The night of the book signing arrived. It had been a long time since I'd seen her, and I wondered what she'd look like. Time had a way of changing people when memory had not. But I knew that wouldn't be the case with Zoe.

Allie's Jazz Bistro at Second and Bainbridge was in walking distance from my loft at Third and Market. Allie, the owner, stood near the bar, eyeing the crowd. She smiled when she saw me.

"Hey, Fred," she greeted me warmly.

"Allie, you're beautiful, as usual."

"Don't start, sugar. I'm old enough to be your big sister," she chuckled. "The author's from Philly. Do you know her?"

"No," I said scanning the room. "I got an invitation from her publicist."

"Oh, Zoe. She's a doll."

"Yeah, we went to Temple together. Have you seen her?"

"She's around here somewhere. Uh-oh. Sounds like I've got competition," Allie joked.

I didn't answer. I gave her a light kiss on the cheek and went looking for Zoe. I spotted her in the crowd, standing near the piano, looking better than I remembered—fuller and more womanly, her chocolate skin glowing. She wore a black strapless dress that conformed to her curves. Her silver and onyx jewelry was as hip as her stylish dress. And she was still sporting that sexy natural. As I walked toward her, she turned and met my gaze.

She spoke before I'd found my voice.

"Fred," she said, reaching for me.

"Zoe," I answered, pulling her to me. "You look incredible."

"So do you. You feel good, too," she said, squeezing my arm.

"I've been running," I admitted, trying not to blush.

"So I started a habit that stuck, huh?" Zoe joked, giving me one of her looks.

"If only you knew," I said.

Then we stepped back and looked at each other. I was glad I'd worn my black linen suit and gray silk T-shirt because we looked like we belonged together. I was freshly showered and shaved, though I'd left the ghost of a beard that I hoped made me look more mature. I'd tried to grow dreadlocks in homage to Zoe's natural, but my hair was too soft for them to take on the powerful look that Zoe would appreciate. Nonetheless, I hoped that she could see that the boy she'd left that day was long gone.

At twenty-seven, the nervous insecurity was erased from her eyes, and her smile was easy. She looked softer and even more inviting. I could feel the familiar stirring in the pit of my stomach.

As it flowed out toward my groin, I remembered my monk's promise, and I fought to calm myself.

"Look," I said, breaking the silence. "About that time before graduation. I was out of line. I shouldn't have tried to . . . It wasn't what you wanted."

Zoe was silent, just looking at me. Then she came toward me and kissed me on the cheek. "Don't leave without me," she said, walking away into the crowd.

I watched her all night as she moved about, schmoozing and running shit. When she stepped up to the mic to introduce the president of a local book club, I envisioned her stepping up to my mic and grabbing it with the same confidence. I shook the thought out of my head, thinking of monasteries. While the book club president introduced the author, Zoe came and stood next to me.

"The author comes across well, doesn't she?"

"Yeah. A lot of authors can't read their own work. She's good, though."

She nodded in agreement.

"So you're doing it, huh?"

"I'm trying," she said, scanning the room.

A few hours later, as bibliophiles filtered out of Allie's, clutching their autographed books, Zoe basked in the afterglow of success.

"Allie, thank you for everything. I'll talk to you soon," Zoe said as we headed out the door.

"Catch you later, Allie."

"All right, Daddy," she said, squeezing my shoulder.

"Keep it up, and I just might stay here."

Zoe pulled me out the door, saying, "Come on, loverboy. Take me to South Street."

We strolled arm in arm up the avenue to a restaurant with an outdoor deck, then we sat along the edge, watching the waves of people ebb and flow near us. After ordering a bottle of wine, we settled in to talk.

"So how's teaching? Is it everything that you thought it would be?" Zoe wanted to know.

"It is. My kids are great, but it does get hard sometimes, though," I answered, leaning back in my seat and getting comfortable.

"How?" Zoe asked, turning her gaze from the crowd of people drifting past to me.

"They're so needy, not just financially, although that's a big factor, but emotionally, too. Sometimes it's draining, but the good days outnumber the bad, so I'm sticking to it." I wanted to talk about Zoe, so I asked, "What about you, Queen of PR? You had a big turnout."

"That's because I have a big mouth," she laughed. "That's definitely an asset in this business. I'm living my dream. No time clock to punch. Good parties. Great money. Fantastic contacts. Freedom."

"It sounds like you have the best of all worlds," I said, proud of her.

"I guess," she responded pensively, taking a sip of her wine.

We sat quietly before I took the plunge, tiptoeing near the line of my oath but not crossing it.

"Are you down with brothers again?" I asked, hoping I sounded casual.

"When I have the time," she admitted, putting down her glass and looking at me.

"Why is it that every time we talk, I end up with more questions than when I started?"

"Because you don't listen closely enough."

"You speak in riddles," I said, frustrated.

"Well, hear my heart," she answered, putting her hand over mine.

I sighed, threw back my wine, refilled the glass, then sat back and looked at Zoe. I wondered what could I do for her that no one else could. What could I give her that was unique? I couldn't believe that I was competing for a small space in her world. For an occasional phone call when she could squeeze me in? For steamy trysts on brief trips to Philly? Fuck it. However she'd have me, I decided that I'd take it. I needed Zoe. I needed the calm that surrounded me when she was with me. I needed the optimism that she brought to my life. To hell with monastic oaths.

I put some cash down on the table and closed my hand around Zoe's, pulling her from her seat. We walked down South Street to Third, turning and heading toward my apartment.

Burning with desire, our fingers formed a lattice as we strolled under the Philadelphia night sky with Zoe whistling "Walk, Don't Run." When we got to my loft, Zoe went into the bathroom while I lit candles that smelled of night rain. John Coltrane's "Naima" filled the dimly lit room, and I sat on a barstool at the counter thinking of Zoe and the future, hoping that the two would collide cosmically.

She emerged from the bathroom with her face scrubbed clean. My stomach quivered as I beheld her natural splendor. She was all woman, and I felt like a vulnerable boy as she approached me. She reached for me through the darkness, and as our hands connected, the physical and emotional distance between us diminished.

I pulled her to me, turning her around as I slowly unzipped her dress. Parting the fabric slowly, I traced a finger down her spine. Easing out of the dress, she turned to face me, and I saw unadulterated innocence on her face. Suddenly, I felt older and wiser, and as I lifted Zoe and carried her to my waiting bed, I needed to show her that I could be the man she desired.

She peeled off my clothes as we kissed slowly, with years of pent-up passion threatening to break through our control. The silk sheets entangled us as she rolled me on my back and began kissing my neck and chest. I'd never had someone suck my nipples before, but that's what she did while stroking my dick. Sliding her body between my legs, she eased down until her face lingered over my throbbing penis. Starting from the base, she licked me like an ice cream cone. Arriving at the head, she flicked her tongue around the rim before taking me fully into her mouth and burying her face in my groin. Up and down she went, creating a vacuum by expelling extra air. She sucked me with a fervor as if to make up for lost time. I began pumping into her mouth slowly, feeling myself being pulled to orgasm. The more I groaned, the harder she sucked, faster and faster, up and down until I came, deep into the back of her throat.

I shifted our positions and had her on her back with her legs around my shoulders. I licked her thin strip of pubic hair, and I inhaled the sweet scent of her, then tasted her juices. She was dripping with wetness. Laughing and moaning, she wiggled her hips in pleasure as I unrolled my tongue, letting it dance all over her clit, which had grown thick with blood. As I alternated between gentle and hard strokes, she responded by bucking her hips and writhing in my mouth. I sensed the first wave of an impending orgasm, and I felt her body beginning to stiffen. When her hips began to shake and I felt the trembling between her legs, I knew I'd pleased Zoe as much as she'd pleased me.

I fell asleep thinking about what I would make her for breakfast, how we'd spend the day. Zoe nestled on my chest. As far as I was concerned, it didn't make a difference whether I had kept my monk's promise or not because I had already been to heaven tonight.

I held her in my arms, and we lay together talking, gathering strength. Zoe mapped out her life's plan for me, giving ages for each milestone. I wondered if there was a mile marker in there for love, but she didn't mention it, so I didn't ask.

* * *

Daylight danced across my bed as I sat up, rubbing my eyes. I walked to the dresser to find some shorts and a T-shirt that would fit Zoe.

"Zoe, some workout clothes are on the bed. I don't know what you're going to do about sneakers, though," I called out.

I pulled my shorts and T-shirt on, then sat on the bed to lace up my own sneakers. I walked out past the drywall divider and scanned the room for her.

"Zoe," I called, walking toward the bathroom. It was empty. Zoe was gone.

I scanned the apartment for a note. Checked my machine for a message but found nothing. All I had of Zoe was the scent of Nite Queen on my sheets.

I sat down on the edge of my bed, put my head in my hands, and cried.

REGINALD HARRIS

Prelude To . . .

*D*amn, man, why these motherfuckers got to be all up in my grill
and shit? Half of Baltimore in here tonight, most of 'em lookin at me.
Don't need none of these tired-ass motherfuckers come up in this bar
all the time lookin at me. Come down here from out Towson, Owings
Mills in the county, someplace, comin downtown lookin for what they
wives can't give 'em. Like that one pretendin not to look when I catch
him. Hunched over, not talkin to nobody, just lookin, tryin to front.
Shit, he want to be alone, what he doin up in Robert's on a Thursday
night, okay? Everybody know this is the place to go to get your drink
on, get set for the weekend. Maybe he new. I don't remember seein him
before . . . but why he act like he want to be alone in here? Look good,
too, for a big guy, clean, sharp, in shape. But he one a them lookin
motherfuckers, tho', all eyes. Sit there, won't never say nothin, even if
he do want to step to you. Can tell that shit from the way he starin at
that beer like it goin to run away on his ass when I gets close to him.
Don't trip, yo, I'm just goin to take a piss. I ain't gonna mess with you
none. But maybe when I comes back, you know? Give the niggah a
chance, right? See what up . . .

*   *   *

Damn, this conference is kicking my ass. I'm sick of it already. Don't know if I can make it one more day. Don't even know why I came in here. I don't need this drink, this noise, this smoke. Just wanted to see some other black guys, I guess. Sitting at that dinner with those vendors last night . . . they give me the creeps. Makes my skin crawl the way they act, always trying to sell even after hours. Laughing in your face but their eyes are dead. Assuming everyone agrees with them, or even knows what the hell they are talking about. I missed this, the music, the rhythm. Seeing the way black men move, dance, laugh, and talk to each other. God, I wish I were home. Not that anyone there would notice. But at least I'd be around people I knew. I guess I should be used to it, but I hate being the stranger all the time. Always the new guy, the one who gets stared at wherever they walk in. Like here. Like that guy down the bar. He looks so familiar . . . was he in that restaurant last night? I don't remember. He keeps looking at me like he knows me or something. I better not stare. Who knows who these people are in here, what's going on, what kind of games are going on all around me. Still, there is something about him . . . shit, he's coming this way. . . . oh, okay, he's just going to the back. I certainly didn't come in here to get into anything, or talk to anybody. Just want to sit and enjoy being around people like me for a change. Try to remember who I am. Get my head back on before tomorrow. I can't wait to get out of this damned town and go home.

* * *

'Scuse me, big guy, didn't mean to bump into you.

That's okay.

Crowded up in this camp.

Yes, yes it is.

Yeah . . .

Uh . . . is it always like this?

Every Thursday night. People like to get they weekend started early.

Hmmm . . .

You not from here? Where you from?

Chicago. I'm originally from St Louis, but I'm living in Chicago.

St. Louis? Yeah . . . I can see that. You got that St. Louis smile.

What the hell does *that* mean?

You guys from the St.–L got a look, a little wild shit in your eyes. Gots that "Country Grammar" and shit.

Oh, yeah, right. Nelly. . . . But you know a lot of other people are from St. Louis, too. Miles Davis was from there . . . well, from Alton, outside St. Louis, but still . . .

. . . See, see, now that's what I'm sayin! Another wild-ass niggah! I'm kiddin', yo, I'm kiddin. My name's Bobby, man.

Kent.

Kent? Like Clark Kent? *Superman* and shit?

It's my mother's maiden name. My friends call me Key. Kent Edwards. K. E.

Cool . . . that's cool. . . . So what bring you up in here, Key?

I'm here for work, for a conference. Combination training, conference and trade show. Been here for almost a week. I leave tomorrow afternoon. I have to go to Charlotte next month for the same thing.

That computer show down the convention center?

That's part of it, yes.

You work with computers?

Yeah. . . .

Yo, you down with computers, right? So, like, look—how come I can't get my scanner to work right? I checked it, see, hooked it up right and everything, okay, but it still don't want to work.

Uh, gee, umm . . . I don't know, Bobby, that could be a lot of things. Scanners can be kinda funny, you know. And they're all slightly different. You have to know exactly what you're dealing with, what software you're using, and everything else. I . . . um . . . I don't really do much work with PCs and scanners, I'm more into the larger systems—local area networks, making sure routers are acting properly, that kind of thing. We also work with the city and different counties back home, working on their systems, making sure parts of the whole state can function. You know?

Oh, oh . . . Oh yeah, right . . . Okay.

Um . . . you're from here?

East Side, near Central.

Okay. And that's where you work, "Webbers?" Is that what your shirt says?

Yeah, it's from the restaurant.

You're a chef?

Nah . . . I could be if I wanted to, right? Some of 'em been showin me a little sumpin sumpin. . . . But it just someplace to make some money so I can go to school. Hey—you, uh, you want another beer?

Yeah, thanks. But I can pay for it. You being a student and all.

Nah, man, don't sweat it. Got paid today. I'm cool. Yo, Miss Darryl! Two lites, man. . . . Thanks.

*   *   *

One look told me all I needed to know. This guy, this kid, he's young: 20 . . . 21, maybe, 22. One hell of a body on this boy, though. Nothing but muscle, dark skin just glowing. . . .I'll bet he's got that body 'cause all he does is work out. No life, probably, just go to work then hit the gym, that's it. He has to have that body 'cause he doesn't have much of a face. Nothing but lines and angles—and that scar. Probably still living with his mother. Yeah, I know this guy, I've seen his kind before. This motherfucker has Trouble written all over him. I don't believe I'm doing this. I must be more tired than I thought. I should've gone back to the hotel an hour ago, to get some sleep. Instead here I am jammed up in this place talking to some thug. If I were home, I wouldn't even give him the time of day. But tonight . . . why not? It's only talk. Isn't that the real reason why I came in here, just to talk to someone. I'm leaving tomorrow afternoon, I'll never see him again, what the fuck? Hell, he probably doesn't even go to the gym. Plays basketball every day, I bet, or runs the streets. Probably started in jail—I can see him getting pulled for selling drugs or something. Shit, he's probably even working now, some kind of hustler, probably trying to work me. Can't figure what kind of game he's playing, though. I don't understand why he's buying me a beer . . . must be some new thing. What the hell, I'll play along, why not. Just keep one hand on my wallet. Sometimes he actually looks almost lost, like a little boy with gentle eyes. Wounded even. A boy with a fucking diesel body, but still . . .

* * *

Where are you going to school?

I ain't in school yet, man. Tryin to get there.

Oh, okay.

I want to get into that College of Art uptown, graphic design program they got up there.

Re . . . really? College of *art?*

Yeah, I always liked to draw, you know? Thought I should get serious, right, see if I can make some money doin what I like to do.

That's great. That's really wonderful. Good luck. Thanks for the beer.

No prob, no prob. Must be nice, your job. Travel around, not have to pay for it.

Well, it's not all free! I have to pay up front most of the time. They'll reimburse me for some things—pay me back, you know.

I know what *"reimburse"* mean, yo. . . .

Yeah, sorry. . . . Uh . . . The job, it, it's okay. It's a job. Sometimes it gets boring, all the travel. I usually don't see too much on these trips beyond the airport, meeting rooms, and the hotel. I seldom get to see what the city I'm in is really like, unless I stay after the sessions are over, or go out ahead of time. And that I have to pay for. When I get to Charlotte, since I know people there, I might see something, but usually I don't.

You found this place, all right. You been here before?

No, it's my first time here. Last night I was heading to this restaurant with a vendor we do a lot of business with, right, and we passed this other bar. I knew by the kind of guys going in there what kind of place it was. . . .

Right, right . . .

. . . So after dinner I go back to the hotel, change, and head back out. But I didn't like it. The music was too fast, Techno, you know? No bass line, no soul.

Word . . . I know where you was. Hate that fuckin place. Only been up in there one time. Was wavin my cash all up in the bartender's white-ass face all night while all these white motherfuckers got served. Bullshit, man.

I know what you mean. I saw only one other black guy in there. And you know what? I said hello to him, right? I mean, I'm just being polite, sort of just to say, "Hey, I'm one, too?" He looked at me like I'd slapped him and damn near ran away.

Yep, word, that's what they like up in there.

So I grabbed a paper from the stack inside the door as I left and looked for a bar listing and a map. This was the only one that said "mainly African-American." I needed to see some black people, you know? So here I am.

I gets so tired of dealing with them down at the restaurant. Arrogant motherfuckers orderin people around, treatin us back in the kitchen like goddamned dogs and shit. When I go out and clear the tables sometimes, them folks just look right through me, like I'm a glass or somethin. Them rich motherfuckers don't even leave no tips for the waitresses, neither, as hard as they busting they asses for 'em and shit. It's fucked up, man. . . . And now niggahs be doin it, too. Give 'em a little money they act like they shit don't stink. Shit's fucked up, man.

I always try to speak to people, even guys clearing the table, just out of courtesy, you know? My parents always told me to be polite to people.

You know that's right, man.

So you're going to go to art school here? I'd thought you'd want to head up to New York. or something. Go where the action is.

I'm a get there. No doubt. Got a friend, Brian, right, moved up there, last year, no, no, two years ago, right? Brian, see, he done told me before I make that move I need to get my shit together, you know? Don't just run on up there, have somethin for 'em, right, bring it to 'em. NYC can kick your ass you ain't ready, man.

That's true. You know, uh . . . you could also go someplace else, like, well, Chicago. I mean, we've got some art schools out there, too, right, not too bad. Great museums. You'd like it there.

You making me an offer, yo? You gonna put me up, I come out there?

Well, no, I mean, I'm just saying—

It's all right, man, it's all right. I'm just messin with you. Don't trip.

Okay. And I'm *not* tripping. But I am serious, though, you really should get out of town, see the world while you're young, you know? First chance I got to get away, I took it. I went to school in Virginia. I could've stayed in St. Louis, but I wanted to see something else, experience what the world was like.

Yeah, yeah, I see what you sayin. I never really been noplace. I been here all my life.

That's a shame. Not even Washington? It's not that far from here.

Well, yeah, everyone goes to D.C., right? But that was just for bus trips to the Smithsonian and all when I was in school. Or hookin up with friends to go down to clubs and shit. Not like just to go and spend some time down there, or someplace else, like you doin.

Well, like I said, my trips aren't all that exciting. Fly in, do what I have to do, fly out. It's gotten tiresome.

Right! Right . . .

And because I'm one of the few blacks working for Tern-Tech, I'm usually the one that gets sent to these things. Shows everyone else how "progressive" they are, right? Makes themselves look good. To me, it only means being the only dark face in a sea of white most of the time. This trip I just couldn't take it anymore. So here I am. . . . Let me buy the beer this time, okay?

Okay.

Two more, please?

* * *

Damn this motherfucker talk white! Ain't met too many niggahs up in here like this, yo. I bet he really want a white man, too, up in here on the DL and shit, fuckin slummin. Nah, he would be over at GCB like he was before, he wanted that. Maybe he in here lookin for somebody to chill with, just to kick it. Probably wants a motherfucker in that fat ass, too. Movin a little stiff even now, like he got a dick shoved up there already. But he ain't stepped to me yet, tho, so what up? And he really talkin to me, too, trying to, listenin to what I'm sayin. Now he singin along to this new Ronnie Size joint. Ain't that some shit. Who is this motherfucker, anyways?

* * *

I guess the bars where you live at must be nicer than this, huh?

Seems like black bars are black bars everywhere, um . . . Bobby. There's a place just like this at home: Same long room, bar along one side, a few tables and chairs on the other, open space in the back. Same crowd on the weekend. Except you all have a pool table back there, we don't. Otherwise, this place seems very familiar, like I *have* been here before. Same music, same guys, only different, like I'm in a dream or something. Some people in here look like guys I'd see back home. Their names are just on the tip of my tongue.

Word?

Yeah. Like you. You look very familiar to me. . . . Sure I haven't seen you somewhere before? Some magazine or something?

Now you shittin me, man . . . I ain't no model.

I don't know, with that body and all underneath that shirt, you could be. You work out, right?

I just play a lot of ball, do a lot of liftin and movin of boxes at work, you know.

Hmmm . . . well, looks like you work out. You look good.

I'm all right. What you do, hit the gym at the hotel where you stay?

Nah. I used to be in good shape, played football in college. But that was a long time ago. Now I think this old body's falling apart.

Old? What you talkin about old. You ain't old, man.

Oh really? How old do you think I am?

Uh . . . you can't be more than . . . thirty? Thirty-five? What? Why you laughin at me?

I just turned *forty-five,* bro . . .

Get the fuck outta here! Dayum, yo, you look *good!*

Thanks . . . I think.

No, no, no, I'm serious. You look real good. No lines in your face and you keep your shit together. Still look like you could be on somebody's team. And no gray hair at all.

That's why I keep it short like this, you know, so you don't see it. I *do* have gray hair.

I don't see none.

Uh . . . it's. . . . Some places. Never mind.

Oh, oh, okay, I get it. . . . someplace your boy at home see but nobody else, right? I get it.

What "boy at home"? I don't have anybody at home.

Come on, Key . . . you got nobody waitin for you when you get in from them trips?

No, I don't. It's not easy, you know. It's not easy finding someone, not easy keeping someone. And since I'm in and out of town so much, I don't think I'd be all that good a partner, either. Always packing or unpacking, I'm never home. Who would want someone like that?

Somebody might.

You find him, Bobby, you let me know, okay? And what about you? Who've you got waiting for you?

Nobody, man. Too many of these motherfuckers out here playin games.

Come on, Bobby . . . I'm sure you've had offers.

Niggahs be stepping to me all the time, talking about how tight I look and shit. But all they want is one thing, you know. Not that I got anything against that, you know what I'm sayin?

Yeah. . . .

But sometime you want somethin more than that, you know. And I ain't no niggah's prize, man.

Sure you are, you're very attractive.

Fuck, man, look in that mirror. I sees what I look like: too dark, fuckin scar across my face . . .

I . . . I wondered about that, but . . .

Got it when I was a kid. Some motherfucker jumped me, cut me before he see he was lookin for somebody else.

Damn . . . that's awful.

They don't play over in them projects, man. It was rough even to just live close to them. You didn't see me cryin when they imploded that shit couple years ago.

I'm sorry . . . But you know, you look . . . well, this sounds like a fucking line . . .

What?

Well I was going to say that you look African, you know? I mean like from the continent, and all? Except for the cornrows, I don't know if they're doing that over there. . . . But you've got that smooth, dark skin, the strong planes in your face. It's almost like you were carved from ebony or something. You have a very strong face. I'm sure you've seen people who look like you in books or on TV shows about Africa. In fact, I was surprised when you spoke to me that you didn't have an accent.

Shit . . .

No, I'm serious. Except for the cornrows, I thought you might be from the motherland.

You think I'm some kind of Mandingo motherfucker, is that what you sayin?

No, no, man, that's not what I'm saying at all.

Just like them people at the restaurant . . . lickin they lips like you was on the menu. Look like they want you to slide your dick out and feed it to them right there at the table for dessert.

No, man, I'm not trying to say anything like that at all. I was trying to pay you a compliment.

Sorry, man. Sorry. I just . . . I guess I just get things kinda turned around and twisted up myself, you know. I know you didn't mean no harm and all. My bad, okay?

Okay. But I think I need to get myself out of here. I've got one more session in the morning, then have to fly out in the afternoon. I need to get to bed, get some sleep.

Yeah, me too. I'm on the crew openin up tomorrow.

*   *   *

Why the hell am I doing this? What's wrong with me? This guy . . . I don't know. He could be anything, this whole thing could be some kind of a come-on, and he could be ready to roll me or something. He looks like he could just as soon fuck me up as fuck me. I try to pay him a compliment, he gets bent out of shape, what's up with that? Black men . . . I don't know. We're so damned sensitive, can't say anything to them . . . us . . . whatever. Now he's looking hurt, like I shot his dog or something. He probably thinks . . . who knows what he thinks. And why do I care what he thinks, anyway? Key, you're too damned much of a nice guy, just like everybody says. Going on these trips when they say jump, being the company's fucking token. Talking to guys like this when you should stay as far away from them as possible. Trying to save the world. Gonna come back and bite you in the ass one day, and you know it. This poor kid . . . he'd be lucky if they let him in the door, he tries to go to that art school. Rough, unpolished, quick-tempered. Wouldn't last five minutes without someone to look out for him up there. Poor guy. Can take care of himself on the streets better than I ever could, but in the suites? In school? Damn, he's just asking for a shitload of trouble for himself.

*   *   *

When were you planning on going to art school, next semester?

Maybe in about a year or so. Got to get my money right and all. I want to pay for most of it myself since it's just me and my moms, right?

What made you want to go to art school, anyway?

My moms. I was always drawin, readin comic books, watchin cartoons. My moms always encouraged me, told me if that's what I liked to do, keep goin. Bought me crayons, pencils, paper . . . took me to the library for drawin books. She thought I could do somethin with it.

That's wonderful.

Yeah, she good people.

I don't know anyone at the schools in Chicago, but I could ask around. I'm sure they have some kind of financial aid, too.

Yeah, that would be cool. And maybe I'd get a chance to do a drawin for you or somethin.

Me? Why would you want to do that?

I been lookin at you from when I came in, right. You got an interestin look man, kinda different.

It's because I'm the only one in here in a buttoned-down shirt. At least I took off the tie. So you were watching me? Bumping into me wasn't an accident.

Busted?

Yep.

You was watchin me, too, so you busted, too, yo. I could tell you was from out of town, too.

You can always tell the new guy.

No, not that. You look different somehow, I don't know. . . . Maybe I kinda always notice guys that're bigger than me, tall and broad like you. And I don't know, you seem like you not tryin to front, neither.

Thanks. There are a lot of guys better looking than me in this place.

Where they at?

Stop it!

For true. You had that "Don't fuck with me" look on your face, tho'.

I didn't think so.

Yep, you did. I didn't know whether I should say somethin to you or not.

I'm glad you did.

So am I, man. You're not as mean as you look.

What?

Kiddin, yo, kiddin. . . .

* * *

He lookin at me like he 'bout to cry and shit. Like ain't nobody talked to him in like forever. Like for all of what he got he still lonely. He go back to his hotel beat his shit off and that it. Ain't had nobody in a long time. Like I been with somebody lately! Hard on a niggah lookin for somebody decent, man. Everybody playin games, just lookin for some dick or somethin. Here this motherfucker come, seem down and all, and he gots to leave tomorrow. Ain't that a bitch? Life be fuckin with a niggah, yo.

*   *   *

You've got some very fine looking men in this town. Like you.

Too many of 'em around here are kind of beat-down lookin. I'm serious about wantin to draw you.

Is this how you pick up guys: "Let me paint your picture?" Is that the line you use?

It ain't no line, man.

Would this be a nude picture?

I can do that, too, now.

Only if the artist was naked, too.

Aw'right, yo, aw'right . . .

I'm just messing with *you* for a change.

Uh huh . . . yeah. . . . Keep it up . . .

Oh, it's up all right.

What?

Nothing. . . . I don't know about guys around here being beat-down, but I'm certainly beat. All this traveling's getting to me.

You talkin to me 'bout me needin to get out of town, what's up with you? Maybe you need to stop goin around to conferences and shit? If you not enjoyin it no more, what's the point?

Oh, I don't know. Money, I guess . . . no, that's not it. I mean I do get paid but . . . I guess I'm just not sure of what else I would do, you know? I mean you, you know what you want: go to school, go into this career, start your life. That's wonderful. Me, I'm at that place where you start wondering what the point of it all is, why you're doing what you're doing. I've even forgotten how I started in this business, or why. I'm just going through the motions. I'm not quite sure where I want to go or what I want to do next.

Damn . . . keep talkin like that and you *are* old, man. Gots to be somethin interests you?

Well, sometimes I volunteer, help my sister out at this training center for kids, you know? Teach them how to use computers, even a little bit about how to repair them. It's fun, but they're kids. All they want to do is play games, you know, go on the Internet and listen to music, watch videos. . . . But some of them are really into it, want to make it a career. Some are even helping out the younger kids with their homework and all. It's really . . . I was about to say "inspiring," but that's such a tired word . . . but I guess that's what it is. Maybe I'd like to do that. Help Linda do that. I think I'd like to do that.

Then why don't you?

I . . . I don't know. You know, I never really thought this through until now, until just now, sitting here, talking to you. That's funny.

Always glad to help a brotha out, you know.

Thanks. You know . . . Bobby, I'm just noticing your eyelashes. You have got to have the longest eyelashes I have ever seen.

Uh . . .

It's a compliment. They're really beautiful. And your cornrows are beautiful, too. I like that design, that zigzag thing you got going on up there.

You got some pretty eyes, too, yo.

Thank you. Bloodshot, probably, I'm beat.

Well, yeah, you do look tired. No offense.

It's okay. It's been a long week. I guess I better get out of here.

How you get here? You couldn't've walked all the way up here from the hotel?

No, I drove. I've got a rental. But thanks for looking out for me.

Maybe I should head out with you and shit, make sure you make it.

No, no, I'm okay. Finish your beer. Thanks.

Hey, man, no problem . . . I'm done.

Uh . . . okay.

*   *   *

Why does he want to follow me to my car? Is he really going to follow me out? I don't understand it. Why did you even bring up art schools in Chicago? So he could come out there and you could teach him English? Please . . . I'm letting the little head do the thinking for the big head. It's that body, I know it, that beautiful skin. It's like I can taste his dark chocolate already. Bobby . . . melts in your mouth, not in your hand. Looks hard on the outside, rich, creamy center. Jesus. I bet he's a screamer, too. Plays that tough guy game to get in and out of his neighborhood but cuts loose behind closed doors. Oh, I shouldn't, I shouldn't . . . that damned router configuration thing tomorrow morning, then the trip to

the airport . . . it's been so damn long, though. I'm not sure if I remember
what to do. Just like riding a bicycle, so they say. Once you learn . . . And
that black ass looks like it would be one hell of a ride. Just don't tell his
homies, right? Yeah, I know the drill. That is, if that's what's really hap-
pening here. If that's what he wants. I'm tired enough I could do either
way, take him to the hotel or just go back alone. Doesn't matter to me,
whatever. . . . God I'm such a fake I even lie to my own self. I'm gonna
regret this . . . but, just look at those lips. . . .

* * *

Been rainin.

Yeah. Seems to have stopped, though.

Look at them streetlights flashin, the way it look in the water
in the middle of the street, them clouds heavy and hard, like they
made of steel.

The lights from the buildings glowing, shining down like stars.
It's beautiful in a way. I love big cities at night. There's always a
hum somewhere, a buzz, some kind of excitement just around
the corner. It really is beautiful.

Word.

This is my car. See, I could've found my way around the corner
on my own.

Hey, no problem, man. The mayor say we gotta keep you
tourists happy. Make y'all wanna come back.

Oh, I want to come back, all right. Are you always this . . .
what's the word I want . . . ? "Friendly" to guys from out of town?
Or maybe I should say "fast" instead of "friendly"?

What you mean, "fast"?

Walking me to my car? "Pretty eyes?" Come on, man. . . .

Shit, man, what about you? "African face and long-ass eye-lashes . . ."

We both of us are full of shit, aren't we?

Speak for youself, yo. I saw you lookin at me in the bar, too. Didn't look like you was goin to say anything.

I probably wasn't, since I have to leave tomorrow. But I don't know, I guess I shouldn't have . . . I mean, I was staring at you, I know.

It was cool.

Maybe I would've said something if you hadn't. I don't know . . . I wish I didn't have that meeting tomorrow morning. We could . . . keep talking . . .

I know what you mean. I got that early shift, too.

Yeah.

Yeah.

Then I have to leave in the afternoon.

Word.

And who knows when I'll be back?

True, true. You shoulda come up to Robert's when you first got here.

But then after I'd met you, who knows how much of the conference I would've gotten to. You seem like a major distraction, like trouble. From the East Side.

I ain't no trouble, man. No trouble at all.

Think about what I said about going someplace else for school. And I was serious about helping you out. Here's my card. Let me write my home number and address on the back.

Got a piece of paper? Give you my cell.

Yeah, I think so. . . . Here.

Thanks.

Keep in touch. If you ever do get out my way, I'll show you around.

Thanks. You don't have to do this, you know. The school thing, I mean.

I know, but I want to. You seem like a good person, a good kid.

I'm twenty years old, man. I ain't no kid no more.

That's what you think.

That's what I *know.*

Well, enjoy being twenty while you can, Bobby. One day you'll look around and you won't be anymore.

You stop thinkin of yourself as being old, yo. I won't believe you old till I see that gray hair you hidin.

Okay, it's a deal. We'll even shake hands on it.

* * *

Soft hands. Nice. Not all hard and callused up like mine. Big solid body. Bet he feel good, too . . . I probably fit right into him, he hold me and shit. Been so long, man, been so long. Gets so tired, man, gets so tired. Don't even want to fuck sometimes, you know what I'm sayin, just lay up with somebody in they arms, holdin you and shit while you sleep. Just holdin you, listenin to the sound in they chest when they talk, like listenin to the radio with some real deep bass. That's all I want sometime, you know, that's all I want. Hang on to me, yo, hold me, man, just hold me . . .

* * *

. . . to have someone in my arms again, to be held. I'm always spin-ning, you know, moving, running. I never stop. Never take the time for anything, or anyone. And I'm so damned scared. What am I afraid of? Not this guy, not Bobby. He is exactly who he is. Me, me, I'm the one who doesn't know what he wants, what to do. And it's not like I've never come into a place and met someone and then flew out. Used to do that all the time. Gave it up because . . . who remembers. And now? Strong hands, nice fingers, but still gentle. Seems strange with that hard face and body. I wish I didn't have to leave tomorrow. I'd love to just wrap him in my arms . . .

* * *

You can let go of my hand whenever you want.

I was 'bout to say that to you, Key.

You got some long-ass fingers, bro.

Big feet, too . . . lemme stop . . . Shit, you ain't the only one wearing size twelves out here, you know what I'm sayin?

Must look pretty strange, two guys holding hands out here on the street, huh?

Not in this neighborhood. Folks are used to this. More.

More?

Yeah, more.

Like what?

Like this. . . .

YOLANDA JOE

Don't Stop 2 You Get Enuf

*D*AMN, *I NEED TO PARTY.*

The thought echoed inside Savannah's brain as she raced her BMW toward the club. Her boss had pissed her off, saddling Savannah with more work than was fair. She smiled at him anyway and thought, *If you're gonna fuck me, you jerk, the least you could do is make it feel good.*

Thinking about fucking always made Savannah think about Van.

Van knew how to make it feel good, oh yes he did.

Savannah began to fidget in the driver's seat just thinking about her ex-boyfriend's milk chocolate skin and that sexy gap between his two front teeth. Six feet tall with a magic wand that swung damn near to his kneecaps, Van oozed sex appeal. When wet and in full thrust Van felt mountainous: sharp and solid, sturdy, as he plunged in and out of Savannah.

She stopped her BMW short at the red light she'd almost run.

Savannah's heart pined. *When we made love we shook the roof, baby.*

She thought back to six months ago, that last night they had been together. Savannah's naked body was clothed only by the moonlight that wrapped itself around her swelling breasts, then slicked its way between her legs. Savannah was proud of her forty-year-old frame with breasts still taut and ripe, succulent nipples; her hips womanly and curvaceous.

Van had loved her body. It was like the body of a twenty-five-year-old, he had often told her.

Guess that's why your black ass ran off with a twenty-one-year-old, Savannah thought.

Her mind replayed their lovemaking. Savannah saw herself spreading her legs for Van, her favorite lover, whose dick filled to the size of a ten-ounce Coke bottle. He would sit back—his dick spearing the air—waiting for Savannah, sliding her inch by inch toward their prime sexual destination. Savannah was getting wet now just thinking about it. She recalled the comforting scent of cologne and sweat: a sure sign that there was a real man in the room. Savannah would slide forward, the silk sheets soft as cold cream against her skin until they'd heated them up. Savannah's neck would damn near snap off rocking hard against the pillow when she and Van got it on. A ball of fire was raging between her legs burrowing deeper and deeper until she wanted to scream. But Savannah didn't scream; she only whispered, *you mother-fucker, you.*

Turn around, Van would then demand, *let me ride this thing out.*

And Savannah would've turned a flip if Van asked her to. He just had it like that. Even now her vagina muscles contracted on hearing Van's command in her head.

Savannah shivered when she felt her body jerk forward from a hard bump from behind. But it wasn't from memory, this was real. Savannah came out of her trance. Her car was being rocked from the rear. Savannah glanced into the rearview mirror at the other driver: he was yelling and waving his hands, pointing up at the green light.

Savannah shook her head wistfully and slammed on the accelerator. *I've gotta stop daydreaming about these once-had lovers. Roxy was right.*

The thought of her best friend made Savannah smile. She was meeting Roxy and her other ace boon-coon Kay at the club.

By the time Savannah drove the remaining half mile and had the valet park her Beamer, she managed to put Van out of her mind. But she had some help; distraction in the form of a sexy little pup spinning the sounds.

"Welcome to Throwback Thursdays, y'all!" the lanky-limbed DJ yelled as he grabbed the mike, his sepia-colored body rippling with muscles. He had on an *oh so tacky it was cool* floppy crocheted hat and a pair of oversized rectangular shades. "I'm Rocking Roger and I'll be jammin this club all night long," he yelled into the mike.

Savannah maneuvered her body through the ebbing crowd. She squeezed left, brushing up against the firm ass of some business type. He grinned at her. But Savannah was too busy to throw a Colgate smile back at the brother; she was on a twofold mission. Savannah wanted to get to the bar and she wanted to scrutinize this new spin-doctor.

"We'll do a little Motown and some Sounds of Philadelphia, too," Rocking Roger promised. "Old-School Rules!"

Yeah right, Savannah thought, *he doesn't look old enough to know a thing about old-school music. Look at him. Probably born in the eighties—check out that boyish body, he's got tender bronzed nipples peeking out of his cut-up T-shirt. And just look at those slim hips, that round butt, and those tight calves. Not a sign of manly spread anywhere. And that 'fro? Too Kobe Bryant nappy. Old-schoolers know how to use a pick! No, ma'am. Rocking Roger is the Great Pretender.*

Savannah chuckled to herself as she continued to slink and slide her way to the bar. There was only one seat left and she was determined to land it. The thumping bass sound pounded inside her ears, driving her forward. Finally Savannah made it to the stool.

"You mounted that baby like a champ," a man behind her observed. He was balding, copper-skinned, fifties, dressed well but sporting a bit of a belly.

I don't want that, she thought, ignoring the high-handed come-on. Lately she hadn't been looking at anyone her age or older. Not after Van left her for that hoochie mama who looked young enough to ride public transportation with a high school bus pass. Hey—maybe that was it. Maybe that was why she'd suddenly begun to eyeball young meat. Maybe Savannah was thinking that two could play that game. She never had before, never had the nerve.

"What you gonna have, sweetness?" the bartender asked.

The bartender, now *he* was old-school; old-school tacky. He had two gold teeth in the front of his mouth that twinkled every time he smiled, which he did entirely too damn much. But Lord, could he make a drink. The martinis tasted like lightning had split open a hive after a swarm of bees finished making love and their juices spilled over and were caught in the glass.

Savannah loved the first sip of a good martini. She always sipped it no hands, scooping out the first swallow of liquor with a curling of the tongue. Savannah adored the way the silky, hot juice filled the soft insides of her mouth. She refused to swallow, nearly gagging with pleasure as she let the drink slowly slip down her throat.

"I wish you'd do me like that," the bartender murmured, leaning in close to Savannah. He grinned, showing off his jeweled teeth.

"Listen, Flash Gordon," Savannah cracked, "our contact is limited to *you pour 'em, I'll drink 'em*. Nothing more."

He stepped back, snaked his tongue out at her and grabbed his crotch in true old-school style.

Savannah shook her head at him, her bobbed hair swinging. "That ain't cute, my man."

"But we are!" a voice sang out from behind her.

Savannah turned to see Roxy and Kay. They'd been best friends since starting out in sales for Beecher and Rowe, the upscale clothing chain whose flagship store was located on the gold coast of Chicago. Kay had recently quit to be an engineer after finishing night school. Roxy was still at Beecher and Rowe full-time, but had risen to manager in the jewelry department. And Savannah was now the lingerie buyer for the entire Midwest region.

"Hey, y'all," Savannah exclaimed as the women hugged. Then, as was their tradition, each pointed out something good about the other.

"Kay," Savannah kicked it off, "you look like you've lost a little weight."

"Been damn near starving myself to death." Kay shook her head and smiled. "Roxy is slimming down, too."

Roxy put her hands on bodacious hips that were perfectly accented by a form-fitting black leather skirt. Her saddle-brown skin was glowing. Roxy had almond-shaped eyes and incredibly long lashes. "I've been working out, girl."

"With a trainer?" Savannah asked.

"*On the trainer!*" Kay joked, squatting a taste before moving her hips back and forth. Kay, barely five feet tall, was so short that it looked like she was buffing the club's hardwood floor with the seat of her skintight jeans.

"UMMMM-huh," the balding fiftyish gentleman leered, "that's why you and this one here," cutting his eyes at Savannah, "are friends. She mounts the horse and you bust the bronco."

Kay rolled her eyes, "Could we get a little space? Girl talk."

He chuckled to himself and edged away, still obviously in their business.

"Like I was about to say," Kay leaned in, talking to her girls, "this trainer Roxy's got is a fine black brother the color of coal with a dick, *she says,* as long and as thick—"

"As I want it to be," Roxy said, cutting her short, then tugging at her matching leather tank top. "Savannah, your new haircut looks good, girl. I like."

"Thank you." Savannah glanced at Roxy's arm. She grabbed her friend's wrist. "Roxy, this Movado watch is out of sight. Five bills?"

"Three with my discount." Roxy grinned.

"Are you grinning about the discount or about this trainer that you've been doing the Ab Slide with?" Savannah teased.

"The Ab Slide, the Ab Rocker, the Ab backside, the Ab six-nine . . . you name it and we've done it," Roxy shot back, beaming. "What about you, Savannah? Got any home fires burning?"

"Ain't no coal been in the oven for a long time," she answered, taking a sip of her drink. Savannah tossed a glance back up at the DJ. He'd taken off his shirt and was now shaking his hips like a blender set on "dice."

Kay was primping in the mirror behind the bar, patting down her no-frills 'fro. She noticed Savannah's trancelike state and followed her gaze. "Savannah, looks like you've got your eye on a sexy little lump of coal right now. Who's the new DJ?"

"The guy at the door said he's visiting from Memphis, related to one of the owners. Kinda young, don'tcha think?" Savannah asked, hoping her friends would agree: anything to stop the stirring in her groin every time she looked in his direction.

Like now.

Rocking Roger was drenched in sweat, jacking his body, dancing as much as DJing. Savannah felt a tingling between her legs like the ghost of sex past was kissing her thighs, reminding her of long-gone lovers. She tried to think of something else, to avert her eyes, anything to stop the surge of warm, wet feeling there. But it was all in vain.

"Yep, Savannah's got a love jones for little Will Robinson," Roxy laughed putting her arm around her friend's shoulder. "I see that mind of yours is lost in space. You should act on your sexual feelings but you won't. You're too much of a coward."

Savannah turned to face Roxy. Her tasteful strapless red dress hugged tightly to her body as she stood up. "Don't you start try-ing to signify Roxy."

"I'm not." Roxy shrugged unfazed as she hopped up onto the bar stool, slipping off one of her high heels. "I just wanted you to get up so I could sit down."

Kay started laughing, diffusing Savannah's anger.

Savannah rolled her eyes, then glanced back over at Rocking Roger, the muscles in his back rippling as he bent down to riffle through a box of albums.

"Mmmmm, look at that boo-tay," Kay lusted. "If I was only fif-teen years younger—baby boy, where were you then."

"He was probably nine years old. But damn then, hello now," Roxy challenged. "Both of y'all are too conservative. Free your-selves sexually and see how much better you'll feel. One of y'all Kizzys should take that young buck home for a one-night stand."

Kay snapped her fingers with a whip of the wrist. "I'm not a coward. I'm just careful."

"I'm not saying don't use a condom—that's Russian roulette, baby, and not a game for me or anyone I care about," Roxy cor-rected, as she slipped her foot back into her shoe. "I'm saying experiment—give yourself a thrill. Hell, *both* of y'all should take him home and wear his young butt out."

"Both of us?" Kay balked, waving the bartender over. "I need a drink for real, now."

"Two women," Savannah laughed, "that's a man's fantasy."

"Good skin-slapping, sweat-dripping, leg-shaking, toe-tapping sex is *everybody's* fantasy." Roxy responded. Then she pretended to be bored, faking a yawn, then cutting her eyes at Savannah and

Kay. "But if y'all don't have the guts, then let's just change the subject to a much tamer conversation."

"You're just gloating 'cause you're finally getting some dick on a full-time basis." Kay took a hefty swig of her drink. "I resent what you're saying and how you're bringing it."

"Why? Because I'm right?" Roxy laughed, looking more at Savannah than at Kay. "Daydreaming about past boyfriends won't satisfy a sister's longing in the present. Will it, Savannah?"

Savannah gave Roxy an evil look but didn't answer.

"Go ahead, act on what would be a primo fantasy," Roxy taunted before beginning to swivel on the stool, dancing to the music. "Do it—that is *if* either one of you have the guts."

Savannah hated it when Roxy needled her, rubbed something in. She loved her friends but Roxy had a nasty habit of knowing how to get under her skin and make a home there. Savannah pulled out her compact, freshened her lipstick, and then smoothed her dress down over her hips before turning to Roxy. "You think you know everything, don't you? Well, watch me work."

As Savannah walked out onto the dance floor, she thought, *Who's afraid? He's only a kid. Surely I could turn him on if I wanted to. Damn being conservative. Van isn't the only one who can interest a sweet young thing, is he?*

Savannah needed to answer that question for herself. So she started dancing in front of the DJ booth. Timidly at first, then more boldly. She talked her way through it in her mind. *I'm clearing a path with these curves; yeah, get back, everybody. Start to jam, girl. Hands above my head; roll the hips down, bend the knees damn near to the floor. C'mon backside, I know you haven't busted a move like this in a while. You remember? Yeah, I'm feelin' it now. My groove is back. Oh Lord, here he comes from around the DJ table. I gotta turn, give Rocking Roger my back so I won't lose my nerve. Look at Kay and Roxy yelling their fool heads off. But who's the fool? Them or me out here on the dance floor? Here I am forty-something trying to seduce a twenty-year-old.*

Savannah closed her eyes. She could feel Rocking Roger pressed hard against her hips, behind, and upper back. His dick was like a cane steady against her body, balancing her. The cane seemed to get wider and longer the more they grooved to the music. Savannah dreamed of smooth skin on skin, their tongues getting lost against each other, the heat fusing their bodies into one. Then she heard the crowd chant, "Go 'head! Go 'head!"

Then suddenly, the cane slipped away.

Savannah turned around to see Rocking Roger and Kay, grinding hard, snaking up and down on the dance floor. Savannah watched as her best friend worked the Youngblood. Kay mouthed the words, "Can't beat 'em, join 'em."

Dare I? Savannah thought. *What the hell?* Savannah hunched her body low and felt a pulling in her thighs. There wasn't a thang sexual about the feeling, either. It was pure pain. Savannah needed to take her raggedy butt to the gym. Still she saddled up to the challenge. Savannah palmed Rocking Roger's round, firm butt and squeezed, pulling herself up against him. It was a Roger sandwich with Kay and Savannah enjoying the feast.

When the music finally finished, the crowd cheered the three-some. Savannah blushed. Rocking Roger had the balls to take a bow. And Kay was jumping up and down like a jack without a box. Then Kay and Savannah hugged and sauntered back over to the bar.

"We showed you," Savannah said, a bit embarrassed at how childish she sounded. *But so what,* Savannah thought, *saying it felt good.*

"You showed yourselves *somewhat,*" Roxy said, reaching for the bottle of Moët that was chilling on the bar in a silver bucket, juicy drops of moisture sliding down the bottle's thick neck. Roxy poured herself a drink. "I'll bet you two won't go all the way."

"What's the bet?" Savannah answered, angry that Roxy was constantly challenging her tonight.

Roxy held out her wrist. "A Movado watch like this for both of you if you go through with it. If not, I want three hundred dollars' worth of lingerie from you, Savannah. Kay, you pay for a case of my favorite champagne. Is it a bet?"

"How do you know we'll tell you the real deal about what happens?" Savannah dropped her eyes, trying not to look up at the DJ table.

"We've never lied to each other before," Roxy reasoned, taking another sip of champagne. "I'm sure we won't start now."

"How do we know he'll even go for it?" Kay said nervously.

"Please," Roxy laughed. "What man wouldn't? But just to be sure, I sent a note over while y'all was getting down, asking him if he wanted a private party with the two ladies who just freaked him on the dance floor."

"You didn't," Kay yelled, then lowered her voice. "You are really tripping tonight."

Savannah just shook her head. "Roxy, you are out of control. We look like hos sending sex party notes back and forth to the DJ."

"A note back would be tacky. I told him to answer yes by playing my favorite dance record."

No sooner than the words left Roxy's ruby red lips, the driving bass beat of the r&b cut "Get Off" began surging throughout the club.

"That's a yes, ladies," Roxy grinned.

Savannah looked over at Rocking Roger, who was sending a sexy smile her way. At the same time, he cranked up the volume. *Oh God,* she thought. Then Savannah had a sudden surge of courage. *Why not? Why be so conservative all the time? Be daring. Be bold.* "Fine," she said, "my place, when the DJ switches shifts. Kay, you go home and get that bad, black lingerie outfit I gave you for Christmas."

"The one with no ass?" Kay asked, although she knew. She raised her eyebrows. "Right on. I'm in, girl."

"You, ringleader," Savannah said, rolling with a bravado she'd never felt before, "give him the address. Kay, make sure you get there before him. I'm going home to get ready."

Roxy clicked her heels together like Dorothy in *The Wizard of Oz,* then high-fived Savannah and Kay. "My girls, this will be the first bet I've ever wanted to lose."

*   *   *

At home, Savannah got to work with a busy stick, her own daring exciting her. Step one: she put red satin sheets on her oval bed, the frame she'd found at a custom bedding shop. Step two:

Savannah put on the most expensive piece of sexy lingerie she owned. Step three: she chilled a bottle of champagne next to the bed and put on a best of the seventies love songs CD. *Where is Kay?* She wondered. They needed to coordinate.

After waiting half an hour, Savannah called Kay and got the answering machine. She called Roxy on her cell. Roxy said Kay had left long ago and that Rocking Roger was well on his way.

Savannah began to panic. Where was Kay? She heard a car pull up in the driveway. *There's that hussy now,* she thought, running down the stairs and pulling open the door. "I didn't think you were coming—"

There stood Roger, minus the floppy hat and shades, leaning against the door, "I'll be coming all night long, I hope."

Savannah swallowed. "Hi."

"Can I come in?" Roger asked. He looked younger and even sexier than he had at the club.

"Of course," Savannah turned quickly and began walking toward her kitchen. Why? She didn't know: to get some water or something before she chickened out. Savannah vowed to kill Kay for backing out on her like this. It was a couple of minutes before Roger followed her into the house.

"Is everything okay?" Savannah asked.

"Yes, I forgot something in my car. That's all." Then Roger grabbed her and started to kiss her passionately.

"Wait, my friend isn't here—I don't think she's coming."

"Well, that shouldn't stop us from getting *our* freak on, should it?" Roger reasoned, and began to run his hands all over Savannah's body.

Her composure gone, she dropped the crystal water glass and it shattered on the floor. Roger scooped Savannah up in his arms and glanced around, "Where?"

Savannah, her hands clasped around his neck, nodded toward the stairs. Roger swiftly climbed the steps as though she weighed nothing. In the bedroom his clothes came off so quickly it was as if Savannah's fingertips were magic wands. His body was to die for—smooth, firm, young perfection. Roger was rocking for real and completely erect. His lips tore at Savannah's neck as if he were a tiger and she a gazelle. Yet she didn't cry out because Savannah didn't want to be rescued. No ma'am. She tried to slow him down by whispering in his ear, "Champagne?" A negative grunt was his only answer as he began to undress her.

Savannah was disappointed that Roger seemed uninterested in foreplay. No holding. No tongue games. But it had been six months since she'd been with Van so the heat between Savannah's legs welcomed this hurried lover wanting, like flames, to devour something to keep itself burning.

The weight of Roger's body pressed against her stomach, taking her breath away. Savannah gasped for air, the coolness filling her throat. The wiry hairs of his chest were brittle against Savannah's tender breasts. Their bodies were dry at first, like the untouched champagne chilling on the nightstand. Savannah felt Roger's fingers, thick, and probing, exploring inside her, his dick a tight knot pressed against her thigh.

Though unused to his type of frenzied lovemaking, Roger was a wonderfully savage lover who beat into submission Savannah's every doubt about his hungry passion. Now completely wet and open, she began to contract the muscles inside her vagina, grabbing and toying with each thrust.

"Oh baby," Roger said, slowing down, enjoying what she was doing.

That's what I'm talking about, Savannah thought, taking the young boy to school a bit. And just when she thought he couldn't go any deeper, he did. It seemed as if the pressure was pushing against her hipbones from the inside out; warm and frothy, the musky scent of their passion filling the bedroom.

Savannah wanted more. Clenching her teeth, she pulled him closer. She grunted and groaned, tearing at the flesh on his back with her manicured nails. Bumping and grinding against one another, they clung to each other, caught up in the volatility of their frantic lovemaking.

When Savannah dared to open her eyes, she realized that they had knocked both the phone and the clock off the nightstand. But they kept on loving one another until their bones ached and a final surge of power shot through them, sapping their strength.

Roger's head slipped forward slowly, landing against the small of her shoulder. His labored breathing came in hot gusts from his flared nostrils, moistening her neck. Savannah's insides felt soft as satin. A smile crept across her face as Roger rolled over next to her.

"You are something else," he moaned, struggling to catch his breath. "Can I smoke?"

"After that fuck you can set the house on fire if you want to," Savannah answered, untangling her legs from his.

The flare of the lighter flicking on, the faint scent of wafting tar, and the sound of Roger blowing the smoke up toward the ceiling all tweaked Savannah's senses, helping her to come down from her sexual high.

"You take all the DJs home or just me?"

"You're my first." Savannah laughed softly, "So, you're visiting from Memphis, huh?"

"For a week, that's all. Then I'm going back home."

"Who are you staying with here in Chicago?"

"My brother, Rick," Roger said, putting his arm around Savannah's shoulder. "He's part owner of the club."

"Is Rick as fine as you?"

"All the honeys seem to think so."

Savannah motioned to the champagne; Roger took another puff, shook his head no.

A young boy like this is already buck wild and the way he makes love? Yeah he's got plenty of women back east and probably has someone here, too. Savannah was thinking hard and fast. *Well, I'd better fill up the old come tank.* Savannah felt mischievous but that didn't stop her from going to work on Roger. She began to stroke Roger's plump right nipple. She ran her tongue along the tip. Out of the corner of her eye, Savannah saw the cigarette smoke cease to a trickle. Roger put her hand on his dick; it was sticky and beginning to slowly inflate like an inner tube.

"You ready to go again?" Savannah asked in a low and lusty voice.

Roger smiled, then flipped her over on her stomach, smacking her gently on the ass. "I'm here to please, just let me run to the bathroom."

Savannah felt him get up.

"Keep your eyes closed baby, and relax and think about the love we've made and the love we're about to make."

Savannah did as she was told but the seconds seemed like an hour, until she felt the weight return to the bed, pressing on her back. Savannah braced for Roger to grab her hips and lift her to all fours.

Instead she got a surprise.

His lips, soft and moist, gently kissed her shoulder blades. A single finger stroked down her back. Savannah moaned softly. "That's sweet, baby," she said.

"That's the only way I like it, sweet."

Savannah felt the bed's weight shift again; this time he was reaching for the champagne. The cork popping sounded like a gunshot. Savannah jumped, surprised because Roger hadn't wanted any champagne before.

"So now you're thirsty," she whispered, turning her head to him.

"Only for you," he answered, his voice, like his touch, gentler than before.

"Can I have some?" Savannah asked, like a little girl.

Roger poured a sip into his mouth, then leaned down and shared it with a kiss. The bubbly stung the inside of Savannah's mouth. She was pleasantly surprised that there was no smoker's taste. The champagne must have covered it.

He gently turned Savannah by the hips until she was facing him. He looked at her breasts with renewed admiration. He kissed each one in appreciation and Savannah felt her heart melting at his tenderness. *How can I ever let this boy go? Savannah thought. So young: yet so sexually diverse.*

He was bringing a whole new style of loving. Savannah was amazed at his remaining energy. He ran his tongue down the center of her stomach, already moist and tight, sending shivers down her body. Savannah, nearly delirious with pleasure, moaned, "Keep going, keep going . . ."

And he did. Savannah felt an explosion inside her; hot and blistering, the room seemed to spin, but a slow looping spin, like being rocked to a sexual lullaby. Easy and full: soft and tender. Her body responded by getting softer and wetter. Savannah wanted to scream out in pleasure, scarcely able to contain herself.

When the last of their lovemaking was finished, Savannah lay back on the bed, dripping with sweat and satisfaction. "That was even better than the first time."

"The second time around always is," he said, reaching for a glass to pour them both some champagne.

"I didn't think you liked champagne."

"Why?"

"Well, I asked you twice before to have some and you said no. I thought you didn't like it."

"Oh," he hesitated, "that was my raunchy side. The soft side of me loves champagne."

He handed Savannah her glass. "I hope you were satisfied tonight," he said, propped up on one elbow, looking down at her.

"Can we do this again, sometime soon, before you go?"

He shook his head and Savannah's heart sank. "Why not? You enjoyed it as much as I did."

"You know I did," he answered, "But it's better to have a night like this only once, when it's perfect, than get together in a relationship and get all twisted and complicated. Let's love it and leave it, baby. I'd rather we remember each other like this."

Damn if this young boy isn't making sense, she thought. Savannah leaned up and gave him a kiss that had all her awakened sensuality in it . . . a kiss that said thank you for making me feel as young as you . . .

He gently caressed Savannah's face. "I have to go."

And although Savannah wanted so much to stop him, she didn't. Spent and feeling like a crowned queen of the Nile she let her servant of love take his leave.

Savannah heard the door downstairs close. Then she heard voices outside her window, in the driveway. *Voices.* Savannah jumped out of the bed and ran to the window. There slapping five was Roger and another man. They were mirror images of one another but the other man had on dress pants and a shirt, his jacket was draped over his shoulder. Savannah stood up, shocked. It all made sense now. That's why their lovemaking had changed so drastically. And that's why one liked champagne and the other had not.

Savannah fell back on the bed, overwhelmed. She'd made love to *two* men tonight. She rolled over and didn't know whether to laugh or to scream. *Oh my God,* she thought. *I could have been killed or something. How could I be so stupid? How could I not pay better attention? They tricked me, those doggish motherfuckers. I oughta call the police,* she thought, and then, on second thought—*what would I say? Excuse me, officer, I just had the best double lay of my entire life, and my body feels caressed and satisfied. I'm sure there's a crime in there somewhere. Can you help me figure it out?*

Savannah sat on the bed and started laughing so hard, tears coursed down her cheeks. Spent from loving and laughing, Savannah reached down and picked up the telephone. It rang as soon as she replaced the receiver on the cradle. Savannah let the answering machine pick up.

"Savannah, it's Roxy. Girl, listen, watch out. I was leaving the club and I heard two of the valet guys talking about Rocking Roger. His twin brother, Rick, is the manager of the club. They were saying that the two of them had this scam going. One of them takes a woman home and finds a way to leave the door open so the other one can sneak in and they switch off. You hear me, Savannah—"

Savannah picked up the phone. "Too late, Roxy. Kay chickened out but it was the best one-night stand I ever had."

"For real?" Roxy exclaimed.

"Yes, girl. And I get my Movado watch, too. It was three-way loving at its best."

"To the victor, my sister, go the spoils," Roxy answered, and the two friends laughed into the night.

REBECCA CARROLL

Mr. Man

As a producer for a popular talk show some years back, I met a lot of celebrities; mostly a lot of white celebrities. Although I liked to look at them just as much as everyone else did, with their chosen faces and cell phone–obsessed entourages, it was when the black celebrities came on the program that I found myself really staring. Every time a black celebrity came into the studio for a taping, I would be overcome by a sort of self-asphyxiating glee. Because what their presence did was to remind me of how black I wanted to be, and of how black I wasn't. I liked to think that on some level they shared a similar feeling, or rather, that they saw me in the same way that white people saw me—as the only black producer of the four who worked on the show, the host of which was also white. I wanted for the black celebrities to see only my skin, stinging as it was with perversely tangled envy, grafted from a deep and silent well of inexperienced blackness. What a relief it must have been, I hoped they would think, for them to see a known and kindred face.

Even more exciting was when I had the opportunity to actually book a segment with a black celebrity. I'd talk to their people with studied indifference, and then invariably, find some less than casual way to let them know that I was black, too. Of course, usually their people were white, which was actually better. It was always easier for me to deal with white people. I had, after all, been raised by white people and was a member of the much-coveted secret society of brown-skinned children adopted by white parents in the 1960s, which touted a very public black platform, while harboring a deeply private and hidden white loyalty. I rode hard on the inherent difficulty of being a white flak representing a black celebrity. How happy they would be to know that the booking producer was also black. "Thank God," I delighted in their thinking, "at least that takes some of the pressure off me to say and do the right thing without offending my client."

It was not very often, however, that I had the opportunity to book a black celebrity, because that would first require getting the host to believe that the guest was notable and talk-worthy enough. Luckily, the trends of the time were in my favor. Puffy had recently donned the cover of *Rolling Stone,* and people were just then beginning to talk about hip-hop as a viable art form. But even better, the hip-hop artists that I wanted to book had recorded the sound track for a current film starring a very popular white celebrity lead. Okay, full disclosure, I had a crush on one of the artists in particular, let's call him Mr. Man, but of course, this had nothing whatsoever to do with my interest in having him on the program, nor did it affect my strong and professional pitch to the host, who went for it with uncharacteristic enthusiasm and green-lit the segment right away.

Getting Mr. Man wasn't that hard, as he was just emerging and his people were anxious to get him some exposure. The second artist was more difficult. He was "famous" and shouldn't be relied on to show up on time, his flak informed me. I gambled with a posture of vested rage and let it course itself evenly and without conviction through the mixed blood in my veins, as I thought about telling her just what and how if she'd even so much as suggested, known, or used the meaning of CP time. And then common sense spun its lithe and winning design as I realized that he was probably guilty of just that. Nonetheless, I was able to book him easily, although whether or not he would be at the taping on time remained to be seen. The third artist, well, he was the star, the real coup. So I pushed and persisted, and was finally able to get him and his people to commit.

On the day of the taping I sat and waited in my cubicle, which felt more claustrophobic than usual. The smell of cheap corporate particleboard seemed almost toxic as I divided my time in the last remaining hours between looking at the clock and, well, looking at the clock. I had several factors to consider. There was Mr. Man, of course, and whether or not he would think I was cute, sexy, attractive, or, more important, black. There was our man of leisure, who I could only imagine would show up an hour late, his pager beeping, his cell phone ringing and his attitude ten miles high. And then there was the star, the one who all my girls were like, "Oh, now, you know you have to tell me if he's as fine as he looks in his videos."

Two hours before the taping, I received a call from his people: "He can't do it. He's not going to do it. It's not the right time." This was very, very bad news. In a moment of what I considered inspired genius on my part, I called in the sound track producer to pinch hit, convincing the host that it was the better way to go, anyway. We would do a one-on-one with the star when his solo album was released in a few months. Miraculously, all three guests—Mr. Man, our man of leisure, and the newly anointed sound track producer—showed up together, and, God bless them, on time.

It was customary for the producers to "meet and greet" their guests in the lobby, and to then lead them to makeup, and then to the greenroom before going to the set. When I saw Mr. Man up close, I was surprised by how vulnerable he looked, because I had expected anger, attitude and inaccessibility. First of all, he came without an entourage. The show taped in a regular corporate building where people had regular corporate jobs. Our program was sort of perceived by the rest of the building as the exotic foreign exchange student who never went back to his own damn country. It then became clear that being on the show intimidated him. It wasn't an interview with *Vibe* or *The Source,* and it definitely wasn't an appearance on BET. He might actually have to complete a sentence.

Still, I am not kidding when I tell you that our eyes met and stayed met for some time as I led him and the other two guests to makeup, and then later, while waiting in the greenroom I swear to God he was lifting my skirt with just his breathing alone. He had beautiful, quiet lips and eyes like pools of velvet pain. Small tracks of sweat glistened across his face, making his skin look like dark chocolate dipped in champagne, and his skin was pulled taut across his cheeks by tight, neat cornrows. He was about six feet tall, slim and broad-shouldered, carrying a strange combination of angst and bravado in his sway.

I knew from my prep work that Mr. Man was from Philadelphia, that he'd always wanted to be famous, and that he'd earned his claim to fame as the lesser noted member of a phenomenally successful hip-hop group less than a year earlier. He bore the pressure of now being on his own like the last bird in the nest, high up on a branch that threatened a deep and irretrievable fall. His confidence was misleading, paper-thin, but oddly seductive. He spoke in murmurs, when he spoke at all, his words dark and hidden, dispatched in jagged drifts of intelligence. As I stood in the greenroom with the guests, glass windows reflecting a bad posture, my lips curled around invisible words, I wished I could be somebody else.

"So," he said, casually, moving neither his mouth nor his body, "how long you been workin' here?"

"Oh, you know," I said, jaw stiff as though never used, "about a year."

"You like it, then?"

"Um, yes, yeah, I do, actually." I realized too late that I'd missed the opportunity to speak in his language, to say it the right way, the black way. Mr. Man nodded slowly, as if to say that it was all right if I worked there and it was all right if I didn't.

For the taping I'd selected a clip from the video of the sound track's hit single, starring Mr. Man, and in which he rips off his Clark Kent–like business suit to reveal the real ghetto Superman underneath. The irony was not lost on me. How I wished it were that simple—that I could rip off either the skin I was born in to free the lonely, smart, and creative white girl underneath, or the white mannerisms I'd inherited from my parents and environment growing up to expose the real black woman I could have been. I watched from the control room as the host threw to the clip and felt, not only pleased by the precision with which I'd cut the clip, but increasingly surreal. I myself, in fact, felt surreal, as if I'd entered into a dream and that I could somehow control the outcome.

As it turned out, I ended up getting on very well, very fast, with the sound-track producer—a lovely, raspy-voiced white woman of about forty, who seemed, in a sad and uncalculating way, something of a pimp to her b-boys in the making. I had no doubts, however, that her intentions were pure. Or, rather, as pure as they could be given that she was the broker of an art form so provocative that it had prompted the launch of a national advisory board with the sole initiative of examining its lyrics. When she invited me to join her and possibly "the guys" for a drink later that night, I was more than happy to oblige.

"Oh, yeah, sweetie, they'll be there. I mean, it's The Four Seasons. Right?" She tossed this whimsically over her shoulder, Jimmy Choo heels click-clacking through the lobby.

I felt slightly washed up after working all day. I stepped outside for some air, buildings tall and exhaust hovering like a vulture, only to be met by a dank and muggy slur of unmotivated oxygen. It was then that I realized that I wouldn't have time to go home to Brooklyn to change before meeting for drinks. I would have to go in what I was wearing, which, thank God, wasn't so bad. I had on a black calf-length skirt and a tight black top (completely out of keeping with what I would normally wear to work, which was jeans and whatever I could find to throw on top), and no underwear, which was standard policy, regardless.

Mr. Man never showed. In fact, none of "the guys" showed. Miss Soundtrack Producer and I, however, had what I believe to be a fine time after we'd both had about eighteen cosmopolitans. She was very encouraging in regard to Mr. Man. She happily gave me the lowdown through pink vodka-puckered lips on what she knew of his personal life, most of which I forgot by the time I got home that night. Lying in bed as I shuffled aimlessly into a strange and unsatisfied slumber, hands slipping in and around my thighs looking for a place to dream, I wondered if I'd ever see him again.

About two weeks later, I got a message on my voice mail: "Hey. You wanna go out or what? Page me." He didn't say his name. He didn't say good-bye. He just hung up when he was done. This was more like it. He sounded like the guy I'd expected to meet the day of the taping. For a minute, I wondered how he had gotten my number, not that it really mattered, but then remembered that during our evening at The Four Seasons, I'd happily given Miss Soundtrack all my vitals short of my social security number. Bless her heart. Miss Soundtrack was suddenly on my Christmas card list.

Obviously, I didn't call him back right away. I saw *Swingers*, okay. No, I practiced considerable restraint and waited the requisite three days before I paged him. Surprisingly, he responded right away. He was out driving around in his Land Rover after a recording session. Word.

"So, whatchoo doin'?" The flesh of my cheek grew hot against the phone, and I suddenly remembered being a teenager in the summertime, when I'd gone to the local dance club in a borrowed town, watched and waited for the black boys to approach, all sweaty, powerful and high from dancing in the spotlight. And when they finally approached and asked me to dance, I'd let my skin and body speak for me, which was more than enough back then.

"Oh, well, I'm just"—I immediately felt stupid for even *thinking* about using the word *chillin'*—"hanging out."

"Oh, you're hanging out, huh?" He enunciated the words *hanging out* in a way that made me feel whiter than usual.

"Yeah."

"Okay. All right. So, whatchoo doin' later?"

"I don't know," I said.

"Where you live?"

"Why?"

"Why you think?"

It went on like that for a while. We ended up deciding to meet for a drink. I chose a very expensive, very chic bar in SoHo, because I'm an elitist snob, and because I knew people who worked there, and well, because shit, I had a way-better-than-average date going on. Mr. Man was parked and waiting for me when I arrived. Summer had ridden its way in on the sweet back of spring. I was wearing a dress that night, something I very rarely do. Dresses and skirts fall under the same fairly prohibitive category as stiletto heels, in my book. I like to know that I can always run fast and far if the situation calls for it. It was a light cotton, lemony-colored dress, which one could very possibly see through if one wanted to. My bare brown shoulders peeked out from under delicate, loose-fitting straps, and the length fell sleepily to my ankles. I felt good in it.

I saw him see me in his rearview mirror as I approached the bar. The streets were dark, people sauntering past in tipsy moods and moonlit sorrows. The smell of the city rose up around us as he stepped out with long, elegant legs dangling ahead of his torso, and then the full of his body. He started toward me, relaxed, composed, straight-faced. I just about died. Standing there, breasts and eyelashes somehow one and the same, tingling in whispers of want, the caps of my knees aching to be touched, and a slight chill passing over my lips, he bent over and kissed me on the cheek before taking my hand in his. Like a perfect gentleman, and not at all like the voice on the phone, he opened the door with the hand that wasn't holding mine, and we entered the bar together. I loved him already.

Recognizing Mr. Man immediately, the young, skinny white hostess met us before the door even had a chance to close. Mr. Man politely asked if we could sit at the downstairs bar, which might be more quiet. Rubbing the knuckles of one hand with the fingers of the other, she smiled eagerly and said, "Oh, yes. Yes, of course. Right this way." At the downstairs bar, young, darkly adorned jetsetters shuffled like shadows in a haze of lifeless smoke. I sat and ordered a cosmopolitan, which was very big that summer, and Mr. Man ordered a Coke. He had recently been cast in his first feature film and had stopped drinking as part of his preparation. We talked some about his upcoming film career, the solo album he was working on, his history with other recording artists, and what I might be able to do for him, as both a writer and a producer, in the event of his imminent stardom.

"You know, I mean, I really like the director on this film. He's like, real innovative, you know? It's not a big part, you know, but it's, like, challenging." *Well, yes, it would be challenging if you've never acted in a movie before,* I thought, but remained attentive.

"It's about, like, these dudes, right, who have like super powers and shit, but are completely misunderstood by society."

How original.

"I was just thinking, you know, you and your show might want to, like, do a story or whatever you got. It's not coming out until next year, you know, movies take a while, like records. But it'll be dope, right, see, because the movie will come out, and then, like, my solo record, too. And it'll be like BLAM!"

I found his enthusiasm endearing.

High on our velvet barstools, knees facing each other and spread wide like grins, Mr. Man moved in closer to me and then turned, slowly looking around us, then back at me. He was disappointed that more people hadn't recognized him, but also pleased that my eyes hadn't once left him. After two and half cosmopolitans for me, and another Coke for him, he paid for the drinks and we got up to leave. As we were heading toward the stairwell, a waiter, a guy I knew, and, I admit, hoped to see, shouted out to me. I'd waited tables with him when I was in between career gigs. I'd had a serious and unabashed crush on him. But he had outright rejected me—

not because he didn't find me attractive, I know that he did, but because he could.

Mr. Man and I turned around at the same time, and as if without thinking, he slipped his fingers through mine and gently drew me toward him. The pretty white boy who had so brazenly cast me aside, was left standing there, probably in shock. Because there I was, perfectly and safely ensconced in the beautiful grip of a man, a celebrity, which, in almost any and all situations, trumps color, class, and gender. And even if Mr. Man had talked about himself all night and was only able to see people, as far as I could tell, on an opportunistic level, in that moment, he wanted to claim me as his.

In the passenger seat of the Land Rover, I propped my bare feet up on the dash and let my dress ride high up on my thighs, while Mr. Man fiddled with the CD player, and casually noted the numbers that showed up on his constantly ringing cell phone. The windows were open and the early summer breeze came into my skin and lungs like a fresh, mirrored glance. As he drove, Mr. Man would occasionally reach over and slide his broad, dark hand up my leg, past my thigh and into the place where it all comes together. And then he'd smile into the road ahead at my quiet gasps for breath.

When we got to my place, I got out of the truck and walked toward my apartment without looking back at him. I heard the weighty slam of his door as I was fishing for my keys, and then suddenly, I felt him against me. The hot pressure of his chest nearly drove through the base of my neck, and my bag and keys almost slid through my fingers as he said, "I've wanted you since the first time I saw you." My breath caught, and the muscles in my abdomen tightened and then released. The palms of his hands moistened my hips before easing up around my waist and then cupping my breasts. I sunk into him for several minutes, then turned and backed into my apartment. "If you want me now, just imagine how much you'll want me later." He drew back away from me, and didn't say his words twice.

The next time he called was midnight about three weeks later. "Whatchoo doin'?"

"It's like midnight, what do you think I'm doing?" Having less time to think about what you're saying is always better.

"Thought I'd roll through for a minute."

"Sure, yeah, come on over." Even if I hadn't been half-asleep, I couldn't think of a reason why he shouldn't.

I buzzed him in less than twenty minutes later. He didn't kiss me, as he had when we'd gone out that dreamy night, but instead, brushed past me and headed straight for the bedroom that was visible in my open loft. As I shook off both sleepiness and fantasy alike, I realized that there was a stranger in my home, and suddenly began to feel a tinge of fear. I didn't think he would hurt me, neither did I think that he would want to cuddle and talk all night, but I did suddenly feel very cognizant of the duality he represented—the young, gifted, and black celebrity about to emerge, and the young, black man who wrote and rapped about anger and payback.

He was on my bed when I walked in. As I stood looking at him lying there, eyes closed, lids fluttering like butterflies, he seemed burdened. Here was my chance, but what do black women do when their black men are burdened? In this fragile and fleeting glimpse, Mr. Man was no longer a celebrity, he was a black man in need of a black woman to soothe, support, and satisfy him. But I had no idea what to do. You see, I'm biracial to white people, and light-skinned black to black people, so having this black man in my bed was loaded for me. Essentially, he wanted to get laid, but I wanted to get purified; baptized in the well of his righteous blackness.

I knelt down on the bed and began to undress him as I kissed his lips, his neck, his fingers, and his shoulders. I became increasingly overwhelmed by insecurity. I desperately wished that I'd had time to get drunk before he'd come over, so that I'd feel less awkward, more sexy, more anonymous, less accountable. Genuinely wanting him didn't seem to help at all, and I longed for that first night together when I'd been lucky enough to be the object of his desire without having to follow through and embarrass the hell out of myself.

Either sensing my insecurity, or just plain tired of waiting, pants halfway down his legs, Mr. Man opened his eyes and his strong hands guided me onto his lap. One hand reaching for the condom he'd laid out on the night table before I'd come in, and the other in between my legs, he sat up and leaned into my face, breathing his own cobwebs of fear, and want for anonymity. His lips opened around mine and then moved across my cheek, leaving the bridge between my nose and mouth warm and wet. It was dark, but the light from the bathroom cast a beam across his face, illuminating what I was, and what I wasn't.

For me, much like dresses and high heels, being on top and giving blow jobs have their own similar category—also somewhat prohibitive. Mr. Man had no time for inhibitions. "You're *hanging out,* is you? Is that right?" he said, his breath just starting to get uneven, digging his strong fingers into my fleshy hips, leading me up and down onto his thighs. I leaned back and looked up at the ceiling. The previous occupant had stuck glow-in-the-dark stars and moons up there. I had never appreciated them. In fact, I hated them. But tonight they were like the point in the room where a ballerina focuses to master her pirouette.

I had no illusions about my part in this experience, and the pleasure I would or would not have. I opened my thighs as I felt the small, merciful window of possible orgasm. When Mr. Man kissed my stomach and the dip of softness where my hip and thigh meet, I felt mercurial and beautiful, and soft moans spilled from my lips. But he was there for himself. A few moments later, he collapsed on top of me, and then slid through the sweat between us onto the bed.

Mr. Man left that night. He didn't even play at making it something it wasn't. It was a consensual and innately prurient one-time encounter. "Page me," he said, and turned to leave, taking his blackness with him. I didn't linger at the door to watch it or him leave, because I'd had it inside of me, all of it— his blackness, his celebrity, and his arrogant, vulnerable, confused, young and burdened self. Despite the awkward moments of truth in my head, I'd enjoyed it. I gave way to the dream, the hype, and the romance, but it all took place in my home and in a body that I own.

Back in my bed, naked and alone, stripped of consciousness and flimsy from primitive bliss, I pushed my body down into the ruffle of disrupted pillows and covers, touched where he'd touched me, and finished what he'd started. Slowly coaxing a loose and constant moistness, then with a tired smile, I felt something like grace.

CONTRIBUTORS

Jenoyne Adams, author of the *Los Angeles Times* best-seller *Resurrecting Mingus* (Simon & Schuster/Free Press, February 2001), is a novelist, poet and journalist. A 1998 PEN Center USA West Emerging Voices fellow, Jenoyne has been featured in programs at the the J. Paul Getty Museum, the Los Angeles County Museum of Art (LACMA), the Essence Music Festival, the National Black Arts Festival, and the Mark Taper Auditorium. She has written for the *Precinct Reporter,* the largest African-American newspaper in San Bernardino County and the *TriCounty Bulletin,* a weekly serving the Orange County area. She is currently completing her second novel, *Selah's Bed.*

Preston L. Allen is a black Caribbean, born in Spanish Honduras on Roatan, an English-speaking island populated with black people. He is the 1998 recipient of the State of Florida's Individual Artist Award in Fiction and the winner of the 2000 Sonja H. Stone Prize in Fiction. He has been anthologized in *Having a Wonderful Time: An Anthology of South Florida Writers* (Simon and Schuster, 1997). His short works have appeared in *Gulf Stream Magazine, The Seattle Review, The Crab Orchard Review, Asili* and

Brown Sugar (Plume, 2001). His short story collection *Churchboys and Other Sinners* will be published shortly by Carolina Wren Press, 2002. He is currently completing the novel *Nadine's Husband,* in which the selection *If He Only Knew* appears. His novel *Hoochie Mama* (Writer's Club Press, 2001) is available on Amazon.com and Barnesandnoble.com. He can be reached at pallenagogy@webtv.net.

Nicole Bailey-Williams is the author of *A Little Piece of Sky* (Sugarene's Press, 2000), which will be reissued by Doubleday / Harlem Moon in 2002. She is an English teacher, a freelance writer, and a contributing writer to *Notable Black American Men* (Gale, 1999), edited by Jessie Carnie Smith. She has been commissioned to write a biography of William P. Young, Pennsylvania's first African-American Secretary of Labor. Bailey-Williams also co-hosts "The Literary Review," a book review that airs on WDAS (1480 AM) in Philadelphia. Born in Philadelphia and raised in the neighboring suburb of Elkins Park, she now lives in Mercer County, New Jersey, with her husband, Gregory.

Rebecca Carroll is an award-winning author and interviewer who has written three books of narrative nonfiction, including *I Know What the Red Clay Looks Like: The Voice and Vision of Black Women Writers* (Carol Southern/Crown, 1994), and *Sugar in the Raw: Voices of Young Black Girls in America* (Crown/Three Rivers, 1997). Carroll has also written a screenplay for the independent production "Smoke and Mirrors," and has a costarring role as "The Interviewer" in writer/filmmaker Sherman Alexie's forthcoming film, *The Business of Fancy Dancing*. A freelance writer, she has written for *Mother Jones, Time Out New York, Elle,* and *USA Weekend,* among others. Carroll is currently at work on her next book, *Race Talk: Celebrity Figures and Cultural Leaders Reflect on America's Racial Consciousness.*

Tananarive Due is the author of four novels, *The Living Blood, The Black Rose, My Soul to Keep* and *The Between.* Her short fiction has appeared in *Dark Matter, Science Fiction & Fantasy* magazine, *Year's Best SF 6,* and *Best Black Women's Erotica.* She has been a finalist for the Horror Writers Association's Bram Stoker Award, and *The Black Rose* was nominated for an NAACP Image Award.

Due's next book, a nonfiction family civil rights memoir entitled *Freedom in the Family* (which she is co-authoring with her mother, Patricia Stephens Due), will be published by One World/Ballantine in 2002. Due lives in Longview, Washington, with her husband, novelist Steven Barnes.

Nelson George is an award-winning author and a native resident of Brooklyn, New York. He has published nine books, including *Where Did Our Love Go: The Rise and Fall of the Motown Sound* (St. Martin's, 1985), *The Death of Rhythm and Blues* (Pantheon, 1988), and *Hip Hop America* (Viking, 1988). His essay collection *Buppies, B-Boys, Baps, & Bohos: Notes on Post Soul Culture* (HarperCollins, 1992), is comprised largely of work from his early '90s *Village Voice* column, "Native Son." A longtime contributor to *Playboy* magazine, George was also Billboard's black-music editor from 1982 to 1989. He has chronicled basketball in

Elevating the Game: Black Men in Basketball (HarperCollins, 1992), and film in *Blackface: African-Americans and the Movies* (HarperCollins, 1994). George has published four novels: *Urban Romance* (Putnam 1993), *Seduced* (Putnam, 1996), *One Woman Short* (Scribner, 2000), and his latest, *Show & Tell* (Scribner, 2001). This year George directed the BET television movie *One Special Moment* and co-wrote the Russell Simmons autobiography *Life & Def* (Crown, 2001). For more information visit www.Nelsongeorge.com.

Michael A. Gonzales as a child once danced on the Apollo stage with James Brown and carried DJ Hollywood's record crates. He has written fiction for *Ego Trip, New York Press, Untold, blackfilm.com, Tale Spin* and *Trace,* and nonfiction for *Vibe, Essence,* and many others. Currently a senior writer at *The Source,* he is finishing *Babies & Fools,* a collection of short stories. He is a contributor to *Brown Sugar.*

Reginald Harris heads the Information Technology Support Department of the Enoch Pratt Library in Baltimore, and edits *Kuumba: Poetry Journal for Black People In the Life.* A recipient of Individual Artist Awards for both Fiction and Poetry from the Maryland State Arts Council, his work has appeared in a variety of publications including *5 AM, African-American Review, Harvard Gay and Lesbian Review,* and *Brown Sugar.*

Yolanda Joe, a graduate of Yale University, studied under Henry Louis Gates. She also won a fellowship to study British Literature at Oxford. She went on to receive an M.S. in Broadcasting from the Columbia School of Journalism. Joe is the author of: *Falling Leaves of Ivy* (Longmeadow Press, 1992), a Blackboard Bestseller; *He Say, She Say* (Doubleday, 1997), a Blackboard and Chicago Tribune Bestseller; *Bebe's By Golly Wow,* (Doubleday, 1998), a Literary Guild selection and a Blackboard Bestseller; and *This Just In . . .* (Doubleday, 2000), a Doubleday, Literary Guild, and Black Expressions book club selection. Joe has also authored a mystery novel, *Details at Ten* (Simon & Schuster, 2000), written under the pen name Ardella Garland. Joe is working on another mystery, *Hit Time* (Simon & Schuster, 2002), as well as another work of fiction. She writes and lives in her hometown of Chicago.

Shawne Johnson was born in Philadelphia, PA, where she now lives with her husband and daughter. She received her undergraduate degree from Bennett College in North Carolina and completed her Masters in English Literature at Temple University in Philadelphia. Johnson was also a United States Peace Corps volunteer in Mozambique, Africa. Her first novel, *Getting Our Breath Back,* is scheduled for release by Dutton/Plume, May 2002.

Sandra Kitt is a best-selling novelist. Considered the foremost African-American writer of romance fiction, she was the first black writer to ever publish with Harlequin. Her first mainstream novel, *The Color of Love* (Signet 1995) was released to critical acclaim and optioned by HBO from a script by Kitt. She has published twenty-five books. Among them, *Close Encounters* (Signet, 2000) was one of the Top Ten Contemporaries for 2000.

Girlfriends, an anthology (HarperCollins, 1999), was nominated for the prestigious NAACP Image Award for Fiction in 1999. A native New Yorker, Sandra is currently an Information Specialist in Astronomy and Astrophysics at the American Museum of Natural History in New York. Sandra has lectured at NYU, Penn State, Sarah Lawrence, and Columbia University. She has appeared on Today, Black Entertainment Television, and Good Morning, America.

Timmothy B. McCann is an ex-collegiate All-American football player and the former owner of a financial planning agency. He also teaches a course on the Art of Commercial Fiction at Santa Fe Community College in Gainesville, Florida. Best known for three highly acclaimed novels, *Until . . .* (Avon, 1999), *Always* (Avon, 2000) and *Forever* (Kensington/Dafina Books, 2000), McCann has just completed his fourth novel, *Emotions* (Dafina Books, 2001) as well as a short story for the upcoming anthology *Proverbs for the People.* He lives in Florida and is the proud father of two beautiful children.

Bernice L. McFadden was born and raised and still lives in Brooklyn, New York. She is the mother of one daughter, R'yane Azsa and the author of three novels, *Sugar* (Dutton, 2001), *The Warmest December* (Dutton, 2001) and *This Bitter Earth* (Dutton, 2002). She is at work on her fourth novel.

Kathleen E. Morris, author of *Speaking in Whispers: African-American Lesbian Erotica* (ThirdSide Press, 1996), is a full-time writer, lecturer and workshop facilitator. Her stories have been anthologized in *Best Lesbian Erotica* 1977 (Cleis Press, 1997), and *Black Silk* (Warner Books, 2002). Ms. Morris has contributed critical, fiction, and nonfiction essays, interviews, and book reviews to *Black Issues Book Review, Venus, Mosaic* and *Lambda Book Review,* among other publications. Ms. Morris has lectured and/or facilitated workshops at several conferences, including *OutWrite* (Boston, MA), *African-American Women Writers Conference* (Washington, D.C.), and the *National Black Arts Festival* (Atlanta, GA). She also facilitates *The Erotic Pen,* a national writing workshop series designed to teach writers of all levels how to tap into their creative and sensual selves through the art of writing. She is currently completing work on *Baptism,* the follow-up volume to *Whispers,* and continuing research for a nonfiction project, *The Orphan's Club: Assuming the Mantle of Power.* "Letters & Remembrances" is excerpted from a book-in-process. She and her partner live in Maryland.

Willie Perdomo is the author of *Where a Nickel Costs a Dime* (Norton, 1996). His work has been included in several anthologies, including *Aloud: An Anthology of Writing from The Nuyorican Poets Café* (Holt, 1995), *Boricuas: An Anthology of Puerto Rican Writing* (One World/Ballantine, 1995), *Listen Up! A Spoken Word Anthology* (Ballantine, 2000) and *Step into a World* (Wiley, 2001). He is the author of a children's book, *Visiting Langston,* illustrated by Bryan Collier (Henry Holt/Books for Young Readers, 2002). He has been featured on several PBS documentaries, including *Words in Your Face* and *The United States of Poetry.* Perdomo is the recipient of the New York Foundation for the Arts Fiction Fellowship 1996 and the NYFA Poetry Fellowship 2001. He also co-wrote an episode for the HBO series *Spicy City* and recorded on *Flippin' the Script: Rap Meets Poetry* (Mouth Almighty Records/Mercury, 1995). He lives in New York City and is completing another collection of poetry, *Smoking Lovely*.

Leone Ross, 32, is an award-winning novelist, short story writer, editor and teacher of fiction writing. She has written two critically acclaimed novels, *All the Blood Is Red* (ARP, 1996) and *Orange Laughter* (Picador USA, 2001). Her work has been widely anthologized in Europe and the USA, and collections include *Dark Matter, Brown Sugar, Catch a Fire, The London Book of Short Stories: Vol. II,* and *The Best of Horror and SciFi: 14th Annual Collection.* Leone is Jamaican and lives in London.

Shay Youngblood is the author of the plays *Shaking the Mess Out of Misery, Talking Bones,* and *Black Power Barbie* and the novels *Soul Kiss* (Riverhead Books, 1997) and *Black Girl in Paris* (Riverhead Books, 2000). She is working on new fiction about food, sex, and dreams.

Zane is the national best-selling author of *Addicted* (Pocket Books, October 2001), *The Heat Seekers* (Pocket Books, June 2002), *The Sex Chronicles: Shattering the Myth* (Strebor Books International, February 2001) and *Shame on It All* (Strebor Books International, February 2001). Her erotic fiction has appeared in several anthologies, including *Best Black Women's*

Erotica (Cleis Press, June 2001) and *Herotica* 7 (Down There Press, January 2002). She is the webmaster of several sites, including EroticaNoir.com and BlackGentlemen.com. Zane is in her mid-thirties and lives in the Washington, D.C., area, where she is a full-time writer and Principal/Publisher of Strebor Books International.

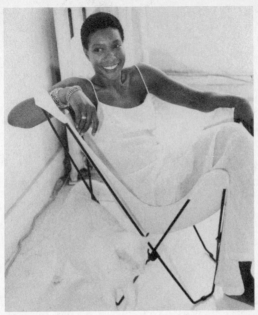

Bob Myers

About the Editor

Carol Taylor, a former Random House book editor, has been in book publishing for over ten years and has worked with many of today's top black writers. She is a contributing writer to *Sacred Fire: The QBR 100 Essential Black Books,* and is the editor of the best-selling, award-winning erotic collection *Brown Sugar.* She is a writer and editor who has been featured in *Ebony, Essence, Black Enterprise,* and *OneWorld,* among many other publications. She lives in New York City and is at work on *Brown Sugar 3* and *4* and on a collection of her own short stories. Taylor is the CEO of Brown Sugar Productions, LLC. She can be reached at BrownSugarProd1@aol.com.